ALONE

Also by Kendra Elliot

Hidden

Chilled

Buried

ALONE

A BONE SECRETS NOVEL

KENDRA ELLIOT

Printed in the United States of America.

Published by Montlake Romance, Seattle

www.apub.com

ISBN-13: 9781477809716
ISBN-10: 1477809716
LCCN: 2013907774

For Lindsay Guzzardo and Jennifer Schober.

Thank you for giving me a chance.

CHAPTER ONE

"I won't miss this part of the job," Victoria heard Dr. James Campbell mutter as he held a blackberry vine out of the way for Lacey and Victoria to pass by.

A discovery of dead bodies had abruptly shortened their Italian dinner at Portland's fabulous Pazzo Ristorante. The trio of coworkers had been relaxing over a lovely Barbaresco when the medical examiner's phone buzzed. He'd taken the call at the table and raised a brow at the women, who'd nodded. Both forensic specialists wanted to accompany him to the crime scene.

Five teenagers were dead in the depths of Forest Park.

Time to go to work.

The guiding police officer who'd met them at the trailhead commented, "A hiker found the scene about four hours ago. Looks pretty fresh. One of the girls was still breathing and they rushed her to the hospital. She's not expected to make it." He paused to take a breath, and the volume of his voice dropped to where Victoria leaned forward to hear him. "I gotta say, this is one of the most disturbing sights I've ever seen." The tough cop looked rattled.

Who would kill so many teenage girls? Victoria Peres shook her head. It was a messed-up world. And working at the medical examiner's office as a forensic anthropologist showed her some of the darkest corners of that world. The indignities and atrocities that people inflicted on other human beings were mind-numbing. The kids were the hardest for her to stomach.

The three of them pointed their flashlights at the dirt path, choosing their footsteps carefully, following the police officer. Luckily the fall rains had paused for the moment, because tonight the forest was intimidating enough. Firs towered overhead, blocking all light from the full moon. Ferns sprouted from tree trunks, drawing nutrition from the bark and thick moss that draped the branches. Victoria had already given thanks that she'd worn her boots to dinner in honor of the fall chill. Still dressed for dinner, the three of them looked out of place for the two-mile hike in the damp woods. It was rare that she accompanied Dr. Campbell to a scene. Her job usually kept her inside the medical examiner's building.

But this was Dr. Campbell's last month on the job. Oregon's ME was ready to retire. And Victoria wanted to spend every working moment she could with him, soaking up his experience, wisdom, and wit. "I can't do anything about the death," Dr. Campbell once told her. "But I can do something about what happens after the death. I can speak for the victims, explain their injuries, and bring justice." It described exactly how Victoria felt about her job. There was a mutual respect between her and Dr. Campbell that made her cross her fingers, hoping she could achieve the same with the new medical examiner.

Dr. Campbell's daughter, Lacey, had told Victoria she'd miss working with her father. Lacey served as the ME's forensic odontologist. She and her father were very close.

Lacey was quiet behind Victoria as they trudged along the dark path. She didn't wonder out loud at the cause of the kids' deaths or bitch about the hike; she was professional. Victoria had worked with the petite forensic specialist for a few years, her respect growing every time one of their cases crossed paths. Only recently had they started using each other's first names.

A soft buzz of conversation touched Victoria's ears and the trail seemed to light up farther ahead. They were nearly there. She swallowed hard as the gnocchi she had eaten twisted in her stomach. Maybe she should have gone home after dinner and let the medical examiner do his job. But she'd be greeted by a lonely house. The evening had been so wonderful between the food and conversation, she'd hated for it to end. She'd decided to tramp a few miles through Portland's five-thousand-acre park to view dead teenagers.

Was something wrong with her?

The trail grew choppy with boot prints and small tire marks from the equipment hauled in to process the scene. They emerged into a clearing lit up with glaring lights, and the quiet hum of conversation stopped. The three of them halted and stared, scanning the surreal setting. Cops stood idle in small groups, observing, while crime-scene techs crawled through the display.

It looked straight out of a cheap horror film.

Off the path about ten yards, five young women lay motionless in a lush bed of ferns, arranged like a wagon wheel, their heads at the center, feet pointed out. The image was simultaneously beautiful and evil. One prong of the wheel was missing—the girl who'd been rushed to the hospital.

A cop thrust a log into Dr. Campbell's hands to sign. He barely glanced at it, his gaze locked on the eerie spectacle.

"Lead all souls to heaven," Lacey whispered.

Victoria Peres felt as if her hands were tied. These poor children still had the flesh covering their bones, unlike her usual subjects at work, but she still had a need to examine them to discover their story.

Five girls gracefully sprawled in the center of a clearing. Their skin harshly exposed by the lighting the crime scene team had brought in. Each girl had long dark hair and they all wore white dresses of different styles. Their hands were all crossed on their stomachs. There was neither blood nor immediate indicator of cause of death, just an unnatural grayness to their skin and lips.

Poison?

The girls looked asleep.

No kiss would wake them.

Victoria pushed her own long hair behind one ear, disturbed by the similarity between the girls' appearances. *Why did they look and dress the same?*

She didn't usually attend a fresh death scene. But she helped wherever her skills were needed. She'd definitely put in her share of hours over the flesh of the freshly deceased and the not-so-freshly deceased. Digging in the burial pits of the mass executions in Kosovo had desensitized her to most situations.

But when James had received the call, her instincts had kicked in. Death was her field. And she possessed a particular set of skills that could get answers for the questions the dead teens presented. She noticed the cops glanced their way, scoping out who'd arrived at the scene. None made eye contact with her. She'd busted enough balls at crime scenes to know they weren't her biggest fans. She didn't care. What mattered was that scenes were handled correctly. Mistakes weren't acceptable.

She looked away from the sorrow on Lacey's face. The odontologist had a big soft spot that she wasn't afraid to reveal. Victoria kept her own sensitivity hidden deep. It wasn't that she didn't feel the sadness of the situation; she simply didn't feel it was professional to show it. And she worked better when she tucked away the feelings.

"Who are they?" James muttered to the cop as he handed the log to Lacey to sign.

"We don't know yet, Dr. Campbell," he answered. "There's no ID with any of the girls. No cell phones, no purses."

"Parents will be looking for their daughters soon," said Lacey. "They can't be over eighteen."

Victoria eyed the stature and build of the bodies, silently agreeing with Lacey's assessment. Parents would expect these kids to be in bed by midnight. She followed Dr. Campbell as he carefully stepped to the closest body and squatted next to a female tech, pulling gloves out of his small kit. Up close, Victoria could see the first girl had applied makeup to cover acne on her chin and wore black liquid eyeliner to give the popular cat-eye look.

Someone's daughter.

Dr. Campbell bent the girl's arm. "Rigor has started. Not fully set yet. Can you roll her onto her side for me, Sarah?" he asked the middle-aged woman, who nodded and gently shifted the dead girl onto her side. He pressed at the purpling skin on her shoulder blades where gravity had guided the blood to settle once her heart had stopped pumping. It didn't blanch. "Livor is set. Have you noticed anything unusual?" Dr. Campbell asked the tech.

The tech grimaced. "Outside of this being a group of dead children? Not yet. It's a very clean site so far. The girls were cold when I got here, and they all look clean front and back. Frankly, it's like a sick fairy tale." Sarah frowned. "They're laid out so perfectly. I mean, even their hair is smoothed down. Someone must have arranged them."

"It's just wrong," Dr. Campbell said as he drew a syringe out of his equipment. Victoria didn't need to see the medical examiner extract the vitreous humor from the girl's eye to determine an accurate time of death. Very few things about the human body bothered her, but a needle in the eye was close to the top of the list. Victoria stood and walked back to where Lacey'd waited at the edge of the scene. Two men had joined Lacey. Victoria recognized them as Oregon State Police detectives from the Major Crimes division. The local police department must have called in the State Police for their help.

"Dr. Peres." The older detective, Mason Callahan, greeted Victoria. His partner, Ray Lusco, nodded at her. Both men had tired eyes and subtle slumps to their shoulders. She hadn't noticed that they'd been working the scene when she arrived. She'd been focused on the death wheel of beautiful girls. But obviously Mason and Ray had already spent several hours in the woods. She'd worked with the detectives several times, their opposite personalities making them perfect partners. Mason was the blunt-spoken salt-and-pepper-haired senior detective, rarely seen without his cowboy boots and hat. Ray was the younger family man, who looked like he should be coaching college football.

It wouldn't take long to get depressed or angry or frustrated at this scene. The absolute futileness of the death of these young women was like a gut punch. It was one of the quieter scenes Victoria had visited, not chatty like some. The tension was thick, and the anger from the cops and workers was palpable.

"No one has reported missing teens tonight?" Lacey was asking, surprise on her face.

Ray shook his head. "Not locally yet. Some males, but no females. It's only eleven. Calls will start coming in. This gives me the creeps. It's like the girls all lay down and fell asleep. No evidence of thrashing about or fighting back."

"What happened?" Lacey asked. "Do you think they drank something?"

Mason tugged on his ever-present cowboy hat. "Possible." He was tight-lipped. Victoria knew he wouldn't speculate out loud.

"No cups," stated Victoria. "Unless you already removed them?"

"Nothing's been removed," answered Ray. "Not by us."

"Ghosts took them," stated the cop with the log. Victoria shifted to read his name. *Dixon.*

The group simply stared at Dixon.

"What?" Dixon met their stares. "Don't you know where we are?"

Victoria saw a flicker of recognition on Lacey's face. The forensic odontologist had grown up in the area. Victoria was originally from a tiny coastal town; she didn't know about Mason and Ray, but judging by their faces, they were clueless about the cop's reference.

"This part of the woods is haunted," Dixon stated solemnly. "All the high-school kids around here avoid this area."

Mason looked disgusted.

Dixon's brows narrowed. "You do know this isn't the first ring of suicides here, right?"

The two Major Crimes detectives called for confirmation. Sure enough. In 1968, six female bodies had been found in Forest Park. Only three of the bodies had been identified. Three had remained unclaimed for decades. Victoria rubbed at her arms in the cold, hugging herself.

How come no one had missed them?

"How is that possible?" she asked the detectives. An hour at the scene hadn't answered any of her questions; it'd only raised more. "How can no one miss three women? I can understand one person who possibly moved here from out of state, living as a transient going unidentified, but three?"

"It was a different era," commented Mason. "I knew there'd been a mass suicide in Forest Park a long time ago, but didn't know where. This place is gigantic. You can believe we'll be looking into it again."

Dr. Campbell stepped up to the group. "I'm done here. It looks like I'll be seeing these young women again. With the air temperature here I'd estimate it's been six to eight hours since death, but I'll have a more accurate window tomorrow after the lab work."

Her heart ached at the regret on his face. She knew he didn't like seeing kids on his table.

"What a case to catch near the end of my career," he added. "I hope to get a clear answer on this one. Soon."

"I didn't realize you were retiring, doctor," Ray said, raising a brow at Mason, who looked stunned.

"I'm looking forward to sleeping in and not getting phone calls in the middle of the night. Or during my dinner."

Both detectives nodded in grim agreement. "Holidays are also bad," said Ray.

"I'll stick around to help transition in the new chief examiner. We've narrowed it down to two applicants. Either will be a good chief."

"You're not promoting from within?" Mason asked.

"Not this time. I've got fine deputy medical examiners, but none of them want the extra responsibility of the position." Dr. Campbell turned and looked over the young women in the ferns. "This case will stick with me for a while."

"Detective Callahan," came a different voice.

The group spun to see the new arrivals in the forest. Another Portland police officer had spoken as he led two men to the scene. One was a man in a dark green uniform with a baseball cap that read RANGER, and the other was a tall civilian in jeans and a heavy jacket. The civilian's face was in the shadows, but Victoria stiffened at his approach. Something about the way he carried himself set off alarms in her head.

"This is Bud Rollins." The police officer gestured at the man in the ranger hat. "He's one of the park rangers and knows this forest inside and out. He's the first guy we call when we need help in here."

Mason shook hands with the slender man. "Sorry to get you out of bed."

"Not a problem. I like to know what's going on in my woods."

The weathered ranger spoke with a soft southern accent, making Victoria blink. The sound was a rarity in the Pacific Northwest. His eyes were kind, and she estimated his age to be in his early fifties. He scanned the scene ahead of him and paled. "Dear Lord. One of them lived?"

"So far," said Mason. "Doesn't look good for her, though."

The second man stepped forward and held his hand out to Detective Callahan.

Victoria couldn't breathe; her gaze locked on the man's face. Every coherent thought vanished from her brain.

"This is Seth Rutledge," said Dr. Campbell as he greeted the man. "Glad you could make it. Dr. Rutledge is one of the applicants for my position. I had the office call him to the scene," Dr. Campbell told Mason as the men shook hands.

Dr. Rutledge met Victoria's eyes. "Hello, Tori."

Everyone looked at Victoria.

Victoria pressed her lips together as she held Dr. Rutledge's gaze, her spine stiff, her hands crammed in her pockets, her ears ringing. "Seth."

Seth gave a half smile, and the shield around Victoria's heart started to crack.

"Been a while, Tori."

Victoria nodded and all ability to speak abandoned her brain.

CHAPTER TWO

Victoria couldn't believe it.

After a decade of silence, Seth Rutledge was standing in front of her with that familiar cryptic smile—the one that never exposed what he was thinking. Suddenly the years were gone, and she felt like she'd just seen him yesterday. When he'd abruptly dumped her for another woman.

Lacey was watching her with an expectant look on her face, indicating she knew something was up and was patiently waiting for an explanation. Victoria wasn't in the mood to share. Her past belonged to her. She didn't need sympathy or more questions from anyone. She scanned the group. Lacey wasn't the only one with the curious look.

"You two know each other?" Dr. Campbell asked.

Trust Dr. Campbell to ask the question on everyone's mind. Even the two detectives looked interested in their history. Few people had facts on Victoria Peres. She liked it that way.

"We were at Stanford at the same time," said Seth. "Haven't really seen much of each other since then."

Not since one night at a conference in Denver.

Victoria saw the same thought in his eyes.

He still thinks about it, too.

"I didn't know you were considering the position here," she heard herself say. How could she have known? She avoided office politics the same way she avoided office socializing. Her dinner with Lacey and Dr. Campbell tonight had been an anomaly. A result of Lacey pressing her and a bit of guilt that her boss was retiring, and she knew she'd be skipping the formal retirement party. A small dinner had seemed logical.

"I've been keeping the process quiet," said Dr. Campbell. "It was time to bring it out into the open, watching him interact with the staff and get a feel for the office. Come take a look at this one, Seth." He gestured at the younger man and headed over to the first girl.

Seth met Victoria's gaze once more and then followed. She watched him walk away, recognizing every distinctive motion of his body. She hadn't thought about him in years. How could he be so immediately familiar?

Her lower back felt damp. How unfair that the one man in the world she couldn't have was the only one who made her feel lovely.

"Wow," murmured Lacey for Victoria's ears. "How attractive is he? He looks like a younger Pierce Brosnan without the crooked teeth. You've got some explaining to do."

"We barely know each other," she lied. *Lacey would notice his teeth.*

"Bullshit."

"I haven't seen him in forever," Victoria amended.

"Well, he looks ready to renew your friendship."

"He's married."

"I didn't see a ring."

Really? "You looked for a ring?" Victoria eyed the other woman.

"Of course. I'm female."

"You're engaged."

"Engaged to the most amazing man in the world. But that doesn't mean I can't wonder about other people's marriage status. I'm not looking for me, but when I see a man who looks like that and is a doctor to boot, I wonder if he's married. Maybe I want to set him up with a good friend." She winked at Victoria.

"He's married," Victoria repeated. She looked past Lacey's shoulder to where Seth squatted with Dr. Campbell next to one of the sad bodies, deep in discussion. The tilt of his head set off sparks of memories, as did the width of his shoulders. Years of separation were evaporating every second. Next she'd be asking him to go for a run, forgetting they hadn't run together in ages. *It's only been five minutes . . . after nearly twenty years.*

Dr. Campbell's words about retiring ricocheted in her head. Could Seth be her next boss?

Oh Lord. *Could she handle that?*

Seth gestured at the dead girl's face, asking a question of the tech at the adjacent body, and Sarah moved over to open the girl's mouth. Dr. Campbell shone his flashlight in the girl's mouth.

"What are they doing?" Lacey muttered, her focus on the two men. The medical examiner looked over his shoulder and gestured at Lacey to join them. If there was a question about something in the mouth, Lacey was the woman to ask. Victoria followed her to the body.

"Whatcha got?" Lacey asked as she bent next to her father.

"She's got something covering her teeth," Seth said.

Lacey peered into the open mouth. "Looks like clear retainers. Can I have a pair of gloves?" she asked Sarah.

Victoria glanced at Seth and was surprised to find him looking directly at her. She met his look squarely. She couldn't get a read on his thoughts. He must have known she worked in the Oregon medical examiner's office, but he couldn't have known she'd be here tonight. Was he surprised? She broke eye contact in time to see Lacey pry one of the clear retainers off the top teeth with a loud snap.

"Not retainers," Lacey commented. "Invisalign. Invisible braces."

Victoria had seen them on TV. The appliances moved teeth into alignment with a series of progressive rigid trays. A feat of dental engineering that hadn't been available when she went through two years of metal orthodontics. "So she'll definitely have some dental records somewhere."

Lacey nodded, her face thoughtful as she studied the two closest girls. "How come they aren't wearing shoes? They don't look poor, the makeup and hair is perfect, nails are manicured . . ." She stopped as Seth abruptly shifted his position to view the soles of the feet.

"Perfectly clean," he stated. "Where in the hell are their shoes? Or did they fly in here?"

★ ★ ★

Seth watched Victoria talk with the other forensic specialist. The woman hadn't changed a bit. Still tall, immaculate, polished long black hair, and all-seeing with those intense brown eyes. Would she have pretended not to know him if he hadn't said anything?

He didn't like his answer.

Victoria Peres had every reason to give him the cold shoulder, yet she was being her professional self. Even in college she'd been ahead of the curve in maturity and poise. She'd stood out in her anatomy class with her intelligent questions. He'd known at once that she was a woman going places.

And she had. She'd traveled the world to study anthropology. Either digging for old bones or observing social situations. He'd read her magazine articles and tracked her professional life online. Then he'd heard about the opening at the Oregon medical examiner's office. His daughter had left for her first year of college, so there was no point in his staying in Sacramento. He applied, hoping to cross paths with the woman he couldn't forget.

When he'd gotten the call about tonight's deaths from the medical examiner's office, he hadn't expected to see her. He'd anticipated a hike in the dark woods and a depressing crime scene. Both of those assumptions had been accurate. Now, being around Victoria was like being around a moving flame in the clearing. He couldn't pull his gaze from her; he kept an eye on her at all times. Even when he turned his back, his senses tracked her. After nearly two decades of not seeing her, he felt like she'd never been gone. There was no learning curve to being in her presence; he instinctively knew what to expect.

The onsite professionals appeared to know her and respect her. The two police detectives had treated her with the utmost courtesy. He wasn't surprised. Victoria was one of those determined people who worked her butt off to achieve her goals. She didn't believe in shortcuts. She'd always succeeded at what she put her mind to.

He turned his attention back to the dead girls.

A fucking waste.

The scene reminded him a bit of the Heaven's Gate cult. In the late nineties nearly forty people had committed suicide together, hoping to catch a ride on a spaceship trailing the Hale-Bopp comet. He remembered photos of rows of neatly arranged bodies in beds, their faces covered with purple cloths and brand-new Nikes on their feet. There'd been a master planner at work who'd brainwashed the group.

Who would do this? Someone was involved. Someone who was still alive, because the girls' shoes didn't walk away by themselves. He had every intention of attending the examinations of these girls.

They were close to Eden's age.

He fought the anger crawling up the back of his throat.

Working on the endless stream of autopsies at the coroner's office in California felt different when the victim was from a crime scene he'd attended. Every body he worked on, he gave his best. But when he'd been present to see the setting of the atrocity, it sparked something inside of him, driving him harder to find justice for the dead.

He'd seen his share of bodies from crimes. It was a factor in what made his job so engrossing. Science meets crime. Science kicks crime's butt. It was a thrill to know he'd helped to bring justice to the assholes of the world who'd believed they'd gotten away with murder. It wasn't glamorous. It wasn't fun. But it was damned interesting, and he saw and learned something fascinating every day.

These girls didn't decide to lie down and die. There was a more powerful hand at work here; he could feel it. And that hand had cleaned up the scene.

"Dr. Rutledge?" Detective Lusco approached him. "Callahan and I are headed out. I just wanted to say good luck with the job selection process." The detective was a big guy, clean cut. He looked like a pro football player turned cop, and Seth estimated the detective's age to be a bit younger than his own. Even though it was the middle of the night, the detective looked as pressed and fresh as someone who'd just arrived at work. Seth looked like he'd just rolled out of bed.

"Thanks. Maybe we'll cross paths again."

"You'll have big shoes to fill. Dr. Campbell has an amazing reputation around here. Hate to see the guy go."

"He's done it longer than a lot of MEs. Wears away at your soul after a while. Probably like being a cop."

"This is the kind of case that does it," said Lusco, taking in the dead girls with a wave of his hand. "The young ones. Always pointless."

"Still no reports of missing teens?"

Lusco shook his head and glanced at his watch. "Shouldn't be much longer. Worried parents are gonna start calling."

Victoria spoke from behind him. "Unless it was one of those organized 'Tell your mom you're sleeping at my house, and I'll tell mine that I'm at your house' type setups." She stepped closer to join their conversation.

Seth studied her profile as she looked at Lusco. Her hair was pulled back in a ponytail, her chin raised and stubborn. Victoria Peres was a woman to be reckoned with. Still.

"Christ. I didn't think of that," said Lusco.

Victoria nodded. "That's because you were never a teen girl. They all did that."

Seth noted she didn't say "We all did that." It was hard to imagine Tori as a teen girl. Even though she'd been nineteen when they first met, she'd always been an adult. Lying to her parents about sleeping at a friend's house wasn't something she'd do.

"You might not get any leads until tomorrow, when the parents start calling each other," she added.

"Tomorrow is really gonna suck," stated Lusco.

Seth silently agreed.

Mason Callahan watched Lacey move away from the bright lights, still bodies, and low conversations into the shadows of the forest. Someone needed a break after the scent of death, he figured. Dr. Campbell often wore her heart on her sleeve. Not like Victoria Peres. You never could tell what she was thinking.

He nearly fell over when Dr. Rutledge called her Tori.

Mason had heard the forensic anthropologist called a lot of things, usually along the lines of Ice Princess and Bone Woman. Hard, unforgiving names. Dr. Peres had a knack for reading bones. Watching her handle the dry bones, scanning them with her fingertips as she felt every bump and valley. The woman knew what she was doing.

Cold was what his fellow officers called the Bone Lady. Antisocial and rigid. Officers who'd stepped a wrong foot in a one of her scenes called her Bitch.

Private, was Mason's assessment.

"Tori" sounded tender coming from Dr. Rutledge.

Holy crap. The Ice Princess had a past.

He shook his head. Victoria Peres was a tall and attractive woman, but there was something very off-putting about the way she interacted with people. Had she been different when she was younger? Dr. Rutledge seemed to know. Mason'd seen the way the doctor's gaze followed Victoria. Yes, there was certainly a history there. Mason cringed. Thinking about getting close to the Ice Princess made him uncomfortable; they had a good working relationship.

He also had a good rapport with Lacey Campbell, but it was different. They were connected beyond a social level. He'd met her briefly a decade ago after she'd nearly become a victim of the Co-Ed Slayer in her college years. Their paths crossed again last winter when she'd identified the remains of the Slayer's last victim and then was targeted by a copycat killer.

Mason followed the path Lacey had made into the forest. Away from the bright lights of the crime scene, it was peaceful. He spotted her leaning against a fir, brushing at her eyes as she tucked a cell phone in her purse.

"You okay?" he asked.

She started, gripping at her purse, then visibly relaxed as she made out his face. "Yes. I'm just getting a breath of fresh air."

Mason nodded. "Not your usual type of scene."

Lacey forced a smile. "True. I probably shouldn't have come. I do better in the sterile environment of the medical examiner's office."

"How is Jack?"

"Good. He's in Japan for work. I was just trying to reach him." Her smile faltered.

"No luck?" His heart ached a bit for the young dentist. She was petite and fragile in appearance, but he knew she had a spine of steel. He'd seen her cry as she held the hand of a parent of a dead child, and he'd seen her focused and training at the gun range, struggling to calm the demons a serial killer had left in her soul.

She'd twice lived through a nightmare. The type that would put most people in a mental ward the first time.

"No," she said.

"What are your thoughts on girls this age? What would drive a teen to do this?"

Lacey blinked at his question, her eyes wide in the dim light.

"You're the youngest female here," Mason expanded. "And you've worked with kids this age, right? In gymnastics lessons? I'm picking your brain for some insight. I've got a son about this age, but girls think differently."

"It's been a few years since I've read *Seventeen* magazine. But I think kids today have the same pressures. Their looks, their friends, being with the right crowd, saying and doing the cool things, wearing the right clothes."

Mason nodded. "But there's more in their lives now. Instant communication. Instant worldwide knowledge. Pictures from around the world show up on their phones to share with their friends. The need to know about everything first."

Lacey drew in a sharp breath. "Do you think someone took pictures? Someone had to have walked away from here. Christ! Do you think there're already pictures circulating of this scene? Do you have someone monitoring social media? Looking for anything macabre?"

Mason knew that once a picture was on the Internet, it would never completely disappear. The source could be taken down, but shares could spread uncontrollably.

"We thought of that. We've got people on it."

She exhaled. "What a mess."

"It could get really ugly. We used to just worry about photographers selling pictures to the media. Now, everyone can be their own media site. Although we definitely would trace where it started."

"I hope no one did that here. Those poor girls. Their families . . . How horrible to know images of your dead daughter were floating around the Internet."

"I'd kill someone if they posted pictures with my kid," Mason stated. And he would. He didn't see much of his son, Jake, because he lived with his mom and stepdad. But Mason did everything he could to keep in close contact with the teen. Some days the hardest thing he did was get that kid to have a conversation with him on the phone. It'd be easy to let him drift away. Mason fought to keep that communication open.

Mason looked back at the white circle in the ferns. Lacey followed his gaze.

"Some parents are about to have the worst day of their lives."

CHAPTER THREE

The TV droned in the background as Trinity poured her bowl of cereal. Her upset stomach from the day before was gone, and she'd woken up starving. She sniffed at her cup of coffee and felt her stomach spin a bit. Okay. Maybe she wasn't totally better. She set it aside. Coffee wasn't really her thing anyway.

Maybe she'd try again tomorrow before school. Today was Sunday, and she didn't need caffeine. In fact, once she finished her cereal, she was headed back to bed. She caught the high-school bus at 7 A.M. each weekday, so she rarely passed up a chance for extra sleep.

Her homework load was insane. Trinity took every advanced class she could, wanting that cheap college credit. Money was tight. It'd always been tight. She was a master at stretching out the life of drugstore makeup and punching up the look of her own clothes. In fact, she had a sweatshirt from Goodwill to alter. She'd spotted the almost-new Hollister hoodie on the men's rack yesterday. It was big and needed to be taken in just a bit. If she got it done today, she could wear it tomorrow. Happier, she plunged her spoon back in her cereal.

The phrase "Forest Park" caught her attention, and she focused on the TV. Black body bags on stretchers were being wheeled out of a trailhead and into waiting ambulances.

Her vision tunneled and sweat started under her arms.

Doors slammed on the back of an ambulance and it drove off. Its lights weren't flashing and its siren was off; it wasn't in a hurry.

Trinity couldn't breathe.

The camera swung back to the trailhead. More stretchers. More bags of death.

". . . the five teenage girls haven't been identified and the sixth in the hospital may not make it," said the broadcaster over the images.

Brooke?

Trinity's hand shook and she dropped her spoon in her cereal. She grabbed her cell phone and fired off a text to Brooke. She waited, heart pounding, lungs tight. Her cereal burned in her gut. Her phone was quiet.

Please, God, no. Please, please, please!

Over the next ten minutes she sent two more texts. Still no answer. That wasn't like Brooke. She was an extremely social high-school senior; the girl took her phone everywhere except into the shower. Not like Trinity. She considered herself to be on the high end of the shy scale. She almost felt honored to be one of Brooke's closest friends. Trinity's friends were few but very tight. Brooke mingled with everyone, but Trinity was part of her inner circle.

Brooke should have texted back by now.

What had happened?

The calls started pouring in during the morning news broadcast. Making his own calls about the dead girls, Detective Mason Callahan was thankful he didn't work at the call center. All night no parents had called, looking for missing kids, but once the body bags appeared on the news, the county's emergency network had been flooded.

Ray hung up his desk phone. "That park ranger from last night showed up downstairs a few minutes ago. He's got a guy with him who saw the girls last night in the forest while they were still alive. The desk sergeant stuck them in an interview room."

Mason stood up and pushed in his chair, grabbing a notepad from the stack on his desk. Finally. Someone who'd seen something. So far the morning had brought empty leads, frustration, and an acid stomach. "Let's get on it." He headed to the door with Ray at his heels, passing a television tuned to local news. Mason caught a glimpse of a reporter in front of the trailhead he'd entered last night.

" . . . parents are flooding nine-one-one saying their kids haven't answered their cells . . . "

"Holy crap. There're only six girls." Ray Lusco ran a hand through his hair. "How come all these parents don't know where their kids are?"

"Don't your kids spend the night with friends?"

"Well, sure. But if my kids don't answer their cell phones, you better damn well believe I'll be calling the parents."

"Both have cells now?" Mason asked. He knew Ray's daughter had made a big deal out of wanting one a year ago, but his son was two years younger, barely in his teens. What would the boy need with a cell?

"Yeah, Ben wanted one after Kirstin got hers. Now it spends most of the time dead on the floor of his room or kicked under his bed. Glad we didn't spend a bunch of money on it. Kirstin is on hers nonstop. Texting. That's all she does. It takes her ten minutes to text a conversation she could have wrapped up in one minute with a phone call."

"What's the fun in making a call?"

Ray snorted. He peeked through a small window in the door of Interview 3. "What the hell?"

Mason couldn't see around Ray's bulk. "What?"

"He's got a dog with him."

"The park ranger?" Mason glanced at his notepad. "Rollins?"

"No, the guy with Rollins." Ray sighed and opened the door, muttering something about allergy medication.

A large shepherd/collie/lab mix eyed both men as they entered the room, but it sat quietly next to its human. Mason didn't think the dog would be a problem, but the body odor in the room was about to choke him. The dog's owner was a transient, brown clothes, brown hair, brown skin. A brown backpack leaned against his legs. Heavy hiking boots were planted on either side of the backpack; the owner's gaze met Mason's.

He's not nuts.

Portland had a large transient population. An ongoing issue for the police, politicians, and people who wanted to help. Mason's encounters with transients had convinced him the majority of the people had mental issues that kept them on the street, unable to function in society. But a few were not mentally ill; they were people who'd purposefully chosen to live a different life or fate had simply dealt them a crappy hand.

Bud Rollins, the park ranger he'd met briefly last night, stood and held out a hand to the detectives. "This is Simon. He saw the girls going into Forest Park last night. I hunted him down this morning to ask if he'd seen anything, because I know he's frequently in that area."

Mason mentally added what Bud didn't say. *Simon lives illegally in the park.*

"What did you see?" Mason asked the brown man.

Mason didn't care if the man had an illegal campsite. He just wanted to know what Simon saw and get a feel for whether or not he was credible.

Ray sneezed.

Simon rubbed his dog's head, his gaze calmly shifting between Mason and Ray. "I saw a teenage girl walking on one of the trails late last night. I followed her and watched for a bit, concerned because she was alone." Simon spoke carefully in a low tone. "The park isn't somewhere young girls should be alone at night."

No shit.

"When she met up with another girl on the trail, I relaxed and was about to leave when I saw one more catch up. I followed the three of them just because I was curious. They were all dressed in white and were clearly excited about something."

"They see you?" asked Ray. "It was pouring last evening. What about coats and umbrellas? How were they able to follow the trails?"

"They all had coats and umbrellas. Flashlights, too."

"If they wore coats, how'd you see the dresses?" Mason asked, searching for inconsistencies.

Simon wasn't rattled. "Their dresses were longer than the coats."

"Did you have a flashlight?" Ray sniffed and wiped at his nose with a tissue.

"Yes, but I rarely use it. I know my way around and batteries are expensive."

"Did you see how they entered the park? Did a vehicle drop them off?"

Simon shook his head. "They were already a half mile in before I came across the first one. No, they didn't see me. At least the girls didn't. It was when the guy—"

"A man was there?" Mason interjected. *Their unknown death scene arranger?*

Simon looked Mason in the eye. "Yes, a man, older than the girls. Tall, thin. He stared into the brush in my direction, so I left. I don't know if he saw me or not. There were three girls with him when I left. I figured they were in a group big enough to be safe."

"You're the Lone Ranger of Forest Park? Watching out for people?" Ray asked.

The transient's mouth twitched on one side. "I've broken up a scuffle or two. Drunken idiots. Usually I keep to myself."

"You know your way around Forest Park in the dark? That's a big place. Thousands of acres." Ray sneezed again.

"I know that section of Forest Park perfectly. I don't venture into the rest that much."

Mason glanced at Bud, who was nodding along with Simon's statements. The park ranger seemed to be comfortable with the man and was taking him at his word. Nothing Simon said had set off any concerns for the park ranger.

"So why follow the girls?" Mason asked. He wasn't getting a predator vibe from Simon. He seemed smart and composed, but some of the sharpest criminals fit that description.

Simon was silent and glanced down at his hand on the dog's head. "I have a daughter."

Mason wondered how long it'd been since he'd seen her.

Bud Rollins spoke up. "Simon's given me a hand a time or two. He didn't want to come down today, but when I explained what'd happened up there, he said he'd describe what he'd seen."

"What else can you tell us about the man? Age? Clothes?" Ray had his pencil poised over his notepad. "Would you recognize him again?"

Simon looked thoughtfully at Ray, paused and then shook his head. "I don't think so. What sticks with me the most is that he was the opposite of the girls. Dressed in black. The girls listened to him, seemed to know him well. He wasn't their age, definitely not teens like they were . . . but not middle-aged either, somewhere in between . . . maybe twenties or thirties?"

"You said they seemed excited?"

Simon nodded. "Chatter, body language."

"You didn't catch any of the conversation?"

He shook his head. "Wasn't close enough."

"Were they carrying anything else?" Ray made a note.

Simon's brows came together. "I think some of the girls may have been carrying a small bag or purse. The man had a large duffel he'd slung over one shoulder. I only saw three girls—you say there were six altogether?"

Mason nodded. "You didn't go look at where they were found?"

"I went to look this morning after hearing about it. Saw the police everywhere and left before I could get anywhere near it. One of the girls survived?" Simon asked.

"So far," Mason said. "Doesn't look good." He glanced at his watch. He hadn't heard an update on the girl at Emanuel Hospital in more than two hours.

"I'm gonna have someone come take a full statement. Tell them everything you can remember, no matter how insignificant it seems," Ray directed. "Anything else you think we need to know right away?"

Simon was silent for a few seconds and then shook his head.

"What's your last name, Simon?" Ray asked.

The room was silent as Simon and Bud exchanged a look.

"Parker," Simon stated, looking calmly at Ray.

Mason held out a hand to the man. "We appreciate your help." Simon stared at Mason's hand for a brief second and then shook it firmly. Ray did the same and the detectives left the room. Mason took a deep breath of fresh air.

"Seems like a decent guy," Ray commented as they headed back to their desks. "Think he has a camp in the forest?"

"Probably," Mason muttered.

"Think he's nuts?"

"No. But I don't know what to make of him. He's a little hard to read. Very mellow, very in control, and thinks before he speaks. Not like the usual transient from the street."

Simon seemed to be a straight shooter, and Mason respected that. But he knew to not rush to judgment. By offering his help, Simon became their first suspect to clear.

"I knew there had to be someone else with that group. What do you think about an older guy possibly influencing a bunch of high-school girls?" Ray asked.

"It's possible. Now tell me why he did it."

Ray was silent for a minute. "Good question. What did he get out of it? He didn't get sex, according to the initial evaluation at the scene. At least last night he didn't. Maybe it was to cover up what he had gotten previously from the group of girls? Dead girls tell no tales?"

Mason's mind raced at a hundred miles per hour. He didn't want to think about a man sexually abusing teen girls. "I'll wait to hear back from the autopsy. It'll show if the girls had been abused."

"Maybe it was consensual sex. Maybe a group—"

"Jesus Christ, Ray. Turn it off." Mason needed to focus on one thing at a time. A sexual angle was a definite possibility, but until he had some evidence indicating that direction, he wouldn't obsess about it. "If you've got an angle to theorize on, write it down. Right now we need to get over to the medical examiner's office and get some autopsy results to point us in a direction. Then we'll put together a history on Simon Parker."

Keys in hand, Victoria grabbed her purse and dashed out her back door. She'd told the medical examiner she'd be in early Sunday morning to help with the girls from the forest. It wasn't early anymore; she'd slept through her alarm. She silently swore. She was never late. She darted down her steps, headed to her garage behind the home, and saw a figure move from the corner of her eye. Blood pressure rocketing, Victoria whirled to face the movement, planted her feet, and pointed her pepper spray in her attacker's direction.

The girl shrieked and tripped backward, hands in the air.

"Trinity!" Victoria's heart stopped as she registered her teen neighbor's face. "You scared me to death!" She lowered the spray and willed her heart to restart. *I nearly sprayed her.* Of course, there were worse things than being nailed with pepper spray. The stuff made your eyes burn and stole your breath until you wanted to puke, but you'd live.

"I'm so sorry, Dr. Peres. I was just about to knock on your front door when I heard you out back."

Victoria blew out a breath. Her neighbor looked truly rattled. Well, that made two of them. Trinity lived a few houses down. Currently a senior in high school, she'd struck up a conversation with Victoria two years ago while she was weeding her yard. When she'd discovered Victoria worked for the medical examiner, she'd begged her to speak to her careers class. Surprisingly, Victoria had a blast interacting with the high-school kids, changing their beliefs that the medical examiner's office was like *CSI* and telling them how it really worked. The teacher asked her to return the following year, saying he'd never seen the kids so fascinated.

Yes, death was fascinating when you studied it at a distance.

Hands-on experience was different.

Still fascinating, but much messier.

Victoria slipped her pepper spray back in her pocket and took a closer look at Trinity. The teen was pale, her eyes red with a look of desperation. "What's wrong?"

In Victoria's opinion, Trinity was a smart girl. Street smart and school smart. She'd been in the foster system since she was ten. Her mother had ended up in prison after too many drug convictions, and Trinity had been bumped through several foster families. Her current situation was stable, and she'd confided that she'd hoped to stick with her foster mom, Katy, through high school. Some of her previous homes had given more stress than help.

"Did you see those girls on TV? The ones found in Forest Park?" Trinity couldn't hold still. She clenched and unclenched her fists. Her blonde ponytail bobbed as her feet shifted and her gaze pleaded with Victoria.

Victoria stiffened. "Did you know them? Do you know what happened?"

"I don't know! My friend Brooke isn't answering her phone. And I know she was going up there last evening. Can you find out the names of the girls who died?"

Victoria swallowed. "They don't know who they are yet. There wasn't any identification with them. What does your friend look like?"

"She's got long dark hair. Blue eyes—"

Victoria's heart fell.

"Oh my gosh!" Trinity froze, her gaze locked on Victoria. "You know? You know what they look like?" The teen looked ready to vomit. "I told her she shouldn't go. The whole situation didn't make sense!"

Victoria placed her hands on Trinity's shoulders and held the teen's terrified gaze. "Yes, they all had long dark hair. Each girl did. But that doesn't mean one of them is your friend. I'm headed to the ME's office now, and I'll see what I can find out. Have you talked to your friend's parents?"

Trinity looked at the ground and her shoulders slumped. "I haven't. Brooke told them she was spending the night with me. I didn't want to get her in trouble if nothing had happened to her."

Victoria tightened her grip. "Listen to me. You're not doing your friend any favors by covering for her if she's doing something dangerous. You don't know where she was last night?"

Trinity shook her head. "She was doing another photo shoot. She told me it was at Forest Park. But she didn't say exactly where."

"A photo shoot? At night?"

"I know, right? That's what didn't make sense." Trinity's voice cracked.

"Who's taking pictures?"

"This guy. I don't know who he is. A friend of hers from a different high school put her in touch with him. He was looking for a girl with long dark hair for modeling. He made Brooke darken hers. He said everything about her was perfect for his pictures, but her hair needed to be a little bit darker."

Red flags were waving in Victoria's head. "Some guy? Another student?"

"I don't know! Brooke never said. I think he was older. He had all sorts of photography equipment and had already done some other photo shoots with Brooke and some other girls—"

"He took pictures of her with other girls? Did you see them?"

Trinity shook her head. "No, I saw pictures of just Brooke. They were really good."

Victoria glanced at her watch. She needed to get Trinity to talk to Detective Callahan. Now. "Do you know Brooke's parents' phone number?"

Trinity shook her head. "I know where she lives."

"Get in the car. We're going to stop by there. And then I'm taking you to talk to the police. Let your foster mom know what's up, okay?"

"I'll call her."

"Trinity." Victoria paused. "Do you have a current picture of Brooke?"

The girl's eyes widened as she nodded. "She texted me one of the professional shots. It's still on my phone."

Victoria doubted the man was a professional. "Good. The police will need to see it." She didn't want to look at the photo. The girls last night were too similar to each other, and they'd blended together in her memory. She was the wrong person to ask if Trinity's friend was one of the bodies.

She'd let someone else break her young neighbor's heart.

CHAPTER FOUR

Victoria passed through the quiet halls of the medical examiner's building. She wasn't early, but she'd beat almost everyone else. According to the cars in the parking lot, only the office manager, Anita, and Dr. Campbell were here along with his assistant, Jerry. She'd left Trinity with Anita to wait for the police detectives, writing up what she knew about her friend's activities last night and a description of Brooke. Usually only a few employees worked the weekends at the ME's, but more people would show up today. The deaths of kids brought an urgency to the job, driving people to search for answers as quickly as possible. She unlocked the door to her tiny office and flipped on the light switch with a sigh, appreciating the peace. It wasn't going to last. Soon the place would be buzzing.

She wouldn't want to be in Dr. Campbell's shoes today. It would be a triple P day. Press, police, and parents. He was already hard at work with the victims.

She estimated she'd had four hours of sleep. She, Lacey, and Dr. Campbell had left the eerie scene close to midnight, but she hadn't crawled into bed until 2 A.M. And then she'd spent the next hour thinking about Seth Rutledge and those girls. It'd been a difficult night. Anyone who'd seen the circle of girls would never forget that image.

The crime scene tech had been right. It'd looked like a fairy tale.

The beautiful girls waiting to be awakened by a prince. But these girls were never going to wake up.

Six sets of parents would endure the worst day of their lives. Hopefully one pair would have a happy ending if their daughter survived. Victoria knew the sixth girl had virtually no blood pressure or respirations when she'd been discovered in the woods. Something chemical had depressed their systems, slowing them down. Victoria suspected phenobarbital overdose. The heart slows, the breathing slows, everything crawls to a stop. It'd take some fast action to overcome. Possibly the surviving girl had been the last to ingest the drug or not taken as much.

Victoria said a silent prayer for the girl and her family.

Last night she'd Googled mass suicide, wondering what other drugs had been used in suicides. Surprisingly, the episodes with the Heaven's Gate cult, Waco, and the women long ago in Portland were the only mass suicides on American soil, but she wondered how many deaths it involved to be classified as "mass." The well-known Jonestown suicides took place in South America, although they involved many Americans.

"Don't drink the Kool-Aid," she mumbled. She'd learned it hadn't been Kool-Aid used in Jonestown, but its less popular cousin, Flavor Aid. *How had Kool-Aid become embedded in American memory?*

She wasn't surprised to find that phenobarbital had been used in Heaven's Gate, but cyanide had been used in Jonestown. Phenobarbital was a little easier to find. It was still widely used worldwide for treating seizures in humans and dogs. And it was low in cost. Unsurprisingly, the main complaint about taking phenobarbital was that it caused sleepiness.

The articles about the long-ago deaths of women in Portland's Forest Park were scarce. She found some old references in *The Oregonian*'s archives, but it'd never been a national story. Maybe there were other mass suicides that hadn't become part of the national memory? Her curiosity was piqued. The detectives had mentioned the old suicide case would be looked at again, and Victoria planned to be one of the lookers. She wanted to be hands-on with this case. Looking for clues to identities in deaths this old fell under her umbrella of expertise.

The anticipation of working on the old puzzle gave her brain an electrical surge. Her fingers ached to examine their bones and uncover their stories. And then find out the relationship to the crime of last night. Who would duplicate the old crime?

The first step was to find out what had been done with the remains of the women. Last night Lacey mentioned three had never been identified or claimed, so that implied the remains could be in a few places. They could be skeletal and in storage, cremated and in storage, or buried. As long ago as this event had occurred, Victoria suspected they'd been buried. She crossed her fingers against cremation.

She sent a message to the office manager asking for help to find the remains. If anyone could hunt down the records, Anita could.

She turned away from her computer with a sigh and shuffled through the files on her desk. She had five new requests to examine bones found by the public. Usually these were bones found in people's backyards or while out on hikes. Ninety-nine percent of the time the bones were from animals. There were eight requests from police departments around the state asking for help with bone identification. Two were highlighted as urgent in relation to missing persons cases. She glanced at the attached photos on one, shaking her head at the close-ups. *Cow?* she scribbled in the margin, eyeing the bulky proximal end of the humerus. Definitely nonhuman, although she could imagine the stocky bone in a hefty troll leg.

Three interoffice cases requested a consultation on open investigations. She scanned through Dr. Campbell's neat notes and, for the hundredth time, regretted his upcoming retirement. *Please let the next ME be as thorough and organized.* Would that person be Seth Rutledge?

She closed the files and massaged her temples. Every thought had flown from her brain last night at the sight of the tall man. She'd instantly transformed into a nervous college freshman staring at the good-looking teaching assistant. Speechless. It'd taken her a good sixty seconds to recover from the shock of Seth's appearance at the crime scene.

Could she work with the man on a daily basis?

Where was his wife? Victoria had confirmed Lacey's observation that Seth didn't wear a ring. But that meant nothing. Many men didn't wear wedding rings, especially if they worked with their hands in the way Seth did.

Had he left Jennifer? What about their daughter, Eden?

Or was the whole family moving north to Portland?

Victoria felt a sharp pain in her left temple. Could she spend each day working with Seth and then watch him go home to his family in the evening? She rubbed at her forehead. Stupid. Getting worked up over a situation that might never happen. She exhaled several times, trying to clear her mind of the thought.

Another male face intruded in her mind's eye. Rory had called her twice this morning. She'd let the calls go to voice mail, but he hadn't left a message, so she didn't call back. She wasn't up to speaking with her ex-husband at the moment, and he could always text if it was important. Issues Rory found important were rarely important to Victoria. And vice versa. Hence the term "ex-husband."

She resolutely pushed back her chair, stood, and pulled on a lab coat. She was wasting brainpower. Bones were waiting for her analysis, and she wasn't going to let an old crush or ex-husband disturb her day. She strode out of her office and nearly ran over Seth Rutledge in the hallway.

Victoria barreled out of her office. If Seth hadn't put out his hands to stop her, she would have plowed into him. Surprised brown eyes met his, and he stood frozen with his hands on her shoulders.

"Hi," he said as his mind short-circuited. *Hi? That's all I can say?*

She licked her lips, and he dropped his grip.

"Sorry about that. I thought you were going to knock me down," Seth said.

"I'm on my way to the lab," she answered.

He watched her throat as she swallowed hard, but she kept her gaze steady with his.

Silence stretched between them.

"You look great, Tori." His tongue finally working, Seth saw that soft lines and angles of her youth had become polished edges. Not hard edges, but mature edges honed by life events. *How much of her life had he missed?* For all the instant recognition he'd felt when he saw her last night, he was painfully aware that he knew nothing of her current life. The only sign that he'd just surprised her was a brief flutter of her eyelashes behind her librarian glasses. Her chin lifted a fraction and he saw shutters close in her eyes.

They'd once meant something to each other.

But he'd fucked things up.

Had time helped her forgive him?

"Good luck with your job interview," she said and moved to pass him.

"Wait!" He touched her arm and she halted, a quizzical look in her eyes. "Can we have lunch together today? Or at least grab coffee later?" The cold shadow in her gaze sank his hopeful heart. His answer regarding her forgiveness shone in her eyes. It wasn't what he'd hoped.

"How is Jennifer?" she asked.

He deserved that. "Fine. We're getting a divorce."

"Divorce?"

"We're getting a divorce," he repeated. The words were still foreign to his tongue.

Brown eyes studied him, and he felt them judge the weight of his statement. "I'm sorry. I hope Eden is doing well."

"She's doing great. She's in her first year at the University of Washington."

A small smile touched Victoria's lips. "I can't believe she's that old. Seems like just yesterday . . . " Her words trailed off, and the smile vanished.

Seth knew what she meant. Seemed like just yesterday his daughter was a toddler, and everything between him and Tori had been swept out from under them. All the dreams and hopes that blossom at the beginning of a fresh relationship. That excitement of something new, something with big potential. Gone in a moment. Taken away without notice.

"Good luck with the job," she said again. This time she pushed by.

He watched her move down the hall, her footsteps echoing in the silence, lengthening the distance between them. For the briefest moment, he'd felt their old comfortableness surround them. At one time they'd been close. Close enough to start tentatively mapping out a life together. With one sentence, he'd shredded their plans.

He sighed and headed to the autopsy suites. Dr. Campbell had said he'd be starting this morning with the teenage girls. Seth wanted to watch the man in action and give a hand if needed. Parents would want answers soon. If Eden was missing, he'd be tearing down the ME's door.

He tried to put the encounter with Tori out of his mind, but her face invaded every thought. Every nerve ending in his body was on fire. He hadn't known that the sight of her would open an avalanche of emotion and memories, knocking him upside the head.

Was it too late to repair the thread he'd severed years ago?

Eighteen years ago

Victoria's anatomy textbook took up half of the table. Her notes took up the other half. She'd spilled coffee on her notes. It hadn't been her fault. A jock had jostled her elbow as he'd pushed by her little table in the crowded coffee shop. She'd recognized him as a

Stanford football player. A rowdy group of students had invaded the little store, raising the decibel level several points. The shop was always loud, but she found it easy to study. Somehow tuning out the noise helped her stay focused.

She concentrated on the drawing of the distal end of the femur in her text, committing to memory the differences of the anterior view from the posterior. She wanted to hold one in her hands and feel the actual ridges. She'd slip into the classroom early tomorrow. A traditional wired-together plastic skeleton stood in the corner of the room. Since they'd started the skeletal system, she sat as close as possible to the grinning form, eyeing the bones as the professor lectured. She couldn't dawdle after class because she immediately had a chemistry class. But going in early was a good option.

She loved college. She loved the independence and the ability to immerse herself in what she found important. High school had so much extracurricular crap that simply didn't matter. What good would pep rallies do for her career? Or student council? They weren't going to get her into medical school. Books and her own determination would.

Her adoptive parents had been very nurturing. They valued education and hard work. They'd brought her up in a structured one-child household, teaching her self-discipline and manners. *What if she hadn't ended up with them? What if she'd ended—*

A tall male pulled out a chair from her table and sat directly across from her. She stared into intense blue eyes and lost her concentration.

Seth Rutledge was sitting at her table.

She tightened her grip on her pencil, her hands suddenly icy. Seth met her gaze and gave a comfortable half smile as if he sat with her every day.

"How's it goin'?" He leaned on his forearms on the table and shifted closer so she could hear him over the noisy hum of surrounding conversations.

Victoria froze.

She'd studied him in class as much as she'd studied the skeleton. As a teaching assistant for her anatomy class, Seth usually sat in one of the front corners of the lecture hall, his profile prime for her gaze. Occasionally he would turn her direction, but she'd hastily shift her gaze to the professor. Seth Rutledge was a bit of a distraction. Tall, athletic, dark-haired, with a genuine smile that made most of the girls in the class focus on him instead of the professor. Victoria had noticed that Seth's line of students with questions during office hours was usually longer than the professor's. And mostly female.

She'd been guilty of stopping in during office hours with a question or two. Seth had always been polite and spot-on with his answers. It'd been more of a test to see if the brain in his head was as gorgeous as the man. As far as she could tell, Seth Rutledge was the real deal. Blessed with smarts and looks. But he didn't seem to have the ego that accompanied the looks.

"You having any problems with that?" He nodded at her text.

Victoria blinked. *Speak.* "No, not at all."

The silence dragged between them. She continued to study his blue eyes. He had the slightest bit of gold around the pupils and his black lashes created perfect frames for the masterpieces.

Speak more!

"I really like this section of the class. I'd rather study the skeletal system than the respiratory system any day." *Much better.* She commanded her lips to give a casual smile. "What are you doing here so late?"

Sometimes Victoria ran down a checklist when she carried on a conversation. Social skills weren't her specialty. She admired women who could talk on and on about anything under the sun, but for her it was a struggle. She was a private person. She spent a lot of time in her head, studying and analyzing the world around her; that didn't mean she wanted to share her thoughts with every person she met. To avoid the tongue-tying conversations, she'd formed a mental checklist. First on the list was to turn the topic back to the other person. She didn't care to talk about herself.

Seth smiled as if he'd recognized her tactic. "I'm usually walking by here about this time of night after using the pool. I live only a block away. I've seen you in here at late hours several times."

He'd noticed her?

"Ah . . . I haven't seen you."

"That's because you've always got your nose buried in a text. No wonder you ace every test."

Elation bubbled in her chest. He'd noticed her *and* he'd noticed her scores. The look in his eyes was frank admiration. Was he flirting? Or was he just being polite? What had driven him to sit at her table? She tilted her head. Sincerity rang true in his voice and gaze.

He's interested in me?

"Do you swim every day?" Victoria repeated rule number one, turning the conversation away from herself.

"Just about. I like to do it in the late evening. The pool isn't crowded and I can focus and think about other things. Helps me sleep, too. I get a weird sort of energy that I need to burn off in the evenings or else I can't sleep. It's a nighttime ritual for me."

"I like to read," said Victoria. "I switch to fiction before I go to sleep, otherwise I lay awake thinking about what I was studying."

Seth nodded. "But what do you like to do for fun?"

"That *is* fun. You're not a reader? Fun doesn't have to be physical."

His eyes crinkled as his grin grew, and she winced at her words.

"That was funny."

Victoria's cheeks heated, but she kept her chin up. Seth continued to grin, and she felt her stomach do a quick series of flips.

"I guess I feel like I read so much for school, the last thing I want to do is read some more," he said. "Usually I'm dying to get out the door and get moving. Apparently that isn't a problem for you?"

She shook her head. "I take a yoga class twice a week, but I can't say I go there with energy to burn."

"I'd ask if you need any extra help in class, but it's pretty apparent that you don't. You could probably do my job."

She studied his face and mentally dissected his last sentence. Why would he ask if she needed help in class? Because . . . "Are you asking me out?" she blurted.

"Yes," he said calmly.

"Isn't that against some sort of rule?"

"Only if I'm a professor." He frowned lightly. "Or are you uncomfortable with the idea of going out with a teaching assistant? I'm not going to screw with your grades or help you out. You don't need help anyway. I don't know why you've asked me the questions you have during office hours. It was pretty clear that you knew the material inside and out."

Victoria held her breath. And held his gaze.

"You're smart, you're gorgeous, you're going places. Why wouldn't I ask you out?"

He thought she was gorgeous? "How many other students from your classes have you asked out?" The question slipped through her lips. It was a bit rude, but she wanted to know. She wasn't falling for the teacher-boinking-the-student scenario.

"None."

"None? Really?"

She must have looked doubtful. He straightened in his chair and repeated firmly, "None. I dated someone back home for a couple of years. We ended it a while ago. I haven't dated anyone else since I've been here at school." His gaze touched her lips, then cheeks and went back to her eyes. "You've been stuck in my head for weeks. I think it started one of the rainy nights I was passing by here. You were studying at this same table, scowling at the text like you were furious with it, and chewing on your lower lip. Did you know you do that in class too? Mainly during tests but sometimes during the lectures. Anyway, I was passing by, considering grabbing a coffee for the cold walk home, and I recognized you from class. Since then . . . " He shook his head, that half smile curling up his right cheek. "Yeah, you stuck in my head."

Victoria stared. If he'd said he was a time traveler, she wouldn't have been more surprised.

In shock, she agreed to a date.

CHAPTER FIVE

"What's a psychological autopsy?" Mason asked as he avoided looking at the young girl on the metal table.

The medical examiner had just mentioned the possible need for an unfamiliar type of autopsy. Dr. Campbell stood back as he watched his assistant stitch together the gaping chest incision that the examiner had created an hour before.

"It's an investigation to discover the state of mind of these girls before their death. Right now I can't even classify these deaths. They could be accidental, suicide, or homicide. I know the results of the tox screen will indicate what stopped their hearts and respiration, but it's not going to tell us how it got in their system. Did someone else put it there, or did they take it willingly?"

Mason was familiar with the NASH classification for deaths. Natural, accidental, suicide, or homicide. Natural was easy to rule out in this case, but the ME had a good point. They needed more information. As soon as these girls were identified, they'd have a place to start. Dr. Campbell had efficiently sped through the first girl's autopsy, from the Y incision, to the tissue samples, to peeling back the scalp to remove part of her skull and examine the brain. When the doctor had moved down the table to take a vaginal swab, anger had burned through Mason. The girl was almost a child, defenseless on the metal table. He offered up a prayer that her soul had left the room and wouldn't witness the indignities her body would suffer. Mason had stared at the light fixture and films through most of the procedure.

Autopsies were impersonal, the essence of the victims departed, but it took a lot of effort for Mason to be present for many of his cases. The autopsy suite was one of his least favorite places in the world. He'd hoped that over the years he would have grown accustomed to the sights and smells; he still waited. Each autopsy rattled him and visually stuck with him. He saw his role in the autopsy suite as honoring the victim. He'd stand at attention, respecting the science that would help bring justice. He was an honor guard starting his work for the victim. Often the victims were alone at their moment of death; they didn't need to be alone for this final affront.

"Who does the psychological autopsy?" he asked.

"I have a couple of psychologists who I've worked with in the past. Usually it's the type of situation where information is needed to settle estate issues or insurance cases. They do in-depth interviews with family, friends, and witnesses. They'll look through social media and emails if they can. Even look at the victim's preference in books and television shows. They have a list of suicide indicators they look for."

Doctor Campbell's definition sounded a lot like Mason and Ray's job. He raised an eyebrow at the doctor.

"Oh, I know." The doctor nodded at him. "That's stuff you'll be doing. But I've got to say, I've never had a case so up in the air from the very start. Did they kill themselves? Did someone give them something lethal without them knowing? Or was it an accident? A bunch of girls trying out something cool they didn't know would take their lives? It's too early to say we'll need one for certain, but I'm going to keep it in mind if we struggle to figure out why this happened." The older man shook his head and Mason sympathized at the sorrow in his eyes. The doctor had four more autopsies to do.

"What's the word on the sixth girl?" the doctor asked.

"I haven't heard anything for a while. So I'll guess 'no change.' I asked them to call immediately if something happened."

Ray stuck his head in the autopsy suite. "I just ran into Dr. Peres," he said with a nod at both men. "She's got a teen neighbor who thinks she knows one of the girls."

"So does half the city," muttered Mason.

"Dr. Peres's neighbor says her friend went to Forest Park for a photography session yesterday and now she can't reach her. Also says the missing girl has long dark hair. The neighbor is out front with Anita." Ray stepped just in the suite and stared at the hair of the young girl on the table. He didn't move any closer. "She told Dr. Peres that there's a photographer who wanted teen girls with long dark hair to model for him."

"Jesus Christ," said Mason. "I wonder if that's who Simon Parker saw with the girls. He didn't say anything about photography equipment, but the man was carrying a bag. That'd be a good hook to get teenage girls to go with you. Doesn't every girl want to be a model at some point?"

Ray nodded. "I know Kirstin loves to watch that model competition show and can't keep her nose out of fashion magazines. Dr. Peres's neighbor goes to high school with the missing girl."

"She ever meet the photographer?"

"No. And Victoria took her to the missing girl's home, but there's no one there, and she doesn't know how to contact the parents. She brought her to the office, so we can talk to her."

"That'll be a starting point. I'll be there as soon as I can," said Mason.

"We've got upset parents starting to arrive," added Ray. "How do you want to handle this?"

Mason looked to the ME.

"I'll have Anita write up a quick questionnaire for the parents to fill out so we can make some immediate eliminations. Questions about height, weight, scars, hair, tattoos, and eye color. What they think their kid was wearing. Plus it'll give these parents something to do. Nothing is worse for them than standing around."

"What about showing photos?" Ray asked. "They're already asking out front."

"Not yet. I've taken good face shots, but that step comes later," Dr. Campbell said. "I want them screened heavily. I won't show these faces to anybody who walks in here because they know a kid who's missing. They need to bring in their own pictures, and if they can get their dentist to email digital dental films on a Sunday, that'd help. I want secondary confirmations, either dental or DNA once we get a positive visual ID. As soon as Lacey gets here, I'll have her put together some preliminary dental findings."

Ray nodded. "I've already started a list of questions to ask the parents, so I'll work with Anita and get Victoria's teen neighbor to fill out a form."

"Scars and unusual things we can note visually will help. Put moles on there, too," Dr. Campbell said. "I've never had a situation with this many similar victims at once. I won't have a screwup like that case back east with two similar-looking teen girls a few years ago. One died in a car wreck while the other one lived, but she was hospitalized and in a coma for a while. A set of parents buried the girl they thought was their daughter. Turns out she was unconscious in the hospital."

Mason faintly remembered the case. "We won't let that happen."

The doctor put a hand in the middle of his back and arched it, grimacing. "I've got some more girls to take care of. This is going to be handled right."

Seth Rutledge stepped into the autopsy suite in full scrubs and gown. He acknowledged the detectives with a nod and greeting. "I can give you a hand," he said to Dr. Campbell.

"Much appreciated," he said. "I can put you to work."

Seth followed Dr. Campbell into the next suite and wondered what Tori was doing. Their brief run-in this morning hadn't gone smoothly. He'd been looking out from a window, waiting for her to arrive. He felt a bit like a stalker, but he'd simply wanted to see her, study her a bit without her knowing. She was still adept at throwing up defenses. It'd been years since they'd crossed paths the last time. A forensics conference in Denver had put them face-to-face for the first time since they split in college.

They'd both been in relationships at the time. Him with Jennifer, and her with Rory. He'd been confident enough to engage her at the conference and suggest dinner. After all, they were both committed to other people. Why couldn't they have a simple meal to catch up? What could go wrong?

What went wrong was too much wine and too much reminiscing.

It'd been one kiss.

Its indications had been explosive.

Seth shook his head, forcing the memory out of his thoughts. The night hadn't ended well, and Tori had left the conference without saying good-bye.

He'd flown back home to Sacramento to his wife, realizing he'd failed her and their daughter. But that failure hadn't occurred in Denver. It'd occurred when he'd agreed to marry Jennifer for the wrong reasons. He'd always known it wasn't the right path for either of them, but it'd seemed the best for their daughter.

How wrong he'd been.

He pictured Tori as she'd walked into the medical examiner's building earlier.

Her looks were slightly exotic with dark eyes too large for her face. Her last name was of Hispanic origin, but she'd always appeared more Mediterranean, more Provençal. She'd eventually told him that she'd been adopted. She'd laughed and said her parents were lucky to adopt a dark-haired daughter instead of a blue-eyed blonde. Fewer questions.

In college, he'd felt instantly connected and later had wondered why he hadn't missed her before he'd known her. Why hadn't the giant hole in his heart been obvious? Once she'd filled that hole, he'd seen his emptiness with clear eyes.

Today he was back to square one with the gaping hole in his soul. Its emptiness resonating every time he thought of her. He missed the woman he'd clicked with so long ago. He placed part of the blame on Jennifer. She'd lied and manipulated him, capturing him where he'd been the most vulnerable. But he could have ended things better with Tori.

Or could he? A breakup sucked no matter how it was handled.

He'd asked "What if?" a million times over the years.

Now he was determined to make amends.

Dr. Campbell's voice entered his thoughts and Seth started. "I'm sorry, what'd you say?"

The older man's eyes narrowed thoughtfully. "You're a million miles away."

Seth smiled. "You don't know the half of it."

"Dr. Peres?"

Dr. Campbell noticed more than he'd let on.

"Yes, she's part of it," he admitted.

"You two have a history? Is it something to keep you from working together?"

The question had been on Seth's mind. "Yes, we have a history. But I don't think it's an issue. It is something I need to talk to her about. If I'm going to make her uncomfortable, then I won't take the position."

Dr. Campbell strolled over to study the X-rays of his next subject. He rubbed at his chin, his gaze on the black-and-white images. "Victoria's the best forensic anthropologist I've ever worked with."

Seth understood what the man hadn't said out loud. "I don't want to hurt her," he replied.

The ME turned and took a long look at Seth. The ME's scrutiny was intense, and Seth fought not to squirm. "You're divorced, right?"

"The divorce process started quite a while ago. They take time."

Dr. Campbell nodded. "Is it going to be messy?"

Seth took a deep breath. "It could get that way. That's part of the reason I left. I need to be away from her while this happens. It doesn't help her to see me. She needs to go on with her life and not trip over me once a week somewhere."

"What about your daughter? She's what, eighteen?" The older man's eyes were fierce, flashing concern for the innocent girl in the divorce

Seth swallowed. "I waited until she was off to college. I've talked with her over and over about the divorce. She's my primary concern, and she's fully aware of the type of person her mother is. She told me she was surprised I stuck it out this long. She says she understands. "

"They always say that. They don't want to hurt you."

"I know. But she's at least accepted it on one level. I don't know if any child of divorce totally gets over it, even in the smoothest divorce. But she's a smart kid, and I really believe she'll get through it. She knows her mother and I still love her. We just can't live in the same house. Or city."

Dr. Campbell studied Seth for a moment, evaluating him as deeply as the X-rays. He had a hunch the doctor didn't miss much. In that case, the ME would see no deception on Seth's part. He'd left a marriage that'd been doomed from day one, and he was simply starting a new chapter in his life.

"I don't know how retirement is going to treat me." Dr. Campbell's tone lightened as he turned back to the films. "I've always had my finger on the pulse of this operation. I know the ins and outs, the dark corners, and where the dead bodies are buried," he joked. "I hope this office and I can adapt to having my input abruptly cut off."

"Maybe you should ease your way out," Seth offered. "Work part time for a while."

Dr. Campbell shook his head. "Sometimes a clean break with a fresh start is the healthiest way to handle the changes in life. People step up to the task when they are faced with challenges. Letting go slowly, hoping to smooth things out, often doesn't help anyone."

Seth silently exhaled, grateful for the doctor's understanding.

Victoria skimmed the email from Anita and silently cheered. There was a reason the woman was the office manager. She could find anything and work miracles. Even though parents and press were clamoring for identities on the dead girls, Anita had managed to hunt down the location of the remains of the women found in Forest Park decades ago.

Victoria was one lucky anthropologist.

The three sets of skeletal remains were boxed in the cold case storage. No cremains.

She fought the urge to do a happy dance in her chair. The women could have been cremated and stored in canisters. Or buried. Instead, someone long ago had reduced the remains down to skeletal and placed them in boxes and stored them away, hoping their mystery could be solved in the future. Now they waited for Victoria to read them and search out answers about their identities.

The main question in the old case still ate at her. How could three women not be claimed? She tapped her glasses on her desk, her chin resting on her hand. Didn't they have families missing them? She'd caught the latest news update, which had expanded to include the event of so long ago. The three who had been identified had previously been runaways or suspected prostitutes. None of them had originally been from the Portland area, but their families had all stated that they'd deliberately left home. Two had fought with their parents and ran off. The third had informed her family she was leaving for greener pastures.

No doubt the similarities of the new case would send reporters digging deep into archives. Perhaps some fresh exposure would trigger memories or reach people who hadn't known about the three unidentified women. In her opinion, the two similar cases had the potential to go viral on the Internet. It had the key ingredients—tragic death, young women, and nearly identical occurrences decades apart.

Ugh. That wasn't the type of publicity the examiner's office needed right now. Hopefully the sensationalism would stay out of the way. She scribbled the reference numbers for the storage room on a scrap of paper, her curiosity level hovering somewhere in the stratosphere.

Her cell phone vibrated on her desk. Intending to ignore the call, she stood and was pushing in her chair when the name on the cell screen caught her eye.

Oh, come on. Not now.

Her ex-husband was calling. Again. She spoke with Rory about once a month since the divorce two years ago. They were still friends—well, they were still acquaintances. She never felt the urge to meet him for a drink, and she only tolerated his phone calls. She classified that type of relationship as an acquaintance. Why was he calling so early on a Sunday? The Rory she knew should be sound asleep from being out too late last night.

Had she mentioned her ex-husband still thought he was in college?

Her hand hovered over the phone. And hit Ignore.

She headed for the storage rooms.

CHAPTER SIX

Trinity sat in the waiting room at the medical examiner's office and tried to make herself disappear. She hunched over her clipboard, glancing occasionally at the growing number of people milling about the room, avoiding eye contact. No one asked her any questions. The growing crowd was mostly adults, and each one or couple had a clipboard with the questionnaire.

The room was tense. Some parents cried, others spoke in hushed tones, and more simply stared into space, their hands in a death grip or clenching a spouse's hand. Cell phone screens were constantly checked and calls made. Trinity's questionnaire about Brooke was finished, but she hadn't turned it in. As long as she didn't hand in the form, Brooke wasn't confirmed as dead. She clung to the clipboard, her fingers icy and her feet numb.

Ever since she'd seen the news on TV, she'd felt like she couldn't get enough oxygen. Her brain was locked away, protected from thinking deeply. A door slammed in her mind if she started to consider Brooke's fate. She'd floated, barely functioning on half power since speaking with Dr. Peres.

In her heart, she knew something was wrong.

Brooke always returned texts.

Trinity read the questionnaire for the hundredth time.

Age

Hair color and length

Eye color

Height

Estimated weight

Any unusual scars, birthmarks? Braces or tattoos?

Clothing last seen wearing

Brooke didn't have braces or tattoos. Trinity didn't know about any scars. The form was so sterile. It didn't allow her to describe Brooke's beauty or laugh. Or explain what a good friend she'd been . . . was. She'd filled in answers that were short and cold. Brooke's sunny smile flooded her brain, and she immediately shut the image down.

Don't think about her.

The parents in the room had filled out their forms as quickly as possible and given them to Anita. Some had demanded to view the girls' bodies and were deftly turned away. Others sat silently in the chairs, staring at their cell phones, sending texts, and waiting. Trinity counted nine tissue boxes in the room. All were getting regular use.

"Oh, thank God!" shrieked a woman staring at her phone. She and her husband leaped up, and she fell into his arms, her shoulders shuddering. He hugged her hard, his head buried in her neck. Pulling apart, they stumbled across the room to Anita's desk, tears spilling down their cheeks.

"My daughter just texted me back. She was at her boyfriend's instead of where she'd told us she was spending the night." The woman's voice cracked as Anita dug through the questionnaires and pulled one out.

"I'll shred this," Anita said to the mother.

"No, I want it," the mother said grimly, holding out her hand. "I want to show her what we went through because of her lies. Maybe she'll learn something."

Anita nodded and handed her the form. The couple headed out the door and all of the other parents watched them through the large windows. Halfway across the parking lot, the mother stopped and turned to her husband. She collapsed against him, her legs visibly shaking. They embraced in the lot, leaning heavily on each other.

The other parents looked away.

Trinity trembled. She wondered if her foster mom was on her way. She'd gone to church, leaving Trinity home with her upset stomach. Katy knew Trinity was with Dr. Peres at the ME's office and had promised she'd arrive as soon as she could. How long would she have to wait? Dr. Peres had said the police wanted to talk with her.

She walked to Anita's desk and quietly laid down the clipboard. The woman gave her a kind smile as she pulled Trinity's form from the board and added it to her stack. "How are you doing, hon?" The woman had a grandmotherly quality that made Trinity want to curl up in her lap.

Trinity forced a smile, feeling her dry lips stretch. "Fine, thank you. Do you know when the police will talk to me?"

Anita's brows came together. "Let me check with Dr. Peres." She glanced at her watch. "Have a seat—"

"Trinity?" A blonde woman in scrubs stepped into the waiting room. "I'm Dr. Campbell. Dr. Peres asked me to get you."

The woman was smaller than Trinity. And she was a doctor? Was she a real doctor or one like Dr. Peres, who studied bones?

Trinity followed the woman out of the waiting room and into the bright hallway.

"One of your friends is missing?" the doctor asked as they moved rapidly down the hall.

Trinity forced her legs to move. A fuzzy cloud still enveloped her senses, requiring extra effort to walk and focus. "I knew she was going to Forest Park yesterday. And now I can't reach her."

Sadness crossed the young doctor's face. "So many girls."

"Have you seen them?" Trinity whispered.

Dr. Campbell halted and turned to face her. "I have," she answered. "And I'll never forget it." Her wide brown eyes were soft with sympathy.

"Are you a doctor like Dr. Peres is a doctor? Or a real doctor?" Trinity blurted.

The woman smiled. "I'm a dentist. I work for the medical examiner as a forensic odontologist. I study their teeth to help identify people."

"So you looked at the fillings and stuff on those girls? And you'll compare them to what their parents and dentists say they had done to their teeth?"

"Exactly."

Trinity tried to remember Brooke's teeth. She couldn't remember anything obvious. They were white and straight like most people's teeth these days. Except her own. Her lower teeth were a little bit crooked, but her foster mom said it wasn't noticeable and that Trinity was lucky to have such good genes she hadn't needed braces. Which was extra-lucky because as a foster kid, dental care was scarce.

"You've already looked at all their teeth? Brooke had perfect teeth . . . in the front, anyway. I don't know if she had any fillings on her back teeth."

Dr. Campbell nodded. "I've looked at four of them so far. For the most part, they have great teeth. What I'd expect to see on healthy, middle-class teen girls." She didn't volunteer any more information.

Trinity slipped her cell phone out of her back pocket. *Would the doctor look at a picture of Brooke?* "Umm . . . would you . . ."

Dr. Campbell placed a hand on her arm, stopping her, her eyes sad. "You can show your pictures to the police, okay? We'll let them figure it out by the evidence, not by me guessing from a picture."

Heart sinking, Trinity dropped her gaze and shoved the phone in her jeans. The doctor was right. She didn't want to hear it *might* be Brooke; she wanted to know the truth.

"Brooke wouldn't kill herself," she said quietly. "They're saying on the news it could be suicide. I know her. She was looking forward to the homecoming dance next week. She had her dress and everything."

Dr. Campbell pressed her lips together. "The reporters are speculating. Don't listen to them. They don't know what happened and they're simply saying what will get the most attention on TV. The police and the medical examiner are the only ones you should listen to."

Trinity looked into her earnest brown eyes and nodded. Dr. Campbell was deadly serious.

"Victoria asked me to bring you to her. The police aren't ready to talk to you, and she was worried about you sitting alone out there. She has a project you can help her with."

"Ah . . . okay." Trinity had no idea how she could be helpful. Maybe the doctor needed some filing done. Or maybe Dr. Peres was simply trying to keep her distracted. She followed Dr. Campbell through a maze of hallways and into a large room that looked like a lab. But this lab had bones. Lots of them. There were three small metal tables, each with a skull and a shallow bin of bones. Dr. Peres was taking bones out of one bin and organizing them on a table.

Sweat sprouted on her temples and Trinity's vision tunneled. Foggily she felt Dr. Campbell grab her arm and push her into a chair. She shoved Trinity's head between her knees. "Take deep breaths."

"Didn't you tell her what we'd be doing?" Dr. Peres asked, concern filling her voice. Her feet moved into Trinity's view and she squatted next to her, her hand on Trinity's shoulder.

"No. I thought I'd let you do that. I didn't know you'd already have the skulls out on the tables when we came in," answered Dr. Campbell.

"Are those . . . are those . . . " Trinity's mouth was too dry to form the words. She stared at the floor as it moved in and out of focus.

"They're real, if that's what you're asking," said Dr. Peres.

Trinity closed her eyes. *How had they removed the flesh so fast?*

"Oh, honey!" Dr. Campbell kneeled and tried to look Trinity in the eye. "These aren't the girls! These are some old skeletons. Dr. Peres thought you might like to help lay them out. She said you were interested in anthropology. I should have warned you!"

Trinity exhaled. *Of course. They wouldn't have cleaned the bones already.* "I'd like to help . . . I think." She lifted her head carefully, expecting to see black shadows rushing her vision again. All seemed clear. Both doctors examined her with concern.

"Maybe another time," Dr. Peres said. She took stock of Trinity's face and frowned. "I can find you a magazine and let you know when the police are ready to talk to you."

"No, really. I'm fine. It was just a shock. Those girls have been on my mind for hours and to step in and see . . . " Trinity scanned the room again and tried to get a grip on her breathing. She could do this. A distraction would be good. One of the skulls faced her, appearing eerie without its jaw and lower teeth. Could she handle touching the bones? It couldn't be much different than the plastic skeleton in her anatomy class. She was interested to see if she could fit the pieces together. It'd be like a giant puzzle.

"Who are they?" she asked.

Dr. Peres turned to study the tables. "Women. They were found in Forest Park several decades ago. In a similar position to how the girls were found last night."

"What?" *It'd happened twice?*

"There were six, just like last night. But with these women no one ever figured out who three of them were," answered Dr. Peres.

"How can that happen? How can no one be looking for them?" Shock roiled through her, and her personal fog cloud vanished.

Dr. Campbell spoke up. "I suspect someone, somewhere missed them. I don't know if back then they were able to get the word out well enough. They didn't have the immediateness of the Internet to inform the world. I wonder if the story ever went beyond the Northwest."

Trinity looked at the skulls in a new light. *Had families been wondering for years what happened?* "You have to figure it out. You have to let their families know," she said to Dr. Peres. "How old are they?"

"They were young women. Late teens or early twenties."

Alarm raced up Trinity's spine. "What do the police think?"

Dr. Campbell gave a sad smile. "I don't know what they think, yet. Dr. Peres is going to assess the remains and see if she can find any indicators for who these women were."

The importance of Dr. Peres's responsibility rendered Trinity speechless. *What was it like to have such an important job?* She studied the tall woman. The doctor didn't look stressed or upset. She looked ready to get to work. Trinity's budding desire to be a fashion designer suddenly seemed trite.

"Why, Victoria," said Dr. Campbell. "From the expression on Trinity's face, I'd say we have a future forensic anthropologist on our hands."

Dr. Peres pulled her gaze away from the closest skull and studied Trinity. Her eyes were warm and a rare smile curved her lips. "It's not a job for everyone." She tilted her head as she considered Trinity's face. "But I think you might do."

A new path to her future rolled out in front of Trinity.

Victoria saw Trinity was wary as she studied Callahan and Lusco across the table. Victoria had snagged a small meeting room at the medical examiner's office for the detectives to have a private talk with the teen. Her foster mom was on her way and had given permission for the men to talk to Trinity as long as Victoria was present.

Trinity had good reason to be suspicious of police; her background was a sad one. Her birth mom had been in and out of jail multiple times for drug use and theft. Trinity had lived with her grandmother part of that time until the state realized Grandma had sticky fingers, too. The mother and grandmother ran a resale business out of their home with the items they stole from local stores. They were as busy as a Walmart. The locals knew where to buy cheap batteries, cigarettes, and skin care; they didn't care if the products were tagged with the grocery store's security sticker.

Callahan and Lusco watched the girl with careful eyes, and Victoria wondered if they saw the same thing she did. Trinity Viders felt like a breath of fresh air in the medical examiner's office. Victoria and the detectives had spent the morning with dead girls, and it was invigorating to see teenage eyes that blinked instead of staring foggily at the ceiling.

Victoria didn't like to judge by appearances, but she appreciated that Trinity didn't dye her hair pitch black or have multiple piercings in her eyebrows. Her blonde hair was neatly pulled back, her chin was up, and she didn't wear makeup except a light layer of mascara. Victoria hoped detectives saw a solid kid in spite of the hell she'd been through.

"We tried to contact Brooke's parents," Lusco started kindly. "No one is at the house. Any ideas where to find them?"

Trinity shook her head. "Maybe they left for the weekend. They don't usually leave Brooke home alone, though . . . of course they thought she was spending the night at my house." Her gaze dropped to her hands clenched in her lap. Victoria noticed she'd bitten her nails to the quick. One outward sign that the girl's emotional state wasn't as calm as she projected. She did a good job keeping herself in control. Her eyes were red, but her gaze was steady.

"Dr. Peres said your friend was meeting a guy in Forest Park?" Callahan asked.

Trinity nodded. "I never met him. He's a photographer. I've seen some of the pictures he's taken of Brooke. And some other girls, but I didn't know them. She posted them on her Facebook wall and texted me one."

"What kind of pictures?" The detective tensed and exchanged glances with Lusco. Victoria remembered their case last summer that involved pictures of small children and a sexual predator.

"The pictures were beautiful," said Trinity. "They were good enough to be in fashion magazines. Or hung on someone's wall. They were light and airy with an overexposed look to them. The girls wore white dresses that sorta faded into the background. It put the emphasis on their faces. I can show you." She pulled her phone out of her pocket and tapped on the screen. "I gave this photo to the lady out front along with the form I filled out on Brooke."

Callahan took the offered phone and stared. Victoria had already seen the photo. It was a stunning picture. Everything was white except for the girl's black hair. Her eyes were closed and she reclined on a white couch in the center of a golden field. There was nothing improper or sexual about the picture. She saw Callahan's chest relax a degree.

"Do you think she was one of them?" Trinity whispered.

Callahan blinked and pulled his gaze away from the picture. He handed the phone to Lusco. Trinity looked nauseous. "I'm sorry, I don't know," Callahan said. "They all had similar hair like this. I just can't tell."

Victoria watched Ray study the image, and his expression suddenly blanked. *Ray thinks he recognizes her.* From her brief time with the bodies, Victoria thought two of the dead girls could possibly be Trinity's friend. It was hard to tell. A body loses much of its character in death. She'd purposefully not tried to compare the picture to the girls. That was up to Dr. Campbell.

"Do you know how your friend met the photographer? Or who else might have been meeting them that night?" Lusco asked.

"I think she met him through Facebook."

"What?" Victoria felt ill. How many horror stories had she heard about girls meeting in person with someone they'd met online?

"He was shooting someone else she knew . . . I don't know who . . . I think she went to a different high school. But when Brooke said she liked the photos, her friend put her in contact with him through Facebook. At least I think it was Facebook. Maybe it was Instagram."

"My daughter has an Instagram account," said Lusco. "I get on there and snoop around occasionally."

Callahan looked at Lusco and raised a brow. "I don't know the ins and outs of Facebook or Instagram. My son keeps telling me to get an account so we can share photos."

"I'll get the cyber guys to look into it," said Lusco, making a notation on his notepad. "Anything else you can remember Brooke said about this guy?"

"She was really excited that he was interested in her. I mean, interested in taking her picture. I didn't like that he told her to darken her hair, but it made the pictures look really good. I remember he'd told her she had the exact look he wanted."

"Look? What did she mean?" asked Callahan.

"I asked that, too. She said he was looking for her age, build, and hair color for a certain photo shoot he was creating for someone."

"So the pictures weren't for him?

Trinity shrugged. "I had the impression there was a client."

"Did he pay her?"

"Not that I know of. I think she would have done it for no money. She was excited that someone thought she was beautiful enough to model." Trinity's eyes moistened and her shoulders sagged. "She was so pretty. She's dead, isn't she?"

Victoria's heart broke, and she wrapped an arm around Trinity's shoulders, wishing her foster mom was there to comfort the girl. Trinity didn't seem to mind and buried her face in Victoria's shoulder.

Ray Lusco kneeled beside Trinity's chair, patting her back. "Hey. We don't know that. But you need to be ready in case that's how it turns out. If it helps at all, it would have been like falling asleep. We don't know what exactly killed them, but I can tell you it wasn't violent."

Trinity nodded, wiping at her eyes. She sniffed, and Callahan nudged the tissue box closer to her. To Victoria, he looked completely out of his element. Plenty of men froze at the sight of a woman's tears. She knew Lusco had a daughter and a wife. He knew how to handle this type of situation.

"We'll find out what happened to these girls. And we'll find out who was responsible." Callahan promised.

Trinity looked up and held his gaze, searching for truth in his eyes. She nodded.

Victoria met Callahan's brown gaze. He was on a mission.

She believed him, too.

CHAPTER SEVEN

Ray hung up the phone on his desk. "That was an odd one. We've got a guy who just came in claiming to know one of the original women who was found in the circle decades ago."

"Seriously? Where the hell's he been all these years?" Mason was irritable after the long morning at the medical examiner's office and glad to be back in the familiarity of his office. Watching beautiful girls get sliced up did that to him. He'd left with an overwhelming sense of urgency to solve their senseless deaths. And figure out what'd happened in the same spot decades before.

Digging into the old case, Mason was amazed at how little information there was on the original women. Like the recent scene, the old photos showed women with long dark hair, wearing white dresses. The bodies were arranged in the same circle. The main difference was the women hadn't been discovered for nearly a week. Back then, Forest Park hadn't been the mecca of popular hiking trails it was now.

The three girls who had been claimed all had similar sketchy histories. They hadn't gotten along with their parents and had run off, or they'd simply wanted a fresh start and left town for a new life. One had been arrested for prostitution in Seattle and Portland in the months before her death. Her arrest photos were in his growing file. Susan Wilbanks had been an attractive young woman from Idaho. Her dark brown eyes had stared blankly at him from the photo, her mouth downturned. She looked like a woman with a lot of regrets.

What had driven her to prostitution?

It bugged the hell out of Mason that no one had stepped forward, looking for the other three women. The detectives from the old case had been unable to draw any connections between the three women who were identified. Besides Susan from Idaho, one had been from Montana and the other from Pendleton in eastern Oregon. The women back then had been slightly older than last night's teens. The original women had been in their early twenties, possibly late teens. He wondered if Dr. Peres had made headway on clues into the women's history. Old bones could tell amazing stories through science and technology in ways they didn't know about in 1968. And if anyone could find something new, Victoria Peres would be that person.

How much crap would they dig through to find the truth? The story was bringing the nuts out of the woodwork, claiming they had information on the old crime.

What were the chances the guy in the lobby was legit?

The desk sergeant had screened walk-ins with stories all morning. This was the first one he'd put through since the transient, Simon Parker. A preliminary search on Simon had turned up an honorable discharge from the military and a work history in construction until three years ago. Mason wondered if an injury had put a halt to the construction jobs. Or was it the recession? No priors, nothing suspicious at all. It confirmed Mason's gut feeling that Simon wasn't their man.

Mason stood up and pushed in his chair. "Let's see what he has to say."

Ray slipped on his sports jacket over his long-sleeved peach Polo shirt. Mason eyed his own wrinkled jacket on the back of his chair and decided to skip it. He followed Ray down the hallway and into the same interview room where they'd talked to Simon.

A man paced the small room as the detectives stepped inside. His hands were clamped behind his back, his shoulders stooped, and his face set with heavy lines that spoke of a life of stress. His hair was a pure white, but his eyebrows were thick and black. Old-man brows. Coarse and spiny. Mason made a mental note to check his own brows when the interview was over. Usually Ray was good about letting him know if he was looking straggly. Ray noticed things like that.

The man eyed them from under the thick brows. His dark gaze assessing. He stepped forward and held out a hand. "Lorenzo Cavallo."

He pegged Lorenzo's age at late seventies. His speech was thickly accented. The detectives both shook hands and introduced themselves. Mason gestured at the chairs and Lorenzo sat heavily, sighing. He had an old manila envelope that he set on the table before him. Mason eyed it as he and Ray sat.

"What can we do for you, Mr. Cavallo?" Ray asked.

"Lorenzo, please. I heard on the news this morning about those young women they found in the forest." Lorenzo met Mason's gaze.

Mason nodded but said nothing.

"The newscasters talked about women who'd been found the same way there a long time ago." Lorenzo lay a gnarled hand on his envelope but didn't open it. "They're saying these young women had long black hair like the women did back then. And that no one had ever identified three of the women from before."

Mason kept his mouth shut. If Lorenzo was fishing for information, he wasn't going to get it from him.

The old man moved his gaze to his envelope, his finger toying with a ripped corner. Mason noticed the envelope was weathered and thin at the edges. It'd lived in someone's storage for a long time.

"My family moved here when I was twenty. There were eight of us. My parents and my younger four sisters and brother. We didn't speak English. Us children picked it up pretty quickly. My parents not so much. They eventually learned enough to get by, but either kept to themselves or socialized with other Italian-speaking families. There weren't many of us in the city back then."

"You lived in Portland?" Ray asked. "And you came from Italy?"

Lorenzo nodded but still kept his gaze and hand on the envelope. Mason noticed he wore a plain gold band on his left hand. He had working man's hands, the nails short and stained. The stain looked permanent.

"My father opened a garage. He knew automobiles. Especially Italian ones, but there weren't many of those here. He learned the American autos very quickly and gained a reputation as an honest man."

Mason looked at Lorenzo's nails again. *Auto grease?*

"My brother and I worked in his shop. We did well."

Mason mentally patted himself on the back.

"One of my sisters did the books. The other girls were much younger and stayed home with my mother." Lorenzo paused, his lips pressed tight as if they were reluctant to pass on the words. "My youngest sister, Lucia, was a disappointment to the family."

What the hell did that mean? Mason raised a brow but kept his jaws shut.

Lorenzo opened and closed his mouth a few times as he tried to phrase his next sentence. "I was gone, you understand, by the time she was grown. I had a family and had moved south to open a garage in Medford. I didn't pay mind to my parents' complaints about her wild ways. I thought they just didn't understand young people, especially American young people. My sisters wanted to be American teens. They wanted to dress and speak like the others they went to school with. My parents struggled to keep up."

Here it comes.

"Lucia had been gone for two weeks by the time my mother told me she'd left. She didn't want me to know. My father was humiliated that his daughter had left him, and he wrote her off, declared she was dead to him. She had a boyfriend and had been out late a few times, but she'd never vanished before. According to my mother, her battles with my father were epic screaming matches. My mother sent her to live with my aunt for a while, hoping she'd settle down and get along with my father when she returned. It didn't work. They fought worse. One day she left, swearing she wasn't returning. And she never did."

Lorenzo looked at Ray then at Mason. "I saw the old photos, grainy from the newspaper, on the news today. I'd never heard of the deaths before. I guess we lived too far away. Medford was very small and a good distance from the big city of Portland."

"Surely your parents or siblings heard of the women's deaths and wondered if one was Lucia," said Ray.

Lorenzo shrugged. "To them, she wasn't missing. She'd left. My parents never spoke of her again."

"But what about your siblings? Your sisters had to wonder what happened?"

Lorenzo gave a sad smile. "You don't know my father. If he said Lucia was dead to the family, then she was. My sisters may have wondered where she went, but as far as the few discussions I've had with them, they've always assumed she'd formed a new life elsewhere."

"No one looked for her? No one asked questions?" Ray sounded flabbergasted.

Lorenzo shook his head. "If they did, I didn't know about it. I had my own family to deal with. Five boys," he added proudly.

Mason wanted to punch the old man. *Holy shit.* What kind of family lets a sister vanish and not ask questions?

When's the last time you talked to your brother? Fuck that. Mason knew his brother was alive and ornery as ever in Washington.

"So you're wondering if one of the women in the past was your sister," Mason stated.

Lorenzo nodded. "The descriptions match. The date matches. Lucia vanished two weeks before the estimated date of those deaths."

"You remember the date your sister left?" Ray asked, one brow rising. Mason had caught the same inconsistency in the man's story. If he hadn't been around and had brushed off his sister's disappearance, why did the date stick in his head?

Lorenzo fiddled with the envelope. "She left on my father's birthday."

Mason nodded. No doubt the father took that very personally and frequently commented on the disrespect. Sounded like something his old man would have done.

Scowling, Lorenzo shoved the envelope across the table to Mason. Mason wondered what kind of relationship he'd had with his father. An immigrant with old country values, trying to survive and keep his history in a new world.

"Those are the only pictures I have of Lucia. They are old, of course. Perhaps there are photos of the dead that were not released to the public. Maybe you have something else that you can compare them to."

"Our best bet would be a DNA sample," said Ray. "We still have the skeletal remains of the women. They can extract DNA and create a comparison."

Lorenzo stared at Ray, his mouth opening slightly, his face flushed. "They were never buried? No prayers said over them?"

Mason shifted in his seat. He wasn't religious, but he tried to respect the beliefs of others. "Uh . . . no. No one knew who they were, let alone their religion. They were kept in the hopes that someday their mystery could be solved." He cleared his throat. "We've already got one of the best forensic anthropologists in the country examining them, looking for identity indicators that our predecessors may have missed or not had the knowledge of."

Lorenzo leaned back in his chair, nodding. Mason could tell the lack of interment upset him, but he'd understood the reasoning.

"Do you remember if Lucia ever broke any bones?" Ray asked, his pencil poised over his notebook. "Or any unusual characteristics about her teeth? I'll get a tech in here to take a cheek swab for DNA if you consent. That will get things moving in the right direction. It can take a few weeks to get results."

Lorenzo gestured at the envelope. "You can see her teeth. I don't remember if any of my sisters ever broke bones. And yes, I'll do the DNA testing."

Mason unfolded the flap of the envelope. It smelled old. Like a bookstore full of used books. He shook the contents out onto the table. Three black-and-white photos slipped out, yellowed and faded with age. Two were small photos with thick white borders. They were family pictures, informal groupings with two adults and six children clustered together. Mason glanced at them and quickly discarded them; the faces were too small. The large school photo was the one he wanted. A beautiful girl met his scrutiny; her strong will shining from her eyes. *Oh, yes. I bet you gave your father hell.* The picture was a formal school shot with her hair in the popular bouffant style of that decade. Dark eyes, dark hair, and distinctively crooked upper front teeth.

Score.

Mason's day brightened. Victoria Peres and Lacey Campbell were going to love the photo.

CHAPTER EIGHT

Victoria opened the back of her vehicle to unpack her gear, feeling clear of the stress of yesterday. Last evening, all the girls had been identified. It'd been a dreadful day, but when the last girl was confirmed, she'd wanted to weep from the relief. Trinity's friend, Brooke, was the girl fighting for her life in a hospital bed. Brooke's parents had returned from a night at the beach to find their daughter near death. But they were the lucky parents.

Dr. Campbell had slowly gone through the questionnaires, eliminating the obvious and setting aside the possibles. It'd narrowed down to nine missing girls who fit the general descriptions. Victoria had heard the other three missing girls had eventually made their way home. All three had spent the night and day with friends, either deliberately avoiding communicating with their parents or blaming dead cell phones.

The five dead girls were beautiful. Victoria and Lacey had looked at their school photos, tears streaming down their faces at the sight of the life and energy that leaped from the pictures. What a waste. Each attended a different local high school, but they all were cut from the same cloth. Vibrant, healthy, cheerful young women, whose parents all swore their daughters had no desire to kill themselves.

It matched what Trinity had said about Brooke. These were girls looking forward to dates next week and college next year.

Someone poisoned them.

Someone deliberately destroyed that beauty and vivaciousness and put it on display for the world.

Victoria was determined to help find out who.

Today she'd woken up with excess energy to burn. She'd been lucky this morning. The sky had been clear for rowing practice, and she hadn't felt a drop of moisture. Well, except from the paddles of the other rowers. Late fall was a crazy time for dragon boat drills, but she loved it. The rowing workout was exhilarating and exhausting at the same time. When the days were clear, like it had been this morning, there was no better place to be than on the Willamette River.

It helped clear her head of sorrow. And anger.

For the past two years, she'd been a part of various dragon boat teams. Occasionally she went out of town for a competition if someone begged her, but she didn't do it to compete; she did it to get out of the house and morgue and be on the water. This morning's two-hour practice had flown by. The air was crisp and cold, and the river was high with the heavy rains from the last two weeks. Lots of rain meant debris on the river, and it stirred up the water into a muddy brown no matter how blue the sky was. When ample rain worked its way from streams and tiny rivers into the Willamette River on its way to the Columbia River and then the Pacific Ocean, it made for treacherous rowing.

Victoria loved the challenge. There was something about being at the water's level and seeing the city and riverbanks from a turtle's-eye view. Mount Hood seemed taller, city skyscrapers seemed mightier, and she simply felt vulnerable and alive. When you spend every day studying the remains of death, getting out into the living elements of the world was essential.

Her next-door neighbor had introduced her to the dragon boats. She and Jeremy had bonded over local wines and his golden retriever when she'd moved into the neighborhood after her split with Rory. Victoria wasn't one to get to know her neighbors, but Jeremy had inserted himself in her life and she'd meekly acquiesced. The seventy-year-old was a force to be reckoned with. Gray-haired, marathoner-lean, and proudly flaming gay. She'd never met anyone like him and had instantly adored him.

He'd dragged her to the dragon boat practices one year when she'd been running herself ragged at work. She'd weakly protested, not wanting to hurt the kind man's feelings, but he'd overruled her. It'd been exactly what she needed. She'd always been a work-out-at-home type of exerciser. She had an elliptical and a treadmill and ran outside when weather permitted. But getting her out on the river in a boat with nineteen other excited rowers had created an addiction.

"Hey, how was the water today?" Jeremy's voice sounded behind her.

Victoria hit the automatic close button on her X5 and faced the man, studying him for signs of worsening health. Jeremy hadn't rowed at all this season. He'd struggled with bronchitis and pneumonia, and she hated to see him as a shell of the vigorous man he'd been six months before. His face was thinner, his movements slower, but his eyes sparkled with life. It was that life that had drawn her to him. He shared it with everyone.

He looks a little better.

Jeremy was usually so spirited; it killed her to see him struggle. She'd never known a grandfather, but she wished she'd had one like Jeremy. He shared his positive energy; he didn't suck it out of others. Victoria had spent too much time with people who left her drained. Jeremy did the opposite.

"Clear and cold," she answered.

His eyes lit up. "In other words, perfect."

"How are you feeling?"

"Fabulous. I'm going to try to get out there next week."

Victoria shook her head. "No. That's too soon. I don't want to see you relapse."

Gray eyebrows narrowed in a playful glare. "You're not my doctor. And I really am feeling better. Was out running errands all day yesterday and even took in a concert the evening before."

Victoria smiled. "Good! I'm glad to see you're coming around. Everyone misses you on the water."

"Ah, they just want someone who does all the work for them. You've been busy, I see. Those girls were all over the television yesterday, and you're all over the paper today."

"What?" Victoria froze.

"Well, maybe that's a bit of an exaggeration." He held up the newspaper. "You're on the front page of the metro section."

Victoria tried not to snatch the paper from his hand. She hated publicity. And the thought of herself in the paper was making her stomach spin. She unfolded the paper and stared at an old photo of herself. It was from a lecture she'd given a few years back at Portland State University. She breathed a small sigh of relief. *The Oregonian* had used the photo before. That meant they didn't have anything fresh from the current investigation. The headline read BONE LADY TACKLES OLD MYSTERY.

Not the Bone Lady moniker again.

Surely the papers could come up with a better name. She skimmed the article. It stated that she was taking a fresh look at the old bones from the original circle of women and briefly rehashed the story. She glanced at the byline. Not Michael Brody. Brody wrote better articles than this; this article said nothing. Brody wrote in-depth investigative articles. She wondered if he was examining the case for the paper. He was a close friend of Lacey Campbell's, and had crossed paths with Victoria a few times. He knew how to push her buttons in a highly irritating way and seemed to enjoy it.

"So you're looking into that old case, eh?"

She looked up. Jeremy studied her closely, and she wondered what her face had revealed. Irritation? Annoyance?

"Yes. I'm hoping to find something that will indicate who those unidentified three women were."

"I remember when that happened. I always thought it was odd that no one stepped forward."

She looked at him with new interest. "You lived in the city back then?"

"Sure. Lived right downtown. It was a different era, you know. Men like me did our best to stay out of the limelight, but we knew where to go to socialize with others like us."

Victoria studied his face. They'd had a few conversations about what it was like to be a gay man in today's society, but Jeremy rarely talked about the old days. Her heart winced in sympathy for the hidden life he'd led.

"We used to talk about that case a lot. Who would murder a bunch of women? Rumors swirled about white slaves and prostitution rings. I always thought it seemed like it had a personal touch. Like someone had arranged them in that circle, you know, put them on display for others to see."

"But why weren't all of them claimed?"

"Maybe folks were too scared to do so. It had that cult-like feeling about it, you know? Something about them being found in a pattern and dressed the same."

Victoria shook her head. Could a cult have hid underground for that many decades in the city?

"I see all the recent girls have been identified." Jeremy nodded at the paper still in Victoria's hands. She handed it back to him, gladly closing the paper on her own photo. "All local girls, but different schools, eh?"

Victoria nodded. "You know Trinity, right? The girl who ended up in the hospital is a close friend of hers."

"Ah, she's a good one, that girl. How's Trinity holding up?"

"She was relieved Brooke lived, but now is terrified she'll die. She spent most of yesterday believing she'd already died."

"It says they didn't figure out who was who until late last night. Were you down there?"

"For a while. It was a nightmare. Lots of parents searching for their kids. Dr. Campbell narrowed it down pretty fast."

"All this new technology, but teenagers still learn the quickest way to hide crap from their parents." Jeremy snorted. "Some things never change. And they're always willing to follow the person who seizes control of their crowd, applying the peer pressure. Usually to their detriment."

"No word on a cult yet," she added with a small smile.

"We'll see," Jeremy said with all seriousness. "There's something that tied all these girls together. And something that ties them to those deaths decades ago. Convincing people to kill themselves takes some sort of brainwashing. Cults know how to do that."

Victoria stiffened. "Who says they killed themselves?"

Jeremy shrugged, rolling his paper into a tight spiral. He tapped his palm with it. "Just speculating. Like they did in the article here." He didn't meet her gaze, his eyes focused down their street. "They'll uncover this mystery. This one and the old one. You'll help them get to the bottom of it."

She hated speculation. She understood its use to form theories to help search for motive and answers, but she didn't care for it being spread around until there was proof. And there was no proof that these girls had taken their own lives. Trinity's tear-streaked face filled her mind.

She was going to figure out who killed these women. All of them.

Trinity sat in another waiting room. Twenty-four hours before, she'd been in the waiting room at the medical examiner's office. This one was better. At least now she knew Brooke was alive. Barely.

Trinity's foster mom, Katy, had disappeared in search of coffee. Trinity thumbed through last week's *People* magazine, its cover shredded and wrinkled, her mind retaining nothing. She'd been given one minute to see her friend. Brooke hadn't opened her eyes. The doctors said they didn't know if she ever would. She'd gone a long time without oxygen. Her body had been in the process of turning itself off when she'd been found. Trinity had heard them talking about a drug that slowed down everything in her body until it simply stopped.

Had it been like falling asleep? Did Brooke know what she'd done?

The cops had asked her if Brooke was suicidal. And her foster mother had asked. And Brooke's parents had asked. Didn't anyone but her know the type of person Brooke was? She'd never do that. She loved her life. She knew she was getting a new pair of UGGs for Christmas; she talked about going to college in California. *Brooke had plans for her life.*

Dying in the middle of a forest with a bunch of other girls wasn't one of them. Trinity was positive of that fact.

Brooke's parents had been in meltdown mode since they'd discovered their daughter was missing. Trinity hadn't been in the medical examiner's office when Brooke's parents had shown up. *Thank goodness.* Brooke's mom's hysterics would have been unbearable. Not that her mom didn't have good reason to be upset, but seeing her hang on her husband and crying nonstop at the hospital freaked Trinity out.

Brooke's father escorted her mother everywhere, holding her up like she had legs of Jell-O.

Jeez, get it together, would you?

Instant guilt flooded her. *How would you feel if your daughter was dying in the next room?* She asked a short prayer for forgiveness. She talked to God occasionally. She figured it didn't hurt. Better to be safe than sorry, right?

Brooke was an only child. If she died her parents had no one.

Trinity's chin lifted. She was an only child and had no one. She'd survived.

Her cell phone vibrated in her back pocket. She studied the text on the screen, her chest tightening.

IS B GOING TO BE OK?

She replied: DON'T KNOW.

She waited and waited for his reply but nothing came. She finally slid the phone back in her pocket, feeling let down. Jason had texted her a few times in the month she'd known him. And all those texts had been questions about Brooke. He was good-looking but clearly not interested in her; he'd wanted to know about her friend. Trinity slumped in her chair and flipped the pages of the magazine. The text had sent her heart pounding one minute and dragging the next.

Why was she interested in a guy who was clearly not interested in her?

Katy sighed as she sat in the chair next to Trinity. "Coffee?" She held a little cup out to Trinity, who nodded and took the cup. Katy moved with quick gestures, reminding Trinity of a sharp-eyed bird. A high-energy, petite woman, her dark eyes missed nothing. Besides fostering, she worked with high-risk women, counseling them on how to get out of abusive relationships. More than once she'd had to leave in the middle of the night to respond to a terrified call from a woman. Trinity sipped, silently gagging at the papery chemical taste of the coffee. She didn't want the coffee; she took it because Katy had been kind enough to think of her. Katy was like that.

Trinity tried to let her know when the small gestures were appreciated.

"Thanks," she mumbled into her coffee.

"Who was texting you?"

Katy saw things. Things a typical teen hoped a parent wouldn't notice. And she had no qualms asking about what she'd seen. Katy had learned to be blunt with her fosters and abuse cases.

"Jason. A friend of Brooke's."

"Friend of yours too? I haven't heard you mention him before."

See?

"Her friend. I've met him once or twice. He doesn't go to our school. I'm surprised he has my number to text me," she lied. *Why was she lying? Was it because it was about a boy she barely knew?*

"Well, that makes no sense," Katy logically pointed out. "You gave him your number or Brooke did for a particular reason. Which is it?"

Once again, Katy wasn't one to let the little details slide.

I should have admitted it in the first place.

"I think he got it when we were arranging a ride to meet at the mall a few weeks ago. I'd forgot about that." *That was better. And the truth.*

"Uh-huh." Katy didn't question any more. In a roundabout way, she'd pointed out that Trinity was lying. And in a roundabout way, Trinity admitted it. Case closed.

A nurse bolted by the waiting area, and two other medical staffers followed within seconds.

Trinity's heart stopped, and she stood to see where they'd gone.

Brooke's room.

The uniformed cop who'd sat outside Brooke's door was on his cell phone, alarm on his face, pacing in and out of Brooke's room as medical staff rushed the room.

It's a code.

Beside her, Katy stood and grasped Trinity's hand, squeezing tight as she watched the personnel fill the room. "Oh, no," she whispered. Trinity's heart echoed her words.

Shrieks from Brooke's mother reached Trinity's ears. She clapped one hand over an ear, unwilling to let go of Katy's grip, but the sounds didn't quiet. They thundered in her head.

Brooke.

CHAPTER NINE

He frowned at the article in the newspaper. They were looking at the old cases again? They'd kept the evidence all these years? He'd assumed the bodies had been cremated or buried. How could the medical examiner's office have room to store unidentified remains for decades? He read the article again, slower this time, squinting in the dim light. It was noon, but the rain clouds and tall trees blocked the sun around his home. And his eyes were old. All of him was old. He hated his old body, the constant pain and unsteadiness. In his youth he'd been strong, a leader people looked up to and asked for guidance.

Now he had only a few followers.

He'd read long ago that unidentified bodies were donated to the medical school. In fact, a few years back there'd been a big issue when the body of a transient had been donated, and then the family had come looking for him. The family had made a big publicity stink, and no doubt the medical examiner had changed the policy. But he was stunned that the three unidentified women were readily available. Would the old bones reveal new facts?

The words on the paper blurred, then sharpened. According to the article, the women had been reduced to simple skeletons. They probably didn't take up much space. Perhaps they had rooms and rooms full of boxes of old skeletons, waiting through the decades for relatives to claim them.

Technology and education had come a long way. Could they identify them with current techniques? He shook his head. Someone had to report them missing first so there would be a record to compare to. And no one was going to report these women.

These women had been abandoned. They were unwanted.

His phone rang and he pushed out of his chair, standing stiffly. He shuffled across the room and picked up the old receiver.

He listened, pondering the problem presented. Someone had made an inquiry into the identity of one of the old cases. Someone he knew very well.

There was no question of what had to be done. He gave his orders and hung up the phone.

Well. So much for his theory that no one would come forward for the old women. Why had Lorenzo spoken now?

Lorenzo would find out how wrong he was.

His gaze rested on the face of the female doctor in the paper. Dr. Victoria Peres. She was obviously a respected expert in her field. In his day, a respected woman took good care of her house and man. His lips formed a sneer. Today's world was on a road to ruin. Kids killing each other, drugs, music, and naked women everywhere. His son had demonstrated on his computer how women plastered images and videos of themselves as they did sinful acts. Shameless. Corrupting the minds of young men everywhere. The United States was going to hell.

This female doctor expected to find something new with these old bones. He couldn't let that happen. He didn't know all of her abilities, but he knew he couldn't allow her to get a good look at the bones. He'd seen TV shows where they tracked down suspects from a single hair. Or a dog's hair. Or saliva on a cup. He couldn't risk present-day technology picking apart the remains of those women.

Old Lorenzo would be dealt with, but how could he fix this new problem? Doing something about the Bone Lady was completely out of the question, so he had to address the bones. He looked at the picture again. Even in the black-and-white print, he could feel the woman's excitement during her lecture to the college class. She'd done well for herself, but in the long run she was just another woman trying to fill a man's role. Part of him admired her for her education and success. The other part was sad for the obvious misfit that she'd become. What man would want to marry such a powerful woman? He knew she'd already failed at one marriage.

She needed to learn to be more deferential and humble.

Then she'd make a man a good wife.

Seth stared into his beer, his shoulders hunched over the polished oak bar. His hotel's restaurant was noisy for 10 P.M. on a Monday night, and he'd instantly decided to sit in the quiet adjacent bar.

He needed peace. It'd been a hell of a forty-eight hours. He'd barely stepped foot in Portland when he'd been summoned to the most tragic scene he'd ever witnessed. Then came the shock of seeing Tori. And then realizing Tori had never forgiven him.

Had he forgiven himself?

Seth took a long swallow of his dark beer and closed his eyes, letting the cool liquid roll over his tongue.

Why did he still play the "what if" game?

He couldn't know how his life would be if he'd stayed with Tori. Possibly he could be a lot happier at this moment. Or he could be a lot more miserable. Eden would be a constant. He'd still love her with all his heart. He prayed he hadn't damaged his daughter by divorcing her mother. And he prayed he hadn't damaged his daughter by staying with her mother for as long as he had. He'd spent almost two decades trapped between a rock and a hard place. And praying a lot.

"This stool taken?"

Seth looked up into the face of Detective Callahan. "Only by you."

The detective perched on the stool and lay his cowboy hat on the bar, running a hand through his salt-and-pepper hair. He looked tired. His face seemed thinner than yesterday, and his jacket was rumpled. But the eyes were still razor sharp.

"It's been a long two days," Seth stated.

"You're telling me," answered the detective. "I hate the ones with kids."

Seth nodded. He'd had too many kids cross his table in his years as a medical examiner. It never got easier. As a father, he saw his daughter's face on each child.

"Come here often?" Seth lamely joked.

The detective snorted. "Actually I do. It's a convenient stop on the way home." He raised a hand at the bartender, who arched an eyebrow at him, and Callahan answered with a nod. The bartender started to pull a draft.

They sipped their beers in silence for a long moment. Seth didn't feel the need to fill the emptiness with talk. He'd crossed paths with the detective twice that day at the ME's building. He'd seen a man on a mission to get the girls' mystery solved. The same mission Seth and Dr. Campbell had been on.

And they'd succeeded in part of their agenda. All six girls had been identified last night. One set of parents was at the hospital, hoping their daughter would wake. Five other sets had gone home to mourn. Many parents were hugging their kids tonight, while others were letting their roaming children understand the type of torture they'd inflicted on their parents.

"At least all the girls were named," said Seth. "For a while there, I was wondering if we would to have a repeat of the old scene. If the media hadn't picked up the story, I suspect we'd still have some unidentified kids."

Callahan nodded. "It's amazing how some parents don't know what their teens are up to." An odd look flashed on Callahan's face, and Seth wondered if the detective had kids.

Do you know where Eden is right this minute?

He didn't. That was part of going to college. He wasn't supposed to wonder about her whereabouts, because college freshman knew how to use a little common sense and look out for themselves. Supposedly. Seth shifted his weight on his barstool, and he fought an overpowering need to call his daughter. Just to hear her voice.

"Christ. My son's in his freshman year in college all the way down in North Carolina. He could go missing for days, and I'd never know he was gone. All I get is an occasional text. Usually asking for money," Callahan commented. "I've called him twice today and he hasn't answered."

"Kids that age don't call. When I want to talk to my daughter, I have to send a text asking if this is a good time to call." Seth frowned. "I should call her tonight." He glanced at his watch. "But she's got a dance class on Monday nights. I don't think she's home yet."

"Yeah, I'd want to touch base with my daughter after days like these, too."

"Do you think it's a copycat killing?" Seth asked.

Callahan frowned and concentrated on dropping the level of his beer for a few moments. He wiped at his mouth with the back of his hand. "I don't know what the hell it is. My mind's been all over the map. If I assume this was orchestrated, and this group didn't decide to commit mass suicide, it doesn't point to a serial killer. Not yet. Not in the textbook sense anyway."

"Textbook?"

"Serial killers often hunt humans for the sexual thrill it gives them. And they want to do it over and over again, believing they can outwit police. Did this scene give someone a sexual thrill? Possibly." He eyed Seth. "According to you guys, none of the girls were touched in a sexual manner."

"No evidence of any sort," agreed Seth.

"So I ask myself, does that mean he'll do it again?" He turned on his stool toward Seth, his face earnest. "Did this thrill him in a way such that he'll want to outdo himself and take it to another level?"

Seth cringed. *What would outdo that scene?*

"Or was he a spree-type killer? That means he'll kill a number of people in different locations, enjoying the journey. But those typically happen in a short period of time. Will he give us another scene tomorrow? Or has he already done it, and we haven't found it?"

The detective was on a roll, the words flowing out of his mouth. Seth wondered how the man stayed sane with the multitude of twisted possibilities surging through his brain. No doubt Callahan questioned how Seth kept his sanity while staring at death all day long.

"Some people would say this was the work of a mass murderer. But those guys usually kill themselves at the scene or hope to go out with suicide by cop." Callahan looked grim. "You guys are pretty sure it'll be a phenobarbital overdose, right?"

"We're waiting on the lab results. But that's what it looks like. They had the remains of a dairy-based liquid in their stomachs and small intestines. We found the same thing in each stomach. There were no injection sites on any of them."

Callahan nodded as Seth spoke. The detective knew all this. Seth was repeating what Dr. Campbell had told the police earlier.

"Last one to drink might be the one who's still alive," stated Callahan.

"Or maybe she had a smaller dose for some reason. It would lessen the effect of the drug in her system." Seth shook his head in wonder. "But what does this tell you about the first set of deaths?"

Callahan snorted. "You see my problem. Two crimes. Decades apart. Who did it? And are they even fucking related?"

"I wish we had good autopsy notes on those old deaths."

The detective nodded in agreement. "You don't know how frequently I've wanted the same thing. But the women were well on their way to decomposition by the time they were found during the hot summer."

"That's one difference," Seth muttered. "The time of year was different. And these were found so much quicker. Was that deliberate? What happened with the hiker who found this second set?"

"He's a student at Portland State," Callahan snorted. "Poor kid's gonna be traumatized for the rest of his life. Didn't seem to have too many sharp tools in his shed to begin with, but now he's nearly a blithering idiot."

"I take it your interview went well."

"We'll talk to him again. He was so shook up he could barely get a word out."

"He's a suspect?" Seth asked.

"He's pretty low on the list."

"Why? I'd think first on the scene would be an automatic high-level suspect."

Callahan took a long drag on his beer and raised a brow at Seth. "I don't recall questioning your slicing and dicing abilities."

Seth's hackles rose. "I'm not questioning how you're doing your job. I'm just trying to understand your process." He felt like he'd had his wrist slapped. Maybe he could have phrased his question better.

"If you don't mind, my brain's a little tired. I don't feel like rehashing my workday for you. And I won't ask you to do the same," the detective said.

The two men sat in silence. Callahan was right, Seth realized. He didn't owe Seth any explanations. If the cops questioned every discovery he made during an autopsy, it'd drive him nuts.

"Sorry," Seth said. "I see where you're coming from."

"I haven't slept," said Callahan. "I want to, but my fucking brain won't turn off. Was hoping to slow it down in here. I need something to take my mind off the case, and it's not easy to do. If I find myself thinking about a different subject, I worry I'm not putting a hundred percent of myself into the case."

"Christ. Give yourself a break. You can't be on duty twenty-four/seven. What do you do to relax?"

"Relax? What the fuck is that?" Callahan gave a half grin. "I know what'll get my mind off work. Tell me about Victoria Peres. I've worked with her for a few years and know as much about her as I did on day one. Namely, I know she's tall and don't piss her off."

The abrupt topic shift sent Seth's beer down the wrong pipe and triggered a coughing fit. Callahan unhelpfully pounded him on the back.

"Tori?"

Callahan's face lit up. "Yeah, how in the hell do you get away with calling her Tori? Most guys I know don't dare call her anything but *Doctor* Peres. But you strolled in and used some cutesy nickname to her face. And she didn't even flinch."

"We've known each other since college. Well, we've lost touch over the years. But we were close once."

"She's close to no one."

Seth's heart hurt at that statement. "Maybe you don't know her that well."

Callahan nodded. "I'll give you that. But I've asked around at the medical examiner's office. The woman doesn't have anything to do with any of them outside of the office. Even little Dr. Campbell, Lacey, doesn't know much about her."

"She's always been a private person."

"I know she was married at one point. A college professor, I believe."

Seth nodded. When they'd crossed paths at that conference years back, she'd had a ring on her finger and they'd talked about their respective spouses. He hadn't asked her what had happened to the marriage. Yet. "Yes, I don't know how that ended."

"She's tough."

"Can you blame her?" Seth clamped his teeth together. He'd said too much. If this cop didn't know Tori's history, it was because Tori didn't want people knowing her past. It was no business of his to share her story.

Callahan's gaze sharpened, and Seth felt him shift into cop interview mode. "What's that supposed to mean?"

"Forget it. If you know nothing about her, then that's how she wants it. But maybe you haven't given her a chance. The Tori I know took a bit of digging to understand. Have you ever put any effort into talking to her? Have you ever asked her a question outside of a case?"

Callahan stared at him. "I don't recall."

"Probably not. Next time ask her what she does in her spare time. And don't let her push you away. It's a natural reaction. Keep at her and I promise you'll be surprised at what you find under that cool exterior."

"You do know her."

"I know her well enough to understand she was dealt a shitty hand a long time ago. A few hands, actually. She grew those prickly defense spines for a reason. A good reason."

Callahan looked fascinated. "Holy shit. The ice doctor has a history. And you were part of it, weren't you?"

"Fuck off."

Callahan grinned. "You aren't the uptight medical examiner you pretend to be, are you?"

"Uptight? I seem uptight?" Seth didn't know how to take that.

"Sure. The morgue is your kingdom, right? No one has the right to question your skills?"

Annoyance bubbled up in his chest, and he fought the urge to tell the detective off. Instead he counted to five and stared down the detective, comprehension dawning. "Jesus Christ. You had me going there. Did you think I'd spill Tori's history because you pissed me off?"

"Ah, it was worth a shot." Callahan winked at him and finished his beer.

Seth chuckled. "I don't ever want to sit across the interview table from you."

"A bar works just as well sometimes. You'd be surprised what people want to reveal. They're usually looking for an excuse to talk."

"Tori's story is her own. Get to know her, and maybe she'll let you in on it."

"But my understanding is that you two haven't seen each other in a long time. Maybe you aren't the Victoria expert you think you are." Callahan pointed at Seth's chest.

The detective had a good point. There was a lot Seth didn't know about the woman he'd once planned to spend the rest of his life with. If he was going to stay in Portland, he and Tori needed to talk.

But would she ever let him inside her walls again?

CHAPTER TEN

Eighteen years ago

His hands shook. Seth stopped and held them out in front of him, palms down. Definite shakes. They looked like he'd been drinking for hours; he *felt* like he'd been drinking for hours, but was experiencing only the bad effects, not the good. He shoved his hands in his coat pockets, continuing down the sidewalk, pushing through the rain. It wasn't cold outside, but damn, he couldn't get warm. He wanted to vomit.

A night of tossing and turning and stressing and thinking had left him exhausted. He'd skipped his classes today, unable to focus. The rest of the day wasn't going to get better. He'd asked Tori to meet him at the coffee shop, the same place he'd first approached her eight months ago. Eight months. It'd been a whirlwind. His senior year had sped by with top grades and a gorgeous, smart girl on his arm. He'd been accepted to the Stanford School of Medicine, and Tori planned to follow in a few years. They knew the path was going to be hard and lean, but they were excited to do it together.

But a wrench had just shattered their plans, and he had to tell Tori today.

Just tell her. Tell her and be done with it. You have no choice.

Some people would say he had a choice. He didn't have to do what he was about to do. But Seth knew if he ever wanted to look himself in the eye, he had to make the right choice. His life wasn't the only one at stake. There was an innocent involved and he had an obligation.

He would be a better man than his father. *His sperm donor.*

That was the type of man Seth would never be. His father had walked out on him when he was two, leaving Seth's mother with no means of support. Seth's biological father was the perfect model of the deadbeat dad. No courts hunted down child support. If they had, it would have been impossible to squeeze money out of a man with none. Growing up, Seth had lied to his friends, saying his father had died when he was an infant. His father never turned up to prove him wrong. He'd spent a few sleepless nights, worrying he'd be caught in the lie, but it never happened. His mother didn't remarry. She'd been crushed by her husband's deception. Her life became a stereotype of depression and alcohol, and she decided she couldn't handle a teenager.

Seth went to live with his mother's brother, whom he'd never met. Dave was single. He'd grudgingly taken the boy, angry at Seth's father for abandoning and mentally destroying his sister.

"Your mother was always a little soft," he'd told Seth when they met. "I knew nothing good was going to come out of her shacking up with that asshole father of yours. But now here you are. Let's see if we can make a man out of you."

For a man with no children, Dave knew how to parent. Tough love, hard work, and responsibility were daily constants in Seth's new life. Coming from a childhood with no guidelines, Seth flourished under Dave's rules. They had their fights, of course, but Seth had always ached for attention from an adult, and Dave filled that need. Seth's previous life had been spent tiptoeing around his mother, avoiding tripping her triggers for depression or anger.

Seth thrived. And grew to recognize the type of person his father had been. Dave was his father's opposite. Dave was involved. Dave gave a shit about Seth's life. Dave taught him to focus his excess energy into swimming, running, and hunting. Now, Seth no longer bounced off the walls at home and school; he could concentrate. And it turned out he was smart. Smart enough to breeze through high school and collect great grades. Smart enough to be accepted to Stanford and smart enough to appreciate what Dave had done in his life.

Yesterday a new path had opened up before him. His chance to make the difference in the life of a child who needed him. Like Dave had done for him. But the decision was going to hurt Victoria.

Seth stopped in front of the shop, staring at the door. She was inside, waiting for him to turn her life upside down. But Victoria was strong, he repeated in his head for the millionth time. Victoria wasn't his mother. Victoria had the tools to continue and create a success with her life.

He sucked in a shuddering breath and opened the door. Warm coffee-scented air breezed over his face and he scanned the shop, his heart thudding in his chest.

There she was.

Beautiful. Elegant. His gaze rested on her face as she studied the text on her table. Just like she'd been doing the first time he'd built up the courage to approach her. Indecision washed over him. *Was he making a mistake?*

As if she'd felt him watching, Tori glanced up. A warm smile filled her face and her eyes danced at the sight of him. Seth felt ill.

It's a mistake. I can't do it.

He'd called Dave in the middle of the night, wrestling with his decision. Dave had sympathized and slowly walked him through what he already knew. He'd never be able to live with himself or be a complete person for Tori if he followed in his father's footsteps. He wouldn't abandon his responsibilities. He gave Tori a weak smile and brushed the rain off his shoulders, moving toward her table.

How was she going to handle this?

Seth took her breath away. Victoria stared at the figure who'd just stepped through the door. He wore the slow half smile that always made her heart flip over. His gaze met hers and his smile grew wider. Then faltered.

She ran a nervous hand over her hair, her own smile weakening.

He brushed the rain off his jacket and moved across the room toward her, working his way between tables in the small shop. She watched him come, admiring the way he pulled the attention of every female in the room. He didn't do anything on purpose; he was just one of those types of guys. He was athletic and casual. Perhaps the fact that he didn't care about how he looked to other women was what drew their eyes. Victoria immediately discarded the thought. No, she'd simply hooked a hottie. A smart, caring hottie. His looks really didn't matter that much to her. What impressed her was inside, his strength of character, his kindness to everyone around him.

She studied him carefully. He'd been sick last night and bailed on their plans to take in a movie. She'd gone with two girlfriends, but had keenly felt his absence. This morning, he looked pale and his eyes were definitely red. Hopefully whatever bug he suffered from wasn't contagious. She pushed her book out of the way and took a sip of coffee, noticing that her hands quivered.

Something was wrong.

He wasn't looking at her. Usually Seth was one big smile and flirting blue eyes. Now, his gaze was on the floor and the sides of his mouth were down. Maybe they should have met at his apartment if he was still sick. He stopped at her table, met her gaze, and Victoria's stomach sank.

Oh Lord. "What happened?" she whispered. Her fingers turned to ice.

He slumped down in a chair and looked at her, defeat showing in his face.

"Are you okay? Do you need to go back home?" The words tumbled out of her mouth. A tornado of disconnect spun through her chest, making it hard to breathe. She'd never seen Seth look so miserable. He leaned forward, grasped her hands and pulled them across the table, gripping tightly.

"We need to talk."

Were there any worse words from your boyfriend's mouth? The phrase triggered Victoria's inner walls to rise, protecting and guarding her heart, and her brain shifted into an eerie calm.

Every physical and emotional defense in her body shot into high gear. *It's bad.* Her icy hands clenched into fists inside his grip.

A woman knows. She didn't have to experience a breakup to know one was about to happen. Seth's eyes pleaded with her to listen, his hands squeezing hers. Victoria was in listening mode, but that didn't mean she was in understanding mode.

"What happened?" she asked again.

"Remember Jennifer?" Seth asked.

Victoria nodded, her gut clenching, acid burning. Jennifer was Seth's old girlfriend from home in Arizona. She'd cheated on him, they'd broken up, and she'd had a baby with her new boyfriend. The woman had moved on quickly. Victoria knew he'd been stung over the cheating and the fast move to another man.

"You knew she had that baby girl?"

Victoria nodded, unease creeping up her spine. A shrill voice inside her head started to scream. *No, Seth, no!* The baby had been born about a month after Victoria and Seth had gotten together.

"The baby is mine. I didn't know. She always swore it was Pete's. He finally had a paternity test, and Eden isn't his daughter. They've broken up and now she says Eden is mine." His eyes pleaded with her, begging her not to judge him.

Victoria breathed out a sigh of relief, stress flooding out of her body. "She's lying. Of course she says it's your baby, but that doesn't mean that it is! We'll get you tested and prove that she's lying to you just like she lied to the other guy." The words rushed out of her mouth.

A false alarm.

Seth was shaking his head. "No, I already had a test done. She told me last week, and I immediately thought the same as you. I laughed it off and went to have my blood drawn here in town. Her doctor called me with the results last night." He crushed her fingers. "I haven't slept since she called; I've had to figure out what to do."

Victoria tried to pull her hands away. "What do you mean, what to do? You don't have to do anything. She dumped you. She chose another guy over you. Why do you need to fix this?" Clanging bells pealed in Victoria's brain.

This isn't happening.

"You don't understand. I can't abandon the baby. We need to be together to raise her."

The pounding sounds in her head escalated. "You don't have to abandon the baby. You can be there for the baby. You might be the biological father, but Jennifer ruined any relationship the two of you could have together," Victoria whispered. "She cut the ties. Why start again with her?"

"She wants me in the baby's life."

"Of course she does. You're the money. You can support them. She's panicked because this other guy has left her and now she doesn't know where to turn. You're a great guy. Any woman is going to want you to be the father of her baby!" Her voice rose and people turned to stare, but she didn't care. She could feel Seth slipping from her and she had to stop it. Her inner foundation rocked, crumbling.

Misery radiated from his face. "Tori, I've made up my mind. I told you what my father did to my mother and me. I can't do that to a child."

"But Seth—"

"I told you, I have to do this. It's the right thing to do. I won't let a kid grow up wondering why her father isn't with her."

"You can still be a part of this child's life—"

"No. I have to *be there.* I never had a man in my life until my uncle came along. I've told you the difference he made for me growing up. I can do that for my daughter. Eden is my daughter." Amazement touched his eyes as he said the words. "I have a daughter, Tori, and the most important thing is that she grows up feeling loved and wanted. I can provide that."

"But what about Jennifer?"

"We can make it work. We did once."

Every connection between them snapped in half, stinging Victoria. "You're dumping me for a woman who left you? Who cheated on you? What about medical school?"

"I'm applying to the University of Arizona."

"That's not Stanford. It won't be the same," Victoria argued.

"It doesn't matter. I can go to medical school and Jennifer can still be near her family, who will help us raise the baby."

What about me? What about us? Victoria shrieked in her head. She stared at Seth. She couldn't say the words out loud. What weight did an eight-month relationship have versus a baby? And Seth's issues about his father's history were heavy on his mind. They always had been.

He's leaving you. He's walking out on you. Exactly what Jennifer did to him.

"You don't know what you're doing. You're choosing an unknown over everything we've planned together." She grasped at straws. The look on his face said there was no changing his mind.

"School gets out in six weeks. I'm going back to Arizona for good," he stated.

Victoria stared at him. His eyes were dead. The life and love that usually shone from them had vanished. *How had he changed overnight? Was this the true Seth?*

"I don't think we should see each other anymore."

"How am I not to see you when you're a TA in my class?"

He winced. "I've asked the professor if it's okay if I'm not present for lectures. I'll be working out of his office more."

He's already made plans how to avoid me.

Her shoulders slumped under the colossal weight. Seth had already emotionally disconnected from her and made the necessary plans to cut her from his life. Her stomach heaved and she swallowed hard. She could cry. She could break down right here in public and make a scene. *She wasn't that type of woman. If this man no longer wanted to be with her, she was going to let him go. She wasn't going to humble herself as a ploy to keep him from his daughter.*

"Why here?" she whispered. "Why did you have to do it in public?"

He shifted in his seat, guilt flooding his face. "I couldn't do it at one of our places. If we were alone and things got too emotional, I was afraid . . . "

He was afraid they'd end up in bed.

Their sex life was good. There was no getting around it. Lying in bed with Seth on a rainy afternoon was heaven. They'd spent hours talking and making love. He'd been her first and had opened a whole new world of intimacy and sharing for her. In the beginning, it'd simply been explosive and exciting, but it'd grown into a tender, loving experience.

And now it was over. No more.

If she could get him in bed, maybe . . .

She rejected the thought; she wasn't a manipulator. She wasn't that kind of woman and she wasn't about to start. She was strong. Seth was done with Seth and Victoria. And her logical brain screamed at her to accept it.

She stood up, shoved her books into her backpack, and pushed in her chair. Slinging her pack over one shoulder, she stared Seth in the eye. "I loved you. I loved you *a lot* and was committed to the future we'd planned together. Good-bye, Seth." She strode out of the coffee shop with her chin up and her heart in pieces on the floor.

Never again.

CHAPTER ELEVEN

Seth noticed Lorenzo Cavallo had managed to rake his leaves in his yard before he died. Lorenzo's home looked like every other small Portland home from the fifties. The entire street had one-story white homes with single-car garages. Only the yards were marginally different. Some with bushes, some with trees, some with nothing. A shiny classic Chevrolet stood visible in Lorenzo's garage. Someone had opened the garage door and the vehicle gleamed against the dreariness of the wet day.

The clouds had been high and gray during Seth's commute to the office. Enough to make him wonder if the day would actually be dry. But his hopes were dashed as black clouds rolled in. Dr. Campbell had assigned him to visit the Cavallo death, doling out assignments among his deputy examiners and himself. It'd been less than a week, and Seth felt like he belonged in the Portland office. His working interview time was almost up. If he was offered the job, he was taking it. No question. He liked Portland. It was quirky, and the ME's office ran like a smoothly oiled machine.

A uniform held a log out to him at the front door. He signed and slipped on a pair of sanitary booties, studying the young officer out of the corner of his eye. He didn't look green or ashen, so hopefully the scene wasn't a bad one. Detectives Callahan and Lusco had already signed the log. It didn't feel like ten hours had passed since he'd parted from Callahan at the bar.

Seth moved down the narrow hall of the house toward the voices in the kitchen. He smelled the familiar odor of death. The coppery scent of blood and the stench of released bowels. A wave of sadness washed through him as he stepped into the kitchen and examined the body on the floor.

Lorenzo Cavallo was covered in blood from head to toe. He wore what Seth thought of as old-man underwear. The white stretchy tank top and baggy white undershorts. Neither had been truly white in a long time; instead they were a bad yellowing cream color. Browning blood stained Lorenzo's silver hair. Detectives Callahan and Lusco leaned against a counter in the tiny kitchen. A female uniformed cop nodded at Seth, and a crime scene tech snapped scene photos.

"Morning, doctor," Callahan greeted him. "Welcome to the party." His grim expression belied his words.

"Morning," Seth answered.

"As soon as you can get us a time of death, we'd appreciate it," Lusco added.

Portland was no different from Sacramento. The cops always wanted that fact first.

Seth stepped over to the corpse, carefully avoiding the blood, and squatted down. Now closer, he could see the tears from a knife through the old man's shirt. And a spot at his temple that looked . . . sunken. Seth scanned his surroundings, looking for a baseball bat or similar weapon. Callahan noticed his gaze.

"Whatever he was stabbed and hit with, the killer took with him," Callahan stated.

"Can you get a picture right here?" Seth asked the photographer as he pointed to a spot just below the ribs on the right side of the body. The old man's tank was ripped wide open as if it'd been prepared for Seth to take his liver temperature. The tech snapped a shot, and Seth made a half-inch slit with his scalpel and slid a thermometer in four inches. He waited and the tech took a shot of the inserted thermometer. Looking around, he noticed Lusco watching in fascination along with the female cop, but Callahan seemed focused on making notes in his pad.

"We just talked with him yesterday," Lusco offered.

"What for?" asked Seth.

"He came in to offer a lead on the old Forest Park case. He thought his sister might be one of the victims," said Lusco.

Seth looked at the body. The old man had been brutalized. *Did someone not like him talking to the police?* "You think it was related to the killings from the other night?"

"Don't know," stated Lusco.

"A neighbor was walking by about seven this morning and noticed his door was wide open," Callahan added. "She came up to the door, rang the bell, yelled his name, and finally entered the house when no one answered. She immediately backed out when she saw he was dead and called nine-one-one."

Seth didn't ask why the neighbor didn't physically check to see if Lorenzo was dead. It was obvious. This was a case of overkill. Seth saw multiple blows to the head and too many stab wounds to count. Any of them could be the cause of death.

Seth took a long look at the furnishings of the little kitchen. "He lived alone?"

"His wife died six years ago," stated the female cop.

"Yesterday in our interview, he didn't mention that. He talked about his life as if his wife was still alive," Lusco said. "We haven't been able to get ahold of any family yet, and the neighbors don't seem to know anything about his sons. I'm a bit surprised. He acted like they were all very close."

Callahan nodded in agreement.

The home showed the touch of a woman, but of a woman who hadn't been around in a long time. The floral prints of the sofa were faded, the picture frames showcased thick dust, and the ashtray overflowed. The house was utterly quiet. It had an aura of waiting for someone. Maybe waiting for the grandkids to pay an overdue visit. Or waiting for the female heart of the house to return.

"I still have guys questioning the neighbors," said the female cop.

Seth took a closer look at the policewoman. Her badge was Portland Police Department and read Goode. Callahan and Lusco were with the state police. There were some police politics at work here. No doubt this had been Portland's crime scene and investigation until someone had discovered the victim had been interviewed by the state police. Goode was keeping her hand firmly on the scene, but allowing state to have its look.

Seth knew from experience that most local departments didn't care to have a different agency step in to lend a hand or take over a case, whether it was the FBI or a state police agency.

Callahan had told him that the Forest Park teenage girls' case had been turned over to OSP, but it'd mainly been a matter of timing. The Portland Police Department was recently overwhelmed with a gang war that had consumed their local resources. OSP didn't have the gang expertise that Portland did. But they knew murder.

Seth's gaze went back to the small plate of ashes on the tiny table in the corner of the kitchen. He sniffed at the body. The usual overwhelming odor of a smoker didn't emerge from the body. "Did you find cigarettes in the home?"

"No. I looked for those," Goode answered. "No cigarettes in the cupboards or drawers of the kitchen. Bedside table drawer is empty. That's a dish from an old china set in the cupboard, not an ashtray. A smoker would have several ashtrays in the house."

Callahan walked over to the ashtray on the table. Seth noticed it didn't have butts left in the pile of ash. Who removes the butts? Goode was right; it wasn't an ashtray. It was a thin china saucer with a bit of worn gold trim on the edges.

"What else did you notice?" Callahan asked Goode.

"He lives alone," she said. "He eats like a bachelor. Lots of white flour and white sugar products. Red meat and frozen dinners. Tons of family pictures on the walls, but they're old ones. Going by the hair and clothing styles, no new photo sessions in at least two decades. He reads Louis L'Amour and Tom Clancy. Sinks were dry when we arrived. No one appears to have cleaned up their bloody hands at them. Hand towels are hanging neatly in place along with bath towels. Same with the kitchen towels."

"What's the room temperature?" Seth asked as he pulled out the thermometer.

"Sixty-five degrees," said Goode.

No heating vents blew directly on the body. Seth did some fast math in his head. "I'll estimate ten to seven hours ago for your time of death. I can narrow that with the lab work. Got all his front photos?" he asked the tech, who nodded. "Help me roll him onto his side."

The two men shoved and pulled to balance Lorenzo on his side. Seth did a quick scan of Lorenzo's back. The tech backed up and snapped more photos of the purpling back tissue. Seth pressed a gloved thumb against the darkened skin. "Livor mortis is fixed." No surprises there based on his time-of-death estimate. The back had no stab wounds.

Seth leaned over the body, distracted by the colored plastic in the corpse's ear. A hearing aid? The color was awfully bright . . . and the shape was wrong. He reached out with the end of his ballpoint pen to carefully move some of the blood-stained hair out of the way. And froze.

His pen matched the color of the plastic in the man's ear.

"Is that—"

"Yes, I think that was a pen." Callahan bent beside Seth. "I was looking at that. Looks like he jammed a pen in his ear and then stomped on it to drive it in farther."

"Holy crap." Seth was speechless.

His ears suddenly ached.

"Someone was angry," he muttered.

Callahan raised a brow at him. "No kidding. This killer would be a profiler's dream. They'd be itching to dissect his brain."

"It's so different from the girls," Seth commented. "That scene was peaceful, almost otherworldly. This is simply brutal. I'd have a hard time believing they were committed by the same person."

"It might simply be someone with two distinct killing motives. Two different reasons and rationales," said Callahan. "I'm not disregarding any theories."

This was a hard, stark scene out of a gore-fest film. The girls in Forest Park belonged in an ethereal fantasy movie, misty and soft.

"This isn't the result of a botched robbery," said Callahan grimly. "Lorenzo Cavallo was murdered deliberately and with a lot of anger. Whether or not it's tied to our girls remains to be seen. But considering he offered insight into the old crime yesterday, I have to consider that someone wasn't happy that he'd volunteered information." He pointed at the pen fragments in the old man's ear. "That's punishment."

"Symbolic, maybe?" Lusco mused.

"Probably not," answered Callahan. "I think it would have been in his mouth if symbolic. As if to shut him up for speaking out. Still, I want that pen when you're done with it, doctor."

"Not a problem," stated Seth. He'd removed odd objects from corpses before. Lightbulbs, kitchen gadgets, and workbench tools. But the crushed pen in the ear was the first of its kind. He stood and heard his right knee pop. As usual. He pulled off his vinyl gloves and set them on the body to keep any evidence with the corpse.

He'd be seeing the man again in a more intimate setting.

CHAPTER TWELVE

Victoria was in her office, typing her notes about the second skeleton, when her email popped up. Noticing it was from Detective Lusco, she immediately opened it and found herself face-to-face with an image of a young woman from another generation. Excitement bubbled inside of her. *Did they have a lead on one of the old remains?*

She slowly read the email, fighting the urge to rush through it. Italian heritage, age twenty. A brother had reported his sister missing yesterday morning. Why had he waited so long? She continued to read Lusco's notes. The brother had consented to a DNA comparison. She scrolled back to the photo and stared at the familiar crooked smile.

She smiled and sent a text to Lacey to meet in her office.

Victoria clicked on her file of lab photos from the three women, and scrolled until she found the teeth views. She studied the upper front teeth carefully in each photo, stopped at the teeth photo of the third skull, and enlarged the shot on her screen.

"Hey, whatcha got?" Lacey breezed in through the open door, a light of curiosity in her eyes. She knew Victoria wouldn't have messaged if she didn't have something good to see.

Victoria arranged the police photo side by side with the photo Lacey had taken of the teeth yesterday, and pushed back from her screen with a flourish. "What do you think?"

The blonde dentist leaned over, resting her hands on the desk as she studied Victoria's screen. Victoria waited impatiently and watched Lacey's eyes flick back and forth between the two photos. Lacey's smile started on one side of her mouth and spread rapidly to the other. "Oh, nice! Where'd you get this old head shot?"

"Lusco and Callahan had someone bring it in yesterday, wondering if one of the women from the old scene could be his sister. He gave a DNA sample, too."

"Excellent. Look how the central incisors overlap." Lacey pulled a dental probe out of her lab coat pocket and held it up to the lovely woman's photo, eyed the angle, and then moved it to the lab's image of the teeth. "The angle and amount of overlap are identical. I'll get a tooth to the lab so they can grind it and extract the DNA for comparison. But I think we've got a great start to figuring out if this is his sister." She grinned at Victoria, who couldn't help returning the infectious smile. "I'd hoped to identify this skull. When I was charting the teeth, I knew this overlap would be recognizable to the right person. I wish everyone had as easily identifiable teeth in photos."

Victoria nodded. To her, most people's teeth always looked about the same. But this woman's were rather distinctive.

"What's her name?" Lacey asked.

Victoria felt a small stab of guilt. She'd breezed right over the name, moving on to the photo in the email. She clicked back to Lusco's letter. "Lucia Cavallo. She was Italian."

"Pretty." Lacey tilted her head as she studied the screen.

Victoria looked at Lucia's eyes, startlingly similar to her own brown, and wondered what had happened in the girl's life that'd brought her to a group death in the quiet woods. Had she chosen the death? Or had she been murdered?

So far, none of the skeletons showed trauma. No nicks on bones from knives nor broken hyoids from strangulation. No gunshots in the skulls. Overall, they were a clean group of women. Two skeletons had well-healed breaks and all were of a normal size, no evidence of malnutrition or disease.

These should have been women who'd gone on to raise families and live normal lives. Not end it on the forest floor.

"Let's go check her out again." Lacey straightened and looked to Victoria.

Victoria recognized the focus in her eyes and the tilt of the jaw. Lacey was a woman on a mission to find answers. Victoria suspected she often appeared the same way. It was the facial expression that made cops move out of her way and techs listen carefully to what she had to say. She followed Lacey to her lab.

The women didn't talk as they strode down the halls. Lacey wasn't prone to useless chatter, and Victoria liked that about her. The two focused on work when they were together, and had found they fostered a similar drive for finding answers. When she'd first met Lacey Campbell, she'd immediately misjudged the dentist to be a blonde bimbo. It'd been a reflexive action. The blonde hair and brown eyes had reminded her of Seth's wife.

Lacey wasn't like that. She was honest, direct, and sharp, with a high level of sensitivity and a bit too much fondness for cats. She didn't seem as intimidated by Victoria as some of her coworkers. They'd discovered they shared an interest in Edwardian English history before it became a trend and a love of Greek food, and both owned television's single season of *Firefly* and mourned its cancellation.

Lacey was the closest thing she had to a tight female friend. Didn't most women have hordes of close friends and run in packs? Victoria had always been the type to have a few intimate friends, usually male. Right now that list included only her neighbor, Jeremy. He knew more about her than anyone.

Except for Seth. Even though they hadn't been around each other in years, he looked at her as if he knew all her private thoughts. He'd always been that way. He'd always been able to read her perfectly. She thought she'd mastered a mask to hide the thoughts in her head, but it'd fallen away when Seth looked at her in the woods.

Her ex-husband, Rory, said she always wore a façade. He claimed he never knew how she was feeling or what she was thinking. She'd said she'd let him know if she was upset, but it wasn't enough. To him, she never looked happy, and he took that as a failing on his part.

What a bunch of bull.

Her happiness didn't rely on her husband's actions. And just because she didn't walk around being ecstatic, it didn't mean she was unhappy. He didn't seem to understand that a person can function in the space between happy and unhappy. That space offered a level of calm and balance. It held an evenness, a place of moderation that allowed her to do her job and go home to forget some of the horrors she'd experienced that day. Some people might drink to forget or seek relief; she preferred to simply exist and accept it.

Rory wanted to party. When they'd first met, he was a breath of fresh air. A stimulant to the life of books and studying and old bones. Rory was fun and outgoing and made her feel important. She fell under the popular college professor of English's spell and married him ten months after they'd met.

Then reality struck. Their oil and water didn't blend. She'd thought she could bring him down to earth, and he'd thought she would lighten up. Deep down, they'd both hoped for a bit of change in themselves and believed the other person could make it happen. Their five-year marriage ended two years ago.

She'd learned a lesson. An obvious facts-of-life lesson. You can't change a person.

You can only change yourself.

"So, how've you been getting along with Seth?"

Victoria fought to not break her stride. "What?"

"Dr. Rutledge. How is it to be working in the same building with him after all these years?" Lacey tried to give an innocent making-conversation look but failed miserably.

"It's fine."

"Fine? That's all you're going to tell me? You haven't seen him in eons, and all you can say is *it's fine*?" Lacey shot her a sideways look. "Sparks blaze when you two are in the same room. It's distracting when I'm trying to chart teeth."

"Sparks?"

"Denying it?"

Victoria felt ambushed. Her mind went into protection mode, and she kept her mouth shut.

Sparks?

Lacey pushed open the door to the lab and headed straight to the shelf with number three's remains. The first skeleton was laid out on a table. Lacey set box number three on a table and removed the lid. "I don't know your history with Dr. Rutledge, but there are a lot of rumors circulating. Why don't you talk about it so people will stop speculating?"

"It's none of their business."

"That's true. Is it an ugly past?"

"It's also none of your business," Victoria said pertly.

Lacey grinned. "You need to talk to someone. Your eyes go all puppy-dog when he walks in the room. I swear you're about to melt when you look at him."

"They do not." Victoria stared at her in shock. *Puppy-dog? Her?*

"How'd you meet?"

"We met in college."

"And?"

"We dated in college. We broke up."

Lacey had a disappointed look. "*Why* did you break up?"

Victoria fumbled for the right words. "It's a long story." She ran a hand over her hair.

The dentist sighed. "I get that. And it's safe to share with me. I won't abuse it."

Victoria studied Lacey's face. She was serious. Everything she knew about Lacey Campbell told her she could trust her with innermost secrets. Victoria simply didn't know how to get the words out. She didn't know how to confide in another woman. In fact, she couldn't remember the last woman she'd admitted a secret to. Her mother? Her roommate in college?

"He dumped me," she blurted out. "He dumped me for another woman he'd gotten pregnant. She was an old girlfriend who he'd believed had a baby with another guy. Turns out he was the father, and she didn't tell him until Eden was seven months old."

Lacey's mouth opened slightly. "How shitty for you."

"Tell me about it."

"You were dating when he got the news he was a father?"

"Yes. We'd been talking of living together. I really believed there was a future there."

"You were in love with him," she stated.

Victoria held her gaze. "Deeply."

Sympathy flashed in Lacey's eyes, and Victoria cringed. She hated pity from someone she respected.

"You haven't seen him since then?"

Victoria pressed her lips together and moved her gaze to the box with the *3* on it.

"Oh. You have! What happened?"

"I'm sorry, Lacey, but—"

"It's okay. You can hold off on that part. For now."

Victoria looked at her. "Thank you."

"I'll expect details later." Lacey smiled warmly at her. "I'm impressed you shared as much as you did. I know it wasn't easy for you. And that was a really crappy thing to have happen to you at that age. To be a college student and believe the world is showing you a nice neat, happy path, and the most important person in your life drops a boulder in your way."

"Exactly."

"I suspect you bounced back nicely. You're kind of like me. I brush off my knees, cry silently inside, and push on, hoping no one saw me trip. Then I promise not to let anyone hurt me that way again. But another man comes along and you open yourself up to be mauled again."

Victoria winced, thinking of her ex-husband.

"You risk getting hurt, but it just takes the right person to make it worth it." A dreamy look entered Lacey's eyes. "The first time I saw Jack, I knew he was special. There's that sense of everything clicking into place, you know? You feel the world shift slightly as it adjusts to lay out your new path with the right man."

Victoria froze. It'd been that way with Seth. Each time. When she'd first seen him at school, when they crossed paths at that conference, and again the other night. So why was the universe being so difficult?

"It's okay to admit you've had your heart broken. Most people have, a time or two. It acknowledges that you are human. Some of us like to think we're superhuman, but we're not. We bleed. Whether it's from a vein or the pain in our heart that no one can see." Lacey gently lifted the skull from the box and smiled at the empty face. "Ohh. I think this is definitely our girl. Let me see the picture."

Victoria turned to the lab computer, thankful for something to do to get out of Lacey's spotlight. Lacey had a point. *Why did she pretend she wasn't human?* Victoria pulled up the image from her email.

Lacey held the skull next to the image. Even Victoria could see the odd front teeth matched. Her gaze went to the eyes and brow ridges of the woman in the photo and then back to the skull. Yes, she could see Lucia in the skull. The DNA tests would make the final call.

Lacey set the skull back in the box. "So pretty," she said softly. "You haven't done a full work-up on this one yet?" she asked Victoria.

She shook her head. "Just some prelim photos and a quick look. I knew when I saw the photo of those teeth that I'd seen them before."

Lacey studied the contents of the box. "There's so much I don't know. I can't see what to look for in a bone. It reminds me of the first time I looked at dental X-rays. All I saw was a weird image in black and white. Now I can judge at a glance what's going on in an X-ray."

"Well, that's why bones are my job, not yours. Go back to school if you want to learn more."

"I'd rather keep watching you."

"Armchair anthropology?"

Lacey lifted out the pelvic girdle and turned it over in her hands, studying the elegant structure. "Why not? You'll show me the important parts, right? Skip all the boring book-learning stuff," she said with a wink.

"And you can show me how to drill decay out of a tooth. I don't need to learn all the technical parts, right?"

"Touché." Lacey smiled.

Victoria smiled in satisfaction. "I'll let the detectives know we have a preliminary match."

Two more to go.

Victoria sipped at her coffee and stared out the break room window at the gray skies. The remains of number three were firmly named in her brain as Lucia. Even if the DNA test came back as not a match, she'd still think of the woman as Lucia.

It was easier sometimes when the bones were nameless and she was still searching for their identity. There was something about knowing the identity of this woman and the knowledge that she'd sat abandoned for decades in a box that was deeply depressing. Would they ever learn why the women had died? Callahan had told her that the decades-old investigation had never found a solid suspect. The only links between the identified women had been their transient status. He'd suspected the remaining three were also a long way from home. He'd discovered that Ted Bundy had been asked about the circle of women. Bundy's admitted murders had started six years after the circle was found, and he'd claimed to know nothing about the Oregon murders. Callahan said the previous investigators hadn't completely ruled out Bundy; he was a known liar, but the circle didn't fit his MO.

She felt Seth step in the room before she heard him clear his throat. As if she was attuned to an invisible frequency he emanated. She turned from the window and held her cheap paper cup of coffee in front of her chest with both hands. A shield.

"Hello, Tori." His voice was hoarse.

Had he known she was in the break room? She studied him from head to toe. For the last few days, she'd avoided looking directly at him, afraid to acknowledge the man he'd become. Did she fear an attraction to him? Did it really matter? The attraction was there; she couldn't deny it. Her heart sped up when she heard his voice. Was that what made her eyes go "puppy-dog," like Lacey mentioned? A dilating of the pupils, perhaps?

"Seth."

Victoria liked what she saw. When it came to Seth, she'd always liked his looks. At that conference, he'd caught her eye from fifty feet away before she'd mentally registered his identity.

A small chip fell off from the wall around her heart. "How's your day so far? Anything fascinating?" she asked.

A startled look entered his eyes.

"What?" Victoria asked.

"You used to always ask me that. Phrased exactly that way."

He was right.

It was an endearment she'd picked up from her parents. One she'd carried on when she dated Seth. And it was one she hadn't used in a long time. She couldn't recall if she'd used it with Rory. She'd developed a habit of not asking about his day because he would roll off a litany of complaints about lazy students and annoying staff. After a long day at the examiner's office, she couldn't bear to hear his bitterness.

But with Seth, it'd suddenly rolled off her tongue. She'd truly wanted to know what he'd done that day.

"I guess I'm a creature of habit," she answered. "Or else nervous."

"Do I make you nervous?" His dark blue eyes held hers.

Lacey was right. He did have a look of Pierce Brosnan about him. He had a leanness to his face sculpted by maturity. She could see the strong bones beneath his cheeks and forehead, and her mind automatically sketched the lines of his skull. It wasn't a morbid thought; it was intimate. She considered it a gift to have the ability to look beyond a person's skin and muscle to their foundation and see its beauty.

"You broke my heart," she said quietly.

There. She'd said it.

Her pain flowed out of her chest, leaving a lingering sense of dizziness. She'd hoarded the pain for too many years. It'd been a crutch. She'd pull out her misery and lean on it to build up her icy walls. Walls to keep everyone at a distance. Now that she'd exposed the old hurt to its source, she was oddly empty. She was exposed, raw. And human.

He'd hurt her, and she'd bled deeply. For a very long time.

He broke their eye contact and inhaled, staring out at the glum rain as she had moments before. "I know." He turned back to her, his eyes darker than a moment ago. "I'm sorry." He started to say more, but abruptly stopped.

She didn't want him to say more; she knew what he'd say.

Eden.

It'd taken some time, but she'd lost the initial anger that a baby had come between them. In fact, she'd been sad that Eden's mother had kept Eden away from Seth at first. He'd missed her birth and the precious first few months of her life. He'd been the first person wronged in their relationship.

Seth had honor. She'd been attracted to that part of his character. Once he started pursuing her in college, he didn't stop. Once he'd made up his mind about his area of study, he'd thrown 100 percent of himself into achieving it. When Victoria found out he had a daughter, she knew she'd lose him. She couldn't stay angry at a man who'd done the right thing. He'd taken responsibility for his daughter and stood beside the mother.

Some men would choose to write a check and see their kid on the weekends. Not Seth. He had to be part of his daughter's life. His father had abandoned him; he couldn't do the same to his daughter. And Jennifer was happy to welcome him back. Who wouldn't want to marry a medical student with a strong sense of commitment?

"Where are you at now?" she asked.

Seth knew exactly what she meant. "I've been living in an apartment for six months. I filed for divorce quite a while ago. It should be nearly done. Emotionally, I've been distant for years. We're working through the actual physical distance."

"How's she handling it?" Victoria's heart started to ice up again. She had to know where Seth and Jennifer stood. Were they really finished?

"Good in some ways. Rotten in others. She'd known it was coming for a long time. That didn't mean she had to like it."

"What are your plans?" She felt like a reporter asking questions.

"Live in Portland. Start life over." His gaze held hers. There was no begging in his look. It was simply a man who'd made up his mind. If he said he was starting over, that was his goal and he'd achieve it.

Victoria's mouth went dry. "You say that like you have the new job."

"If I don't get the position, there's room here for another deputy examiner. Either way, I'm here to stay."

The air left the small break room. She drew shallow breaths. "You left once," she whispered, her fingers tightening on her coffee cup.

"It won't happen again."

Why didn't his words reassure her?

"I don't know what to think," she blurted. "What are you saying?"

His gaze softened. "I'm saying let's get to know each other again. We've got all the time in the world. Are you seeing someone? What happened with Rory?"

Victoria's mind sped into overdrive, spinning out of control while her body froze in position. Seth wanted to start over. She'd known it the minute she'd seen him in the rain that night.

He wants me back.

I can't do it. Or can I?

"It wasn't right. We realized we made a mistake. It's been finished for two years." She wanted to scream that she wasn't seeing anyone, that Rory was only a passing thought, and that she'd gladly take Seth back in a heartbeat.

The logical part of her mind overruled. Seth had to lay a lot of groundwork before she'd risk her heart again.

He nodded. "I understand mistakes."

"I need to get back to work," she said and pushed by him out of the stifling room. She brushed his upper arm as she scooted around him through the doorway and felt his heat penetrate through her lab coat. She strode blindly down the hallway in the general direction of her lab, her brain spinning in confusion.

Seth wanted her back.

Could she do it? Was her heart worth it?

As she rounded the last corner before her lab, the fire alarm sounded. The siren screamed and she stuck her fingers in her ears. Looking down the hall, she saw the pant leg and shoe of a man as he vanished out the emergency exit at the end of the building.

Did he trip the alarm by going out the door? Or was he getting out because of the alarm?

She sniffed the air. No smoke.

Ears ringing, she did a quick peek in the three rooms in her hall, finding nothing to set off the alarm. She jogged back to the main hall, meeting up with a half-dozen employees, questioning and shouting over the din.

The alarm abruptly shut off.

The group exhaled.

"Everyone okay?" she asked.

A chorus of yeses and head nodding answered her.

"Who set off the alarm?" asked Seth from directly behind her.

Victoria glanced over her shoulder, comforted by his tall presence. He nodded at her but kept his attention on the small group. They looked at each other, shaking their heads.

"Everyone here?" Seth asked.

"Yes, this is everyone who's in the building at the moment," Anita answered, stepping through the door from her office. "Both Dr. Campbells left for lunch. I shut down the alarm."

Trust Anita to have her finger on the pulse of the office. Victoria wondered if Dr. Campbell knew how rare a gem ran his office.

"No smoke anywhere?" Seth asked. "Have all the labs been checked? All the suites? Storage?"

Everyone exchanged looks again.

"I checked all the rooms at my end," Victoria spoke.

"Same with the suites," added Jerry, Dr. Campbell's assistant. "I looked in each one when the alarm started. I'll go do a quick run through the labs."

Seth nodded at him and the large man vanished.

"Anyone know what tripped the alarm?"

Everyone shook their heads.

"Wait a minute." Victoria turned to Anita. "Someone went out the emergency door down the hall from my lab. I saw the door as it was closing. You sure everyone's here?"

Anita scanned the surrounding faces. "Yes." Nods from the group agreed.

Victoria looked at Seth, tension twisting in her stomach. "Go out the front of the building and around to the east side and see if you spot anyone. I'll go back down the hall."

Seth was already headed toward the front lobby. "Take someone with you," he shouted over his shoulder.

Victoria glanced to Anita, who nodded, and both women jogged back toward the lab.

"Who do you think you saw?" Anita was out of breath by the tenth step.

"Don't know. I think it was a man. Looked like a male shoe and jeans. I didn't see higher than a knee."

They came up to the door with the ALARM WILL SOUND WHEN OPENED sticker above the broad silver bar handle.

"Will the alarm go off again if I open it?" she asked Anita.

She shook her head. "I deactivated the whole system."

"Fire trucks aren't going to show up, are they?"

"Shit! I need to go call them. They've probably called to confirm the alarm by now. Damn it!" The older woman hustled back down the hall.

Victoria pushed open the heavy door and stepped into the drizzle of the day. Portland was in one of those months where it seemed the sky would never be blue again. Record amounts of rain fell in the past ten days and the F-word was on every weather forecaster's lips: *flooding.*

She looked right and left, but saw nothing but wet grass, concrete, and employee vehicles. Seth appeared on her right as he rounded the corner of the building from the front.

"See anyone?"

She shook her head.

"Me neither." He stopped beside her, stepping under the small overhang to avoid the majority of the drops. It didn't help; the wind guided the falling water onto them. He blew out a breath, scanning the lot, and Victoria watched his breath steam in the air. The sudden quiet and stillness of the outdoors made the alarm incident seem distant.

"What exactly did you see?" he asked.

She repeated her story.

"So someone was in the building. Do you think they triggered the alarm by going through the door?"

"It's a good possibility. We should see if Jerry found anything in the labs."

Seth nodded, beads of moisture sticking in his hair. He ran a hand over the dark dampness, making it spike up a bit, and he suddenly looked ten years younger.

Victoria's lungs tightened at the sight. *He looks like when we first met.*

CHAPTER THIRTEEN

Tori regarded him, her eyes wide and her gaze distant, as they stood in the light rain.

"What's wrong?" he asked.

She blinked and the moment was gone. "Nothing. Just . . . " She didn't finish.

He brushed a raindrop off her cheek. "It's not raining hard, but it's that type of dense misting rain that absolutely soaks everything."

She nodded in agreement, still quiet. Her gaze held his, but her walls had risen. A second before, she'd looked like the Tori of their youth. Wide-eyed and curious about the world. Now she was Dr. Peres. Quiet, observing, and impenetrable.

He liked this serious woman, but he missed the inquisitive girl of the past. He had a hunch the old Tori was below the prickly surface. The surface others like Mason Callahan saw and caused them to make snap judgments.

Was it his fault she had such walls?

He no longer saw her physical changes over the last two decades; now he felt her essence and it was a familiar place. His body and mind remembered it. He leaned closer, his focus on her lips, catching the scent of her hair stirred up by the soft rain. Her pupils dilated slightly. She inhaled abruptly, turned away, and stepped back inside the building.

Okay . . .

He followed her inside, wishing she'd held still for five seconds longer, and saw she was striding toward her lab. "Hey! Hang on a minute." Tori stopped and turned to face him. If he'd thought she had walls up before, she now had brick walls with steel supports guarding her thoughts. The stop sign she projected halted him in his tracks. Her chest heaved slightly, her lips clamped together, her eyes searching his.

Seth didn't know what to say to her.

I was about to kiss her outside.

And she ran away.

"I'm sorry," he started lamely. "I didn't mean—"

"Forget it."

"No, I don't think you underst—"

"I don't understand? You think I'm confused because the man I fell in love with almost two decades ago has shown up on my doorstep and wants to pick up where we left off? What's not to understand about that?"

She had a point.

"You are under my skin, Seth. I know that. But that doesn't mean I'm going to blindly trust you again and offer my heart up on a platter for you to do with as you please. I've made mistakes. Big ones. One named Seth and one named Rory. Those weren't slap-a-Band-Aid-on-it mistakes. Those were long-years-of-soul-searching mistakes. Do you think I'm going to jump in for round two with you on a whim?"

She put her hand on her lab door and shoved. The door swung in and stopped with a *thunk* as it slammed into something.

"Ouch!"

"Oh, Christ." Tori peeked into the room. "What are you doing in here?"

Over her shoulder, Seth could see part of a man who stood on the other side of the door. He moved and Tori managed to push the door the rest of the way open. A tall blond stranger in a wet peacoat met Seth's gaze. The man's green eyes were instantly suspicious and guarded.

"Anita said you were down here. She said the fire alarms had gone off?" The stranger didn't drop Seth's eye contact, but the question was obviously for Tori.

"Yes, we're still checking around." She glanced back at Seth, her brows narrowing.

"Rory, this is Dr. Rutledge. He's considering Dr. Campbell's position."

Rory? Her ex?

"Ah. Dr. Campbell has always been a favorite of mine. Those are some big shoes to fill." The man held his hand out to Seth, the majority of his suspicion gone in his gaze. Seth shook his hand.

Did his name not ring a bell with her ex? Or had she never mentioned him?

An odd sense of disappointment swept over him. When he'd ended it with Tori, she must have written him out of her life story. Could he blame her? What'd he expect? To be shared as part of her history as the one who got away? More likely he was the one who'd ripped out and stomped on her heart. He wouldn't share that story with anyone, either.

The three of them stood there for an awkward second, not speaking, just looking from one to another.

Seth forced out some words. "Well, it doesn't look like there's any sign of a fire or smoke from this room."

Tori jerked slightly as if pulled out of a trance and gazed around the room. "Um. No. It looks—wait a minute." She strode past Rory and stopped at some boxes on one of her metal tables. "What the hell?"

Seth didn't like her angry tone. He moved beside her. "What's wrong?"

"Someone went through these."

Three boxes were strewn across the table. All their lids off. The yellowed color of bone visible in each one. Several bones were loose on the table.

"God damn it!" Tori picked up the loose pieces. "Someone's mixed them together."

"Aren't they coded?" Seth asked.

She nodded. "But a lot of the numbers had faded to nothing over the years. I'd touched up some of them but not all."

Seth peered in a box. Two pelvises. That obviously wasn't right. He lifted them both out, feeling Tori's watchful gaze on his movements. "I can read the numbers on both of these. Why would someone try to mix them up?"

A cold chill passed through him and he turned to stare at Rory. The man had his hands in his pockets and was staring at the bones in obvious distaste. He moved his gaze to meet Seth's. Comprehension dawned in the man's eyes.

"Jesus! Don't look at me. I'd stepped in here a few seconds before she whacked me with the door."

"He didn't do this." Tori defended her ex. She snorted. "Rory doesn't care for bones."

"They give me the creeps."

How in the hell had Tori ended up with someone like this?

"And you married an anthropologist?" he asked Rory.

The man shrugged. "She didn't bring her work home with her very often." Another light of comprehension crossed his face. "I see she's mentioned me." His lips twisted wryly and he looked at Tori. "Tell any good stories?"

"I don't tell stories," she stated quietly. "Why are you here, Rory?"

Rory looked at Seth, plainly unhappy that there was a witness to his discussion with his ex-wife. "Can we talk somewhere?"

Tori glanced at the pelvises in Seth's hands. "I can't now. I need to get these back in order. And we need to figure out who did this." She met Seth's gaze. "I told you I saw someone going out the back door. Do you think this is what he was doing?"

"Someone broke into your lab? How can they get past Anita?" Rory asked.

"Good point," added Seth. "Are there cameras anywhere?"

Tori shook her head. "I need to do an inventory right away." She carefully dug through one of the boxes, muttering under her breath.

Seth studied the coding on his two pieces and placed one in the correct box. Tori dug through the box his second pelvis belonged in.

"Damn it. Two left femurs." She stared at the bones in her hands. "I can read the code on this one." She squinted at the other. "This one's too fuzzy."

"We'll get it straightened out. Do you need help?" Seth set the pelvis in her box, and Tori's gaze followed his hands.

"Wait a minute." She quickly scanned the box and then moved to another one, gaze searching. "Look in that box over there. Is there a skull?"

Seth looked and shook his head.

All the skulls were missing.

Tori swore and rubbed at her forehead. "Damn it. Someone doesn't want them identified."

Mason could tell Dr. Peres was steaming mad about the break-in. Those brown eyes of hers shot daggers in every direction she looked. She didn't rant and rave, but held it in. Her ramrod-straight posture and tight jaw told him how deeply the mess affected her. Seth's words about the bone doctor rang in his head, as she described what was missing.

Takes a bit of digging to get to know her.

Mason admired the anthropologist. She knew her shit and didn't complain about hard work. He'd been to more than one scene where the woman was deep in the dirt for hours to find answers for him and for the families. He studied her face as she explained about the teeth on the skull she was 99 percent certain was Lorenzo Cavallo's missing sister. The Bone Lady cared. She gave a rip about a woman who'd been dead for decades. That was something he didn't see every day. Her frustration with the missing bones was plain in her speech.

"I'd like to strangle someone," Dr. Peres said frankly. "There's never been a break-in here, but today they steal my bones? What really pisses me off is that I hadn't done the full exam on some of the missing pieces. I have photos and X-rays, thank God. But I didn't get to spend the in-depth time with them that I like to."

"You can tell a lot from the X-rays, right?" Ray Lusco asked.

She nodded. "Age, breaks, ancestry, health. A number of things. But nothing is better than having the actual bones in my hands."

Mason glanced at the other two men in the room. Seth Rutledge stood silently, arms across his chest, feet planted firmly, his gaze locked on Dr. Peres's face as she spoke. Next to him stood the ex. Mason had never met Rory Gibbs. But what he'd learned in the last fifteen minutes told him he hadn't missed out. Other than a brief greeting and introduction, Mason hadn't spoken to the man, but he'd watched him carefully. Rory Gibbs couldn't stand still. He shifted his weight constantly, scanned the room, and eyed Seth Rutledge with annoyance. Dr. Rutledge ignored him.

The man had no focus, Mason decided. And he was a college professor? He was as antsy as a student during a lecture on dirt. What had Victoria Peres seen in the guy? Mason was perturbed by his adult ADHD vibe. In Mason's experience, men who couldn't stand or sit still were usually guilty about something.

"You didn't see anyone around?" Mason directed his question to Rory. Victoria had finished her description of the leg and foot she'd seen darting out the door. Good thing Lusco had been taking careful notes. Mason's mental notes were on Rory Gibbs.

Rory looked at him. "No. Nothing. Anita gestured me toward the back, saying Victoria was back by her lab. Anita was on the phone, speaking to someone about an alarm that'd just gone off. I know my way around. I've been here a lot."

Mason waited.

"Well, not recently. Not since we divorced." Rory shot a glance at Victoria.

Mason followed his gaze. Dr. Peres's face was perfectly blank. Her previous frustration about the break-in carefully shielded along with her feelings about her ex-husband.

"Why were you here today?" Mason asked.

"I wanted to talk to Victoria."

Mason waited again, watching the college professor adjust his balance and clench his fingers together. He judged Rory Gibbs to be the type of man who didn't like silence and would fill in the holes.

"I wanted to know more about those girls who died. When I saw their names on the news, I realized two of them had been previous students of mine."

Mason's gut started to buzz. *The prof knew two victims?* "These girls were all in high school. You teach at the community college, right?"

Rory nodded. "English. All levels. We get lots of high-school students taking lower-level classes during the summer sessions. Gets it out of the way. Cheaper for the parents and one less class for their load during freshman year."

"Were the girls in the same class?" Lusco spoke up.

Rory shook his head. "I already looked at my records. I wanted to be certain that I was right when I saw their names. They both took a one-hundred-level English class last summer, but on different days."

"Did you check for the other girls' names?"

"I only looked at last summer's classes, but I didn't see any other names from the news."

"Who'd you teach?"

"Brooke Sheardon and Glory McCarthy."

"Why'd you remember them?" Mason asked. "I'd think that the names and faces would blur together after a while."

Rory moved his feet. "That's true. But Glory's name stuck in my head. It's an odd one. And I had her in a summer session. We'd joked about her plans for the Fourth of July."

"And Brooke?"

"I didn't remember her until I looked at the class roster."

"Were the girls friends?" Lusco had his pencil speeding along his notepad.

"I have no idea. I don't remember anything about them except for the Fourth of July conversation."

"They're attractive girls," Mason prodded.

Rory stared at him. "What's your point?"

"Usually men remember pretty girls." He held the college professor's gaze, infusing his comment with a hint of slime.

"What the hell?" Dr. Peres spit the words. "What are you saying, Callahan?"

"I'm just trying to prod his memory a bit. If the girls hung out together through the college, that'd be the first connection we've managed to establish. Actually you're the first connection we've found, Professor Gibbs. We haven't been able to tie them together at all."

"If they'd been in the same class, I'd say that's a connection," Rory argued. "But being in different classes on different days is pretty weak."

"No, not the class. You. You're the common denominator." Mason showed the professor his teeth. "I'm glad we ran into you today."

Mason swore Gibbs's face paled two shades.

He knew he shouldn't poke at people like that, but the professor rubbed him the wrong way.

"Is Brooke improving?" Dr. Peres spoke up.

"She gave everyone a bad scare yesterday," Lusco answered. "Put her parents and the hospital staff into a panic, but she pulled through. Still not conscious."

"Any change in her prognosis?" Dr. Rutledge asked.

"No change. Touch and go."

"The first funeral is later today," stated Dr. Peres softly. "I'd planned to go until the break-in happened. Lacey is going."

Mason nodded. "We'll have police there. In uniform and in plainclothes."

"Why plainclothes? I'd think the parents would appreciate a blue turnout that's as big as possible." The professor's skin color was back to normal.

"These men will be working. Filming the attendees."

"Oh. I've heard killers will attend their victims' funerals. Is that what you're looking for?" Rory tilted his head as he spoke, his gaze intent on Mason.

"The service today is more for the public," Mason stated, ignoring his question. "It's not an actual funeral. It's so the people who didn't know the girls can give their respects to the family. Actual interment will be private."

"This case has struck a huge chord with the community. The church will be packed. You're probably looking at thousands of people," Dr. Rutledge added. "That's a lot of faces to look through."

"I'm kinda hoping the rain keeps some people away," said Mason.

Victoria gave a half smile. "If Oregonians stayed home when it rained, we'd never get out."

"Three of the smaller rivers have already spilled over their banks," Lusco spoke. "I drove through a foot of water not far from my neighborhood. They've got roads closed in some of the areas and people are already picking up sandbags."

"Tired of the rain," Mason added. He turned back to Dr. Peres. "Will you be able to get an inventory of what's missing by this evening?"

She nodded. "I think so. Each bone was coded at one point, but a lot of the numbers have faded. Hopefully I can put together something pretty accurate. This was deliberate, you know. The only reason to steal skulls is to try to hide their identity. Nothing tells us more in anthropology. With a skull, I can tell sex, race, and age range, and match dental records. Or even have a forensic sculptor create a likeness from clay or computer images. Full identification from any other bone takes a rare specific incident. Like a broken femur with a matching X-ray. I wish I'd gotten a closer look at the last skeleton."

"Let me know when you're done. I want to know exactly what's missing." Mason turned to the college professor. "How about we set up a time for you to come talk to us at the office?"

Mason enjoyed watching the color drain from the man's face again.

CHAPTER FOURTEEN

Trinity tugged on her hood to protect her face from the rain. She followed in the slow-moving procession of foot traffic outside the memorial at the church, feeling a bit like a cow in a cattle drive and fighting the urge to moo. She'd decided to attend the public service for Glory McCarthy and be thankful that it wasn't a service for Brooke. Not yet.

When Brooke coded at the hospital yesterday, Trinity thought she was dead. She'd fallen into her foster mom's arms and bawled like a baby, the stress of the previous forty-eight hours catching up with her. Instead, Brooke had pulled through. But would she ever wake?

Was she going to have brain damage? Would she remember Trinity?

She gripped Katy's hand tighter. Her foster mom had agreed they should attend even though Trinity hadn't known Glory. They came to show Glory's family that people cared. And they came to pray for Brooke's recovery. It felt like half the city of Portland had turned out. They slowly moved into the huge church. It was one of those megachurches. They didn't have pews; they used folding chairs, and it could hold thousands of worshipers at one time. Trinity pushed back her hood and stared at the huge images of Glory flashing on the screen at the front.

She had the same long dark hair as Brooke, but her eyes were a deep green. Trinity stopped in place as she watched the slide show. Glory and her three siblings, Glory as a baby, Glory and her parents. Trinity felt Katy glance at her. She knew Trinity longed for a tight-knit family.

But right now, Trinity was simply content to be healthy and holding hands with an awesome foster mom. She squeezed Katy's hand. She didn't want to trade places with anyone. A rumbling behind her made her realize she was holding up the line, and she looked for a place to sit. The chairs were all full; it was standing room only.

"Let's go stand over there." Katy pointed to the right, pulling her that way, and Trinity followed.

A tall figure stood out in the packed masses and made eye contact with her.

Jason. Her heart gave a mini double *thump.*

Did he go to Glory's school?

She hadn't heard from him since his texts about Brooke at the hospital.

Jason was good-looking. There was no getting around it. She'd always thought Brooke was lucky to catch his attention.

He raised a brow at her and smiled. Her heart continued its tiny dance. *He'd acknowledged her!* The kid standing next to him elbowed him in the side. Trinity tried to see who he was standing with, but the other teen wasn't looking her way. Three more steps and Jason was lost in the crowd. She craned her neck, unsuccessfully searching for him again. The crowd was dense. She and Katy squeezed between groups of mourners, searching for an open spot.

Katy reached a small clearing near the far wall and let out a sigh. "Let's try here. We can still see pretty good."

Everywhere Trinity looked, she saw strangers. There were tons of teens, but she didn't know them. Groups of crying girls and stoic guys. Parents who wiped at their eyes and grandparents with small children on their laps. She suspected most of the people didn't know Glory nor the other girls. She was witnessing a community in pain, leaning on one another for support.

She noticed the police who stood at the edges of the room. There were several different uniforms. Trinity recognized the Portland police and Multnomah County, but she couldn't make out the others. A dozen different police precincts were represented. Another sign of the public coming together. Everyone experienced pain when young people died.

"Trinity?" She felt a light tap on her shoulder and turned to see the brown eyes of Dr. Campbell from the medical examiner's office. "I knew that was you."

"Hi, Dr. Campbell."

"Call me Lacey," the pretty blonde said. She gestured at the tall couple with her. "This is my friend Michael and his fiancée, Jamie."

The couple smiled, and Trinity tried not to stare at Jamie's amazing pale green eyes as she introduced them to her foster mom. Michael seemed like an intense type of guy. He had an arm tight around Jamie, but Trinity noticed he often touched Lacey's shoulder in a sisterly sort of way. Lacey's eyes were red, the lids puffy. Sorta like 80 percent of the other people around her.

"It's nice you came, Trinity. How is Brooke doing?" Lacey asked.

"The same," Trinity whispered. An image of Brooke in her hospital bed filled her mind. Every day she looked thinner and thinner. She was being fed through a tube of some sort, but Trinity didn't think it was enough. She looked away from the sympathy in Lacey's eyes.

"I can't stand this," muttered Michael. "Children shouldn't die before their parents." Jamie nodded and she leaned her head on his shoulder.

His words struck a chord with Trinity. Was anything more true? Parents shouldn't bury their children; it should be the other way around. That was how life was intended to be. Yet, her own mother had walked away from raising her daughter. How does a mother do that? Didn't it go against their chemical makeup?

In therapy she'd learned her mother was mentally ill. Drugs and alcohol made her problem worse. She understood why her mother had acted as she had, but that didn't make it hurt less. Her grandmother was also an alcoholic. Trinity's therapist and she had spent hours discussing whether alcohol would be an issue for her.

"It's easy to say 'I'll never drink,' but harder to achieve it and stick to it," her doctor had said. "You must be hyperaware that you might be susceptible to an addiction. Millions of people have no issue with alcohol, but some appear to be predisposed to addiction. And it's showing its ugly face in your mother and grandmother. You need to learn from what you've seen. Many addicts don't have the luxury of this strong warning."

Trinity swore to heed that warning. She would never be her mother.

The service started. Next to her, Katy frequently wiped at her eyes. Trinity felt her phone vibrate in her coat pocket. Unable to ignore it, she pulled it out.

I'm already addicted to something. My phone. Not good.

It was a text from Jason. Heart speeding up, she opened the message.

WHAT'S THE WORD ON B?

Unable to help herself, she tapped out a reply. NO CHANGE. HAD A SCARE YESTERDAY BUT SHE MADE IT.

She waited. No reply. Feeling disappointed, she slipped the phone back in her pocket and tried to listen. Glory's uncle was speaking, but Trinity couldn't focus on his words. The pictures of Glory's family sucked up her attention. A big family. Aunts, uncles, grandparents, tons of cousins. What was it like to grow up with so many people who care about you?

Murmurs started near the back of the church. Trinity tried to ignore it, but they grew louder. Katy craned her head to look past Trinity in the direction of the noise, a frown on her face. Voices escalated and more heads turned to look. Trinity couldn't see. It came from the dense crowd standing near the main doors.

Voices grew to shouts and people started moving. Glory's uncle stopped talking.

Katy grabbed her hand and Trinity heard Michael swear under his breath. A half-dozen men yelled, and Trinity saw people start shoving.

Did someone just throw a punch?

Michael's hand landed on her shoulder and gave her a firm push. "We're getting out of here. Go. Now!" He thrust Jamie in the direction of a side door and pulled Lacey after him. Lacey tugged at Trinity's sleeve, and she followed.

"Follow him," Katy commanded. Trinity pushed between the other mourners. All focus was on the rowdy crowd in the back. Police bulldozed past her, heading toward the riot. One woman slammed her shoulder against Trinity's, trying to move toward the fighting group.

"Sorry!" Trinity shouted at the passing woman's back.

Katy gripped Trinity's shoulders, pushed and steered her after Michael. "Don't stop!"

A riot in a church?

Panic rose in her throat as more people pressed against her. Trinity felt like she was swimming upstream. She kept her gaze on Michael's back and pressed on. He shoved open the side door and the group spilled out into the gray rain. More people sped out behind them.

"What happened? What was going on in there?" she blurted, gasping for air.

Michael hustled them to a semidry spot under a tree. "Everyone okay?"

The other three women looked as rattled as Trinity felt.

"I don't know what happened, but a group of teenage boys started it. As soon as they started pushing and punching, I was getting us out of there," Michael stated, his eyes grim. "That was too close of quarters for a fight. They can get out of hand fast."

"But that wasn't a bar," Lacey exclaimed. "That was a church! A memorial service! What the hell happened in there?"

"I wasn't waiting to find out."

A gunshot echoed from the church.

"To the truck! Now!" Michael commanded. He pointed, grabbed Jamie's hand, and ran. Trinity caught a frantic look from Jamie and ran after them, bent over in imitation of Michael. She heard Lacey and Katy's pounding footsteps directly behind her, splashing in the puddles.

"Go, go, go!" Katy yelled behind her.

A gun?

Trinity ran.

CHAPTER FIFTEEN

Seth blinked and squinted at the computer screen in the medical examiner's office, but the webpage still said the same thing.

Sixty-eight percent.

Eden had a D in chemistry.

How can that be?

Eden got straight As. No exceptions. What the hell was wrong with her chemistry class? He swallowed and studied the rest of her grades. Three Cs and a B. What was going on? They weren't final grades; they reflected where she stood at the middle of the term. But still . . . a D? He reached for his cell phone, trying to get a grip on his temper. He knew college wasn't like high school and didn't grade the same, but Eden was sharp. She had the skills to succeed. He dialed her cell.

Why hadn't she told him she was struggling?

He'd meant to check her grades for weeks, but he'd been wrapped up in the hope for the new job. Maybe he should have looked at them earlier. Was it too late to improve them?

Her phone continued to ring. He held his breath. Voice mail. He hung up.

He stared at the computer screen for another thirty seconds, mind racing. Maybe it was a good thing she hadn't answered. He was a bit worked up and might not listen well. He glanced at his watch. Seven P.M.

He sent a text: CALL ME.

He blew out a breath and leaned back in his chair. The numbers taunted him from the screen. Two of the Cs were nearly Ds.

Was the divorce upsetting her?

A million questions raced through his mind and he mentally set them aside. He needed to talk with her before he jumped to conclusions. Looking at the calendar, he realized it'd been more than a week since he spoken with his daughter. That wasn't like her. He'd called a few times but had never reached her. He scrolled through his texts. Two days ago, she'd said she'd call him that evening. He checked his call log for missed calls.

Nothing.

All the texts before that were typical teen. Had to get to class, had to study, out with friends.

No time to talk to Dad.

He tossed his cell on the desk. Was he overreacting? How often did he talk to his uncle when he was at college? Once a month? Maybe?

The grades worried him. That wasn't like Eden.

Should he text Jennifer? Ask if she'd heard anything? His phone taunted him from the desk. Everybody was a simple click away these days. Even Jennifer. But he was trying to create distance between them, get her adjusted to not hearing from him. Contacting her about every little issue wasn't going to help. The final divorce papers had arrived this afternoon for him to sign. No doubt Jennifer had received them, too. This was not the best day to get in touch.

If he didn't hear back from Eden by tomorrow, he'd contact Jennifer.

Decision made. He hated postponing issues, but there was nothing he could fix tonight unless Eden called him.

"Seth? Are you in there?"

The panic in Victoria's voice from the hallway had Seth out of his seat. She dashed into the office, alarm in her eyes. "What's wrong?"

The Tori he remembered didn't raise her voice. And he doubted this new one did either.

"There was a shooting at the memorial for Glory McCarthy." She rushed her words, her chest heaving.

"What? Just now?"

"Jerry called me. He saw it on the news. He wanted to know if Lacey was there."

"She went, right?" Seth asked.

"She told me she was going. I've tried to call her, and I've texted her." Victoria looked at her phone again. "I haven't heard back."

"Did the news say anyone was killed?"

"Just bumps and bruises so far."

Seth took a deep breath. "That's good. Let's see what's going on." He sat down and pulled up the website for a local news station. "There's a whopping five sentences on their page that says nothing new. And the story was posted ten minutes ago. I don't think they know much yet."

"Trinity was going, too."

Seth looked at her face, leaning close over his shoulder to read the screen. Her pupils were dilated, making her eyes darker than normal. This close he could see every eyelash.

"Why would someone do that? So utterly stupid." She pressed her lips together and lines formed between her eyebrows. "How many people were there?"

"It says the place was packed, but police caught the gunman. Lots of cops were there just to show support, so that was lucky. Sounds like half of Portland attended."

Victoria's phone gave a delicate melody. "Lacey?" she asked into the phone.

Seth heard a female respond on the other end. The lines eased out of Victoria's face.

"Did you see Trinity?" The lines eased further. "Oh, thank God. What happened?"

Seth's spine relaxed. The teenager had been through a lot lately. He liked to see Tori's fondness for the girl.

How would she get along with Eden?

She closed her eyes as she listened, her posture visibly sagging in relief.

"Where are you?" she asked Lacey. "How's Trinity holding up?"

Victoria opened her eyes, meeting Seth's gaze. He'd been studying her, taking advantage of the moment.

She listened intently. "Yes, that doesn't surprise me one bit. Poor thing."

"Poor thing" wasn't a good description of Trinity in Seth's book. He'd seen a scrappy kid, who listened and looked very carefully before she spoke or moved. She seemed to have a good head on her shoulders.

"Have you talked to the police?" She paused. "None of you saw anything?"

A minute later she'd wrapped up the conversation. Seth refreshed the news webpage. No new results.

"She said a fight broke out. It may have possibly started between some teens. Michael hustled them out of the building before the shot was fired."

"Who's Michael?" Seth asked.

"A pain in the ass. But he's actually okay for a reporter."

"A reporter?" Seth avoided reporters on principle.

"Investigative reporter for *The Oregonian*. He and Lacey go way back. If I'd been at that memorial and someone started shooting, he's the guy I'd want on my side."

"A reporter?" Seth repeated.

"Doesn't seem right, does it? You'll understand when you meet him."

"You say that like I'm about to meet him."

She nodded. "You are. Something about being at the scene of a shooting has Michael's curiosity piqued about the death of the girls in Forest Park. We're about to be interviewed."

"I don't want to talk to the press." Seth had learned in his years as a medical examiner to not talk to the press. A press conference was fine, preferably without press questions if possible. But a one-on-one with a reporter about a huge case? That's how people got fired. Or humiliated in the paper.

"Of course not, no one does. But this guy can find anybody and anything."

"So it's not for an article?"

"No. If there's anyone who can dig up information on those old murders or these new ones, he's the guy. I think the police have their hands full trying to solve the recent case. And Detective Callahan knows him. The two of them have worked together before. I don't think it'll hurt."

"You called them murders. You don't think there's even a possibility they're suicides?"

She shook her head. "Callahan told me they can't find anything in the girls' history for the past weeks that indicates they were thinking of suicide. No good-bye notes, no depression, no giving away of items, no weird statements on Facebook about life or love. All the friends and family the police have interviewed swear up and down that their friends had things in their lives they were looking forward to. Usually someone will say they'd been down or talking about weird topics. Callahan said he'd strongly suspected murder in the first place, considering how that scene was staged. No shoes, remember?"

Seth nodded, remembering the clean bare feet.

"Someone walked away," she said grimly.

Victoria felt stifled. Lacey had a lovely large home, but stress flowed from the group who'd escaped the shooting an hour earlier. Lacey opened a third bottle of wine for the adults and the tensions slowly dropped along with the wine level. Trinity sipped sparingly at a Sprite; she still looked rattled. Victoria was on her first glass of wine, letting the others use the alcohol to unwind. She preferred to stay on her toes in a group. This crew was just the five who'd attended the service plus herself and Seth. Even though they were relatively close acquaintances, she still wouldn't risk lowering her guard.

She'd dealt with Michael Brody a few times. Enough to know he was freakishly smart and deceptively casual. She glanced at Seth beside her on Lacey's couch. He'd taken to Michael right away and vice versa. There were a lot of similarities in the men. Height, stature, intelligence. But Seth's calm didn't give her the annoying friction that Michael's pushy sharpness did.

Right now, some of that pushy sharpness was needed to investigate the history of the dead Forest Park women. Both sets of them. Michael had the nose to do it, and Victoria was all about using him for her own purposes to find some answers. Trinity was under his scrutiny at the moment. Surprisingly, he'd taken a soft tactic with the teen, who gazed at him with a bit of hero worship that made Michael's fiancée, Jamie, hide a smile.

"I didn't know Glory," Trinity repeated. "And I didn't see anyone at the service I knew except for Dr. Campbell and Jason."

Michael's gaze narrowed. "Who is Jason?"

Trinity gave a half-hearted jerk of her shoulder. "I met him through Brooke. He goes to Harrison High School. He was there with some other guys I didn't recognize."

"Were they standing toward the back?" asked Michael. "Back where the noise started coming from?"

Trinity wrinkled her nose. "Kind of near the entry doors. It was so squished in there. I only saw him for a moment before we moved over to where you guys stood. He could have been anywhere by the time the fight started."

"What's his last name?" asked Seth.

"I have no idea. I do have his phone number. We text sometimes. Well, he's texted me to ask how Brooke is doing."

Victoria's heart softened at the crack in Trinity's voice as she said Brooke's name. Victoria knew the doctors were guarded about the teen's prognosis. Her brain had been oxygen starved; there was no way to assess the damage yet.

Trinity passed her phone to Seth, who thumbed through her contacts.

"You don't think he's involved in the shooting, do you?" she asked Michael.

"I don't know. Police haven't released the name of the shooter, but rumors say they arrested a teenager. I have someone looking into it," he said.

Victoria glanced at Lacey, who gave a small eye roll. Michael had a tendency to break the rules and push the boundaries of the law where he saw fit. No doubt his "someone" was a cop buddy or a person who shouldn't be passing information to a reporter.

Trinity looked tired. Her foster mom sat beside her, occasionally patting her back or holding her hand. Katy knew how to manage teen girls. Victoria gave a small prayer of thanks for her own adoptive parents. Birth was a gamble. You never knew what kind of parents you'd end up with. She'd been lucky, and it appeared Trinity was in good hands after her rotten first decade.

Michael's hawk-like gaze turned to Victoria. "Tell me again what happened at your break-in."

"All three skulls were taken. I was in the middle of inventorying everything when this occurred, and now I'll have to go through it again and make certain nothing else is missing."

"Lacey mentioned the remains had been mixed together. How can you tell what belongs to who?"

"Skeletal remains are immediately printed with their case number. Every piece. Sadly they used pencil back then, so some of the numbers are nearly illegible or completely missing. I'd touched up several but not all. I'm making an educated guess at the rest."

"So they may not be completely right," he stated.

"I'm getting it as close as I can." The question didn't bother her. No one else would be able to solve the puzzle of the missing pieces better than her. She had faith in her abilities. She may not be perfectly accurate, but show her someone who could do better.

"If anyone can figure it out, Tori can," Seth added. He reached out and squeezed her hand. He'd tensed slightly during Michael's questioning, a defensive tone now in his voice.

Michael turned his probing gaze Seth's way. He met it with utter calm. "You've worked with her for less than a week."

"I know her reputation. She's one of the best in the country. And I know her character." His spine straightened another inch, his molars clenched.

His hand tightened around Victoria's. When he'd taken it, she'd felt a calming warmth flow from his touch. It'd felt normal. It hadn't felt like he'd been absent for nearly eighteen years. It'd seemed completely natural for him to touch her in reassurance, and for it to work.

Victoria struggled to remember sitting next to Rory and holding his hand, but the memories were surprisingly far away for a marriage of five years. She'd filed Rory and their life together into a mental box and firmly closed the lid. She'd thought she'd done the same with Seth, but suddenly it was all back at the surface. How had eighteen years vanished?

She blinked and realized Michael was looking at her expectantly, the echo of a question lingering in the room. She'd heard nothing.

"I'm sorry, what?"

His lips turned up in amusement. "How long were you out of the room?"

"It couldn't have been more than thirty minutes. I'd taken a break and got something to eat, and I was on my way back to the lab when the alarm went off."

"Which was caused by the door opening. Could he have heard you coming back and decided to leave?"

"He could have easily heard my shoes. Everything echoes in those hallways."

"I wonder if he'd planned to do more damage or if you interrupted him." Seth rubbed at his chin, a thoughtful look in his eye.

Victoria nodded.

"I still can't believe no one else has come forward during these years to claim the other women. They must have parents or even children who wondered what happened to them," said Seth. "How can a family member simply accept that a sister or mother vanished? Maybe the children were told their mothers had died."

"I was adopted," said Victoria. "If I hadn't grown up knowing my mother was dead, I would have searched."

"Maybe a trusted parent told them their mother was dead," speculated Michael. "Have you seen your mother's death certificate?"

Her brain shot into jet speed as she froze. She'd never seen a death certificate. She'd never doubted her adoptive parents' word. Victoria couldn't speak.

Awareness flowed in Michael's gaze as he took in her silence. "I'm sorry. My nature is to question everything. Doesn't matter the source. If I hear it from one person, I need to have it verified by two other people or sources."

"My parents wouldn't lie to me," Victoria choked out. But her mind was racing in circles. *Would her parents lie to her? Parents lie to children all the time.*

"I know what you mean," said Trinity. "My mother and grandmother told me my birth father was dead. When I was placed with Katy, I had her look into it. He wasn't dead. He was in prison and had signed off all rights. After a lot of time with my therapist, I made the decision not to get to know him. He didn't seem like the type of person I wanted influencing my life."

Katy wrapped an arm around the girl and gave her a warm hug. Trinity rested her head on Katy's shoulder for a brief second, her eyes sad.

Trinity may have made her decision, Victoria thought, but obviously it was a hard one. It must haunt her daily.

Now will I always wonder? Did my parents lie to me? Could my birth parents still be alive?

Her thoughts must have been plain on her face, because Seth spoke.

"We'll help you find out."

"Thank you," Victoria said. A bit of guilt prickled at her, because she doubted the people who'd raised her. Both had passed away more than a decade ago, but she still thanked them every day for giving her a good upbringing.

"It's okay to wonder," Trinity said. "You're human."

"It's not that," said Victoria. "It's making me doubt everything my adoptive parents told me. And that doesn't sit well with me. They were good people." She felt a tear run from the corner of her eye. She wiped at it. Her defenses were crumbling. And she couldn't blame it on a single slow glass of wine. "Oregon has a law that anyone over twenty-one can request their original birth certificate with their birth parents' names on it. In adoptions, the original birth certificates are sealed. I requested mine a few years back." She took a long shaky breath. "But the state said they have no record of mine. My parents had died by then, so I had no one to ask about it. I've just gone on with the identity they built for me. All I know is my adoption was arranged through a tiny church that my parents attended for a while in Seaport, near the coast."

"Ah, shit. I'm sorry, Victoria," Michael said, dismay clouding his face. "Have you contacted the church to ask for their personal records?"

She noticed he didn't call her "Vicki," the nickname he used to poke at her. That was truly a heartfelt apology from Michael Brody. She didn't know who she was. She had no record of who her birth parents were. The state couldn't find a record of her adoption, and she'd taken her adoptive parents at their word. "No," she whispered. *Why hadn't she? She'd thought about doing it but never followed through. Was she scared they'd have no record either?*

Seth transferred her hand into his other one and wrapped his arm around her, pulling her close on the couch. Victoria didn't fight it. In fact, she wanted to lay her head on his shoulder like Trinity had done with Katy. A huge wave of emotions bubbled up in her throat. Embarrassment at crying in front of six people, doubt about her parents, confusion over Seth, relief that Lacey and Trinity were okay, anger over the break-in.

If anyone deserved a second glass of wine, she did.

CHAPTER SIXTEEN

Mason rubbed at the back of his neck. *Holy shit, they'd been lucky.*

Gunfire in a large crowd rarely ended well. But everyone was breathing a sigh of relief that the gunman had been tackled and arrested immediately by the police present. His department wasn't handling the case. The shooter was probably lucky that the Clackamas County Sheriff's Office had him. Judging by Ray's scowl, he would have slowly torn off the young punk's limbs.

Ray pounded on his keyboard, probably imagining it was the face of the teen who was presently being grilled by the county police.

What had the kid been thinking?

One of the county detectives had told Mason that the teen's friends were the ones who'd initially disarmed him. They didn't know if the kid actually intended to shoot someone or just show off. It didn't matter to Mason. An event that big would guarantee that several people were carrying concealed. In addition to the fifty officers who were present, Mason guessed there were another twenty handgun carriers in the crowd. Legitimate, law-abiding citizens. He had no beef with them. He fully respected the public's right to arm themselves. But not a stupid teenager's rights, who pulled out a gun in the middle of a crowd.

"You're shaking your head," Ray said from his desk.

"Fucking idiot."

"You're reading my mind."

"It could have been a disaster. One on the news for the next two weeks."

Ray snorted. "No point in worrying about what could have happened." His desk phone rang and he picked it up. "Lusco."

Mason directed his focus back to the Forest Park girls. They were getting nowhere fast. Lorenzo Cavallo's death and the theft at the ME's office had to be related to the original case, but forensics was still processing the evidence and so far hadn't found any obvious leads. Rory Gibbs would be in tomorrow to talk to them about the girls from his English class, but Mason didn't have high hopes for the interview.

What were they missing?

Maybe they should take another look at the cult theory. But there weren't any underground whispers. Usually if a group is involved, someone starts talking. There'd been one freak who'd come forward, saying it was related to an invisible spacecraft passing by the earth. He'd meant to catch a ride that night, but had drank too much to remember to kill himself. Now he'd missed his ride and they wouldn't be back for another fifty years. Mason had read the statement and nearly rolled on the floor. God bless the cop who'd taken it and managed to write it up without inserting a single ounce of sarcasm.

He still snickered about it at odd moments.

He knew cults thrived. They didn't have to be large. They just needed a group of impressionable people and a charismatic leader. There was a mansion on several acres outside of one of the hick towns on the edge of the Portland tri-county area. Mason had heard the rumors of the large number of people living there. Locals were nosy and gossipy, saying that the people never left the estate, kept to themselves, and had all their supplies trucked in.

The rumors grew so large that the local sheriff finally paid a friendly visit. He'd found an old couple who simply kept to themselves. No masses of live-ins. No orgies or drugs. Two old people who'd decided to build themselves a fabulous home. And rescue cats. But they didn't put them up for adoption. They kept them all. The place was crawling with cats. Supplies were trucked in. Mainly cat litter and cat food. A small group of staff received room and board to care for the cats. Mason liked cats. Just not that many cats.

He wondered if the mansion smelled.

He shuffled the papers on his desk, glancing at the clock. Nearly 9 P.M. He was hitting that wall of uselessness where his mind wandered and nothing got done. Time to leave for the night. Things had slowed to a stall on the girls. The search for the girls' cell phones had turned up nothing. The cell phone carriers were all cooperating. But the girls' phones had stopped sending signals before they died. Someone had the forethought to remove the batteries. Last locations were all near Forest Park. Ray had run a comparison on the text and cell numbers from the different carriers, looking for common numbers. The girls had called and texted each other, but there didn't seem to be another common number that was unaccounted for.

How had they communicated with the organizer?

Mason had a mental image of the organizer as a tall thin man, walking away from the circle of unmoving girls; their shoes, phones, and purses in his bag.

Two girls had home landlines. No common calls.

Their Facebook, Instagram, Twitter, and what-the-fuck-other social media accounts had been searched. No flags were found outside of the girls all being "friends." Some of the girls had more than a thousand friends, which blew Mason's mind. Ray informed him that teens often didn't actually know their "friends." They just gobbled up friend invitations from friends of their friends, trying to build an impressive number.

An ego boost. That was a concept Mason understood.

Ray had also pointed out that most social media messages could easily be deleted. But would all six girls be consistent with their deletions? Somewhere there had to be a digital footprint left by one of the girls that would point to their killer.

The computer forensics guys were searching the home computers and laptops for evidence, but they didn't expect results for at least another week. The amount of data had to be overwhelming.

The remaining public memorial services had been canceled. No one wanted a repeat of today. The community couldn't mourn when they were checking the stranger next to them to see if he carried a weapon. The tragedy of the day had escalated to a whole new level. Because of some punk teen.

Ray hung up his phone. "That was Clackamas County. They haven't been able to talk much to the kid they arrested. They're waiting on his lawyer."

Mason sighed. "He's said nothing?"

"Nothing. But his buddy is talking."

That got Mason's attention. "And?"

"The kid with the gun is Kyle Carey. He went to school with Glory McCarthy. His buddy says Kyle was interested in McCarthy, but the two had never connected."

"Interested? Like he had a crush on her?"

"Yeah, that's the impression I got. Anyway, the friend saw Kyle pull the gun out of his coat during the service. That's when the scuffle started. He'd told him to put it away and the other kid refused. Other people around Kyle argued with him, too, but Kyle wouldn't listen. So the friend tried to wrestle it away."

"Aw, shit. Seriously?"

"That's when the shot was fired."

"Christ, that could have killed someone!"

"The friend thinks his own finger was on the trigger when the gun was fired. County says he's pretty shook up that he'll receive the blame for the shot being fired."

"That's why you don't grab at someone's gun in a crowd." Mason shook his head. The kid had good intentions, but sometimes the best intentions don't work out the way you want. Sometimes someone dies. "Did the friend say why Kyle had a gun?"

Ray frowned. "That's where it gets a bit odd. The friend—his name is Jason—thinks Kyle brought it, hoping to figure out the person responsible for Glory's death."

"What? Kyle knows something that we don't?" *Who on earth did Kyle expect to see?*

"Jason said Kyle got really agitated when he spotted a girl at the service. That's when words were exchanged and the gun came out."

"This sounds more like an argument over another girl instead of Kyle wanting to shoot whoever he thinks killed Glory McCarthy."

Ray nodded and he gave a grim smile. "Ready for the twist?"

"Ah fuck, another one?"

"Kyle got agitated when he spotted Trinity Viders."

Mason was silent as his mind did laps trying to catch up to Ray's statement. "Our Trinity? The girl with Victoria Peres?"

Ray nodded. "That's the one."

"She was at the service?"

"According to this Jason kid."

Mason stared at Ray. "Think Trinity might have more to tell us?"

"Only one way to find out."

CHAPTER SEVENTEEN

"What the hell happened?" The old man tried not to shout on the phone.

The reports of the shooting were all over the late-night news. He stared at his TV, a graphic of the memorial service overlaid with a gun hung behind the newscaster's left shoulder. The female newscaster frowned as she related the story, her disapproval ringing in her tone. *. . . a teenager pulled out a gun in the middle of a packed crowd saying farewell to Glory McCarthy . . .*

Guns were the hot topic at the moment. A new rash of public shootings had escalated the subject to the top of every lawmaker's list. Big changes were in the works.

"I don't know. I haven't been able to get any information, Father." Leo's voice cracked slightly.

Idiot.

"It's bad enough you were seen at the medical examiner's today. Now this?" the old man asked.

"It wasn't our fault."

"Why was he there? He was told to avoid the services. Police tape those, specifically looking for familiar faces."

"Jason wanted to go with his friends. He thought it would look bad if he didn't."

The old man blew out a breath. "I gave specific orders to not go to the memorial services. You should have told me what he was doing."

"I didn't know."

"That's no excuse."

The line was silent.

Yes, his son couldn't be expected to prevent what he didn't know was happening. That meant he needed to watch Jason closely.

"You need to know what my grandson is doing. Keep a tighter rein on his activities. Do you know where he is all hours of the day?" He didn't care if the question seemed unfair. They were in a crisis mode. There could be no more mistakes. "Our success stems from our control. It's important that no one step out of line. And it's up to us to enforce it."

"He'd said he was going to a friend's house. He's always at someone's home."

"Then it's time to curb his activities. Who's in control in your home? You or Jason? You can't let him run freely about the city doing as he pleases. He's shown he can't be trusted. It's time to crack down."

Why did he have to give this talk? Leo knew the rules. He knew he was directly responsible for Jason's actions. "How are you going to fix the problem at the medical examiner's?" the old man asked.

"I don't think there is a problem. I got what we needed and confused the scene to mislead them. It will take them days to sort it out."

"You're making assumptions. They're professionals. You know the bones have been assigned to Victoria Peres. She's renowned for her anthropology skills. It may be as simple as an easy crossword puzzle for her."

The line went silent again. Let him think on that. The old man didn't tolerate sloppy work or assumptions made on no information. Let him sweat under his father's praise for the woman's work. Maybe it would push him to try a little harder. Nothing like a bit of rivalry.

"What did you do with the bones?"

"They're safe," Leo answered with confidence.

The old man closed his eyes. *Had this man learned nothing from him?* "Where are the bones?"

A pause. "At the house."

"Where your boy can find them?"

Another pause. "He won't find them."

Jesus Christ. "Boys can find anything. Especially deliberately hidden things. Remove them at once. I want them here."

Leo cleared his throat. "Yes, sir."

That was better. A little respect. Perhaps the fault did lie with himself. Had he been too lax on his flock? Was he growing too soft in his old age?

"Where is Jason now?"

"Ummm. I'm not sure. He's not answering his phone. I've told him to call me at once."

"He's not obeying well, is he? I want to see him. Tomorrow. First thing in the morning."

"Ahh. Okay. I'll try to find him."

The old man's blood pressure rose. "Find him now! And get those bones over here tonight. What is wrong with you? I've never seen you so incompetent before. Can't you find his location with his phone?"

"I've tried. He must have powered down his phone. I'll be able to tell the minute he turns it back on."

"So he's avoiding you. He knows how to keep you off his back." The old man's mind raced. Jason was becoming a big problem. The stunt he'd pulled last week had brought national attention to the deaths of long ago. *What was the boy up to? He'd never been so defiant before.*

"I'll find him," Leo said assuredly.

Liar. The old man had no confidence in his son. Within twenty-four hours, he'd managed to destroy any trust and respect he'd built in the old man's eyes. This was an important time for them. He needed to rely on people who'd proved themselves to be trustworthy, and this man was rapidly sliding down the ladder.

"Get those bones over here now," he ordered.

"On my way, Father."

The old man broke the connection and turned his attention back to the television. Memorial attendees were being interviewed. Their stories were jumbled and confused and offered no insight into the terror that'd happened inside the building. One gun, two guns, three guns. *Figure it out, people!* How could the eyewitness accounts be so different? He answered his own question; no doubt these were not eyewitnesses, but people who simply wanted their faces on TV. They may have been present, but they didn't see anything.

What was he going to do with Leo? And the boy? His heart hurt at the thought of punishing them. But they'd broken the rules. The boy had broken a direct order. And the father had failed by not keeping the boy in control.

He'd meted out punishment several times. His other son, the oldest boy, had been an issue for many years. He'd demonstrated as a child that his mind didn't work correctly. The old man had read that improper upbringing during a boy's formative years could add to adult issues. But these were brothers. How could one turn out normal and the other so malicious? Was the lack of a mother that important?

He shuddered at the memory of his last encounter with the evil brother. He'd defied him, hoarding a precious necklace that had belonged to his dead mother. The boy had been eighteen at the time, and had shown a history of mental instability. The elders had urged him to do something to control the boy. He'd given him chance after chance, many more than any human deserved. When he'd been ordered to return the necklace to the family coffers, the young man had refused, clinging to the necklace and the memory of a mother he'd never known.

They'd faced each other down in the kitchen. For a long moment, he'd been slightly intimidated by the health and bulk of the youth standing up to his order to return the necklace, but he saw the hesitation in his eyes. Deep down he was afraid to defy his father.

"Give me the necklace," he'd commanded.

"It is mine. It is all that is left of her. I have a right to it, Father," he'd answered through clenched teeth. The hesitation in his gaze wavered, morphing into anger.

"I hold all the keepsakes. No one person can have them."

"You are one person. Do you hear how you contradict yourself? Your rules are nothing but contradictions. They make no sense."

"Give it to me now."

The young man lunged, thrusting the necklace into the garbage disposal and hitting the button above the countertop. The gnashing sounds of metal shredding shrieked through the kitchen.

"No!" he shouted, lunging at the sink.

His son pushed him away. "If I can't have it, no one can."

The old man had frozen, staring into the malevolent eyes. *He has to be put down. We can't have one like him in our midst.* "You shoved me," he shouted over the din. It was the least of the man's offenses but the most immediate.

The doubt and hesitation flickered in the young man's eyes again. "I'm sorry, Father."

The old man had shaken his head. It was too late; the actions with the necklace had sealed his fate. They all had to follow the rules.

He let out a long sigh, willing the memory of that other man to fade, tapping his fingers on the arm of his easy chair.

He had to take action again. He couldn't lose face in the eyes of the few followers he had left. He needed to assert that he was still in control. He might be old, but he hadn't lost his power. His bones ached on a daily basis, but with years came wisdom, right? In that case, no one was wiser than him.

Why was Jason striking out at him the way he had?

Sweat pooled under his arms. Had Jason discovered the shed?

Everyone had secrets. His were firmly locked away inside the shed and out in the forest. He wasn't proud of his weakness; he'd worked hard to control his urges. Even the shed looked innocent to a casual observer, but with a little digging, his world could be turned upside down.

His grandson could destroy him.

He was physically too weak to make any changes in the shed now. It was a rare day when he could walk out there without panting for breath.

He needed to see Jason.

Leo ended the call with his father.

How dense could the old man be? Did he see nothing?

The elder was losing it. For someone who'd led people for decades, the man was no longer logical. Perhaps it was simply aging. Perhaps his brain was rotting from the inside. How else could you explain the man's actions over the years?

Why did his father still shove Victoria Peres in his face? Anger burned up his throat. The woman was an abomination. Women shouldn't do what she does. She pranced around the country, showing off her knowledge, speaking at colleges, speaking at national seminars. That was a role for a man.

He knew she'd failed in her marriage. No doubt she'd driven the man away with her unfemale aggressiveness.

Someone needed to use a heavy hand with her. Show her how an obedient woman should act.

He paced the small bedroom in his house. It should be his role. He had the right to show her how a woman should act. His father hadn't stepped forward to take care of it. Didn't that mean the responsibility fell to him?

Excitement shot through him, like a stimulant had been injected into his veins.

He wanted her to know that he'd snagged her skulls out from under her watchful eye. He needed her to know that she wasn't the perfect woman she presented herself as. He wanted the satisfaction of seeing her fear him, admire him. His eyes closed. He could see her dressed in the flowing white dresses of the dead teens, her long black hair spread out on the ground around her, her skin a bloodless white.

He stopped and stared in the small mirror above his dresser. He had to give the stolen skulls to his father. But he knew where to find more. A lot more.

He wanted to send Victoria a message that she was being watched. What better delivery system than bones?

The pounding rain made the streets hard for Seth to see in the dark. Lack of street lighting simply made it worse. At least the traffic was light. At this late hour, few cars were on the road. Seth squinted and slowed his car, turning his wipers up to full blast. They whipped back and forth across his windshield, attacking the rain that dared to land upon the surface.

"I love this weather," Tori said from the passenger's seat. Seth wanted to look at her but didn't dare take his eyes from the road.

"I didn't know it could rain like this. This is crazy."

"But being indoors while it rains like this gives you that cozy, safe feeling."

Seth wanted to argue that they weren't indoors, and he was feeling anything but safe driving on a road that he could barely see. His steering wheel gave a small shudder and he felt the tires hydroplane.

"Jesus Christ," he muttered. The moment was gone before his startled brain could think how to react. He struggled to remember what to do when a vehicle hydroplaned.

Foot off the gas. Don't hit the brakes.

He risked a glance at Tori. She was staring straight ahead, a serene look on her face. He wondered if she'd even felt him lose control of the car. The last time he'd seen her this mellow was during their dinner that night at the conference in Denver.

He'd spotted her at registration. He saw her from the back. She was bundled up in a coat, but he'd known right away it was her. His gaze had instantly locked on to the woman with the long black hair. Something about the way she carried herself had resonated in his bones. *He knew her.* He'd moved slowly in her direction, not letting her out of his sight as she accepted her badge and bag from the registrar. As she turned, she'd looked right at him and not blinked, her gaze locked with his. She hadn't seemed surprised; perhaps she'd spotted him earlier and not reached out? It didn't matter. All he wanted was to spend time with her.

They'd played it cool. Greeting each other like old acquaintances and agreeing to dinner like you would with an old friend to catch up. During the meal, she'd been pleasant but reserved. They'd shared the events of their lives, talking about their spouses, work, and Eden. They'd danced around the causes of the actual breakup, but she'd oohed and aahed over his pictures of his daughter with no anger or jealousy on her face. He'd hoped she could respect that he'd made the right choice. But after the dinner as they walked back to her hotel room, she'd stopped him in the hall at her door and looked deep into his eyes.

"I've always wondered if you thought about me. If you'd wondered what you walked away from. I know you love your daughter, but do you ever wonder what could have been with us?"

It'd been a surreal moment. One he blamed on wine and the removal of themselves from their real lives. That's what happens at conferences. People are separated from their everyday routines and feel free to take steps they wouldn't usually take.

She'd been gorgeous. Her eyes large and dark in the dim light, and she'd worn heels and a sexy dress. She'd never dressed that way in college. He was seeing Tori the woman wielding all her feminine weapons for the first time. And she took his breath away. She'd fulfilled all the potential she'd demonstrated in school. Smart, respected in her field, and all woman.

"Every fucking day," he'd uttered. And it was true. Things had never clicked with Jennifer; he'd often wondered what he'd walked away from.

Her eyes had closed as he spoke, and she'd exhaled, her shoulders slumping the tiniest bit, as if she'd held her breath for his answer. He stared at her mouth for a long second and then kissed her. He slid his hand around the back of her neck, closing the space between their bodies as he pressed her backward into the hallway wall. She wobbled in the heels as his body met hers from hip to chest, their lines melting into each other. The moment lasted forever as he explored her mouth and sank both his hands into her hair. Silk. Pure smooth silk. She gave a small moan in the back of her throat and relaxed against him.

His brain shot into overdrive and all rational thought exited. "Open your door," he whispered against her lips.

She stiffened under his hands.

Seth froze. *Too far.*

He slowly extricated himself from her heat, holding her gaze. Anger and then sorrow shone in her eyes.

"I'm sorry," she mouthed. No sound came from her lips.

"Tori," he started, but she broke their eye contact and dug in her purse. She pulled out her room key, her hands shaking.

"We shouldn't have had dinner." Her words tripped over themselves. "I thought I could do this. I thought we could talk about old times and everything would be fine. I didn't know we would end up like this. I won't do that to my husband, and you shouldn't do it to Jennifer and Eden." She turned her back to him and fumbled with the door lock, trying to find the slot for her key. "I screwed up. I shouldn't have let it go this far."

"It's not your fault, Tori," he'd said, feeling utterly helpless. Why had he considered going in her room? He wanted to shoot himself. "I didn't mean it."

She looked over her shoulder at him, her eyes angry. "You just needed some sex?"

"No, that's not what I meant. Christ, I don't know what I want."

She pushed her door open and turned to face him, blocking him from the room. Her chin was up, her eyes fiery. "We're both married, so I'd say we know what we want. We made our choices long ago. Well, *you* made the choice for us."

His heart cracked at her words and the angry tone. Here was the elephant that'd been in the room with them at dinner. They'd delicately danced around the topic, but now she'd ripped it open and laid it before him. A gulf widened between them, spread apart by his past decision. He couldn't fix it now.

"We're married. And I think we're both happy for the most part. I won't apologize for something I did long ago. I made the only choice I could," he answered.

Her face had paled, all emotion disappearing behind a cool mask. "Good night." She stepped backward and shut the door in his face. He'd stood there for a long moment, hearing her heels click across the floor in her room, and then there was silence.

In the car, Seth knew Victoria was slightly buzzed from her wine at Lacey's. She hadn't eaten dinner that evening and had said she rarely drank more than one glass of wine. After the emotional group at Lacey's house, he'd offered to drive her home and she'd readily accepted. She'd given Lacey and Trinity a hug good-bye. From Lacey's faintly surprised look, he'd gathered that Tori wasn't a hugger.

He was learning about her in bits and pieces. Watching her interact with other people was the most telling. Tonight had been an eye-opener.

Seeing her break down over the thought of her adoptive parents lying about her birth parents had told him two things. First, that Tori adored and had utterly trusted the wonderful people who'd brought her up. Second, that she had a stiff upper lip around her friends. When Michael Brody looked crushed at the sight of Tori in tears, Seth knew she'd never shown that side to anyone. Lacey had looked stricken, and Trinity had been moved to tears in sympathy.

The people around Tori cared deeply for her but never saw below her shell. A shell she kept up nonstop. Until tonight. Even now it was still down, a relaxed state about her that was no doubt created by two glasses of white wine.

He wished it didn't take wine to tear it down.

"How long ago did your parents pass?" He'd never met her adoptive parents. He remembered her phone calls home from college; she'd seemed very close to her mother, calling at least once a week to check in and see what was up.

"I was twenty-five. Mama died and then Daddy three months later. I swear he died of a broken heart. He was never the same after she passed."

"I didn't know you'd been so young. I remember you'd told me your parents were older."

"They were in their seventies when they passed."

"That's young. It may not have seemed so when you were twenty-five, but personally I find that to be young. No doubt the perspective of what is old changes as we age."

"Definitely," she agreed.

They lapsed into a comfortable silence.

"You'll finish the inventory tomorrow?" he asked to fill the quiet.

"Yes, shouldn't take me long. As long as there are no more interruptions."

"Have you learned anything in general about the women? That was a different era."

"I wish I could say I have. Lacey made a general observation that they had a lot of amalgam fillings. Something you'd expect to see from that era. She said some of the dentistry was quite poor. Poor enough to make her wonder if it wasn't American. But she mentioned that dental techniques had come a long way in the past fifty years and perhaps that it was simply a dentist who wasn't very skilled."

"Have the police considered that the women weren't from the US?" That was a fresh angle Seth hadn't thought about. Were they looking at a bunch of trafficked women?

"I don't know. I imagine so. I think they're still struggling to come up with a working theory. Heaven knows there are enough rumors around."

"Doesn't foreign dentistry look different than American? I've heard the jokes about British dentistry. They probably weren't from third world countries if they had fillings. I'd imagine they wouldn't have the access to care and possibly their diets wouldn't even bring on the amounts of decay caused by American meals of processed food."

"That would be a question for Lacey."

"I like her," Seth added. "I liked the couple I met tonight, too. Jamie and Michael seem to be good together."

Victoria gave a soft snort. "If she can put up with his mouth, then it's a match made in heaven. Sarcasm is his second language."

"You were never one for sarcasm," Seth agreed. "I still remember you staring down some jerk from your anatomy class who thought he was the funniest guy on campus. You didn't even blink when he tried to be funny."

"I remember that. He wasn't funny. He was an idiot."

"Michael doesn't seem like an idiot."

"He's not. He's one of those super-smart people who are missing part of the filter between their brain and mouth sometimes." She paused. "He means well."

Seth figured that was the best compliment Michael Brody was going to get from Tori. Actually, he suspected it was a form of high praise.

"You'll use his help to verify if your birth parents are dead?"

A long moment of silence filled the vehicle. "I will. If I don't look into it, I'll always wonder. But how had I gone so long without questioning anything they'd told me?"

Seth hated to hear her doubt herself. "I suspect that's a testament to how great your adoptive parents were. No doubt you'll find out everything happened as they said."

She told him to turn at the next street, and he knew they were getting close to her home. Part of him wished the drive was longer. A different part of him wanted to follow her into her house and pick up where they'd left off long ago.

He glanced at her from the corner of his eye. It was wishful thinking on his part. He slowed down as the street turned into a residential neighborhood. The street was dark and quiet. Lights off in most of the homes. Unsurprising, considering it was nearly midnight.

Tori was quiet in her seat, and he wondered if she wanted the ride to be longer, too. Tonight had been good. They'd spent a few hours in each other's company, and he wanted more. Yes, the evening had started with a crisis, and Tori had gone through a few rough moments at Lacey's home, but overall he'd loved being with her. It didn't matter what they did together, he was relaxed and at peace when she was beside him.

The road curved sharply, and Tori gasped, her hand grabbing at the door as she straightened in her seat. He hit the brakes. "What? What is it?" Seth scanned the empty road in the dark, looking for a person or cat.

"My house is on fire!"

He looked in the direction she'd pointed, his pulse rate skyrocketing. A flickering light shone through a wide broken window on the first floor of her house.

"Call nine-one-one now!" he ordered. He jerked the wheel and parked the car in front of her house, flung open his door, and got out. Tori lunged out her door and started toward the house. He grabbed her arm. "Wait! What are you doing?"

She jerked to a stop and stared at her home.

Flames danced inside the home. The fire seemed localized to one area. No other flames showed in the upstairs windows. She seemed transfixed by the flames.

"Could anyone be in there? No pets, right?"

She shook her head.

"I'll make sure." He turned her face toward his. Her eyes didn't seem to focus. "Call nine-one-one *now.* I'll check around. Is there a hose somewhere?"

She pulled her phone out of her pocket and dialed. "It's in the garage. Don't you dare go in there."

"I won't," he promised and ran up the porch stairs.

He punched the doorbell three times and pounded on the front door. "Anyone here?" he shouted. He pounded on the door again. *At least it's raining. Everything is soaked. It shouldn't spread outdoors.*

A rushing sound and faint roar came from the flames, but no voices. The front window was shattered. He glanced at the flower bed in front of the window, seeing just a few pieces of broken glass. Most of the glass must be inside. *Someone broke the window from the outside.* He gave a small breath of relief. Someone hadn't broken it out, trying to escape.

The hole wasn't large enough for a person to get through, so he didn't think anyone had broken in. It looked like something had been thrown through the window.

Something thrown to start the fire? Was it started on purpose?

He glanced back at Victoria. She was still on the phone, gesturing with wide hand movements as she talked. He waved at the side of the house, indicating he was going around back. She nodded and pointed at him like a mother does when her kid is in big trouble.

He got the message. *Be careful.*

Not a problem. He had no desire to step inside a burning house.

CHAPTER EIGHTEEN

Victoria pulled her coat's collar up over her nose. The scent of the smoke permeated the air in her neighborhood. The fire was out, but firemen still filled her house. Katy and Trinity had arrived fifteen minutes after Victoria and Seth. They'd been headed home from Lacey's and had stopped, the street blocked by fire trucks.

Katy wrapped her arms around Trinity as she stared at Victoria's smoking home.

The home didn't look too bad from the outside. The fire had been put out quickly. There was probably more smoke and water damage inside the home than anything else. Thank goodness there were companies that specialized in cleaning up that sort of mess.

It's just a house. Things can be replaced.

She sucked in a deep breath.

The firemen had made a disaster in the front yard, which had already been a swamp from the constant rains. Smoke scarred the outside walls where it had poured out the front window. Bulky shadows of men moved inside while others tramped in and out of the home, putting away their equipment.

A small crowd had gathered in the street, under the protection of the giant firs, avoiding the pounding rain. Katy had run to her house and returned with three oversized umbrellas, standard equipment for life in Portland.

Seth held one over his and Victoria's heads, his other arm wrapped around her shoulders, watching the movements of the firemen. "What a fucking mess," he muttered.

She nodded. It was an understatement. How long would it take to get her house back to livable shape? How would they remove the scent of smoke?

"They said something containing an accelerant had been thrown through the window. It was deliberate," Seth added.

Victoria numbly nodded again. "Arson" was the word on everyone's lips now. The firemen hadn't let her in the house yet. They'd promised she could go in to collect a few things soon. *Would any of her clothes be wearable?* Katy had immediately informed her she'd be staying with them. In a mind fog, she'd agreed.

As if she could sleep tonight.

What a horrible day. For all of them. A deep shudder sped through her body, and Seth pulled her closer. "Cold?" he asked.

"Yes." It was a good enough reason. Seth was like a furnace. She could feel his body heat seep through his coat and into hers, warming her skin. She needed more of it. Most of her body was freezing. Even her brain felt like it'd been lightly coated with ice; it was numb. Watching Seth pound on the door of the burning home had raised a level of alarm in her that she'd never experienced. He hadn't been in much danger, but seeing him run toward the fire as she stayed back had ripped a raw spot on her heart.

She'd wanted to keep him safe. And the lack of control over the situation hadn't sat well with her. She'd been shaking by the time he'd returned from investigating the back of the home. While he'd been out of her sight and she'd spoken with the 911 operator, she'd never felt so powerless.

What was he doing to her? Part of her wanted to shove his arm off her shoulders, while the other half of her wanted to burrow deep into his coat and hide her face, pretending nothing bad was happening.

He pulled out his phone and started subtly taking pictures of the people who were watching.

"What are you doing?" she whispered. She had a hunch, but why didn't he leave it to the investigators?

"Fire starters like to see their handiwork," he stated. "I haven't noticed anyone else shooting the crowd yet. Why wait? I'll offer the pictures later."

Three police cars and two fire trucks blocked her street. Not many people were gawking. It was about the number she'd expect on her quiet street at one in the morning. Several people were headed back into their homes. The excitement over for the night.

"If I was setting a fire, I wouldn't stand and watch where someone could notice me."

"They like to try to blend into the crowds. We had a serial firebug two years ago in Sacramento." He pressed his lips into a tight line, and Victoria wondered how many burned bodies he'd dealt with.

"It started off with empty buildings and rapidly escalated. I spent some time reading up on what makes these guys tick."

"I've never understood the appeal."

"It's control and excitement factors. With the single act of lighting a match, they can regulate events that aren't normally controlled. They manage to orchestrate the fire, the exciting arrival of the loud fire engines, the creation of the fascinated crowds, and the thrill of the destruction. At first they're satisfied with property destruction. But many move on to destruction of life. They get a taste of the excitement and need to feed it. It takes more and more to satisfy their needs."

"Christ. It's like a serial killer who can't stop killing."

"Very similar. Sometimes there's even a sexual release that comes with seeing their power—"

"That's enough." Victoria cut him off. She didn't need to hear about that aspect. She had enough on her mind.

Seth raised a brow at her. "Too much for you?"

"No. Some things I don't need to research. I work in the ME's office, I hear enough about the deviants out there. And see some of their results."

"It's really a fascinating area of study."

"I'm good. Thanks. I'll stick to bones." She sought for a topic change and glanced at the dwindling crowd. "I think most of these people are my neighbors."

"You *think*?"

"I haven't met everyone. And even the ones I have, I don't recognize unless they're standing in front of their house. Occasionally someone will greet me in the grocery store, and I'll be totally lost about how I know them."

"She's getting better. Didn't know anyone for the first year she was here." A new voice entered their conversation. "Everyone okay? No one got hurt?"

Victoria turned to see her neighbor, Jeremy. He held a small umbrella over his gray head. He wore a brightly colored housecoat and rubber boots. The sight of the man gave her heart a much-needed happy jump.

"Seth, this is my *neighbor,* Jeremy. No one was home, thank goodness."

The men shook hands.

"Seth Rutledge. I work with Victoria," Seth added.

"You the new medical examiner?"

"Not yet. I'm currently in the middle of a working interview for the position."

Sharp eyes studied Seth as he placed his arm back around Victoria's shoulders. She tried not to cringe. Jeremy was always threatening to introduce her to the straight men he knew, but she always declined. "Soooo, I guess I missed quite a bit while I was laid up with that bug."

Seth gave his slow half smile. "Don't tell me you're the person to ask about the latest goings-on in Tori's life."

Jeremy's eyes narrowed. "Tori, eh? Sounds like you and I need to have a glass of wine and a long talk, Dr. Rutledge."

"Deal."

"Not tonight, we won't," Victoria quickly added. "You're not a hundred percent yet, Jeremy. And I don't like you running around in the middle of the night in the cold."

"Heck. I don't sleep anymore at my age, anyway." He met Seth's gaze. "See how she mothers me? Doesn't let a man have any fun."

"Did you see the fire before the fire department got here?" Victoria asked, shifting his focus away from herself. "Hear or see anyone around?"

Jeremy shook his head. "Nothing. I was watching TV and didn't know anything was up until the trucks came screeching up the street. Who called it in?"

"We did. Seth was driving me home when I spotted it."

"Home, eh?" The old man's eyes sparkled in the dim light.

"Stop that," Victoria ordered. She felt a laugh rumble through Seth's chest.

"Victoria, I think we're ready to go," Katy said as she and Trinity approached. Trinity looked exhausted and half-dead on her feet.

"I'll be there as soon as they let me grab a few things," Victoria said.

Trinity seemed deflated, like half the oxygen had been sucked out of her cells. The girl was in desperate need of sleep. Victoria moved out from under Seth's arm, feeling the cold air wash over the spots he'd warmed. She touched Trinity's arm. The girl met her gaze and gave a wan smile. "You two head to the house. I'll be there in a minute."

"Wait a minute, Ms. Peres?" One of the firemen stepped up to their circle.

"Yes?" Victoria said.

The fireman glanced at the group. "I need to ask you about something we found inside. We're wondering if it belongs to you."

"What's that?"

"Maybe you could step aside with me for a minute?"

Victoria looked at her neighbors and Seth. "There's no one here to hide anything from. What did you find?"

"We think the window was broken with a large rock we found inside. Then they threw in an accelerant in some sort of lit glass bottle."

"Right. They told me this already," Victoria said impatiently.

"Did you have any bones in that front room?" the fireman asked.

"Bones? No. You found bones? Like someone was in there?" Victoria's brain shot into high alert.

Trinity gasped.

"No, not a body. Just a skull. Looks real, but I'm no expert."

"I am," said Victoria firmly. "Let me see it."

The fireman raised an eyebrow at her. "This skull was on the floor close to where the fire started. If it didn't belong to you, it was probably thrown in with the accelerant. Now it's evidence."

"Dr. Peres is the forensic anthropologist for the medical examiner's office," Seth interjected before Victoria could speak. "The skull will probably end up in her hands for confirmation anyway. Let her save you some time and tell you if they're human or fake."

The fireman studied Victoria for a long moment. "Okay. One look. No touching." He turned and raised a hand to another fireman by the truck, gesturing for him to bring something over. The second man walked over with a large paper bag and handed it to the first. He opened it for Victoria to peer inside. Her heart speeding up, she peeked in the bag. Too dark. She smelled a familiar scent. Burned bone. Seth held up his cell phone and shone its light in the bag.

A woman's skull glowed. Its lack of brow ridges and small size stated its sex. Its fused seams and teeth stated its maturity.

I knew it.

A small part of her knew it would turn out to be one of her skulls.

Whoever had burned her house had stolen her bones. *But why?*

"It's human. Female," she reported. "And please contact Detective Callahan at OSP, because I suspect it's related to a case he's working on."

"What?" The fireman and Katy spoke at the same time. Jeremy took a step closer to look in the bag, shaking his head. Victoria noticed Seth was silent and knew he'd had the same suspicions as she.

"Just one skull? That was all?" Seth asked.

The fireman nodded, an odd look on his face. "You expected more?"

Seth shrugged.

"It was stolen from your lab?" Katy asked Victoria. She looked stricken. "Why was it thrown in your house along with starting a fire?"

Victoria had no answer. The fireman left with his bag and startling information. Victoria's mind spun. *Why? Why return the skull like that? Assuming it's one of the skulls that was taken.* She wouldn't know for certain until she compared it to the photos and X-rays. But why would they steal it and then return it?

"Does someone know where you live?" Seth said under his breath for her ears only.

"I don't know." Her brain hurt. "I need to talk to Callahan."

"We're heading in," Katy said. "We both need bed."

"Go ahead," said Victoria. "I'll be right there."

The two women walked away. Trinity's feet dragged in her boots.

Victoria turned back to Seth and Jeremy. "I need to go. Seth, I'll see you tomorrow. Jeremy, get back to bed."

"Yes, Tori." Jeremy winked at her with his use of Seth's nickname. "Good to meet you, Dr. Rutledge." He headed in the direction of his house.

Victoria didn't have the energy to reprimand him. *Does it really matter?* She sighed, placing all thoughts of the skull out of her head. There was nothing she could do about it tonight. She looked at her ruined home and tried not to cry. There was nothing she could do about that tonight either.

She'd check in with the police tomorrow. And find someone to clean up her house. The mental checklist to restore her home came to a screeching halt. *Tomorrow. Take care of it tomorrow.* She was too exhausted to think about it.

She looked up at Seth, seeking a distraction from the voices in her head. It was nice to have to look up at a man. Most men were about the same height as her or a little shorter. Something about a taller man made her feel a bit feminine. Few things did.

He rested the umbrella against his shoulder, angling it to keep the both of them dry, and met her gaze, studying her face.

For a long moment, Victoria didn't hear the mumblings of the firemen and onlookers. The rain splashing on the street was the only sound. Seth's eyes were dark in the poor light, and she wished she could see their beautiful blue shade. How many times had they stood like this on campus long ago? It felt completely familiar and comforting.

She didn't want to let him go home.

Seth reached out a hand and brushed back her hair. "The rain sparkles in your hair."

"It makes it frizz," Victoria added unhelpfully. *What a stupid statement.*

Seth's smile grew. "I remember how you hated the dampness in the air at school sometimes." His brows angled down. "I remember a lot of things. Sometimes it feels like it was just yesterday, our days together. I have to think hard to remember a lifetime has passed. That Eden has grown from a toddler into a young woman. Almost the same age you were when we met. How is that possible? My daughter is still a girl. You were a woman."

"I suspect it is all in the eyes of the beholder."

He smoothed her hair again. "Tori . . . "

She closed her eyes at his touch on her hair and the memories washed over her. He'd loved to touch her long hair. So many nights they'd spent together simply watching TV in bed while he ran his fingers through her hair. It'd been soothing and relaxing. After they'd split up, she'd struggled to fall asleep for months and suspected part of her issue had been the loss of the soothing gesture before she slept.

She felt him gather her hair into his fist at the back of her neck and gently tug her head backward. She arched her head back, her eyes still closed. Rain hit her forehead and eyelids, shocking her with its chill. He must have moved the umbrella, because more drops hit her mouth and neck. She shuddered and parted her lips.

She felt his heat touch her lips before his mouth pressed against hers. Warmth blasted through the sensitive nerve endings of her lips and shot down to her toes. She lit up inside.

Seth.

His mouth commanded hers, leading the kiss, challenging her to keep pace. His fingers pressed into her scalp, stroking in a way that made her want to crawl inside him and avoid the world. Nothing compared to being touched and kissed by Seth. Nothing.

He'd always had this power over her. The power to make everything around her disappear until only he existed. Nothing had changed between them. Only the calendar marked the years. Their souls and minds ignored the fact that time had passed and acted as if they'd never been separated.

After a long moment he pulled back, and she was exposed to the rain again. Her eyes opened, meeting his gaze. He'd lowered the umbrella so they both stood in the cold wet. It wasn't a pounding, soaking rain at the moment. It was a good rain. Soft and gentle, the type that refreshes. She needed the coolness to offset his heat.

She watched a drop run down his cheek and bounce off his coat, feeling the same action repeated on her face.

She didn't care. Right now, the Pacific Northwest could throw whatever type of weather it wanted at her, and it wouldn't change that all she wanted to do was stand next to Seth Rutledge.

She wanted to forget that she needed to go to work tomorrow, forget her house had been deliberately damaged, and forget her lab had been robbed. She wanted three days and nights alone with him to immerse herself in him. She wanted to talk and eat and have glorious sex without interruption. The way they used to. She wanted to talk about the future and map out their plans. She sucked in a giant breath, feeling the cold touch the bottom of her lungs.

"I should go," he said.

Were there any sadder words?

"I know," she answered. Inside her brain screamed for him not to leave again. The cold had exposed her, opened wide her vulnerable center, ripe for a man to easily destroy with the wrong words. Or salve with the right ones.

"I don't want to. Not tonight. Not any night again."

His words were a balm that smoothed her raw nerves.

"I don't want to ever hurt you again," he whispered. "I know that can be hard to accept, but I hope you will. I want another chance. And I think you do, too. What we had never died. It was hibernating until our summer could come again."

But what a long cold winter it'd been.

"I never stopped loving you, Tori. That's the honest truth. If I could go back in time, I'd figure out a way to do right by both you and Eden. I was wrong to sacrifice you the way I did."

"Shhh. Don't talk about it. It's long in the past and there's nothing you can do about it now." She didn't like the distress in his eyes.

"I've thought about it for years. I've been haunted by it. I did the worst thing a man could ever do to the woman he loved—"

"You were young. We both were. You thought you were doing the right thing at the time. I forgave you a long time ago." It wasn't until the words were out of her mouth that Victoria realized how true they were. She had forgiven the young man who'd been driven by a sense of honor to take care of his daughter.

"I forgave you," she repeated for her sake as well as his. "And you're here now."

He exhaled, and she felt his shoulders relax as he briefly shut his eyes. "You don't know how much that means to me. I've felt like I've had a curse over my head for almost two decades."

Victoria felt a weightlessness flow through her body. She'd been carrying the curse, too. He moved forward and kissed her again, pulling her tight against him. Current shot through her body where she pressed against him. Her mouth knew his taste and feel; it'd never forgotten. She sank into the kiss, almost giddy with the elation he'd caused. She and Seth hadn't meant to be apart. The universe had realigned to place them together again.

Her house might be damaged, but she had her soul mate back.

CHAPTER NINETEEN

Trinity woke, instantly alarmed and confused, blinking at her surroundings.

Katy's spare room.

Katy had given Dr. Peres Trinity's room because of the nice big bed. Trinity had slept on the daybed. She inhaled deeply and caught the scent of smoke. She pulled a handful of hair across her nose. Yep. Odors cling to hair.

How bad was Dr. Peres's house? Were all her things ruined? How would they get the scent of smoke out of the home? Hair and clothes could be washed, but she didn't think that would be sufficient for the carpet and furniture.

Poor Dr. Peres.

She'd spent a lot of energy reassuring Trinity yesterday. First after the shooting, and then after the fire. She'd talked about insurance and claims adjusters and companies who specialize in taking care of disasters just like her home, trying to put Trinity at ease as she worried for her neighbor.

A small vibration sent her hunting for her phone.

The sight of a text from Jason made her heart pound. *Silly. He's probably asking about Brooke.* She opened the message.

R U OK?

He was asking about her? Her heart raced a bit faster as another text came through.

DID U SEE WHAT HAPPENED AT THE SERVICE?

She texted back. I'M GOOD. NO. RAN OUT. WHAT HAPPENED?

IDIOT WITH GUN. TRIED TO GET IT AWAY.

She sucked in a breath. Jason had been in the middle of that mess? And tried to disarm someone? *Seriously?* U DID THAT? WHY?

I'M WORRIED. I TOUCHED THE TRIGGER. DON'T WANT POLICE THINKING I PULLED IT.

Alarm rang in her head. He'd touched the trigger? What if he had actually caused the weapon to fire? DID YOU GO TO THE POLICE?

THEY BROUGHT ME IN. TOLD THEM. DON'T KNOW IF THEY BELIEVE.

Why was he telling her? Did he really have no one else to talk to? ARE YOU STILL AT THE STATION?

NO. AT A FRIEND'S. GOTTA GO.

Why was he at a friend's at eight in the morning? If she'd been taken to the police station, Katy would have dragged her ass home afterward. Maybe he didn't have a good home to go to. Trinity could sympathize with that. Her last two foster homes had been less than supportive. She'd been left alone to do as she pleased and had found the home atmosphere to be stress-filled and temperamental. She'd spent as much time at friends' homes as possible.

She got up and wrapped a throw around her shoulders. Quietly opening the door, she peered into the hall. Listening closely, she heard kitchen-type noises. Someone was up. She padded to the kitchen.

Dr. Peres stood at the sink, her back to Trinity, filling the coffee pot. Trinity's stomach rumbled. The woman didn't look like a successful professional with a career in the macabre. Dressed in soft yoga pants and a thin long-sleeved T-shirt with her feet bare and her hair pulled back in a messy knot, she looked like someone's mom.

"Mother" wasn't a word Trinity would ever use to describe the doctor. Even when Dr. Peres had spoken at her school, she'd been the consummate professional.

Dr. Peres shoved the pot into the brewer and hit a button. Trinity cleared her throat, causing the doctor to immediately turn.

"You're up." Dr. Peres's brown eyes widened and she gave a warm smile. "I woke at the crack of dawn and was totally restless, so I made scones. I don't think Katy will mind that I invaded her kitchen." She pulled a tray out of the oven and a delicious scent filled the kitchen.

"Ohh. That smells awesome." It really did.

Her words made the doctor smile. She cut a triangle out of the huge baked lump and placed it on a plate, shoving it into Trinity's hands. "Sit," she ordered. "Want coffee or milk?"

Trinity sat. "Milk, please." She took a bite of warm yummi-ness and sighed.

The doctor placed the milk in front of her and sat across from her, watching her eat.

Trinity was instantly self-conscious. "Are you having some?"

"I will in a minute. I never bake or cook for anybody, so forgive me if I stare for a little bit."

Pity washed over her. "That's kinda sad. Don't you have some siblings somewhere?"

The doctor gave a small smile. "No. It was just me and my parents. I'm divorced, so I haven't done much cooking since then." She poured a cup of coffee from the barely full carafe, making Trinity cringe at the thought of tasting that super-potent coffee.

Dr. Peres sat and took a huge bite of scone. And smiled. "It always tastes better when there's someone to eat it with. It's a waste to bake this just for me."

"I love to bake," said Trinity. "But Katy doesn't like it. She says it's too tempting to have cake and cookies around."

Dr. Peres smiled. "Yes, I understand that logic. Should we wake her up?"

Trinity shook her head. "I wouldn't be surprised if she was up half the night."

"You're right. I know I had a hard time getting to sleep." The doctor stabbed at her scone with her fork. Trinity wondered if she'd slept at all.

"Have you been outside? Have you seen the house today?" Trinity asked.

"I can't see much from here. I went out to get the paper, but it's pouring rain, and all I could see was the blue tarp where they covered the window. I can still smell the smoke outside."

"I don't know if they'll ever get rid of the smell." Trinity sniffed at her hair again. "I stink."

"Yes, I showered last night, but I can still smell it on me."

"You got some clothes?"

"Yes, I dug these out of the very bottom of my dresser." The doctor sniffed at a sleeve.

"I really like Dr. Rutledge," said Trinity. "He likes you a lot, too. Are you dating?"

Did Dr. Peres just blush?

Trinity wasn't certain about the blush, but the doctor dropped eye contact. Exactly what her friends did when they were slightly embarrassed or someone mentioned a guy they liked.

"I wouldn't say we're dating. We did at one point. He's back in my life now after a very long absence, and we're still feeling things out, trying to see where to go with this."

"Well, he's pretty clear about what he wants. Everyone last night could tell."

Dr. Peres met her gaze. "What?"

"He likes you a lot. He puts out that protective vibe around you. It was weird to see it last night."

Trinity's phone vibrated in her pocket. Dr. Peres met her gaze and smiled. "Go ahead. I'm going to see if Katy's up yet."

Trinity nodded and pulled out her phone. Jason again.

DO U HAVE A CAR? COULD U COME GET ME?

She stared at the screen. Why her? R U OK?

There was a long pause after her text. She took a few bites of her scone, but it seemed to have lost its flavor. *Why would Jason ask her for help? They barely knew each other.*

AVOIDING SOMEONE. HE KNOWS ALL MY FRIENDS. NEED TO GO SOMEWHERE ELSE.

Trinity's mind spun. Who was he hiding from? His parents? Were they angry about the shooting? But were they mad in a concerned-parent way or a want-to-beat-on-him-asshole-parent way? She knew nothing of Jason's family situation.

IS SOMEONE GOING TO HURT YOU? She cringed as she sent the text, but she needed to be frank. Would he answer truthfully?

A full minute went by. Had she offended him? Or was he laughing at her? Showing her text to his friends and laughing at what a dork she was for being concerned about him?

She finished her milk and strode to the fridge for a refill. Jason and his friends could go to hell for all she cared. He obviously hung with some idiots if one of them pulled out a gun at a memorial service. And the only reason he'd reached out to her was because he was interested in Brooke, and she was Brooke's best friend. Everyone knew you made nice with the best friend if you wanted to get in—

Her phone vibrated on the kitchen table, and she nearly slopped the milk she was pouring. She set down the carton and grabbed the phone, mixed emotions rolling through her. What did she owe this guy? Nothing.

IT'S POSSIBLE. I DID SOMETHING I WAS TOLD NOT TO. THEY PUNISH.

She swallowed hard. *They?* His parents? Did "punish" mean taking away his phone or using a belt on him? Part of her was cautious; he could be lying about everything.

I'M SORRY. I CAN'T HELP U. PLZ LET ME KNOW WHAT HAPPENS.

She hit Send and sighed. Some people might think she was a crappy friend for not helping him out, but what could she do? She'd have to ask permission to use Katy's old second car and then explain why she needed it. And she hardly knew Jason. Surely there was someone else he could ask.

"Katy is sound asleep." Dr. Peres padded into the kitchen. She did a double take at Trinity's expression. "Are you okay?"

"I think so. I have a friend who asked for something, but I really don't know him that well . . . not at all, actually. I'd like to help if I could, but . . . " She didn't know how to describe it.

The doctor studied her face. "You don't know him? But he chose you to ask? Why you?"

Trinity squirmed. "I think he's avoiding his parents. And the parents don't know me."

"You just answered your own question." Dr. Peres topped off her coffee. "A friend doesn't ask you to help him avoid his parents. He needs to face his parents."

"But what if his parents are wrong? What if they're mean?"

The doctor sat down, wrapped both hands around her mug, and her brown eyes softened as she held Trinity's gaze. "Most parents have their kids' best interests at heart. I'm sure it hasn't always been that way for you, but you've seen the exceptions instead of the majority."

"But . . . what if he's truly scared they might hurt him?"

Her eyes narrowed. "Did your friend say that?"

"Not exactly." Trinity looked away. Jason had been deliberately vague. Possibly he was trying to manipulate her. For all she knew, he just wanted a ride to the mall to meet his friends.

"What did he say?"

"He said they punish."

Dr. Peres was silent for a long moment. "If he fears he is going to be hurt, he needs to go to the police. Or a school counselor. It's wrong of him to ask you for help. It was probably the easiest of his choices of where to ask for help, but the least effective."

Trinity studied the tabletop. She'd been scared of her real mother. But she'd never hit her or hurt her. Not physically. Emotionally and mentally, she'd been battered by both her mother and grandmother.

They'd neglected every aspect of raising a child. Even the most basic. Trinity qualified for the free lunch program at the school, but her mother never registered her. She had good friends who shared their lunches, believing they were sneaking it behind the teacher's back. Sharing food wasn't allowed.

But the teacher had noticed and privately asked her about lunch. Trinity had tried to laugh it off, saying she wasn't hungry during the day, when in truth she was starving. Often she'd had fast food leftovers for breakfast. How many times had she eaten cold fries? Or empty-calorie junk food left out on the table from her mother's late-night binges? She ate whatever she could find. Opened any can.

She stared at the remains of her scone. Baked for her. Baked by someone who was excited to share it with her. The crumbs blurred.

What if Jason was in a similar situation? He didn't seem hungry, but what if he was abused in other ways?

Her sharp-eyed teacher had made a report. Child welfare had paid a visit. The empty fridge and cupboards didn't please them. When Trinity couldn't tell them what she'd eaten in the last twenty-four hours, they were even more unhappy. She was rushed to a doctor who clucked her tongue over her weight and then took her to a house where there was always food. It wasn't the healthiest food, but it felt like living in a grocery store.

"How old is your friend?"

"He's a senior."

"Then he's old enough to ask the right people for help. It's not your responsibility to try to save him. Just guide him in the right direction."

She was right. Trinity thumbed a quick text to Jason with the doctor's advice then shoved the phone aside. Part of her wanted to run to him and do everything in her power—which wasn't much—to make him feel better. Her therapist had told her she was a natural nurturer and protector. It would always be inherent in her to help others, even to her own detriment. She had to learn to weigh the consequences and ask if she was hurting herself in order to make someone happy.

"You look miserable," Dr. Peres said quietly.

Trinity exhaled. "You're right. It's not my problem. I'm sure there's someone better suited to really helping him."

"Good girl. I wish I'd been that smart at your age."

"That means I should be heading up NASA by the time I'm your age."

Dr. Peres laughed, and Trinity was struck by how beautiful she was.

CHAPTER TWENTY

"Johnson Creek flooded again," Ray Lusco stated as he dropped his bag on his desk. "I didn't think I was ever going to make it to work."

"Are you surprised?" Mason asked his partner. He glanced at the time on his computer. Ray was barely five minutes late.

"Of course not. But the sucker is always the biggest headache around. Messes up traffic something awful."

"I worry more about the people who live by it. I don't know why they don't move. Seems like we see the same homes on the news every time."

"This is going to be a bad storm. When I watched the weather last night, there's no letup in the coming week. We're already breaking the rainfall records for this month. They're lucky that landslide in the West Hills last night didn't hurt anyone." Mason frowned. At least they wouldn't be crying drought next summer like this past hot summer. The snowpack in the Cascade Mountains benefited from the excessive rain.

"The dirt is oversaturated with water. All the slopes are treacherous. I'm stunned at the number of people who build homes on the sides of the hills around here. Who wants to wake up and find your neighbor's kitchen has slid into your garage? Hate the rain." Ray scowled.

"Did you ever get ahold of Trinity Viders's guardian? Does she know we want to talk to the girl again?" Mason was done talking rain.

"I left a message for her last night. Haven't heard back yet. I told her I had some questions."

"There's a teenager angle to these latest deaths that I think we're missing completely. I feel like there's something just out of our reach. Something that these kids know about and they're not sharing with adults yet." Mason hadn't realized this fact until he'd said the words out loud. Something was hovering just out of his awareness, something about the deaths and the teenagers that he couldn't grasp. And he suspected talking to these kids was where they needed to focus.

Ray studied him. "You think some of these teens know what is going on?"

Mason thought for a minute. His stomach was doing an odd tingle that told him he was speculating in the right direction. "I think they're not telling us everything. I feel like we're only getting part of the story. Either the kids are covering for each other or they're scared of something."

"They're teenagers. Of course they aren't telling us everything."

Mason tapped a pen on his desk. "What about Lorenzo Cavallo's family? Where are all those sons he was so proud of? Four boys?"

"Five," corrected Ray. He scowled as he flipped through a small notebook. "I've called three of them. I left messages at two homes, and at the third, the wife said she'd have her husband call me back. I haven't heard a word. I'm still trying to locate the other two. I was hoping to get numbers from the other brothers."

"That doesn't sound right."

"I agree with you there. I'll check to see if someone has requested the body. Maybe some family has come out of the woodwork. We gave clearance for the release yesterday. Forensics and the medical examiner have everything they need." Ray picked up his desk phone.

Mason looked at the blue pen in his hand and slowly set it aside. He needed to look over the reports from the medical examiner. How would Dr. Rutledge describe the pen jammed in Lorenzo's ear? His stomach did a slow roll. The lab should have the original pen by now, and no doubt it was in a long line of backed-up evidence waiting to be processed.

Mason adjusted his reading glasses and dug to find his notes from the Cavallo house. It was rare that he didn't trust his memory with scene recall, but he had to admit he'd been a bit distracted during this particular case. The pen jammed in the ear had rattled him. And the absolute loneliness of the home. He hated the thought that Lorenzo had died alone without contact from his family for years. He scanned his notes. Nothing jumped out at him. The follow-up with the family members was the priority. Where the fuck were they? *Why hadn't they called back*?

Ray hung up the phone. "No one has inquired about Cavallo." His tone was grim.

Mason felt nauseous. That old man. Living alone for years and now the abandonment continued in death. Anger flared in his chest. "Jesus Christ. Give me the numbers you have for those kids of his. I'll have a word with them."

Ray handed him a slip of paper. "I'm stunned. What would drive away an entire family?"

"It'd have to be something big for all five kids to shun their father. Seems like there's always one who will look out for the parent no matter what the feud is."

"But remember when we talked to him? He spoke of his kids like he saw them every day. That was a proud father. Apparently the kids aren't reciprocating the feelings."

"If they're still breathing, I intend to find out why."

"Christ. I didn't think of that."

"What?"

"Maybe something's happened at their homes, too."

Mason froze as the number he'd called rang and rang in his ear. He'd been using an expression of speech with his comment about breathing, but Ray had an excellent point. "No one's answering this one. I'll try the rest, but get their addresses and get someone to check on their homes immediately. Are they local?"

"I think at least two of them are." Ray looked pale.

"Figure out where the other phone numbers are located and we'll get the local departments to check on them." Mason swallowed hard, images of more pens floating in his head. "You said you talked to someone at one of the homes?"

"Yes, I assume it was a wife." Ray was already dialing dispatch.

Mason wiped at his forehead. Hopefully the numbers Ray had were landlines. That'd make the addresses easier to search. *Christ.* He didn't want more deaths associated with this case. He dialed the other number and listened to it ring.

Why no voice mail or answering machine?

"Hello?" A woman's quiet voice answered after countless rings.

Mason rattled off his identity and asked to speak to Mr. Cavallo.

"I'm sorry, he is very sick and can't speak on the phone right now. May I take a message?" The voice was all politeness.

"Are you who my partner, Ray Lusco, spoke to the other day? And asked to have him call us back?"

"Yes, I spoke to a police officer the other day. My husband is still sick."

"Mrs. Cavallo, are you aware your husband's father, Lorenzo Cavallo, was murdered? We are trying to notify the family."

The phone was silent and Mason wondered if she'd hung up.

"Yes." The woman paused. "We'd heard."

Mason waited. *That was all she had to say?* "Who is going to claim his body? He's still at the morgue."

The woman paused again. "Do we have to?"

Mason straightened in his chair. "What?"

"Are we legally obligated to do something? Just because we're related?"

He was speechless. "Ah . . . I don't think so. Your husband won't feel differently?"

She gave a humorless laugh. "I'm positive. He hasn't spoken to his father in years."

"Perhaps one of the other brothers will want to take charge."

The laugh again. "That is doubtful, but you're welcome to try."

Mason tightened his grip on the phone. "Mrs. Cavallo, I don't understand. When I spoke with your father-in-law a few days ago, he seemed very proud of his children. He mentioned them several times. What happened to this family?"

"I'm sorry, Detective Callahan. I can't help you."

The phone clicked in his ear.

He slowly set the receiver back in its holder. What had Lorenzo Cavallo done to his sons?

"You reach someone?" Ray asked.

"Yeah." Mason relayed the odd conversation.

"What the hell?" Ray wrinkled his forehead. "I don't understand."

"That makes two of us."

"I'm still sending a uniform over there," Ray added. "I want someone to actually lay eyes on and talk to these fabulous sons of Lorenzo's, so we know they're still breathing."

"Good idea," muttered Mason. Had all the sons turned their backs on their father? What could cause that kind of divide in a family?

"What the hell?" Ray muttered, staring at his computer screen. "Did you look at this email from Victoria Peres?"

"No, I haven't looked yet today." Mason waited as long as possible to open his email in the morning, because once he did, it seemed like he got nothing done. He liked to clean up yesterday's leftovers before adding more pork to the pot.

"You really should scan through first thing in the morning," Ray rebuked. "You might see something important." It was a regular argument that Mason chalked up to organizational differences. "It was sent to both of us."

"Well, then I didn't need to see it first thing, right? You're on it." Logic. "And if it was really important and something I needed to know right away, she would have called." More logic.

Ray gave him the evil eye. "An arsonist hit Victoria Peres's house last night."

Shock spiked Mason's spine. "What? Anyone hurt?"

"No. She wasn't home." Ray studied his screen. "Victoria says a skeletal female skull was found inside the home not far from the rock that broke the window. Someone threw in both items before a Molotov cocktail–type device to start the fire. Damage to the home was minimal."

"She think that's one of her missing skulls?"

"She wants to find out. Naturally, they didn't let her walk off with it last night. Do you have anything from the Portland Fire Department? I don't yet. She says she told them to contact us."

Mason opened his email, his guilt prickling because he'd missed Victoria's message. He would have opened it ten minutes earlier. That wouldn't have helped much. Christ. He'd received forty new emails overnight. *This* was why he preferred not to look. "I don't see anything."

"I'll reach out to them and get that skull on her table. I think she had X-rays. She should be able to tell if it's one of the missing."

"Why in the hell was it thrown in her house?" Mason asked, mentally adding an arson element to his odd case.

Mason clicked on Victoria's email. Not surprisingly, it read like a report. Facts stated in chronological order. Some questions at the end. She and Seth Rutledge discovered the fire after midnight? *What was the medical examiner doing with Dr. Peres at that time of night?* Mason smiled.

"What's so funny?" Ray asked.

"Nothin'. Just wondering what Seth Rutledge was doing over there at that time of night."

"Christ. Get your head out of the gutter. She's a nice lady." Ray sounded doubtful. "Nice lady" was a term rarely used to describe the Bone Lady.

"Well, she and that medical examiner have a past. I don't know exactly what, but he's looking to get the fires going again, I believe." He chuckled at his pun.

Ray snorted. "Lame."

"But the skulls were stolen. Why give one back?"

"Maybe the thief didn't need that one."

"Why?" Mason pressed.

Ray struggled to theorize and threw up his hands. "Beats me. Maybe someone else was returning it. But why do it along with arson?"

Mason shook his head. "We still need to talk to Trinity about the shooting last night. This is another reason to get the girl in here ASAP. One boy says the shooter got riled because he saw Trinity Viders."

"Well, at least we know the shooter didn't set that fire. He was still in holding at that time."

"Maybe he has friends." *More teenagers.*

CHAPTER TWENTY-ONE

No doubt Leo's message with the skull had made its point. The woman was as vulnerable as the rest of the world. The location of her home was not a secret. Her profession was not untouchable. Her safety was not a given. She should be feeling rattled. He could ruin her career and destroy whatever she held precious.

Adrenaline surged in Leo's bloodstream. The nicotine from his cigarette pulsed through his veins. He was unstoppable.

Old Cesare often shoved the woman's success in his face. For a man who seemed to believe women were best kept barefoot and pregnant, he had a bit of an obsession with the success of Victoria Peres. He took pride in the woman's achievements as if they were his own, but in the same breath tore her down, claiming she was a misfit and a disgrace.

Considering the identity of her mother, he understood Cesare's point.

He'd decided it was time for Victoria Peres to learn about her mother and had put the wheels in motion yesterday. Her present bone investigation had been entangled, her home security compromised. What would discovering the truth about her roots do to her psyche?

Two people knew the truth about Victoria's mother: himself and Cesare. Cesare believed only he held the knowledge. But the man shouldn't keep written records. The man had a lot to learn about living a secret life. He'd been sloppy. His hiding places weak. Cesare had managed to fool his congregation for years, but Leo had easily discovered the truth. If you're going to hide an alternative life, don't leave dead women in your shed.

He blew a lungful of smoke into the air. The ceiling of the tiny bedroom grew fainter through the gray-blue haze. He set his cigarette in the ashtray and tucked his hands under his head as he rested on the bed. Last night had gone as planned. He'd hoped the fire would have burned more of the home, but he'd made his point. She wasn't safe.

The first time he'd found a body in the shed, he'd nearly wet himself. She'd had long dark hair. The feature was a fetish of Cesare's, and he decided to adopt it as one of his own. He'd been snooping, noticing the man often made trips to the shed at all times of the night. His father kept the door padlocked, but he had watched to see where Cesare kept the key. One early morning, he'd decided to look for himself.

She'd been dead for a while. He could smell the rot.

Why had Cesare been visiting a dead body?

The handcuffs were carelessly cast aside. The mattress foul. The room showed signs of occupancy. A water bucket, a waste bucket. Some empty cracker boxes. More handcuffs and rope attached to various metal rings in the walls and floors. The room had been strengthened. From the outside, it looked like a shed about to collapse. Inside the walls were closer than they should be. A sign of thick space between the inner and outer wall, no doubt filled with an insulating material. He'd tapped on a wall. They'd been dense two-by-eights. A room meant to imprison.

The next day he'd returned, and the woman had vanished. A few days of wandering in the woods behind Cesare's home had revealed a plot of freshly turned dirt. Nearby were other sunken depressions in the ground. He'd read that an amateur grave will first be a raised area of dirt, but then sink where the torso collapses as it rots, leaving the concavity. He'd counted five possible sites.

Cesare wasn't the holy man he presented to his flock.

He'd kept his knowledge to himself, watching as the old man preached to the dwindling congregation. Now the group was small, mostly older men like Cesare whose wives had abandoned them to their faith, unable to live the oppressive role their husbands laid out for them.

Leo wondered if Cesare had always been so bitter toward women, or if it'd grown after his own wife left. Had he intensified his hatred because of what his wife had done to him?

He'd snooped thoroughly through the shed and discovered a locked fire box of photos. The key hadn't been hard to find. Cesare kept his keys in the same drawer he'd used all his life. His confidence in keeping his secrets safe was laughable.

The pictures were of women. Some dead, some still alive. All with long dark hair and white dresses. But the photos that struck him the most were of the circle. The women laid out as if they were daisy petals. Their white dresses echoing the flower. Some pictures showed them flush with life. But others showed their cheeks and eyes starting to sink as they lay lifeless in their circle day after day.

How many days in a row had Cesare returned to photograph the women?

He pictured Victoria Peres in the circle. Her life's essence destroyed.

Not yet.

First he wanted to emotionally rip her to shreds.

The bones were done. Victoria stretched the kinks out of her back, shuddering at the series of loud cracks. Everything was inventoried. Samples were removed for testing. Full records written and photographed. Frustratingly, she hadn't found an earth-shattering lead to use as a tool to hunt down the women's identities. From an anthropologist's perspective, these were a bunch of nondescript women. Sadly missing their skulls.

She closed her eyes for a long moment.

It was a process she'd done since her first anatomy class: imagining her own bones without their flesh. She could see her skull. Its forehead high, its eye sockets slightly angular, and the zygomatic arches high and well defined. Cool and bare. Lifeless.

"Need some sleep?"

Victoria smiled as she opened her eyes. *Seth's voice.* It was low and rumbly and sexy. It'd taken her all of one second to get used to hearing it again. That first night in Forest Park, the sound of his voice rang in her ears like hearing a beloved song from long ago. At first the sound was a small, stunning surprise, and then came the realization that she knew every melody and lyric.

She turned. He'd changed out of scrubs and lab coat into a faded pair of jeans. His hair was slightly messy, and she knew instantly he'd been running a hand through it in mild frustration. But his eyes looked happy and relaxed. *Hmmm.*

"What's up?" She could tell he had news. He was so easy to read.

"Anita asked me to give you this. It just came via messenger." He handed over the white cardboard document envelope.

Victoria glanced at the front, verifying it was for her. *Weird. No return address.*

She ripped open the envelope and shook the single sheet of paper onto her desk. Seth leaned against her doorjamb, his arms crossed, casually watching. She flipped over the paper. It had two sentences.

Your mother's name is Isabel Favero.

The second line was an address in Portland.

Victoria's vision tunneled on the paper, reading the name over and over. Seth spoke as if from a great distance. She couldn't move.

My mother?

Is this a joke?

Isabel Favero.

"Tori!" His tone grabbed her attention. "What is that?" He moved behind her and read, his hands heavy on her shoulders.

"What the hell?"

Her thoughts exactly.

"I thought someone had died, by the look on your face. Can I see that?"

She nodded, and Seth tugged the paper from her frozen fingers.

My mother?

Seth glanced at the back of the paper. Blank. "I don't think this is how Michael would deliver any information he found, right?"

Victoria shook her head. "No. He'd call."

Seth picked up the messenger envelope. "I'll call them and find out who had this delivered." Frowning, he pulled out his cell and started tapping, searching for the messenger service number. "I don't like this. Who would send you something like this?"

"I don't know." Victoria shook her head. Her spinning brain made her stomach queasy. She leaned forward on her desk. *Why now? Why send this within a day of her wondering about her birth mother?* She listened as Seth spoke on the phone. He wasn't getting an answer he liked.

"A walk-in," he told her as he ended his call. "He paid cash. Now they're noticing the form he filled out has a bunch of bogus information."

"He?" Victoria asked.

Seth nodded. "They couldn't tell me much about how he looks. Hat, jacket, jeans, and wet. Just like everyone else in Portland today. And they don't have cameras." Seth ran his finger down the edge of the paper. "Chances are this is a hoax."

"I know. So it should be easy to disprove."

"Let's call that reporter friend of yours. See what he can dig up on this name and address first."

"He's not my friend."

"I'll call. And then we might go for a drive."

Victoria agreed.

It seemed like forever before Michael got his information back to Seth. Victoria sat in her desk chair, unable to keep her feet or hands still. She tapped pencils and pens. She crossed and uncrossed her legs as Seth talked to Michael on the phone. She'd left the matter in his hands. Ever since the note, her mind had been unable to form a coherent thought. Two mantras blasted a path through her brain.

Is this my mother?

Who is doing this and why?

Seth was doing a lot of "Uh-huh" and "Hmmm" on the phone, scribbling notes on a pad with his cell tucked between his shoulder and ear. Every now and then he'd meet her gaze, his fiercely serious as he listened to Michael.

He hung up and Victoria held her breath.

Seth looked at his pad. "There really is an Isabel Favero and this is the address listed for her. She doesn't own the home; she rents. She is fifty-five, single, and currently unemployed."

He looked at Victoria and frowned. "Breathe," he ordered.

She inhaled and pressed her lips together. *So far, nothing had ruled it a prank.*

"She's been married three times and has four children. None appear to live with her."

Possibly five.

Do I have siblings?

"She has a past address in Seaport."

Victoria straightened in her chair. *Where I was adopted.*

"The address is the same as the church where your parents attended. The church burned down twenty-five years ago."

Victoria nodded. She'd remembered that. Her parents had been upset that their previous church had burned, and a very young Victoria had questioned what had happened to the grandpa-like pastor. Her parents had assured her no one was hurt. But she'd always wondered if the kind old man had rebuilt his church somewhere else. "Wait. She lived at the church? I don't understand."

"Could be a number of things. Maybe she worked there and got her mail there. Maybe she just needed some sort of mailing address. It was pretty rural out there at the time. I doubt she actually lived in the building."

Nerves bubbled up inside of her. They weren't excitement nerves or dread nerves. Simply sheer stimulation. This day had taken an odd turn of events. "I haven't heard anything to rule her out."

Seth nodded. "I agree." He paused and stared at his pad.

"What? What else did you find out?"

Seth licked his lips. "Brody pulled up her driver's license photo."

"And?"

"He says there could be a resemblance. Black hair, brown eyes."

Victoria swallowed hard. "Oh my God. This might be real," she whispered.

Seth squatted in front of her chair, his hands on her thighs, his eyes earnest. "Listen. No hopes up, okay? Someone could have engineered this. I don't know why, but don't rule it out, okay?"

"I need to go see. I have to know." She ran a hand through her hair. She'd never wanted anything so badly in her life. The "not knowing" made her want to vomit.

"Okay, let's go take a look at the address." He took her hand and helped her out of the chair.

She knew he hadn't missed the icy sweat on her palms.

CHAPTER TWENTY-TWO

"What do you mean, you don't know where Jason is?" The old man stared at Leo. His worthless excuse for a son was sniveling, terrified of him.

"I've checked with all his friends. I went to their homes and looked. I don't know where he slept last night." He looked around the room, avoiding his father's gaze.

The old man moved in his seat, wishing he could stand up easier. The pain in his legs was a constant companion. Drugstore painkillers no longer helped. And he would never visit a doctor. They asked too many questions and threw drugs at every problem. Medical nonsense. God gave him pain; why would he fight against God's will? Suffering was part of life.

Today's society spent too much effort to avoid suffering. Pain was good for the soul.

He wouldn't allow his son the pleasure of watching him struggle to stand, but he didn't like the fact that his son was looking down at him. It created a subtle advantage. He preferred to have the higher ground during this type of discussion.

"And . . . and there's one more thing," his son whispered.

The old man looked up. That tone didn't bode well, and his son looked like he wanted to melt into the carpet. Anger flared in his chest. "Well?" he barked. "What is it? What else has happened?"

His son twisted his hands together, misery in his expression. "The bones. When I went to get the skulls, they were gone."

"The bones you stole?" he roared. A red haze narrowed his vision. *He'd lost the skulls?* "Jason took them?"

"I . . . I don't know. I don't know who else could have found them. No one else comes in our house, so it must have been him." His son looked ready to cry. "I'm sorry, Father."

The old man hated him. How had he fathered such a weakling? "The boy has the bones. There's no question in my mind. We need to get them back and—" He broke off, a new idea pushing its way into his brain.

What if they told the police the boy had the bones? Let him take the blame for the break-in.

He sucked in a deep breath. Was it plausible? Would that work? Let the police hunt down the boy. Who would the police believe, a rebellious teenager or two adults? His mind spun with the possibilities. Would the skulls lead back to him? Or could they present it as a stupid teen prank?

His son studied him quizzically, but he stayed silent.

"Wait a minute," the father mumbled. "I think I have an idea."

The man nodded eagerly, his gaze hopeful.

The father looked out the window, mentally exploring every avenue this thought had opened. *Jason had already been questioned by the police in the shooting yesterday. This would shine more light on what he's done. But where would it lead?*

Who knows what kinds of stories Jason would tell? Would anyone take them seriously? It didn't matter. The risk was too high. All it took was one curious cop to take a closer look at the boy's family.

"Damn it!"

His son's eyes grew round, knowing his father never swore and didn't allow swearing in his presence, a subject the grandfather and Jason had butted heads on before. There were other words for expressing anger. Foul language was a lazy man's tool.

"I'd thought it might work," he muttered. It would have solved two problems. The police could have located Jason and the bones for him. But the risk was unacceptable.

Who could he ask to bring Jason in? His son was worthless. There was no one he trusted. Not anymore.

He'd have to make the boy want to come to him.

Leo stepped out onto the front porch of his father's house and blew out a breath. Steam hung in the cold air, making him crave a cigarette. The tall firs surrounding the home held his gaze. *Should he tell his father the truth?*

Pride rushed through him. Part of him loved fooling his father, but part of him craved his father's acknowledgment of his brilliance. His father truly believed he was a spineless weakling.

Someday he'd know the truth. Someday his father would be stunned at his son's strength.

But when?

He'd learned not to show his strength from watching his older brother. His brother had been the strong one. One who stood up to their father. And he'd paid for it with his life. Back then Leo had sworn to let his father believe he was cowardly and pathetic.

Leo enjoyed the game. He wasn't ready to surrender yet. He had the upper hand, and his father simply didn't know, blinded by his anger over Jason.

Where was Jason?

His son had thrown a kink in his plans. Seeing the skulls missing had angered him. Why had Jason taken them? Had he simply wanted to show them off to his friends? Brag about the disgusting find in his father's room?

Or did Jason suspect?

What was the boy up to?

Trinity stopped the car in front of a tiny house on the west side of Hillsboro and squinted through the rain at the house number. This was the place. What a dump. No wonder he didn't want to stay here any longer. A piece of plywood over one window and the yard looked severely unloved. It needed serious time with a weed whacker and a lawn mower.

Should she go to the door? Honk? She glanced at her watch. She was only ten minutes late. He should still be here and hopefully watching for her. She saw a curtain move at one of the front windows. Someone had spotted her. Good. She didn't want to dash through the sheets of water or leap over the giant puddle that blocked the walkway to the front door.

The door opened and Jason stepped out. He slung a backpack over his shoulder and pulled up the hood on his jacket. He moved down the walk and easily avoided the mini-lake with his long legs. He opened the back door to the car, thrust his wet pack into the backseat, and slammed the door. The passenger door opened and he slid into the seat, pushing back his hood and filling Katy's little car with his size. Trinity swallowed hard. *Should she be helping him?* He suddenly seemed very large, and she became aware of how powerless she was if he turned out to not be a nice guy.

Don't pick up strangers.

He's not a stranger, she argued. He was Brooke's friend. Trinity had hung out with him and a few friends that time at the mall. He seemed normal. Nothing set off alarms in her head except for his need to avoid his parents. How much trouble was he in?

"Hi. Thanks for coming to get me." He shoved his hair off his forehead and gave her a grim smile, his brown eyes serious. Cigarette smoke clung to him and permeated the air in the car.

Trinity studied his face. He looked stressed. Something big was up. "No problem. You sounded really concerned."

"Yeah, my dad is furious with me for going to that service yesterday." He looked out the window, avoiding her eyes.

Trinity had a hunch he hadn't told her the full truth. The service may have been part of it, but that wasn't the complete story. "I don't get it. Why would he care if you went to the service of a friend? That doesn't seem right."

Jason looked at her, obviously struggling with how much to share. He ran his hand over his hair again, and she noticed his fingernails looked identical to hers: chewed to the quick. *Let it go. For now.*

"Never mind. Parents don't make sense sometimes." She started the car. "Where are we going?"

Relief filled Jason's face. "Thanks. Can we go get some lunch? There was like no food in there at all."

Trinity wasn't hungry. Dr. Peres's scones sat in her stomach. She glanced at Jason as she pulled away from the curb. His jacket was soaked from his short dash through the rain, and he smelled like he'd recently showered. The car smelled of soap underneath the tobacco scent. Still, something about him being in the car with her felt good. He was plainly stressed, and she wanted to help. She remembered what Dr. Peres had said about taking his problems to a responsible adult. She'd help him find the right person as soon as he shared his real problem.

"Hey," she said. "I got a text from Brooke's mom this morning. She said Brooke opened her eyes and even squeezed her hand on command a few times. I guess the doctors are really excited about that."

Jason leaned his head back on the seat and closed his eyes. "Thank God. You don't know how worried I was about her."

A mild spike of jealousy poked Trinity in the chest, and she felt guilty. How could she be jealous of someone who'd almost died? "I think it's a good sign. Hopefully she'll keep getting better and better."

Jason opened his eyes and straightened. "Yes, at least one of them might make it." He started to chew on a nail.

"You seemed really concerned. I didn't think you and Brooke knew each other all that well," Trinity pried, keeping her eyes on the road. As far as she knew, Brooke and Jason had only casually met a few times.

"Yeah, I guess I didn't know her that well. But she seemed like a really nice girl."

Trinity frowned. That told her nothing of their relationship. "You knew Glory, too, right?"

"Yeah, she went to my school. She was in one of my classes."

"It's weird how all the girls who died went to different schools."

Jason looked out his side window, now biting the cuticle of his finger. "Yeah. Weird."

"Brooke told me you put her in touch with the photographer who took those gorgeous pictures of her."

He whipped his head around to her, alarm on his face. "She told you that? Did you tell anyone else?" His words rushed out, his face pale.

Panic shot through Trinity. *I pushed the wrong button.* "I don't know. I don't think I told anyone else. I didn't know it was a secret."

"It's not a secret," Jason said stiffly.

He's lying. She tried to remember exactly what she'd told the police detectives. She'd told them Brooke had gone to Forest Park for a photography session. Had she told them how Brooke had been contacted by the photographer?

"I think I told the police she met the photographer through Facebook or Instagram. Is that how you originally met Brooke?"

Jason nodded. "We had some mutual friends on Facebook. I think she'd commented on someone's portrait and we started chatting."

"You're the photographer?"

"God, no!"

Trinity cringed at the horror in his voice. "Then you know who took the pictures?"

Jason was silent for ten seconds. "I don't know what happened."

That didn't answer my question. She focused on the other traffic, but watched Jason out of the corner of her eye. He hadn't stopped biting his nails. She didn't know how he had anything left to bite. "Fast food okay?"

"God, yes." He sounded starved.

Twenty minutes later, with a huge bacon cheeseburger and most of a large-sized fry order in his stomach, Jason leaned back in his chair as he pushed aside his tray. "Do you know where I could stay for a few days?"

Trinity's heart sank. "I don't. We have a houseguest because my neighbor's house caught fire last night."

"What?" Concern filled his eyes. "What fire?"

Trinity relayed the events of the night before.

"Shit. That really sucks. And they think it was done on purpose?"

"Well, something didn't accidentally fly through her window to start a fire."

Jason sucked on his straw, looking thoughtful. "Did they say what was used to start it?"

"No. An accelerant. They didn't know exactly what it was, but the firefighters said they could smell it last night. So it was probably something like gasoline, I'd guess."

"Why would someone do that?"

"Beats me." Trinity shivered. Her words sounded strong, but the thought of a fire starting while Victoria had been asleep made her stomach burn.

"It's bad enough Kyle was stupid enough to pull out a gun at that service. Someone could have been killed. That's two bad accidents that you were pretty close to in one day." Jason's eyes were full of concern, but Trinity could tell his mind was ticking. He was thinking hard about something.

"Why did he bring a gun? Was he a friend of yours?"

"Sorta. We've known each other forever. More like a distant relative than a friend." Jason frowned like he didn't know how to describe his relationship with the boy.

"Why on earth did he have a gun? And what made him pull it out?"

Jason met her gaze, his brown eyes quizzical. "I asked him the same thing, but he didn't tell me. All I know is that he got irate when he saw you."

"*Me*?" Trinity squeaked. "What? Why?" *She didn't even know who Kyle was. And he pulled out a gun? Because of her?*

"He spotted you and started getting really agitated. Mumbling under his breath."

"I don't even know who he is. Are you sure?"

"He pointed at you, swearing under his breath."

Trinity stared at Jason. "Seriously? I don't understand. He was going to shoot at me?"

Jason exhaled, resting his weight on his forearms on the table. "That's what I thought was about to happen. That's why I tried to get him to put it away."

"That's crazy. He must have been pointing at someone else."

Jason rubbed at his eyes, looking exhausted. "Kyle hasn't been himself for a few months. All he talks about is how society is corrupt and that all young women are going to hell for their wild behaviors. He looks down on everyone."

"So he has the right to shoot someone? Was he going to punish me for my hemline being too short? Is that his idea of proper behavior?"

Jason gave a half smile. "Actually, you're not far off. I was watching TV the other day, and when he came in, all he did was rip apart the female actresses. How they were a bunch of sluts and immoral."

"He's on a religious kick?"

The smile disappeared. "Religions are supposed to be about love, not hate. He's full of hate and anger. It's like he's trying to elevate himself by putting others down."

"Putting others down by shooting them? Like it's his job to kill people because he thinks they're sinning?" Trinity said. *Was that why he pulled out a gun?*

"I don't know what he was thinking."

"That makes two of us," Trinity muttered. "Your friend has mental issues. Now what? Do you need a ride home? Have you talked to your parents?"

"I live with my dad. They divorced a long time ago. My mom lives in Idaho. But no, I don't want to go there. My dad has been acting weird. He and my grandpa have been fighting."

"Does your grandpa live with you guys?" Trinity sympathized with his home life. Just because your real parents were still around, it didn't mean life was easier.

"Nah, he's got a place on the way to the coast. Lives out in the middle of nowhere, but my dad goes out there a lot. My grandfather's health isn't the best."

"I'm sorry. That has to really suck."

"He's a cranky old man." Jason focused angry brown eyes on Trinity. "I think he's an asshole. If he dies, I'm not going to cry about it."

Trinity stared at him. *What could she say to that?* "That's horrible. But I kinda get it. My grandmother wouldn't win any prizes either. I lived with her for a while. She wasn't mean. She just didn't care."

Jason plunged the last of his fries into his pool of ketchup. "He's the one making my life miserable right now. Both he and my dad. Talk about crazy people. Sometimes they make Kyle look normal."

Trinity took a deep breath. "You said something about punishment in your text today. What did you mean?"

Jason scowled at his fries before pushing them in his mouth. "I can't be around them right now. Something is up and my grandpa is on the warpath. I could hear him yelling at my dad over the phone when he found out I went to Glory's service."

"Why would he care?"

Jason was silent. She could see his mind flipping through the possibilities. "I'm not sure," he said slowly. He traced a pattern in his ketchup with his last fry. His phone gave a chirp and he looked at the text. Trinity averted her eyes from the screen, trying to not care even though she was dying of curiosity.

His expression darkened.

"What's wrong?" she asked.

He met her gaze, an emotional struggle on his face. "What happened?" she asked again, her chest tightening.

"My grandfather pulling strings," he said, spitting out the words.

"What does he want you to do?" she whispered. The anger on his face alarmed her. Maybe giving him a ride wasn't her brightest move. Her mind spun. Could she make an excuse to leave? Tell him to find another friend to come get him? Why hadn't she listened to Dr. Peres? Her mouth went dry. "Maybe someone else should be driving you," she said slowly.

He looked stunned, his anger evaporating. "You can't?" His expression changed 180 degrees.

Guilt wracked her. "Uh . . . yeah, it's okay. It looked like you needed to address something with your grandfather and maybe that'd go easier if I wasn't here. You know?" *Please tell me someone else can come get you.*

"There's just some stuff I need to drop off at his place. I didn't want to do it today, but he's insisting. It's not like I have to talk with him. Just drop the stuff and go." He raised a brow at her. "Is that okay?"

"Oh . . . I guess. But this is the one who lives on the way to the beach? How far?" Trinity tried to remember how much gas was in Katy's old car.

"It's not too bad from here. I'll give you some gas money."

Again he hadn't directly answered her question. Since she'd picked him up on the west end of Hillsboro, it meant they were on a straight shot to the coast.

"You think that'd be okay?" he asked.

"Of course," Trinity said. He smiled at her, and she felt her breath catch. His anger was gone. Why had she been so scared for that split second? And he seemed to want to spend the day with her. She wasn't going to let that pass by. Katy hadn't asked how long she'd be gone when she left this morning. Katy trusted her with her old second car.

He stood and flung the backpack that he'd refused to leave in the car over his shoulder. Odd clanking sounded in the bag. Jason reached behind him to pat the sides of the bag, checking for openings. His fingers found an open zipper and yanked it closed, covering Trinity's brief view of a camera's lens cap.

CHAPTER TWENTY-THREE

Victoria sat silently in Seth's passenger seat. Possibilities raced through her mind. She'd envisioned knocking on the door and falling into her happy mother's arms, as her mother sobbed about the baby who'd been taken from her. She'd thought of driving by and never going back. What if the address was fake? What if it was a prank? What if the woman hated her?

She was nauseous.

Seth squeezed her hand. He'd held her hand the entire time in the car, making her worry as he merged onto the freeway. "We'll just take a look. Maybe knock on the door. Don't get your hopes up about anything," he reminded her.

Victoria nodded. He'd said the same thing a half-dozen times. He was as nervous as she was.

"You're sighing," Seth stated.

"I know. I can't help it. I swear every nerve I have is on edge."

"Lack of sleep and the possibility of seeing your birth mother will do that to anyone."

The GPS announced they'd arrived at their destination. Seth parked across the street at the curb and turned off the car.

Victoria studied the small home. They were in an old neighborhood in southeast Portland. The lots were close together and the homes looked incredibly tiny. And run-down. Even she could tell the home needed a new roof. A chain-link fence bordered the yard, keeping trespassers from stepping foot in the straggly grass.

Her heart sank. This was no childhood dream home.

The home's door opened and a woman stepped out. Victoria held her breath. The woman headed for the mailbox unit on their side of the street, letters in her hand. She was tall and too thin, and a cigarette dangled from her side of the mouth. Her black hair was heavily streaked with gray. Victoria heard Seth draw in a breath.

"Holy cow," he breathed.

Victoria could see it. The woman's carriage was identical to hers. She put her hand on the car handle and pulled, before she could talk herself out of it. She stepped out of the car, ignoring Seth's whispers to stop. She moved toward the woman, a light drizzle of rain dusting her face.

"Excuse me," she said to the woman as she locked her mail slot with a key.

The woman turned, eyeing her suspiciously. "Yes?"

She had brown eyes like Victoria, but her face was heavily lined. An obvious smoker. Michael had said the woman was in her fifties; this woman appeared to be in her late sixties. Life had beaten her down. "Are you Isabel Favero?"

The woman stared. "Who wants to know?"

Victoria's mind blanked. *What should she say? Your possible daughter?* She couldn't speak. Seth appeared beside her and greeted the woman.

"I'm Seth Rutledge. I'm a pathologist at the medical examiner's office. You must have seen from the news that we're dealing with the recent murders of those teen girls and reevaluating the remains from the old killings decades before, right?" He took Victoria's hand again.

"What about it?" Isabel said rudely. She crossed one arm over her chest and fiddled with her cigarette.

"We've managed to identify one of the older sets of remains," Seth said quickly. "Are you familiar with the name Lucia Cavallo? She used to live in your house."

Victoria froze. *Apparently Seth could think fast on his feet.* Isabel eyed Seth. "What's that have to do with me?"

He gave a charming grin. "Nothing, of course. Our research showed the home is in your name now, but we wanted to just get a feel for the woman's past. It helps to see things sometimes, you know. Like where she lived."

Victoria wanted to melt into the sidewalk. *What kind of bullshit was Seth feeding her?*

Isabel pointed her cigarette at Seth. "You can't look in my house," she snapped.

Seth held up both his hands. "I wouldn't dream of asking. I just wanted to let you know why we were in front of your house. Some people are instantly suspicious."

"You got ID?" She glared at both of them.

Seth pulled out his wallet, and Victoria did the same. The women peered at their identification from the medical examiner's offices. She took a good look at Victoria's picture and then her face and handed it back. Victoria held her gaze for a split second, searching for any kind of recognition in the woman's eyes. She saw nothing. Isabel spent longer with Seth's.

"This is from California."

"I'm in the process of moving to the Oregon office," answered Seth.

She handed back his identification. "I don't know nothing about that name you said. You figure out who killed all those women back then?"

"Not yet." Victoria found her voice.

Isabel sniffed. "Some psycho asshole, probably. People are crazy." She took a puff on her cigarette and blew it to the side.

Victoria wanted to leave. She wanted to run away and forget she'd ever seen this woman.

"Whole world is full of crazy jerks. Men who take advantage of young women. Those women probably trusted the man who killed them." Isabel glared at Seth.

"Maybe it'll turn out to be a woman who did it," Seth suggested.

"Maybe. I'll put my money on a man. Those poor women got screwed over, and he walked away scot free for decades, because no one gives a rip."

"That's not true," Victoria interjected. "You don't know how hard the police are working to figure this out. Even decades ago they struggled to find the killer."

Isabel gave a condescending sneer. "Aren't you the optimist? Men rule this world, honey. That's how it's always been. You may have some big position, but who's your boss? A man, right?"

"Well, yes. But—"

"Proves my point." Isabel turned her focus back to Seth, Victoria written off. "Stay away from my house," she ordered. She spun and headed back to her home.

Victoria couldn't move. *What just happened?*

"The police will probably be in touch," Seth said to the retreating back.

"I got nothin' for them," Isabel tossed over her shoulder.

You have nothing for me.

Victoria's numb feet tripped on her way to the car. She slammed her door closed and started to shake uncontrollably. Seth started the motor and cranked up the heat, pointing all the vents at her. She buried her fisted hands between her legs and fought down the nausea. Bile burned the back of her throat. *That wasn't her mother.* The woman sauntered back across the street and vanished in her palace.

Not my mother.

I help people. I don't have that anger in me.

Possibly Isabel was her mother by blood, but she would never be her mother in spirit. Victoria fought to recall the memories of her adoptive parents. Their beautiful faces danced through her memory and tears burned down her cheeks.

"I did not like her," Seth stated. His hands gripped the wheel as he drove straight ahead. "If that was your birth mother, you inherited nothing from her. *Nothing at all.*" He pounded his palm on the steering wheel in time with his last three words. "Damn it! I knew this wasn't a good idea."

"No, I'm glad we came," Victoria said. "I had to know."

"You didn't find out anything. Without testing, you don't know if that's your mother."

She breathed deep, seeking calm. "I know who my mother is."

"No! You can't say—"

"My mother died when I was in my twenties. She and my father loved me and brought me up to love the people around me." She looked at Seth. His profile was hard and angry. He brushed at an eye with the back of his hand, and her heart swelled.

He hurt for her.

She loved him for it. And for a dozen other reasons. She didn't need to know who gave birth to her, for her to feel like a complete person. Seth had made her feel whole.

He abruptly pulled to the curb and stopped, throwing the car in park. He turned and faced her, grabbing her hands and looking her directly in the eye. "You are nothing like that woman, Tori. You are all that is good in people. You help and you care. Look at how you've touched Trinity's life. Look how you've touched *my* life. I've been empty for the last eighteen years, but a week with you has made me feel alive again."

"I know! You don't have to convince me. You bring out a side of me that I've stifled for nearly two decades." She smiled through her tears.

"I made a mistake letting you do this."

"No, this wasn't a mistake. I've lost nothing. I still have the parents I had. For an hour today, I knew there was a chance I would find a birth mother I'd hardly ever wondered about. I just met a person who can add nothing to my life." She breathed deep and looked at him. "But I've found the person who adds everything. Knowing you're here makes what happened this morning not matter."

She held his gaze. The inside of the car was silent. She wanted nothing more than to climb inside of him and lose herself.

"I don't want to go back to the office," she heard herself whisper.

He held her gaze a second longer. "My place?" he asked quietly.

"Yes." She needed him to hold her.

He shifted the car back into drive.

Fifteen minutes later, they'd parked in the city center, catching a lucky spot on the street.

He reached out and took her hand as they walked down the wet sidewalk. Victoria tensed, unused to the sensation of hand-holding in public. She cast a few nervous glances at passersby, who ignored them. She slowly relaxed. His hand was warm and strong. Something about having a man reach out and claim her in such a casual yet powerful way gave her goose bumps. It hadn't been like this when they were younger. Perhaps she'd taken too much for granted. They'd almost been kids. Romance at her age was a whole new experience.

"I had some news I wanted to share with you earlier, but since that letter showed up, I'd put it out of my mind."

"What happened?

"I mailed off the signed divorce documents to my lawyer today."

"You didn't tell me you had them." She glanced at him, scanning for any sorrow in his face. Shouldn't a divorce be a sad time? Hers had been depressing. Even though she'd known it was the absolute right thing to do, it'd seemed like a big symbol of failure. Seth didn't look the slightest bit sad. In fact, he looked very relaxed. "How do you feel about that?"

Seth smiled. "Jennifer and I have been working toward this for a long time. Everything has been pretty amicable, but the legal part took forever. In my head, we've been divorced for a long time. This made it real." He abruptly stopped in front of the Italian restaurant where she'd eaten with Lacey and Dr. Campbell. "I'm staying here." The restaurant occupied the bottom level of one of Portland's finer boutique hotels.

"Great hotel."

"It's old. But they've got fantastic rooms. The windows in mine are incredible. They look like they belong in a large sun room."

He'd understood when she'd said she didn't want to go back to work. He'd driven straight to downtown Portland, neither of them speaking, but knowing exactly what they both needed.

He gripped her hand. He hadn't let go. The space in the elevator seemed to shrink as they silently waited for the upward trek to finish. She studied Seth out of the corner of her eye, her heart expanding at the sight of the rugged profile. Right now, she felt like she'd spent the last ten years with him at her side.

He made her relax. It'd been a roller-coaster of twenty-four hours. Her house was fire, smoke, and water damaged. She'd met a horrible woman who was possibly her birth mother. But being next to Seth made it all bearable.

They stepped off the elevator and moved down the hall to his room.

"Don't let me forget to grab my cell phone," Seth said.

"How on earth did you forget one of your phones? I'd feel like I left my right arm behind."

"That's exactly what it's felt like all morning. It's driving me crazy. I should know better. I've been carrying a work phone and personal phone for about five years, but somehow I will leave one behind sometimes." He held his key card to the lock and pushed the door open, holding it for her to walk through.

Light beckoned to her and she moved forward, dropping his hand, her eyes wide at the sight of the windows that wrapped up and over a portion of the ceiling. "It's like staying in an atrium."

Seth laughed. "I feel like the whole city can see me in here. But I really don't care. Who's going to recognize me?"

"It is really exposed." Victoria studied the buildings across the street. "Their windows look straight in here. At least there's a good distance. They'd need a telescope for details."

"I've given them a few shows."

She whirled around to face him, an exclamation on her lips, until she saw he was teasing. An image of him parading naked for the viewers crossed her mind. A laugh bubbled out of her chest. How long had it been since she laughed like that?

He watched her carefully, a big grin on his face, but his eyes reflected a soul-deep level of adoration. "God, I've missed you, Tori."

She held his gaze, her stomach warming and trembling in a good way. He moved closer, taking both of her hands and squeezing tightly. His heart was clear in his gaze. He meant every word. Abruptly he pulled her to him, wrapping his arms firmly about her, burying his face in her hair, and she felt a shudder go through him. "It's been too long."

Her insides dissolved and absorbed into his heat. She moved her lips against his neck and nestled her face against the roughness of his skin. His stubble stimulating the most sensitive skin on her body. She inhaled his scent, and a calm flowed through her. It was a masculine scent, one she wanted to breathe forever.

She didn't notice her tears until she tasted them.

Seth noticed. He pulled back and lifted her chin, his gaze considering her face. "Aw, Tori. Why do you cry? Was it that awful woman? Don't think about her." His voice was a low rumble, a sound she knew meant his emotions were very, very close to the surface.

"I didn't know I was."

He wiped at her tear tracks. "Don't cry. Nothing makes me cry except the sight of your tears. Should we not be up here?"

She shook her head at him. "I want to be here."

"Are you sure? We don't have to do this." He held her gaze, his blue eyes earnest. He'd given her the ability to stop it. Tension radiated from his body. He wanted her. Badly.

She laughed, choking on the salty moisture in her swollen throat. *Stop? Now?* At this very moment there was nothing more she wanted more than to feel his warm skin pressed against every inch of hers. She craved it. She needed it. She needed to make the morning disappear and lose herself in Seth.

She moved into him and pressed her mouth softly against his. He hesitated a fraction of a second and then wrapped his hand around the base of her skull and moved hungrily into the kiss. His mouth was hot, and she tasted her tears as her tongue moved against his. Fresh tears spilled from her closed eyes.

He brushed at her tears, keeping his mouth against hers. His hand stroked down her face, his fingertips wet. "I've dreamed for years about this," he muttered against her mouth. "Ever since I kissed you in Denver, I knew my life would never be complete without you in it."

She pressed her forehead against his. His words echoed in her heart, chipping away at the walls she'd created when he left her. Protective walls. But now they no longer had a purpose and they were crumbling.

"I'd accepted that I'd always have a space in my heart in which only you would fit. I was prepared to go through life simply learning to live with it." His voice dropped. "I'd believed I'd destroyed everything beyond repair. You were married. I knew I needed to move on."

He pushed her coat off her shoulders and let it drop to the floor. She was instantly cold and shivered, moving her body against the length of his. She wanted his body against her from her toes to her lips. She tucked her arms under his coat, wrapping her arms around to his back.

"Take your clothes off," he whispered in her ear. His lips trailed the arch of her ear, his teeth biting gently at her earlobe. Lightning shot through her.

He didn't need to ask twice.

She pulled back and held his gaze as she ripped her sweater over her head. His eyes widened, his gaze locked on her unsexy T-shirt bra. She took a deep breath as power filled her chest. *That's right. Take a good look at what you've been missing.* She gave a slow smile, reveling in the need on his face. Yes, he wanted her.

She kicked off her boots and slid off her jeans, all while holding his gaze. Seth stood motionless, and she wondered if he held his breath. His stare moved down her body, stopping on the simple white thong. She tilted her head, giving him a minute to look his fill. She didn't have doubts about her body. She rowed. She ate well. "Long" and "lean" were common adjectives used to describe her. Seth appeared to approve.

"Strip," she ordered, biting back a laugh at the elated shock that crossed his face. It was instantly replaced with a smug grin.

"Yes, ma'am."

He stripped.

She hungrily watched him work off his layers of clothing. She glanced out the wall of windows, wondering if they were providing lunchtime entertainment for the office building across the street. Looking at Seth dropping his last layer, she didn't care. Let them watch. Why not give them something to tell their neighbors about?

With a rapid move, Seth tackled her onto her back on the huge bed. She wrestled the down comforter out of the way, loving the cool sheets on her skin. Her skin temperature had shot up in the last minute, her body craving the man.

"My God, you're gorgeous." Seth lay beside her, propped up on one elbow as his gaze traveled her body. He was pressed against her from toes to shoulder, just as she'd wanted.

He was beautiful, too. Was that an appropriate word to describe a man? Subtle hints of muscle showed everywhere. She liked that he wasn't jacked like some men. He was just Seth. A memory prickled, and she reached up to trail her nails through his hair, tracing his scalp, and his eyes closed, bliss on his face. *Yep, he still likes that.*

He abruptly pulled her face to him and kissed her. His mouth moved from hers, up her face, to her hairline, and then down to her neck. She squirmed as her skin tingled under his lips. His hands were everywhere, stroking and pressing, finding all the places he'd once loved to touch her. She sighed. She simply wanted to spend the rest of the day here in bed with this man. The office was gone. Bones were gone. Stress was gone.

"You don't know how long I've wanted to do this again," he muttered as he worked his mouth down her stomach. "I can't be in the same room with you without being bombarded by need for you. Do you know what the last few days have been like? Seeing you at work? Christ. I thought I was going insane."

She sank her hands into his hair, gliding her nails along his scalp and making him moan. He kissed his way across her belly and released the front clasp to her bra. Her breasts spilled out and he exhaled as he gently stroked one and then the other. He slid off her thong and flung it behind him.

"Hang on." He sat up, and she missed his body heat. He stretched over to the nightstand and removed a condom from the drawer.

He has condoms? Victoria stared at him.

He gave her a sheepish look. "I was looking ahead."

"When did you buy those?" Her mind froze. Should she be happy? Scared? Insulted?

"The day after I saw you."

"What?"

"Let's say I was cautiously optimistic." He gave a sexy grin and further scrambled her brain.

"Well, I didn't . . . I didn't give you . . . Why—"

He cut her off with a deep kiss, and she no longer cared why or when he'd done it. The sight of her had driven him to buy condoms. She should be flattered, right?

"If I had the slightest chance with you, I wasn't going to blow it by not being prepared," he whispered.

She reached down and wrapped her hands around his hard length. He hissed and closed his eyes. "Yes, touch me, please." He was silky and smooth under her fingers. She watched the alternating agony and pleasure dance across his face as she handled him. He pressed the condom into her hand. She opened it and rolled it on him, as he watched her with a dreamy look. She ran one hand up his chest, massaging with deep pressure. Her other hand pleasuring him, keeping that lustful look in his eyes that made her feel like the most powerful woman in the world.

She'd buried herself in her work, seeking that sort of power. Wanting her colleagues to admire her skills and leaning on her successes to give her satisfaction in her life. It didn't matter how anyone else saw her, she knew. It was about what she meant to one man, and what he meant to her.

She moved on top of him, sitting on his stomach, and his eyes lit up. Seth made her feel sexy and female, a feeling she didn't get very often. She arched her back, making her breasts lift. Could anyone across the street see them? A naughty part of her hoped so. She felt a bit like showing off. It was safe here, just the two of them. The expanse of gray wet skies filled the room with light, exposing everything.

Seth ran a hand up one of her thighs. "You're beautiful, Tori."

Her heart swelled. She shifted her weight and pressed his covered tip against her opening. And then met his wide eyes. His jaw was locked, one hand gripping the sheets. The other dug into her thigh, almost hurting her in his excitement. She pressed down, watching him. His lids fell closed as his chin lifted, digging the back of his head into the pillow. His legs and stomach tensed.

She looked back to Seth, a wide smile on his face. He met her gaze and clamped his hands on her hips, grinding himself in deep. She gasped for breath, small fires shooting up her backbone.

"I love you, Tori," he forced out from clenched teeth.

She froze, her hands on his. "I've always loved you, Seth."

He stopped moving beneath her. "I'm not going to let you get away again. This is it. You and me. Moving forward from here. Together. Agreed?"

She tried to shift her hips beneath his grip, but he held her tightly in place. Part of her wanted to leap off and hide. But that urge was rapidly smothered by an overwhelming need to stay with him permanently.

"I won't leave you," she said softly. She felt the last bit of her walls dissolve.

Seth rolled them over, his hands tighter on her hips. Suddenly she was on his pillow with his eyes inches from hers, his look fierce. He was still deep inside her and he pushed harder, emphasizing his words as he spoke. "You and me. We're going to live out the rest of our lives together, driving each other crazy, okay?"

Moisture filled her eyes. He was giving her exactly what her heart had ached for. She nodded through her tears.

She was lost in his eyes, feeling his hands touch everywhere on her body. She wanted to let him take every inch of her that she offered up before him. His words rang through her head. *The rest of our lives.* They'd been said before, but they'd been nearly children at that time. Now the words held a power, a truthfulness. They were coming from a man who knew what he wanted.

She surrendered to Seth's pleasure. In her heart and in her body.

CHAPTER TWENTY-FOUR

Seth opened his eyes as a rare burst of sunshine touched his face. By the time he'd realized that Tori was curled up at his side, the sun was gone, hidden again behind dark gray clouds. Tori nestled into him, his arm gripping her tightly even in his sleep. With her eyes shut and hair mussed, she looked totally innocent and approachable, a look she rarely projected during waking hours. He was glad she'd relaxed. She'd been stressed for a solid day.

He still regretted taking her to see that witch this morning. She could blow it off all she wanted, but watching her go through the excitement of meeting her possible mother and then the absolute desolation had nearly cracked him.

He wouldn't believe that woman was her mother. The two women couldn't be more different. It'd take DNA to prove it to him.

He doubted Tori would ever request that Isabel give a sample. It appeared Tori had no desire to ever contact the woman again. Who could blame her?

He glanced at the clock on the side table and silently moaned. Two hours had vanished. He probably had a half-dozen calls and texts from people wondering what'd happened to him. He slowly untangled from Tori. She rolled to her other side and burrowed into a pillow.

He sat up, watching her, and smiled. She made his soul happy, and brought a calmness he'd missed for years. Even though he needed to get back to work, he really didn't care that much. They were together and moving forward on the same path.

Finally.

When he'd first seen her he'd wanted her back in his life with a fierceness that'd surprised him. When they were together, the universe made sense. Everything moved in harmony. He rubbed a hand over the stubble that'd formed on his chin, feeling slightly sheepish at his fanciful thoughts, but damn if they didn't make a hell of a lot of sense at the moment. Would he hear angels sing next?

He got up and looked for his jeans he'd worn yesterday, finding them on a hook on the back of the bathroom door. With his personal phone in the back pocket. He sighed at the feel of the case against his palm. He hated having to carry two cell phones. How had he left it behind? He'd been in a funk all morning. The other cell phone he carried on loan from the medical examiner's office didn't have all his personal contacts on it.

He opened the screen, frowning at the number of text messages and missed calls. *Shit.*

Jennifer.

He scrolled through her texts, panic tightening his chest.

Her texts had started last night, saying she couldn't reach Eden. Then her texts stated Eden's roommate claimed Eden had gone home two days ago.

Sweat broke out on Seth's neck. *Two days ago?* Where was she?

He ignored the voice mails from Jennifer and called her. She picked up on the second ring.

"Where have you been? I've been trying to reach you since last night!" Jennifer's anger burned through the line.

He ignored her anger. Jennifer reacted to every situation with anger. Even when something good was going on, she found a reason to get upset and pass the emotion to the people around her. It'd been part of what destroyed their marriage. He couldn't be around someone who was angry nonstop. "My phone was on silent last night, and I didn't listen to your voice mails yet. What's going on?"

"Damn you, why haven't you called me?" More heat.

"I left my phone at home. I just got it. *What happened?*"

"Eden is here. She's okay."

"What? How'd she get there?" Seth was stunned. Sacramento was a good seven hundred miles from Seattle. *Had she flown*?

"Some friend drove her here. She's dropped out of school."

Shock and then guilt flooded through Seth. *Was that what Eden had wanted to talk to him about? Should he have put more effort into reaching out to her?* "She can't drop out of school. It's only been a few months."

"Well, she's *understandably* upset with the divorce." Jennifer dug into his heart with her words.

"I talked to her about it," Seth said, his heart pounding in his chest. "She said she understood." Eden had reacted calmly during their talks about the divorce. Had she been hiding how she really felt? When he'd helped drop her off at college she'd seemed happy and looking forward to campus life. What had changed? His hands were ice.

"You know how she is. She doesn't like to upset you, and she doesn't let anyone know how she really feels." Again Jennifer stabbed at him with her words. *This is all your fault.*

"But she's willing to upset you? Are you sure she's okay?" He looked at his watch. He needed to check the flights to Sacramento.

"Yes, she's depressed. She didn't like being alone up there."

"That doesn't sound like Eden." Seth had never seen his daughter act the slightest bit depressed. And when he left her in Seattle, she was already hitting it off with her roommate. He tried to see past Jennifer's words and anger. "What's really going on?"

"I just told you she's upset about the divorce. I don't know if I can go through with it if it's going to rip her up like this. I'm not like you."

Her words burned Seth's brain. He ran a hand through his hair, glancing in the bathroom mirror. *He wasn't the selfish asshole Jennifer thought he was.* He firmly put the thought away. He knew he and Jennifer had done the right thing. But Eden was in need of some extra support.

Tori stepped into the bathroom, a concerned look on her face. She'd pulled on her sweater and underwear. "What's happened?" she mouthed at him.

Jennifer yelled at him from the phone, her voice no doubt carrying to Tori's ears. Confusion reigned in his head

Seth stared at her. The woman he'd wanted all his life stood in front of him. But his daughter was crying out for help. He didn't know what to say.

Tori blinked, wariness entering her gaze.

"I'll be there on the next flight," he spoke.

Tori's brows shot up. "What's going on?" she asked.

"Who's that?" snapped Jennifer. "And Eden doesn't want to see you right now. Give her a few days with me and then come down."

And let you poison her mind against me?

"I'm coming down. Don't tell me I can't see my daughter."

"Eden's in Sacramento?" Tori whispered, alarm crossing her face. "Why?"

"She doesn't want you here right now. She needs time to clear her brain," Jennifer spit out.

"Let me talk to her," Seth ordered. He had to hear it from Eden's mouth. She'd always been her mother's girl. Jennifer was who she ran to when she had issues. It'd worked. Jennifer identified with Eden because her brain was permanently stuck in that teen mentality.

He heard Jennifer speak to someone in the background, and then Eden's quiet voice filled the line. "Daddy?" The sound of her word soothed his heart and he closed his eyes for a second. Nothing touched him deeper than hearing his little girl call him Daddy. And it told him she was all right.

"What's wrong, Eden? Why did you leave school?" Thankfully Eden hadn't inherited the irrationality of her mother. He could ask questions and get true answers without anger getting in the way.

"I didn't like it. I was lonely all the time."

"You should have called me. I was only a few hours away." His heart broke at the sorrow in her voice.

"I know. And I did call but I wasn't going to ask you to leave work to come see me. I know you're trying to get a new job."

"Ahh, honey. That doesn't matter. I'd drop everything if you needed something. I don't want you upset because we're getting divorced. You're my first priority, you know."

Tori started to leave, but he reached out and grabbed her arm. "Stay," he whispered. She shook her head, her mask firmly in place. She didn't want to interfere in his family business. She pulled her arm out of his grip and went back to the bedroom.

"I'm okay, Daddy. I just wanted to go home for a while."

"I'm going to come down and see you."

"No. I don't want you to do that! You need to focus on your job interview. I'd feel horrible if you missed out on the job because you left." She pleaded with him.

Seth was torn. "Your mom says you're upset about the divorce."

"No, I'm not. I just don't know if going so far away for college was the right thing for me. I couldn't think about anything else except home. And it rains there a lot. It was always gray. I knew it was going to be wet, but I didn't expect it to be *that* wet," she said plaintively.

"You need sunshine like your mom," Seth admitted. It was true. "Are you sure about me not coming down? I feel like I should see you."

"When will you know about your job? Can you come after that?" Eden asked.

"It should be soon, and then I'll head down. Are you sure you're okay with the divorce? Why did your mom say that was a reason for you leaving school?"

"Dad, *really*?" Eden snorted in the phone.

Seth was relieved and saddened at the same time. Eden could see right through her mother's tactics. Jennifer thrived on making Seth feel guilty for every little possible thing. He extracted more promises from Eden about calling him regularly and enrolling in the local community college.

He hung up the phone and sighed, rubbing at his eyes. He'd ridden a roller-coaster all morning. First signing the divorce papers, finding that horrible woman who might be Tori's birth mother, making love to Tori, and then the absolute terror when he'd believed his daughter was missing. But the lowest of all was when Jennifer tried to make him think he'd emotionally ripped up their daughter by filing for divorce. Jennifer knew how to push his buttons. She never accepted blame for anything. She would twist every situation to make him look like the bad guy instead of sharing blame.

His relationship with Tori was a good thing. Even Eden would see that.

He wanted to introduce Tori to Eden. He wanted to show his daughter how two adults should have a relationship. Eden had watched him and Jennifer avoid each other for years. He fervently hoped her views of marriage weren't too skewed.

He tossed the phone on the bathroom counter and went to look for Tori. A few minutes in her arms would bring the world back into balance. He found her fully dressed and making the bed.

He stared, stunned. "What are you doing?"

"I'm heading back." She didn't look at him as she arranged the pillows.

"Well, hang on. I need a shower, don't you?" His stomach coiled in an odd sinking sensation. "I'll just be a few minutes." He turned to grab a rapid shower, but she touched his arm, stopping him cold. He met her gaze and saw she had all barriers at full attention.

"I'll get a cab," she stated.

"No, wait. What's going on?" Seth could feel her slipping away. *What just happened?* "Are you upset I brought you up here? That we had sex? Because that was one of the best decisions I've made in a long time. I don't regret it one bit."

Tori shook her head. "No, it was good."

Good? "It was fucking fantastic," he corrected.

Her smile didn't touch her eyes. "It was good. But you have another life that you need to get back to. They need you." She turned to leave.

He grabbed her arm. "I need *you*." *This wasn't happening to him. He wasn't letting her walk away.*

She made a show of glaring at his hand on her arm. He relaxed his grip but didn't let go. Neither of them had spouses now. He had no reason to let her out that door. He was going to fight for her.

"Your daughter needs you. I won't stand in the way of that."

"You're not!"

"She should be your first priority!"

Seth heard an echo of his earlier words to Eden. "She is. I will be there whenever she has need of me, but she's an adult now. She told me not to come, and I believe she doesn't need me to hold her hand while she gets over her homesickness. I don't need to wash her bloody knees when she falls.

"I love my daughter. No one will take her place, but she's my *daughter,* not the woman I want to spend my life with. She's learning how to navigate in the world, and she hit a stumbling block. Her mother can soothe her."

Tori studied his face, her gaze flicking back and forth between his eyes.

Did she believe him? "Eden had a rough couple of months. She's run back home. But I'm not going anywhere. I'm here to get this job and move forward with us." He smiled. "I came here with the first goal, but the second was added the moment I saw you. We're moving in the right direction, and you're not going to run away again."

"I didn't run away. I was married. So were you! With a child!" She pulled her arm out of his grasp, but the determined look in her eye was faltering.

He was getting through to her. "Exactly. There's nothing holding us apart. And I'm not going to let your fears damage the start we've made."

"My fears," she stuttered.

"Yes, *yours.* You're going to have to get used to the fact that I'm not going away. I'm here for you. I don't care what kind of crap we have to deal with. I've got some relationship baggage with an ex-wife and you've got some with an ex-husband, but I think we're both mature adults. I'm not going to run at the first sign of adversity. And I won't let you either."

She swallowed and her shoulders relaxed a fraction.

He exhaled, but his mind was still spinning. *Holy shit, that was close.*

Victoria studied his face. Seth was determined. As determined as she'd ever seen him. They were both too rational to allow a misunderstanding to undermine what they wanted. He'd told Eden she was his first priority, and Victoria had felt like an intruder. Hell, she'd felt like "the other woman" even though they were both single and available. Her first instinct had been to disappear.

She would have been in a cab by now if he hadn't grabbed her arm.

She was thankful he'd held on. At that precise moment, she'd needed to know he wanted her. Her anger had shot up that he'd manhandled her, but right then her mind hadn't been rational. She'd been ready to run without asking him what'd happened on the phone.

What did she want? Didn't she want to have a future with him? Is that why she'd tried to vanish? Was she not fully committed to moving forward with him? She drew in a shuddering breath.

"I love you, Seth. But—"

"There are no buts," he cut her off.

"Yes, there *are*," she asserted. "You've been here a week and we've rushed headlong into this. We both need to take a careful—"

"Damn it, Tori. Do you hear yourself? Can't you go with your heart? Why are you doubting yourself? You know as well as I do that we belong together. Why do we need to analyze everything first? We're not in relationships with anyone else. I'm not wanted by the police. I've got good credit and a clean medical history. What else do you need to think about? I *love you!*" he shouted, lifting his arms in exasperation.

A naked man was shouting at her.

Tears welled. She brushed at her eyes, frustrated at the sudden surge. Where was her self-control? The last few days had ripped her open. Next she'd be texting cute pictures of kittens to her friends. She felt like she stood on a precarious peak, and the wind blew at her from every direction, trying to push her off balance. Her emotional balance was threatened.

Seth put his hands on his hips and stared at her, waiting. Did he know how hard it was to argue with him when he was naked?

He stood as if dressed in a suit, completely unconcerned with how he looked. He'd always been fearless in front of her.

She sucked in a ragged breath. "I love you, too. I got rattled. I heard you talking to your daughter, and I felt like I'd interfered somehow . . . that *we'd* interfered, messing up your priorities. I was just trying to make it easier for you."

Sadness filled his eyes. "Ah, Tori. Not having you won't make anything easier. I know how to love my daughter. Being with you won't interfere with that. You need to trust me on this," he pleaded.

She shut off her rational brain and stepped into his arms. Inhaling, she smelled her scent on his skin. He smelled like her, and she liked it. She'd marked him, and he'd firmly imprinted on her heart.

"We're going to make this work," he promised.

CHAPTER TWENTY-FIVE

"Okay, that was one of the weirder interviews I've ever done," Ray stated as he and Mason ducked out of the downpour and inside a noisy Starbucks. Mason couldn't agree more. They brushed the rain off their shoulders, wiped their feet on the soaking wet mat, and stepped carefully across the damp tiles to the long line.

Perpetual rain in Portland had a way of driving people out of their homes and into businesses. Residents grew restless with the drizzle and needed interaction, even if that contact was simply reading a book in a coffeehouse with a bunch of strangers. Mason scanned the seated crowd, seeking Michael Brody's tall frame. No luck yet. The reporter had asked for a meeting.

"I feel like I need a shower. Or something to wash all the conspiracy theories out of my head," Ray muttered. "So far, Cavallo's progeny are a bunch of nuts."

Mason nodded. They'd spent twenty minutes talking in circles with Nico Cavallo. Nico was the second son they'd tracked down. The first son was still too ill to talk with police, according to his wife-of-few-words. Flu, she'd claimed. At least they'd actually proved that the man existed. Instead of sending over a uniform to check, Ray and Mason had decided to pop in themselves. A quiet woman had shown them a feverish man.

She'd given Mason the creeps, rarely making eye contact. A lot of people were intimidated by the badge, but this woman appeared to be cowed by humans in general. She'd given them the address of another son. Mason asked her to call ahead and inform Nico that two detectives would like to discuss his father's murder. Her eyes had widened, fear crossing her face.

It'd been a look that'd haunted Mason for the last hour. "Do you think she was scared of calling her brother-in-law? Scared of telling him she'd given his address to us? Or was it the mention of murder?" he'd asked Ray as they dashed down her walkway to Ray's vehicle.

"She knew he was murdered. That wasn't news. I gotta think it's something about the brother-in-law."

Nico Cavallo was his father's clone from twenty years before. He had the same coloring, mannerisms, and proud speech. He'd greeted the detectives at his door and led them into a formal but severely dated living room of orange and green. Ray and Mason had sat politely and accepted his offer of tea.

Then Nico had cordially rebuffed every question they'd asked about his father.

Mason thought the guy should be in politics. Their inquiries were answered with questions.

Nico's primary concern was the company cleaning his father's home. That was it. He showed no interest in helping them discover who'd murdered his father. He wanted to know when the cleaners would be finished and when the house would be released.

"It's the site of a murder," Ray had spit out, shock on his face.

"Well, we still need to get it on the market. Do prospective buyers have to be informed someone was killed there? That would affect the home's value." Nico took a careful sip of his tea.

Mason was stunned. *What was wrong with this family?*

"Uh . . . that might be part of disclosure laws. You'll have to ask your Realtor," Ray answered helpfully. "Now, about your father—"

Nico waved a hand at him. "I haven't talked to my father in years."

"You live in the same city. Surely you had some family gatherings or heard about him from your brothers." Mason ached for any sign that this family gave a rat's ass about the murdered Lorenzo.

Nico gave a casual shrug. "My wife would go clean his house occasionally. She hasn't gone for a while. She didn't care for him."

Judging by the state of Lorenzo's house during the murder scene, Nico's wife hadn't been there in several years. "Can we speak to your wife?" he asked.

"No, she doesn't have anything to tell you."

Mason looked at Ray. Ray stared back. *What the hell?*

"I'd like to hear from her that she has nothing to tell us," Mason said politely, gritting his teeth. Nico Cavallo was as much of a dinosaur as his father. People called Mason old-fashioned sometimes, but at least he pretended to live in this century.

"She has nothing to say," Nico stated. He met Mason's gaze over his teacup, his eyes calm. "Now, how long before the home can be put on the market?"

Ray scooted forward on his chair, leaning conversationally toward Nico and clearing his throat.

Good luck, Ray.

"Mr. Cavallo," Ray began. "I don't think you realize why we're here. We're not here to help plan your future; we're here to find out who killed your father. Anything you can tell us about your father's social circle or daily interactions would be very helpful. I hate to think that there's a murderer wandering around this city, possibly interested in your family."

Mason watched Nico carefully. The man hadn't flinched during Ray's plea, but his eyes had narrowed slightly at the mention of his family.

"My family will be fine. I seriously doubt someone would target me. Why would they?" he replied stiffly.

Ray jumped on the question. "You're not worried? This doesn't read like a random attack. There was nothing stolen from your father's house. Robbery probably wasn't the motive. It felt very personal to me. Why would that be?"

"I don't know. Isn't that your job to find the answers? I already told you I didn't keep in touch with my father. I don't know what he's been doing for the last ten years."

"When he came in and talked to us, he mentioned his sons several times. I saw a proud father. He said nothing of being estranged from his family. Why did you shun him for the last ten years?" Ray pushed.

"You're asking personal questions. Things that have nothing to do with his death."

Ray waited. Nico's teacup rattled as he set it back in its saucer.

"We didn't get along," Nico added. He clamped his mouth shut and turned his gaze to Mason, his message clear. He was done talking to the police. He stood. "I'm sorry I haven't been of more help to you, detectives. But I can't tell you what I don't know."

Mason and Ray slowly stood, the interview clearly over.

Outside Nico's home, Ray had commented, "He's lying. He has a good hunch why his father was killed."

Mason had completely agreed.

Sipping on his coffee at Starbucks, Mason let his mind sift through the interview. "I wish his wife had come in. I could hear someone clinking dishes in the kitchen. I assume that was her."

Ray leaned back in his chair, stretching out long legs. "I wanted to pound on his face because of his attitude about her input."

"Sounded just like his father," commented Mason. "Apparently they'd been close enough at one point, so he could hand down his asshole views on women."

"I don't get how attitudes like that survive today. Don't people watch TV? Don't they interact with their community? Especially here in Portland. I mean, this is where changes in America's behaviors begin, right? Portland always has it first, whether it's the newest foodie trend or social behavior. Doesn't mean it's guaranteed to catch on. But you can't live here without being exposed to new shit." Ray looked perplexed.

"Succinctly put," Mason agreed. "Portland is where new shit is shoved in the face of the mainstream. But there are always pockets of people who don't like change." *Like me.* "Takes a while for stuff to catch on."

"But surely no one believes that whole 'Me Tarzan, you Jane' crap. We've come further than that, right?"

"Are you listening to yourself?" Mason wanted to smack him in the head. Ray talked about the way he wanted the world to behave, not how it did. "How many battered women do our people deal with every day? How much domestic abuse? I think communities try to fool themselves that we've moved beyond that, but the fact is *it's still there.* Every fucking day. And maybe the Cavallos don't beat on their women, but they sure as hell beat them down in other ways."

Mason slipped out of his coat, feeling overly warm. "How'd we end up with this family where the women are second-class citizens? At first I wrote it off as Lorenzo's old-time culture, but damn it, it was handed down to his kids, who've trained their wives to hide and not speak to strangers. It's like they were brought up in another country. I don't fucking get it."

Ray stared glumly at his latte.

Mason knew he hadn't burst any bubble for Ray. He'd simply brought him back to earth. "All we can do is teach our kids to treat people well." Mason stepped off his soapbox and scorched his tongue with a big sip of coffee. The pain felt good.

"And catch the assholes who abuse," Ray added.

"Damn right."

They drank in silence, looking out the window as water streamed down the glass in rivers. Puddles littered the parking lot. Not puddles, lakes. Mason eyed the hundred-foot-tall firs waving in the wind. According to the latest forecast, they were in for strong winds over the next two days. He'd rolled his barbecue into his garage before leaving for work that morning. He didn't want the wind to turn it into a missile to blast through his glass slider to the deck.

But the biggest risk to the city and homes was the firs. Portland was thoroughly soaked. A strong windstorm after heavy rains was a recipe for disaster. Trees would topple everywhere, taking out power lines and putting fresh skylights in houses. He'd avoided buying a home with firs on the property. He'd already experienced a fir taking out the fence at his previous house. If the wind had blown a different direction, his son's nursery would have been toast.

A chair scraped the floor and Michael Brody sat down at their table. The tall man brushed at his sleeve, sending a fine spray of water over their coffee.

"Watch it." Mason made a show of wiping his coffee lid off with a napkin. He'd been watching the parking lot. How had he missed the reporter's entrance?

"Brody," Ray greeted him with a toothy smile. He liked the pushy reporter. Mason simply tolerated the man. He respected Brody because he knew how to get shit done, but he found the reporter's laid-back view of privacy and basic law to be grating. He waited impatiently while Ray and Brody discussed the acidity and flavor of the coffee of the day.

It's coffee! Just drink it!

Michael turned sharp green eyes on Mason as if he'd heard his thought. "Where are you at with identifying the three women from the old Forest Park killings?"

No pleasantries for me?

Mason appreciated the reporter's directness. Brody knew better than to discuss off-topic crap with him. Ray was the one for that stuff. In an abrupt moment of clarity, Mason realized that the reporter had a powerful gift of reading people. Mason had worked for years on his skills; it was a tool that came in handy when dealing with suspects. Not for the first time, he cursed the reporter for not putting his skills where they could be utilized. Like at any police department in the state. Brody preferred to use them for his own devices.

Mason sipped his coffee, considering his words. Discussions with Brody called for discretion. "You asking because you care, or because you're writing something?"

Brody didn't blink. "This is for me. The old deaths are clearly tied to the new deaths, and the new deaths are tied to shots fired at the service I was at yesterday. I'm not cool with that."

Who is?

"We've identified one, well, she's ninety-nine percent identified. Her brother came forward with an inquiry that put us on the right track. Then he was murdered."

Mason was rewarded as Brody's eyes widened slightly.

"The Italian guy in southeast Portland?"

Did he just pull that out of his ass? What the hell? The reporter had an uncanny knack for putting two and two together. "That's the one," Mason admitted, fighting the urge to sulk.

Brody held his gaze for a long moment. Mason could nearly hear the gears spinning in his mind. "You know Victoria Peres asked me to help find her birth parents."

Mason nodded.

"Her adoption was arranged by a church on the coast. This church placed quite a few babies back then. But it burned down about twenty-five years ago. At the time the property was owned by Lorenzo Cavallo. He was next on my research list when I found out this morning he'd been murdered yesterday after talking to you guys about the case. I didn't know he'd offered information about a missing sister."

"He ran the church?" Ray asked.

"No, just owned the land. He sold it ten years later. There's a small strip mall in its place that struggles to hold tenants."

"What else do you know about that old church?" Mason asked.

Brody leaned on their table, his gaze moving between Mason and Ray. "I'm not finding much. Old articles paint it as a small unique congregation. No denomination affiliation."

"It has to belong to some branch of faith," argued Ray.

Brody nodded. "You'd think so. It sounds like it was created more from a community of people who followed their pastor. I guess you'd call him a pastor. In my honest opinion, it's got cult written all over it. A cult masquerading as a church. Everything seems to circle around one man."

"Lorenzo Cavallo?" Ray asked.

Brody shook his head. "No, I think he was a member. Probably bought the land for the church. The pastor was a Cesare Abbadelli."

"Italian?" Mason asked. *Like Lorenzo Cavallo?*

"Sounds like it," agreed Brody.

"The priest," said Ray. "The little priest."

Brody and Mason stared at him.

"That's what Abbadelli means. Hey, Jillian's grandfather was Italian. Don't look at me like that." He frowned and took a sip of his coffee.

"And Cesare is a form of Caesar, right?" added Mason. "That's a powerful name. Priest and Caesar all rolled into one. This guy still alive?"

"I don't know yet."

Mason was surprised to hear the reporter say those words. And he didn't look frustrated or embarrassed. Lesser men would have talked around it or bluffed their way through the question. His estimation went up a notch.

Ray was making careful notes on his pad. "I'll look into it, too."

"I haven't told you the fun part." Brody grinned.

Ray's head lifted. "What?"

"Victoria got an anonymous note this morning with the name of a woman the sender claimed was her birth mother."

Mason stared at the reporter, wondering if he was pulling his leg.

"Seriously?" asked Ray.

"Yep. Seth called me, asking me to check out the name and address. I gotta say, from what I could see on the driver's license, the woman could be related. *And* she had a previous address in Seaport. One we were just talking about."

Mason's brain couldn't keep up. "That address for that church? The woman lived at the church?"

"Who knows? But she was out there close to the time when Victoria was born," answered Brody.

"But why?" asked Ray. "Why tell Victoria in an anonymous note? What's the motive to do that?"

"That's the million-dollar question. Victoria and Seth were going to take a drive out to this woman's Portland address this morning. I haven't heard how it went."

"That's crazy. Why did someone contact her out of the blue like that?" Mason asked.

"Maybe I stirred something up with my questions." Brody frowned. "I don't see what I could have done, but the timing is pretty coincidental."

"You find the father yet?" asked Ray.

"Next on my list," replied Brody. "I'm waiting for a phone call any minute."

Mason stood and picked up his cowboy hat from the chair next to him. He held his hand out to Brody. "You gonna go dig under some more rocks?"

Brody rose to his feet, shaking Mason's hand. "My favorite pastime."

Mason's phone rang. "Callahan."

"Detective Callahan, this is Katy Morris. Trinity Viders's foster mom."

Surprise shot through Mason. "Yes, Ms. Morris, I've left you a few messages, we'd like to talk with Trinity—"

"This is about Trinity. She left early this morning and I can't reach her. Her cell phone is off."

"Now, Ms. Morris—" Mason started.

"I know, detective," Katy said shortly. "It hasn't been long. But this isn't like Trinity. She borrowed my car, saying she would only be a few hours, and now it's late afternoon. After the shooting yesterday, my panic monitor is in high gear. *Something is wrong.*"

"Did she say where she was going?"

"She said she had to pick up a friend who needed a ride. I didn't pry." Her voice cracked. "She's a good kid, detective. She has boundaries and she sticks to them. Something must have happened."

"You've called her friends?" Mason sympathized for the woman, but there wasn't a heck of a lot he could legally do at the moment.

"Yes. All of them. No one has heard from her."

"I'll see what I can do. Give me your plate number and a description of your car." He scribbled on a table napkin as Katy spoke. Ray turned it to read it, already dialing his cell phone to get the word out. "What about a boyfriend? She seeing anybody? Did you call him?"

There was a short pause. "She doesn't have a boyfriend," said Katy.

She didn't sound convinced.

"Maybe you better give her girlfriends another call and press harder about the boy issue. I could see them trying to cover for her if you're not supposed to know about a boy."

Ray nodded emphatically. *The guru of female teen behavior.*

Mason ended the call. The woman's worry had triggered acid to irritate his stomach. He treated it with a last sip of cold Starbucks coffee. His burn intensified.

"I don't like this," Brody stated. He'd listened to Mason's side of the conversation with his feet spread apart and his arms across his chest. His scowl had intensified with every second. "That girl seemed responsible to me."

Mason raised an eyebrow. "Big words from a man without kids. We're talking about teenage girls. There are no rules."

His ear to his phone, Ray nodded again, pointing at Mason, agreeing.

"Either way," said Mason. "I've added Trinity Viders to my list for the day. I want to know where she is."

CHAPTER TWENTY-SIX

"Turn here," Jason stated, squinting through the windshield. He pointed to her left.

Trinity slowed the car, looking for a turnoff, her nose nearly touching the top of the steering wheel. Their current road had steadily deteriorated. It was more gravel than blacktop. Hell, it was more mud than blacktop. She didn't know if they'd officially passed out of the state forest, but it didn't matter. The skyscraping firs still blocked the sky.

They'd headed west on Highway 26 toward the coast, driven up and over the mountain range, but then turned off after the highway had almost returned to sea level. According to a highway sign, they'd summited the range at sixteen hundred feet, but the mountains rose up higher around the road. It wasn't much of a highway; a lot of the time the road was two lanes. Thankfully there'd been almost no traffic.

The other drivers were smart, Trinity admitted. Who would be on the road in this wet mess? She expected to see an ark float by at any minute. Yesterday, there'd been mudslides in the West Hills of Portland and in one of the coastal communities, moving homes and wrecking barns. The rain showed no sign of letting up, smashing records for the month. Wind whipped the firs lining the roads, scattering forest debris.

She'd said a prayer as she drove through a tunnel on the highway. The tunnel had been dedicated to a highway worker who died years back when part of the tunnel roof collapsed as he inspected it for water damage. She'd whispered one prayer for his soul and one for her safe passage. Today she'd fought the urge to close her eyes as she drove through; not a good idea.

She spotted the turn, marked by a tiny street sign, and carefully guided the car through the ruts. "This is crazy. How much farther is it?"

"Not too far."

"You've been saying that since we left."

"It just seems longer because you have to drive so slow."

Trinity bit her tongue. Damn right she was going slow. She was terrified that one of the ruts would be deeper than it looked. The road was nearly all standing water. It was hard to see. Rain pounded the roof of the car, huge drops falling from the firs. She could barely hear Jason's words.

Why had she agreed to drive him to his grandfather's? Katy was going to have a fit when she saw the dirty car. Maybe the rain would wash it off by the time she got home. She glanced at the clock in the dash. She hadn't checked in with Katy since that morning. The time with Jason had flown by, and she'd totally spaced on her responsibility.

"Would you look at my phone in my purse? See if Katy's called me?" she asked Jason.

He turned and snagged her purse from the backseat, and then gingerly poked through it until he pulled out her cell. He pressed the screen a few times and frowned. "Your phone's dead. Do you have a car charger?"

"No, it's in the other car." *Crap. Katy was going to have her head.* "Can I use your phone to call her when we get there?"

"Yeah. Not a problem." He set her purse in the backseat.

"She's going to kill me," she muttered.

"You didn't tell her where you were going?" he asked.

"No. And usually I'm not gone this long. Not without checking in, anyway."

"My dad doesn't care where I go, let alone if I check in," he said.

Trinity studied him out of the corner of her eye. Jason's face was glum. She'd felt like that before. Where no one cared what the hell happened to you. Katy's rules had taken a bit of getting used to, but Trinity realized it felt good to have someone give a rip about where you were. "If you didn't show up one night, he'd worry."

Jason looked out his side window. She saw his jaw move.

"I can't hear you."

He turned. "I said I wasn't sure of that."

"He's your dad. Of course he cares what happens to you. What about your mom?"

"My mom left years ago. She divorced my dad and left when I was five. I don't really remember her. She lives in Idaho now. She remarried."

"Right, you told me that. She doesn't keep in touch?" Trinity was prying, but her curiosity was piqued.

Jason shrugged. "I get a birthday card. But my dad always opens them and reads them first. He says he doesn't want her telling me any lies about him. " He paused. "I've seen him take letters before. Letters that were addressed to me. When I asked for them, he said he read them first and they were full of lies. That she was trying to turn me against him."

Trinity struggled to understand. "I don't get it. What could she say that would make a difference? She's the one who left, right?"

Jason wiped at his nose and shifted in his seat. "Kyle's mom left, too."

"Kyle with the gun?"

"Yeah, I told you we'd kinda grown up together. Our parents hung out together. Kyle's mom left about two years ago. He's always been really angry with her about it."

Trinity didn't know what to say. Kyle plainly needed therapy. Did his father not see it? "Kyle needs help."

"Yeah, but that's not allowed."

"What?" She pulled her gaze from the swamped road to actually look right at him. "What's that mean?"

Jason squirmed. "Grandpa doesn't think he needs it."

"What does your grandfather have to do with Kyle?"

Jason was silent, and Trinity focused on the road. *That's not allowed.* It reminded her of when he'd said "they punish." What kind of family had Jason grown up in? "You said Kyle wasn't family, right?"

"Not really. We sorta belonged to the same church. But I don't go anymore. At least I try not to. My grandfather runs the whole thing. It's hard to say I don't belong to his church, because I feel like I'm denying he's my grandfather."

Her brows shot up. It was most Jason had ever said about his family. Everything else had come in bits and pieces. Now it was making a bit more sense. "What church is it?"

"Nothing you'd ever heard of. It's small. And it's gotten smaller over the years. Now it just feels like a bunch of men who get together to talk about the old days."

"What do the women do?"

"They don't usually meet with them. The women sorta do their own thing."

"Well, that sounds archaic."

Jason nodded emphatically. "It is. All their attitudes about women are straight out of the Dark Ages."

"Seriously? There're still groups around that support that crap?"

"I think it's one of the reasons my mom left."

Trinity could barely hear him over the pounding rain. "And it would explain why your dad feels he has the right to restrict conversations between the two of you. Wow. I can't imagine being married to someone who was that high-handed." She looked at Jason, wondering if he'd ever talked to anyone else about his mom.

He abruptly grabbed the steering wheel, terror filling his face. "*Watch out!*"

She spun her gaze back to the road, her hands clenching the wheel as she hit the brakes. The road had vanished. A river flowed where the road had been a moment ago.

It was too late.

The car lifted and shuddered, moving to the left. She stomped on the brake, steering right. The car gently sank a few inches and jolted as her tires touched bottom. She hit the gas, praying she had traction. Twenty feet ahead, she could see the outline of the road.

The engine raced and then abruptly stopped.

Water in the engine.

The car jerked and swayed, the water lifting and pushing it to the left again. The water rushed around the car. Jason shouted, but she didn't understand. She turned the key.

Nothing happened.

"*It won't start!*"

Cold water touched her feet. She gasped, lifting them. She could barely see the water that flowed into the car from under her door.

"Holy crap!" Jason scrambled in his seat, lifting his feet. He turned to his door, yanking on the door handle. It wouldn't open.

A small part of her brain acknowledged that the water outside the vehicle kept the door from opening. She peered out her door window. The water wasn't high; it was just over the bottom of the door, enough to get water into the car and keep the doors from opening easily. The rear end of the car started to shift, turning the car to face the water.

Should she roll down the window?

"Should we crawl out?" she shouted at Jason. His eyes were wide in panic as he met her gaze. He couldn't speak.

Frustration shot through her, muting some of her own panic. Jason wasn't going to rescue them. She squinted through the windshield. It wasn't too far to dry land. But how strong was the current? Should they get out or stay in the vehicle?

"Was there a river here?" she yelled.

"No. There's never been water here," he hollered back.

She felt a bit better, knowing they weren't in the middle of a riverbed. Somewhere there'd simply been too much buildup of rain, and it'd followed the path of least resistance. And it'd found her car.

The vehicle rocked sharply, spinning ninety degrees.

Trinity shrieked.

CHAPTER TWENTY-SEVEN

Victoria watched Katy end her call.

"What happened? Where's Trinity?" Victoria glanced at the clock on Katy's microwave. Almost 4 P.M. "Was that the police?" She placed her briefcase on the kitchen desk as she slipped out of her wet coat. She'd managed to get an hour of work in at the office after her hotel break with Seth. She'd returned to Katy's to grab her things and go back to Seth's hotel. She was tired and ready for a quiet evening watching TV from the bed with Seth.

Katy jumped, clearly unaware Victoria had entered the kitchen during the conversation. She turned teary eyes Victoria's way.

"I don't know. This isn't like her. She always calls when she's going to be late, but she's been gone all day, and I can't reach her. That was the police. I called Detective Callahan."

"Good." Victoria slid into a chair at the kitchen table next to Katy. She gripped one of the woman's hands, holding her gaze. "She's going to be okay. Her phone's probably dead and maybe she's having some car issues."

"But she hasn't called. She always calls when she's gone this long," Katy repeated. "Surely she could ask someone to use a cell phone." Her eyes were red-rimmed. "After all the crap she's been through in the last week, I don't like this. Something is wrong."

"I heard you say she doesn't have a boyfriend. Are you sure that's true?"

The woman snorted. "I can't say what's true anymore. You were a teenage girl once. Did you always tell your parents the truth?" Victoria saw her eyes shadow a bit as she recalled Victoria's circumstance with her parents.

"Actually, I almost always did. But I've learned I was an exception to that teen girl rule," she said slowly. "You know, Trinity asked me some odd questions about a friend this morning." She thought hard to remember the conversation. "And it was a boy she was asking me about."

Katy studied her. "She's said nothing to me about a boy."

Victoria had a small sting of guilt. "I think I was in the right place at the right time. If you'd been in the room, no doubt she would have asked you. Anyway, she said he'd asked her to do something, and she wasn't comfortable."

Katy sat up straighter, her hand stiffening in Victoria's. "What did he ask her to do?" Panic rang in her tone.

"No! Nothing sexual. Not like that. I didn't get that vibe from the conversation at all." She crinkled her nose in thought, looking out the window. "It had to do with his parents. He was trying to avoid them and asked her for help. She'd told me she didn't know him that well."

"Then why did he ask her?"

"That's what I asked her. I told her he must have closer friends he could ask. She did say he was worried about some sort of punishment from his parents."

Katy didn't relax. "How horrible to put that sort of guilty request on her. But I don't think she took your advice. She gave someone a ride this morning, and I've talked to all her girlfriends. None of them have heard from her."

"Maybe the thing to ask them is if she has a new boyfriend or has been talking about a boy."

"That's what Detective Callahan said, too," Katy admitted. "But I'm afraid she's in trouble." She looked at the kitchen window. "This rain has been insane. There's flooding all over the place. Maybe she got stranded." Her voice lowered. "What if someone took her somewhere? What if whoever she gave a ride to had different ideas?"

The door between the garage and kitchen opened. Seth entered, stomping his wet shoes on her large mat. "Katy, you had a street drain clogged out front. I managed to move the debris with a branch. The thing was packed with leaves. That lake out there should vanish in a minute." He looked up, his gaze flickering from the women's grasped hands to their faces. "What's happened?"

"Trinity's missing. No one's seen her since this morning and her phone is either off or dead," Victoria stated.

His eyes filled with concern, and he shrugged out of his wet coat. "You've talked to her friends?"

Katy patiently updated him. His frown grew deeper as he listened.

"This isn't right." He squeezed Katy's shoulder, holding her gaze. "We'll find her."

Victoria's heart melted. *He's a good man.*

"I'm freaking out," said Katy, her eyes wide. "What if the same person who killed those girls got Trinity? She told the police Brooke was with a photographer. What if he decided Trinity saw or knows too much about him? What if this person contacted her for a ride?" Hysteria elevated her tone.

Victoria bit her lip. Why hadn't she asked Trinity more questions this morning instead of giving advice? Police had theorized a man had used the photography cover to recruit the girls. What if Trinity had fallen for a similar ploy?

Katy stood. "I'm going to go call her friends again. God help them if I find out one of them is hiding Trinity's relationship with a boy or knows more about this photographer. They better understand how serious this is." She left the room.

"This isn't good," Seth said. He pulled Victoria out of her chair and into his arms in a deep hug, kissing her forehead. "God, I'm glad my Eden made it home safe and sound. And I'm thankful I was blissfully unaware she was missing for a few hours when her mom couldn't reach her. I would have been sick with worry. Exactly how Katy is feeling right now."

"I'm worried," Victoria whispered into his neck. "I'm afraid she might have done something stupid, trying to help this friend. What if it wasn't a friend? What if Katy is right that someone is upset with what she told the police?"

Her cell phone vibrated inside her big bag. She reluctantly pulled out of Seth's arms to address it. An unfamiliar number showed on her screen. *Trinity?*

"Hello?"

"Ms. Peres?" An old man's voice came through her cell. "My name is Cecil Adams. A reporter contacted me, saying he was helping you search for your birth parents."

Victoria's heart jumped. "Yes. Michael Brody is helping me."

"That was his name. He called me asking about some records of the Leader's Way church. He was wondering if any of the records still existed from when they used to organize adoptions."

"Yes. I knew mine was through the Leader's Way church from the coast." Her parents had continued to attend until she was nearly ten. Her memories were faint.

"Well, I've kept a lot of things. You're not the first to come searching for adoption records over the years. I've helped out a few times."

Victoria exhaled. *Would he have a record of her parents' names? Would Isabel Favero be on it?*

"Are you the pastor?"

Seth was watching her conversation closely. She covered the phone with her hand. "Michael found someone with the church records," she whispered. His eyes lit up and she tilted the phone away from her ear so he could hear the other half of the conversation.

"Oh, no. He passed away a while back. The records have been stored in my barn since the fire destroyed the original building twenty-five years ago."

"They've been in a barn that long? Are they legible?" Images of water damage and mold crept into her mind. She remembered the church had burned soon after her parents had left.

"Oh, yes. It's dry and the containers are waterproof. Last time I dug through them was about six months ago. Everything looked good."

"Do you think you could go look for—"

"I can't get up the ladder these days," Cecil cut her off. "I've got a bit of a bad leg. You'd have to do the looking yourself. Or get someone to bring them down for you. Sorry about that."

Victoria paused, her mind racing. She and Seth could easily handle it. Seth met her gaze, reading her mind, and nodded.

"Are you available tomorrow? We could come out in the morning," she said.

"Oh, that's too bad." Disappointment rang in his voice. "I'm flying out at the crack of dawn tomorrow. But I'll be back in about two weeks if you want to set up a time for then."

Her heart fell through the floor. Could she wait two weeks?

"Ask him if we could come tonight," Seth whispered.

"Mr. Adams, what about this evening? Where are you located? I have someone I could bring with me tonight to take a quick look if that works for you."

"I'm about ten miles east of the coastline. Just over the Coast Range on Highway 26."

Victoria did some quick calculations. "We could probably be there in about forty minutes."

"Are you sure you want to come out in this weather? It's pretty stormy tonight," Cecil spoke slower, a bit of hesitation and regret in his voice.

"You don't even have to leave the house," Victoria said rapidly. "Just point us in the right direction." Right now she didn't care if they were imposing; she wanted a look at those records tonight.

"Now, you realize these aren't legal documents, right?" Cecil said. "These are just some simple church ledgers. But it's probably enough to give you some leads on your birth parents."

Would something in there name her mother? What about a father? There was no guarantee that her answers were in a box in someone's barn. But she'd never know until she looked. "We'd really like to come out tonight, Mr. Adams."

He gave her his address and Victoria promised to see him within the hour. She ended the call, adrenaline buzzing through her veins.

"What about Trinity?" Seth asked. "Are you okay leaving Katy right now?"

"All I'd be able to do is hold Katy's hand. I think all three of us know that won't do a heck of a lot."

"What's going on?" Katy asked as she stepped back in the room.

"We've got a lead on some church records that might list my birth parents," Victoria told her. "We're going to run out there tonight if you're okay with that. Otherwise we can't see the records for two weeks."

"Of course," answered Katy. "Sitting here doing nothing isn't helping Trinity. I'm doing enough sitting around waiting for the phone to ring. All of us don't need to participate. I've got more calls to make, and I know how to reach you if I need to."

"That's what I thought. We're going to meet a guy from Leader's Way church and see what he has."

"Leader's Way?" Katy's brows shot up. "That was the church? Those guys?"

Seth scowled. "You know them?"

"I've met some of the castoffs. Women seem to have a third-class citizen role in that organization."

"I thought the church no longer existed. It burned down quite a while back," Victoria stated.

"The building may have been gone, but the teachings lived on. What a bunch of pigs. They don't care for me. I've held a few women's hands as they made the decision to break ties with their families because of the belief system of that church. I have a hard time calling it a church. It's more of a bunch of old men sitting around telling women to stay barefoot and pregnant."

"I think that's one of the reasons my parents left," Victoria said slowly. "I remember hearing them discuss what the role of a woman should be. My mother wanted me to be more. I think things had started to change in the church back then. It'd suddenly gotten stricter. They moved closer to Portland and never went back."

"Sounds like they made a good move," said Seth. "I can't see you growing up in an environment like that."

"Me neither." Victoria straightened her back and squeezed Seth's hand. "Let's go. I want to look in that guy's barn."

CHAPTER TWENTY-EIGHT

Victoria was thankful for her SUV as she blew past an eighteen-wheeler. The spray from the truck's tires would have blinded the driver of a lower-sitting car. Her wipers sped up to double time to rid her windshield of the truck's moisture. Her vehicle's tires grabbed the road, breaking through the moving layer of water that coated its surface. Her GPS indicated they were close to the turnoff.

"I didn't know the roads were going to be this bad when I begged him to let us come out tonight," she muttered to Seth.

"Let's just get it done. One less thing to think about. You don't want to spend the next two weeks wondering what might be in Cecil Adams's barn, do you?"

"No," she admitted. She slowed and turned off the highway. "Jesus Christ, it's dark."

Her vehicle bumped along the rough road. She clenched the wheel and put her faith in German engineering.

"I'm glad we didn't take my rental." Seth grabbed at the handle above his head as the SUV rocked. "Mine wouldn't have managed this at all."

Victoria set her jaw and pushed forward. "This can't be right."

"According to the GPS, we turn again in another mile. Then it's not much farther along that road."

"Who lives out in the woods like this? This is nuts."

"People who like their privacy."

"I like my privacy. You don't see me abandoning society and living like a hermit."

"Maybe it just seems bad because it's dark and wet. I bet it's really nice out here during the summer."

"Hmph." Victoria's wipers sped up to double time again. She yanked at the wheel, avoiding a boulder. "Jesus. Did you see that? Where did that come from? It was right in the middle of the road."

"Maybe the water pushed it. Or it rolled down the hill." He bent over to look up the steep slope. It was a solid wall of ascending firs. "It could have come from up there. Everything is soaked. Look at all the debris in the road."

He was right. The road was a mess of tree branches and tiny streams shooting across the lane. All the rain was seeking the easiest way to the ocean level and pushing aside anything in its way. The dirt was beyond soaking in the rain. Instead, the water hit the ground and immediately searched for the lowest territory, creating lakes where there'd been meadows.

She followed the GPS's polite directions to take the next turn. And promptly wanted the conditions of the previous road.

"Whose idea was this?" she mumbled.

"Can we blame Brody?" asked Seth.

"I'll go with that."

She stood on the brakes and Seth lunged forward in his seat, his seatbelt keeping him from shooting through the windshield. "Look at that!" She pointed. She'd spotted the car up ahead and off to her left. The sedan was wedged against a group of ancient firs, water flowing over its tires. Water flooded the road before her, flowing down the hillside and streaming in the direction of the sedan. Something moved.

"Someone's inside!" Seth exclaimed.

Victoria backed up a fraction, turned her wheel, and moved forward, shining her headlights on the car. She caught her breath. "Is that Trinity's car?"

Seth opened his door.

"Wait. You can't go out in that!" She grabbed at his arm and looked back at the car. Hands and a face pressed against the glass of the passenger side window. The window started to lower and she could see a male teen. Trinity's face appeared over his shoulder, both kids waving at the headlights.

Shock rocked through Victoria, but then she breathed a sigh of relief. "That's her. I don't think that car is going anywhere. It's stuck against those trees. We've got to call Katy."

"You call her. I'll figure out how to get them out of that water."

Seth stepped out into the downpour, peering at the car. Trinity drove an older sedan. The kids looked like they were okay but scared. Victoria was right that they weren't going anywhere. He guessed the water had lifted them off the road and carried them twenty feet into a mass of tree trunks. He looked up. The trees swayed in the growing winds. *How firmly were they rooted?* He didn't want to think what would happen if the trees toppled.

Why in hell was Trinity way out here?

Water soaked through his shoes. He wasn't standing in the mini-river that had moved Trinity's car, but by Victoria's vehicle it was at least three inches deep. The road dipped slightly where the water rushed across the choppy blacktop, acting as a funnel for all the rain landing in the steep thousand feet of elevation to his right. The rushing water looked about eighteen inches deep. *Why had she tried to cross?*

She probably hadn't seen it. Even Victoria had to stand on the brakes to keep from driving into the water. He glanced at her SUV. It could probably cross safely. He waved at the kids. There was no way they could hear him over the rush of the water. He gave a thumbs-up and a hang-on gesture and then ducked back in Victoria's SUV.

"I think it's raining harder up here than back in the city," he said.

"The Coast Range always gets an insane amount of rain. Floods the coastal towns and highways with its runoff." She was tapping her cell. "I got Katy's voice mail. I don't know if she's on the phone or what. But I told her we found Trinity and she's okay. Cell reception is horrible. I had to try three times to get the call to go through." She glanced at him and her expression hardened. "That bad?"

"I don't know how we're going to get them out. The water is fast, and I can't tell how deep it is in spots."

"I called nine-one-one and reported it too. I told them there's a car trapped in the water. They'll send a fire truck with heavy rescue equipment."

"Christ, I hope they can find us."

"They locked on to my signal. She said she could tell where I was."

"Good. Thank God for modern technology."

"Yes, except I was cut off. I've tried to call back and can't get reception."

"Shit. Think they got our location clear enough?"

She took a deep breath. "I think so." She set her phone on the console.

He took her hand, squeezing it tight as he studied the kids in the car. They'd rolled up their window partway, but he could see two sets of eyes pointed in their direction. They were scared to death. "How much water do you think is in their car?"

She was staring too. "I don't know. It's getting higher, isn't it? We've got to do something."

"Do you have any rope? Or anything like that in here?"

"Yes." Her eyes lit up, and she opened her car door.

Seth hopped out and went to the back of the SUV, where she'd lifted the hatch, covering them from the pounding drops. Next to her boat paddle and life jacket, she had a coil of yellow synthetic rope. She tugged on a length. "It's strong. Do you think it's long enough?"

Seth took the rope. "This'll work. I'll take a look at the front."

He moved into the blinding headlights and kneeled, looking for something to anchor the rope. "Perfect," he muttered, spotting a thick metal loop that screamed for a rope to be hooked through it. He brushed the water out of his eyes and ran the rope through the loop, yanking with his body weight to test its strength. He knotted it and stood, turning to check the kids. The water was higher on the sedan's door. "Shit." Victoria watched him from the driver's seat. He moved to her lowered window. "Can you get closer?"

She nodded and inched her vehicle forward. Seth watched her front tires move into the deeper water. The rain splattered through her window, her knuckles white on the steering wheel. "I'll go a little closer," she said.

"Let me see how far this gets me first." Seth looped the rope around his waist and secured it. He turned to move into the water. Reaching out, Victoria grabbed his arm.

"Be careful." Her eyes were huge.

"I will." He held her gaze. "Back up if you see me go under. That water is fast. I don't want to be slammed into the trees. And keep trying to reach nine-one-one again."

She nodded, her lips pressed together.

Seth stepped into the water, and it soaked his ankles. *Fuck, that is cold.* He pushed deeper to mid-shin, his focus on the sedan, his brain shrieking at the icy temperature. How could water feel colder than ice? The rush of the water was steady but not impossible to navigate. He felt for every foothold before shifting his weight into that step.

The ground shifted from underneath his shoe as he stepped off the road and into the softer dirt. He flung out his arms for balance and the water moved above his knee.

That was close. He didn't look behind him for Tori's reaction. He could feel her gaze boring a hole in his back. The windows in the sedan were steaming up, but he saw two sets of wide eyes watching him through the barely opened window. *Maybe this wasn't the smartest idea. Should they wait for help?* The water was nearly lapping at the door handle. The sedan had ended up in a depression at the base of the trees, slightly lower than the roadway.

Fuck it. Going in.

He lunged through the final ten feet of water, letting the water propel him forward, and slammed against the passenger door. "Hey, guys!" The water rushed around his thighs. Trinity's face was wet from the rain. Or was that tears? "Ready to get out of here?" The boy rolled the window completely down.

"God, yes. Get her out first," the boy said. "Are you sure it's safe?"

Hell, no. "I'll tie her to me. I think we'll be okay."

Trinity crawled into a sitting position in the window of the door, her feet dangling over the side. Seth untied his rope and looped it around her waist, bracing his knees against the car door.

"There isn't enough to tie to you!" Trinity shouted over the roar of the water.

Seth already knew that. "I'll hang on tight."

"No, I'll go back then throw the rope to you. No one should go through that without it!"

"We'll be fine."

Trinity's expression showed she didn't believe him. But she slid down into the water, gasping at the temperature. She wasn't tall. The cold water was nearly to her crotch. Seth gripped the rope with both hands, refusing to look at Tori. She would be throwing a fit that he wasn't tied. "Follow me." He pressed forward, angling for the side of the runoff river. Every step felt like he pushed through deep mud. He tightened up the rope and pulled himself forward. Trinity grabbed at the back of his belt, and he wavered. He caught his balance and plowed ahead, each step getting shallower.

They reached the SUV and Victoria jumped out, ripping the rope off Trinity. "Are you okay?"

The girl's teeth chattered in answer, but she nodded. Seth's teeth were chattering, too. With numb hands, he tried to tie the rope around his waist again. He felt like he'd run a marathon.

"Just throw him the rope," Victoria suggested. "He's a big kid. He can tie a knot."

Seth looked at the kid. He was already outside the car in the water, hanging on to the door for balance as the water rushed around his lower thighs. He was a lot taller than Trinity. Victoria grabbed the rope out of Seth's hands and flung it in the kid's direction. The rope landed in the water and was instantly swept into the teen's hands.

"Jason! Be careful!" Trinity shouted, cupping her mouth. Jason looked up and nodded, rapidly tying the rope around his waist.

Seth watched him. *Knot it again.* He gestured for Jason to tie it better, but the teen wasn't looking at him. He let go of the car and moved forward. Shock crossed Jason's face as he realized how difficult it was to push against the current. He tightened his grip on the rope and pulled, his legs slowly moving through the fast water.

Victoria climbed back in the driver's seat, her gaze locked on Jason. Trinity clasped her hands together below her chin, shivering. Seth grabbed the rope at the SUV, pulling the boy closer.

Jason wobbled, lost his balance, and fell. The rope was yanked out of Seth's hands. Jason vanished under the water, but his head bobbed up, mouth gasping for air. The water pushed up into his face as it streamed past him.

"Stand back!" Victoria shouted. Seth and Trinity jumped out of the way as she backed up the vehicle. The water formed a wake around Jason as Victoria dragged him into shallow water. Seth pulled him up out of the cold, shivering and sputtering.

"I tripped." Jason spit out a mouthful of water.

"We noticed," Seth said as he inspected the teen. His jeans were ripped at the knees and fresh blood flowed, but he didn't seem too hurt.

"Are you okay?" Trinity untied the rope with shaking hands. "You're bleeding."

Jason looked at his knees. "I can't even feel it."

"We need to get him to a hospital," Victoria announced. She pulled off his wet coat. "Take off your shirt." She shed her thick jacket and held it out to him. Jason stripped to his bare chest and pulled on her jacket. The teen shivered violently.

"I don't need a hospital," he argued. "I'm just wet." He inspected a knee. "These are scrapes, nothing bad. My grandfather lives a hundred yards away. I can dry off there and get warm."

"How far is the closest hospital?" Seth asked.

Victoria shrugged. "Back in town. There's probably an emergency care center in Seaside."

"I'm fine," Jason insisted through blue lips. "I just need to get dry and warmed up."

"Wait, your grandfather lives up the road?" Victoria asked.

"Yes, he was expecting us. That's where we were headed when her car got swept off the road," Jason added, rubbing his hands up and down his arms through Victoria's coat. Trinity nodded in agreement.

"Does he have an old barn?" Victoria questioned.

Jason's teeth rattled as he bobbed his head.

Seth couldn't feel his feet, and Jason had to be colder. The sooner they warmed up the better. "Sounds like we're headed to the same place. Let's go." He eyed the water level across the road. "I think we're good. This thing is a lot higher off the ground than Trinity's car. The deepest part is the hollow Trinity's car swept into. Stick to the opposite side of the road."

They piled into her SUV, and Seth cranked up the heat to full blast. Victoria slowly drove through the rushing water. Her vehicle's heavy weight keeping the tires securely on the road. Seth exhaled as they broke out of the water. "Christ. I don't want to ever swim again."

"Me neither," added Jason from the backseat. "You'll see my grandfather's place a ways up on the left."

"Anyone else live out here?" Seth asked. "This is really secluded."

"There're a few homes. You'd have to drive another mile or so."

"Over the river and through the woods," muttered Victoria. Seth snorted.

"There it is!" said Jason.

Seth spotted a faint light ahead on his left.

Please let the heat be working.

CHAPTER TWENTY-NINE

Mason was ready to leave the office and call it a day. Ray was on the phone, getting a grocery list from the wife for a stop on his way home. Mason knew he still had at least a dozen frozen dinners and pizzas in his freezer, so he had no need to stop at the grocery store. As long as he had something to put in the microwave and coffee for the morning, he was good. There'd been a time when he and his ex had discussed dinner plans every day and what to feed Jake. He didn't really miss it. Food should be uncomplicated, not requiring thought and planning. Sure, he was shoveling chemicals and processed crap into his body. But who wanted to live forever?

He'd passed on the description of Katy's car, but outside of recommending a BOLO, there wasn't a lot he could do. He was slipping his coat on when his desk phone rang.

"Callahan."

"Glad I caught you, detective," came the voice of the front desk sergeant. "There's a woman here asking to talk to you about the Lorenzo Cavallo case. Says he was her father-in-law."

Mason's ears perked up. Which daughter-in-law had finally come forward? "Send her up." He took his coat back off and draped it over the back of his chair, giving Ray a signal to wrap up his call.

Ray covered part of his cell. "What is it?"

"Got a Cavallo daughter-in-law who wants to talk."

Ray's eyes lit up, but then he grimaced, pointing at his phone.

Yep, tell the wife you're gonna be late again.

Mason dug through a stack of papers on his messy desk, looking for his notes on the original interview with Lorenzo Cavallo. Sadly, the old man had been murdered before finding out that his sister was one of the original circle women. Maybe that was for the best. Would this daughter-in-law care? If she did, would she be able to do anything about it?

A uniform opened the hall door, let a woman through, and pointed at Callahan. Mason studied her as he moved across the room. Mousy was his first impression. Large brown eyes rapidly took in the room, her gaze skittering from object to object as if she expected them to bite. Her hair was gray, and she clutched a purse to her waist like Mason was about to snatch it. Her red rubber boots were her only piece of color on her outfit. The boots looked huge, like she'd had to borrow them to go out in the rain.

"Mrs. Cavallo?" Mason held out his hand, and she gingerly shook it.

She was terrified.

What had propelled this woman out of her comfort zone?

"I'm Detective Callahan." He led her back to his desk and gestured at a chair. Ray had stepped away to wrap up his call. His wife understood late hours and changed plans came with the job, but that didn't mean she had to like it.

"Esther Cavallo." She looked straight at him as she sat down, and Mason saw a spark of determination in her eyes.

"You're married to one of Lorenzo's sons?"

"Yes, Nico is my husband. You were at our house today. I apologize for my bad manners in not greeting you as a guest." She swallowed hard.

"Ah . . . that's quite all right. No harm done."

"Nico didn't know if your visit was going to be appropriate."

Appropriate for what? For a woman's ears? Like he and Ray were going to drop a bunch of f-bombs that might sully Nico's wife? "That's understandable." *In the Dark Ages.* "What can I do for you?"

"It's about Lucia."

Mason waited.

Esther toyed at her purse clasp, her fingers tracing its metal prongs. "Lucia was one of those women found so long ago, right? You've identified her?"

"That's right. We're ninety-nine percent certain it is her. Lorenzo left a DNA sample for us to compare, and we're waiting on those results. But based on some dental findings, we believe it's her."

Esther nodded.

"Did you know Lucia?"

"Oh, no." Esther shook her head. "Nico was only a boy when his aunt left."

Mason abruptly realized the woman in front of him couldn't be older than fifty. She acted two decades older.

"But there were always stories about his wild aunt. The other family members would always whisper about her. She was the one who'd been sent away."

"I thought she ran off after a fight with her father."

"The men described it that way. But the women knew. She'd been punished for her behavior."

Ray sat down at the desk across from Mason and nodded at Esther. "Punished? Punished how?"

Esther stared at him with wide eyes.

"Mrs. Cavallo, this is Detective Ray Lusco. Ray, this is Nico Cavallo's wife." Mason spoke up before she took flight. "Maybe you better tell us about the rumors of Lucia's behavior and punishment."

For the next ten minutes, Mason listened and gently led the woman through a story that sounded straight out of a third world country. Women treated as belongings, men who dominated, and a man who ruled over all of them.

"This took place here?" Ray asked in disbelief at one point. "In Oregon?"

Esther nodded emphatically. "The church dissolved when Nico was a teen. His mother sometimes told me stories about the old days, when she was encouraged to not speak to men other than her husband. She never learned to drive or handle any money. The men did everything. A woman's role was to serve her husband. But Lucia didn't like it."

"Mrs. Cavallo, why are you telling us now? Aren't you worried about getting in trouble?" Mason wanted to say *getting in trouble with your husband*, but couldn't form the words. How had women lived with this oppression?

"Because it's not right that Lucia is not laid to rest. Her bones should not be in a box somewhere. And no matter what bad blood there is between Lorenzo and his sons, at least one of them should be stepping forward to claim his body. They may have avoided him for the past decade, but they should not continue to punish him in death."

Esther was a woman with principles.

"What do you think happened to Lucia?" Ray asked softly.

She held his gaze. "I think she was killed. She and those other five women."

"Who did this?"

"Cesare Abbadelli. No one dared speak against him."

The same man that Michael Brody discovered ran the church and who arranged the adoptions.

"The minister?" Ray asked.

She nodded.

"Mrs. Cavallo," Mason asked carefully, his brain spinning. "Do you know anything about adoptions arranged by that church?"

The woman paled. "What of it?"

"We have a friend who was put up for adoption through this church. She's trying to find her birth parents. Where did the babies come from who were put up for adoption?"

Esther stared at him. "Some were of the church," she whispered. "The unmarried women who got pregnant. Others came from the surrounding area. Girls who got in trouble and didn't know what to do."

Mason looked at Ray. *A different era. Yes, this church was in a rural and rather isolated area, but was there nowhere else for the women to turn?*

"Why do you think the minister killed Lucia?" Mason prodded.

Esther looked at her hands, strangling her bag in her lap. "I don't know."

Mason believed this terrified woman was reaching out to him to share what she knew. He just had to guide it out of her. Gently.

"Mrs. Cavallo . . . why do you suspect Cesare Abbadelli was responsible for those women's deaths?" he asked calmly.

"It was whispered." Her gaze slowly lifted from her purse, meeting Mason's. "The other women of the church whispered behind closed doors that Cesare was weak when it came to women. And that he hated his weakness, blaming the women who created it. His own wife vanished decades ago. No one asked questions. He said she ran off with another man."

"She left before or after the first circle of women?" Ray asked softly.

Mason's heart was pounding, and he fought to slow his breathing. The conversation had a fragile edge to it that could shatter at the wrong question or tone. He didn't want to scare Esther away.

"After. I don't know when. Maybe ten years. And his other son vanished when he was about twenty. He'd been a rebellious boy. Cesare had a difficult time keeping him in line."

What had this man done to his family?

He glanced at Ray's composed face. Ray's shirt pocket twitched over his heart, revealing his rapid heartbeat. *Ray's thinking it, too. We've got a serial killer on our hands, hiding behind the guise of a pastor.*

"Rumors spoke of women who came to the church. Runaways, women seeking a safe place." Mason leaned forward to hear Esther's soft words. "They'd stay at the church for a few weeks, getting back on their feet, and then vanish again. Even the ones who expressed desire to put down roots in that community. They never stayed. All left and never returned. Never communicated with the friends they'd made in their short stay."

Mason thought back to the previously identified women from the old circle. All women in transition. Had they sought out the church as a sanctuary only to find a hell?

"Who do you think killed the girls last week?" Ray asked Esther.

She slowly shook her head. "I don't know. It was exactly as the scene before, but Abbadelli is an old man now. How could he orchestrate it? But I don't know who else could be evil enough to do such a thing."

"Abbadelli is still alive?" Ray asked.

"Yes. Lorenzo continued to follow him even though he'd moved to the southern part of the state for a while. Nico and his brothers stopped talking with their father when he railed at them to attend Abbadelli's sermons twice a week after he'd moved back to this area."

Sermons twice a week? That sounded like a lot of preaching in Mason's mind.

"Lorenzo apparently was a dedicated member of Abbadelli's flock," Mason stated. "Could he have killed those young women if Abbadelli ordered it?"

Esther shrugged. "I don't know. How would he convince the girls to do as he says? He was an old man, too."

Mason agreed. He didn't see Lorenzo as the type of man to convince a bunch of young women to meet him in Forest Park at night. "From an eyewitness account, we're looking for a younger man. Possibly one who does photography."

Recognition flashed in Esther's eyes. "Abbadelli's grandson is a photographer for his school paper. My nephew knows him. He goes to the same high school as Kyle."

Ray pulled a tiny notebook out of his pocket and rapidly flipped through it. He halted on a page and ran his finger down his notes, stopping on a line. "Kyle. Is Kyle Carey your nephew? The one arrested for the shooting at the memorial service?" he asked.

Esther's shoulders slumped slightly. "He is. I don't know what he was thinking. He told us he spotted the woman who convinced his mother, Jackie, to leave her family at that memorial service. He was very upset, but he wasn't going to shoot anyone."

"Wait a minute? He wasn't upset at a teenage girl? His focus was on an adult who he blamed for his family falling apart?" Callahan interjected.

Ray put two and two together. "Katy Morris? She counsels women in crisis situations and was there with Trinity. Could she have worked with his mother?"

Esther was nodding. "That name sounds familiar. Kyle tries to follow Abbadelli. Tries to bring back Abbadelli's teachings. He has been very angry since his mother left. She couldn't take any more of her husband's rules. I doubt anyone can blame a counselor for her actions. I've heard Kyle say we should return to the old ways."

"The old ways of beating down your wife?" Mason spit out.

"He is a boy. Right now he sees Abbadelli as some sort of symbol to admire. But he is friends with Abbadelli's grandson. Perhaps the two of them . . . " She trailed off, a nauseous expression covering her face. "Perhaps together they . . . " She couldn't finish.

Mason completed her thought in his head. *Perhaps together they decided to punish today's young women.*

"Jesus Christ," said Ray. "They're just teens. Why would they do that? To get the old guy's admiration? Maybe he orchestrated it. Manipulated the teens."

"Abbadelli is definitely the pastor Brody was looking for. He wasn't sure if he was dead or not. Do you know where he lives?" he asked Esther.

"He lives where he's always lived," she said simply. "We don't go near him. My husband doesn't want to remember his years in that church."

"I wouldn't call it a church," said Mason. "This has cult written all over it. And Abbadelli is the aging Manson."

Esther's lips whitened. "Yes," she whispered. "I would call it a cult. They don't follow a religion. They follow the teachings of one mortal man. A very bad man. No one knew for certain if he killed all those women so long ago. It was only rumors. There was no proof. And if someone reported him, what would happen to their family? Would they die, too?" Esther wiped at her eyes. "I have to imagine they were all too scared of him."

Mason's gut was on fire. He wanted to hit someone. Preferably Cesare Abbadelli. And some of his spineless followers. Families had looked the other way as a madman possibly murdered women seeking help. And possibly his own wife and son? *How could they do nothing?*

"You said he lives where he's always lived. Where is that?"

"I don't know. He has a place in the forest. Some land near the coast."

Ray straightened. "Wait a minute. Like out Highway 26? Over the Coast Range?"

"Yes, I believe that is where Nico said he lives."

Mason looked at Ray. "What's wrong?"

"Brody emailed me earlier. He said he'd located someone from the church who had some of the old church records and had passed Victoria Peres's contact information to him. She'd told him she would head out there tonight. Brody didn't say it was the pastor of the church, but I know the address is out in the middle of nowhere on the way to the coast. I think he found Abbadelli. But why didn't he say so?"

"I don't think he goes by Abbadelli anymore. I think he's changed his name to something else," added Esther. "I don't know what name."

"Get someone out to that address. And call Dr. Peres. See if she's headed out there yet."

His buzzing phone distracted him. "Callahan."

"Detective, it's Katy Morris again. I wanted to let you know we found Trinity, but thank you for your concern."

Mason had nearly forgotten about the teen since the Abbadelli revelations. "Ms. Morris, we were just talking about you. Did you ever work with a Jackie Carey in your practice?"

Katy paused. "Yes, why?"

"That was her son with the gun at the memorial service. Is it possible he'd be angry if he saw you?"

Katy coughed. "Angry is putting it mildly, detective. Are you saying seeing me is what set off that teen?"

"It's possible," said Mason.

"Well, I told them to get him into counseling. Damn it! I knew that kid was a ticking bomb. I'm glad they've got him now. Maybe he'll get the attention he needs."

"I don't understand what's going on in teenage brains these days. But Trinity has been found? She turned up okay?" Mason asked.

"Yes, the car was washed off a road, but she and the boy with her are okay."

"Thank God. So there *was* a boy. Is the car damaged badly?"

"I don't know. Victoria Peres found her on the other side of the Coast Range. Can you believe that? She left me a message, but I haven't been able to reach her. I think there's no signal."

Every alarm went off in Mason's head. "Coast Range? Where was she going?"

"Beats the hell out of me. We'll be having a deep discussion about this incident."

"Who was the boy she was with?"

"I don't know that either," Katy admitted.

Mason looked at Ray. "Trinity Viders was found by Victoria Peres on the other side of the Coast Range. With a teen boy. How much do you want to bet it's Abbadelli's grandson?"

"Jason?" Esther asked. "She's with him?" Fear filled her face. "I wouldn't trust him. He must be taking her to his grandfather. What are they going to do to her?"

"And it sounds like Dr. Peres found a link to the birth records' source. In the same place," Ray stated. His face was grim.

"Detective, what are you talking about?" Katy asked, concern filling her voice.

"Dr. Peres didn't tell you exactly where she'd found Trinity?" he asked.

"No. All she said was that they'd spotted her car and were getting her out. She did say she'd called nine-one-one."

"They will know where her call came from. We'll trace them through their system." He tipped the phone away from his ear and gestured to Ray. "Dr. Peres placed a nine-one-one call about the car being washed off the road. See if they got a reading on her location."

"What is going on?" Katy nearly yelled. "Is Trinity all right?"

"We're going to find out, Ms. Morris."

Mason mentally crossed his fingers.

CHAPTER THIRTY

"Are you sure you're okay?" Victoria asked again. She didn't like the amount of blood that was soaking through Jason's jeans below his knees. He'd climbed out of her SUV in slow motion, moving gingerly, trying not to bump his legs on the truck door. Seth came around the front of the vehicle, stopped next to Victoria, and squinted at Jason's pants in the dim light.

"Wow. You're really bleeding."

Jason swallowed hard and looked at the front door of the little house. They'd stopped in front of an old A-frame cabin that looked straight out of a campground from the 1950s. Victoria could make out some smaller outbuildings scattered around the forested property, but this was the only one with lights on inside.

The entire area was dark. The rain clouds and firs shadowed the area, creating an atmosphere of midnight when in reality, the sun had set only an hour ago. The cabin was built on a slightly elevated piece of ground, avoiding the possibility of flooding like the low area they'd crossed minutes before. The Coast Range sloped up behind the cabin, giving the impression that it grew out of the back of the residence.

Victoria followed Jason's gaze to the cabin. "Are you sure someone's home?"

"Yes, I talked to him earlier."

"Maybe you should be the one to knock. Although I think he's expecting me, too. Is your grandfather Cecil Adams?" Victoria asked.

Jason met her gaze, and she didn't like the level of alarm in his eyes. "Yes, why are you seeing him?"

"Supposedly he's got some old documentation of church records. Possibly some adoption references. I'm trying to verify my birth parents." Victoria watched his face carefully. Why was the teen so alarmed? "Does that sound like something he'd have?"

"I don't really know." Jason looked away, picking at his jeans.

Why is he lying to me?

"Did your grandfather belong to a church that burned down a long time ago?" Seth asked, his brows nearly touching each other as he studied the young man. *Seth sees it, too.*

"Beats me." Jason bent to examine the bloody denim around his knee.

Victoria turned toward the house as the squeak of hinges caught her attention. She turned in time to see a flash from a shotgun muzzle and was deafened by the immediate roar.

Seth tackled her from behind, crushing her into the mud.

★★★

Seth saw the old man step out the door with his double-barreled shotgun pointed in their direction. The boom sounded in his ears as he rushed at Victoria, hitting her in the shoulders and landing on top of her, covering her head with his hands. Trinity cried out, as Jason pushed her aside, knocking her down.

"Nonno! Stop it! It's me!" the teen yelled at the old man.

"Jason?" the man asked.

"Damn it, Nonno! What are you doing? You knew I was coming."

"Don't swear at me, boy! I expected you and the girl. Who else is with you?"

Seth studied the white-bearded old man from his position on Victoria's back. He was squinting in the dim light, and Seth suspected he'd shot over their heads, not directly at them. "Mr. Adams?" Seth asked.

The gun moved toward Seth. "Who wants to know?"

"My name is Seth. Victoria Peres is with me. I think you were going to show us some paperwork in your barn?" The old man was silent, and Seth wondered if he'd forgotten about their meeting already. Was he sane? At the worst he had one round left in the shotgun. Judging by his stiff movements, it'd take a few moments to reload. "Are you going to put away that gun?"

"Are you armed?" Mr. Adams asked.

"No," said Seth, immediately wishing he'd kept his mouth shut. But the old man lowered the gun a little, pointing it behind them instead of directly at them. Seth exhaled and Victoria squirmed underneath him.

"Get off of me," she hissed.

He moved. "Sorry."

"It's okay. But my wrist cracked when we went down." Pain rang in her voice. She pushed up with her right hand, tucking her left close to her chest. Mud covered the front of her clothing and one side of her face.

He wiped at her face with his sleeve. "What do you mean, cracked?" Dread tightened his chest.

"I'm not sure. I heard it and I can feel it." She looked at the old man by the front door and raised her voice. "Mr. Adams, you said you were okay with us coming out tonight, right?"

"Lady, I don't know what you're talking about."

Victoria caught her breath. "I just talked to you on the phone. Less than an hour ago. You have some old church records we were going to look at."

The old man stared at her, squinting in the poor light. "What'd he say your name was?"

"Victoria Peres." The twin barrels returned to point directly at her.

"Peres? The lady doctor?" Adams asked.

"Yes. I have a doctorate in forensic anthropology. I'm not a medical doctor."

A grin cracked the man's face. She didn't like it. It wasn't a happy grin. It was an I'm-a-crazy-bastard grin.

"Why do you think he can help with some paperwork?" Jason asked, his voice low. "He's an old man. He doesn't know anything."

Seth looked at the teen. Jason was helping Trinity wipe off the mud just like he'd done for Victoria. There was an urgency in the boy's voice that made the hair stiffen on the back of his neck. "Why not?"

"You guys should just leave. He can't help you. Get Trinity out of here, too."

"Why did you bring her out here then?"

"I didn't know he was going to be in one of his crazy moods," Jason stated. "It's best to leave him alone when he's got the gun out."

No kidding.

"Maybe we should come back another day," Seth whispered to Victoria.

"No. We're here. I want to see what he's got."

"Jason probably knows when it's best to leave his grandfather alone. I think we should listen to him."

Another gun roared and Victoria flung herself back to the ground with Seth a split second behind her. His ears rang, and he mentally checked his limbs for injuries.

"Jesus Christ, Dad. What the hell?" Jason yelled.

Dimly Seth noted that the second gunshot had come from behind them. Looking back, he saw a tall, thin figure with a similar shotgun who'd just blasted a hole in Victoria's rear tire. Panic flared in his lungs.

"Don't blaspheme," the figure said.

Jason's dad?

"Why did you do that?" the teen yelled at his father.

The man said nothing. Seth couldn't make out his face in the dark, but he could plainly see the shotgun focused on him and Victoria. Two barrels again. Images of the crazy men in *Deliverance* spun in his brain.

"Oh my God," Victoria whispered. "What is this?"

"I've no fucking idea," Seth said under his breath. "How are we going to get out of here?"

"I don't care if my tire's shot out. I'll drive on it if that's the only way out," she whispered.

"Be quiet," the thin man ordered. "Get up."

Seth stood, keeping the man in his view, and carefully helped Victoria to her feet. Jason helped Trinity up and moved between her and his father. "You need to let them go."

"I don't think so." His head turned toward Victoria. "I've been waiting for her."

Seth froze. What did he want with Tori?

Pain radiated up Victoria's arm. *Shit.* The slightest movement or twist made her eyes roll back in her head. Definitely broken. She'd heard the snap when Seth landed on her. But at the moment, her arm was the least of her concerns. Two crazy men with shotguns took priority.

"What is going on?" she mumbled to Seth, who supported her with her other arm. Rain and mud soaked her jeans.

"I don't think Jason's grandfather is happy to see you."

"I got that. But why?"

"Women shouldn't do what you do," came a voice behind her.

She glanced over her shoulder and saw the tall, thin man with his gun's muzzle at Trinity's back. He didn't wear a hat or hood, and water streamed down his face. He gave no sign that he felt it.

"It's not normal," he added.

"What do I do?" she asked him.

"Look at bones. Those people are dead. You shouldn't be handling them like they were pots and pans." His voice rumbled in anger.

Fire ripped up her spine. "I give every death the respect it deserves! I don't throw their remains around like pots. My job is to figure out why they died and who is to be held responsible."

"Why is anyone responsible? Perhaps they deserved to die."

A new chill started in Victoria's stomach and filled her lungs.

Was he their killer of the circle of women from forty-five years ago? She dismissed the thought. He was too young to have committed that crime. She slowly turned her head to look at the grandfather. *He was not.*

The old man was still staring at her, his gun trained on her and Seth. He'd recognized her name. How? From the paper? "Are you Cecil Adams?" She directed her voice at the porch.

"That's one of my names."

"And the other?" she asked.

"At one time I was Cesare Abbadelli. Americans struggled with that name. No one blinked when I changed it to Adams."

Memories poked at her brain. "You were the pastor. My parents went to your church. I remember that it had burned down and I remember you." She could picture a kind old man, sort of like Santa Claus. But now he was Santa with a gun.

"As I remember you," he stated.

"That's enough talking!" Jason's father snapped.

Victoria leaned on Seth as she turned to look at the angry man. "We need to leave."

"Absolutely not." He moved his gun closer to the back of Trinity's head. Her blonde ponytail dripped rainwater onto her back.

Ice grew in Victoria's gut. Facing her, Trinity couldn't see behind her but Victoria's expression must have alarmed her. Her eyes filled. Both women looked at Jason. The boy appeared stunned.

"Dad, what are you doing?"

"I want you to take them to the shed."

"No, why—" began Jason.

"Don't question me, boy!" he snarled.

"Jason," Trinity started. "Why—"

"Quiet!" roared his father. "Move them, now!"

"No," stated Trinity. Jason's father slammed her in the head with his shotgun muzzle, and she cried out, making Victoria cringe. Seth started in Trinity's direction, but Victoria grabbed his arm with her good hand, locking gazes with the younger gunman. Fear and anger shone from his eyes.

He's crazy.

She held tight to Seth.

"Get back." Leo separated Trinity and Jason. "Stand with the girl," he ordered Victoria.

Every cell in Victoria's body screamed not to leave Seth. She let go of his arm, holding his gaze. She felt like she was being ripped from her foundation. As long as she stayed by Seth she was safe. She turned her head so neither of the gunmen could see her lips move. "There's a gun in the console," she whispered. She usually kept the small handgun in her duffel for boating, ever since she'd been accosted by transients at the waterfront one morning. She'd moved it to her console when she emptied the duffel last week. Seth's eyes widened the smallest bit and he gave a small nod.

"Leo!" shouted Abbadelli. "What are you doing?"

"What I should have done a long time ago. I'm taking control of this family. You served long enough. It's time for new blood."

Abbadelli's jaw dropped. "Leo?"

"Do you think you're the only one who can have power?" Leo stared at his father, a challenge in his eyes. "I've been watching you all my life. I've learned from the best."

Victoria cringed. Leo's hatred for his father shone on his face. *What had the man done to his son?*

She joined Trinity, whose tears streamed down her cheeks. Her hand was pressed to the side of her head where Leo had hit her. Blood oozed between her fingers, mixing with the rain that drenched them all. The blood was a dark stain against her light hair. She silently met Victoria's gaze.

She was terrified.

What had they walked into?

"Lock them in the shed." Leo dug in his pocket and held out a key to Jason. "Careful opening the door, the other one might try to get out. Bring me back the key."

Other one?

Leo looked at the two dripping women. "I'll come give you instructions in a minute."

No one moved.

Leo moved behind Jason and punched him in the kidney with the butt of his weapon. The boy gasped and fell to his knees. He moaned and collapsed into the mud. Leo kicked him in the other kidney with his boot. "Next time do what you're told!"

Seth took one step in Leo's direction only to come face to face with the muzzle of his shotgun.

"Don't move!"

Seth raised his hands. And froze.

"Now!" Leo bellowed at Jason. Jason lurched up from the ground, resting his hands on his thighs, and then took a few shaky steps, his back hunched in pain, to take the key from his father's hand. His father pulled a pistol out of the inside of his coat and held it out toward the boy. "Use this." Jason took it with weak hands.

Jason turned to the women, meeting Trinity's gaze. *I'm sorry,* he mouthed at her. Trinity simply stared at him.

"Go that way," Jason directed, pointing to the right of the house with the pistol. Victoria and Trinity looked at each other and back at Jason. Neither moved.

"Move or I'll shoot her brains out," Leo said calmly, pressing the muzzle of his shotgun into the back of Trinity's head. She gasped.

Victoria grabbed her hand and tugged her in the direction Jason had indicated. Trinity followed. Victoria glanced over her shoulder at Leo. Disgust exuded from his gaze. She nearly tripped in alarm.

Why did he hate them?

Seth watched Victoria and Trinity walk away, fighting every instinct to grab the barrels of Leo's shotgun and deck him with it. But Leo was watching him. Closely.

When Leo struck his son, the shock hit Seth.

They were in trouble. *Big trouble.*

The old man on the porch. Abbadelli. He looked just as shocked by Leo's actions. He now leaned against one of the porch rails, his focus with the shotgun not as precise as minutes before.

"Looks like you surprised your father," said Seth to Leo.

The thin man jerked and glared at Seth. "Shut up."

Seth raised a brow. And said nothing. Both sets of fathers and sons were at odds. That was clear.

"You're the one who Victoria talked to on the phone, aren't you?" Seth injected an amazed tone into his voice. *Butter him up.*

Leo sneered.

"You posed as your father to get her out here, why?" Seth pressed.

"It was time. He's let her go on for too long and not done anything about it," Leo answered. "Move to the porch." He waved his shotgun in Seth's direction.

Seth raised his hands and walked toward Abbadelli, where he waited on the porch. The old man was breathing hard, his face red below his white hair. "Your father doesn't look too good, Leo. Your chest hurt?" he asked Abbadelli.

"Shut up," Abbadelli snapped. "What is wrong with you?" he gasped at Leo.

"You've shoved her in my face for the last time," Leo said from behind Seth.

Seth stopped at the bottom of the steps, looking up at the old man, worrying he was about to have a heart attack.

"Shoved who?" Abbadelli spit out between breaths.

"The woman! Peres. You've bragged for years about her success in my face."

Seth blinked. *Years?*

The shotgun jammed into his back, and Seth stumbled onto the first step. "Get up there. In that chair."

Seth slowly moved up the step. Abbadelli had recovered enough to keep his shotgun aimed at his progress. The rain stopped beating on his head as he moved under the roof, but drops landing on the ground grew louder, their noise echoing off the wood siding of the cabin.

He sat in the chair.

"Get me some rope," Leo ordered his father. Abbadelli disappeared into the house, as Leo stood on the top step, his gun trained on Seth's head. The two men stared at each other.

"What will happen to Victoria and Trinity?" Seth asked.

Leo's eyes lit up, making the skin on Seth's neck crawl. *Jesus Christ. So that is what crazy looks like.*

"They'll be tied up for a while." Leo laughed at his private joke.

Sweat dripped from Seth's armpits. The air was cold, but he was about to overheat. Everything around him was soaking wet, but his mouth rivaled a desert. *Keep your head.*

Abbadelli stepped out of the cabin, a length of rope in his hands. "Tie him to the chair," Leo ordered. "Tie it tight."

Seth's hands were pulled behind him and through the rungs of the back of the chair. He winced as the rope burned his wrist as Abbadelli strictly followed Leo's orders. The chair was no flimsy discount chair. It was a heavy-duty solid wood construction that looked like it'd been on the Abbadelli porch since the Second World War. Seth wouldn't be busting any boards trying to escape. Abbadelli tied a second loop tight around his waist.

"Where's Jason?" Abbadelli asked as he yanked on the ropes to test.

"He's not back yet."

"You trust him with those women?" Abbadelli asked.

"He'll do as he's told."

Abbadelli snorted. "I used to say that about you."

Seth heard a tone of pride in the old man's voice. *So now he's impressed that his son is a criminal?*

"I let you believe what I wanted you to believe," Leo said smugly.

Abbadelli straightened from his knot-tying job. "I believed Jason had killed those girls last week. You didn't do anything to correct me."

Leo's face lit up in crazy mode again, setting off alarms in Seth's head. "I knew you'd figure it out eventually. I wanted to show you I had more steel than you believed."

Leo had been seeking Daddy's approval? That was why those girls were killed?

"You needed to see what I was capable of. You always said I had none of you in me, only Mama in me. I wanted you to know you were wrong."

"So you killed children?" Seth challenged. "What kind of man kills children to prove a point?"

Leo shifted his hold on his shotgun to a batter's stance and swung the gun at Seth's head. The tip caught Seth's cheekbone before he could whip his face out of the way. The crunch sickened his stomach and pain burned along his cheek. Blood dripped onto his shirt.

He ground his eyes shut, the pain reverberating through his skull.

Don't taunt the killer.

Leo got close to his face. "My father created a work of art with the bodies of those women decades ago. It was damned beautiful. Like a white flower. I never got it out of my head." He reached out with a finger and jabbed at Seth's cheekbone. Fire shot though his face and his tears mixed with his blood.

"How?" asked Seth. "How were you able to get those girls to trust and follow you?"

The man kept his face close to Seth's, grinning as he studied his handiwork below Seth's eye. "That was easy. Every girl wants to know she's beautiful. I found some through Jason's Facebook account, and that led to others. Teen girls post pictures of themselves everywhere. It was easy to find the look I wanted. I'd set up a professional page through Facebook months before, showcasing some of the work I'd done. It was so easy to get their attention; they all wanted the chance to look beautiful on film. Whores. Sluts, all of them."

They were children. People's daughters.

"Now. Drink this." Leo slid a flask out of his back pocket and shook it before unscrewing the cap. Seth didn't think he was sharing a companionable shot of whiskey.

"What's that?"

"Something to make you sleep."

Phenobarbital. What he'd found in the girls' stomachs.

He turned his face away.

"Hold his head! Plug his nose!" Leo ordered.

Seth's head was grabbed and braced against Abbadelli's stomach. Leo snagged Seth's chin with one hand and pushed the metal against his lips, cutting the soft flesh and scraping his teeth. He thrashed his head back and forth. Someone's finger dug into his ripped flesh over his cheekbone and he screamed. Leo sloshed the liquid in his mouth. Seth spit and thrashed some more, but some liquid slid down his throat. He tried to gag, envisioning every nasty stench that'd ever crossed his table. He was unsuccessful.

"That's enough," Leo snapped. He stood back, panting, his eyes flashing in anger. Behind Seth, Abbadelli panted harder. "I'll just have to convince him to have a nice long drink." He set the flask on the railing. "Ready for a show that'll make you beg me to let you drink?" Leo looked at his father. "Watch him," he ordered. He turned and dashed down the porch steps into the dark night.

He's getting Victoria.

Seth wondered if he should have drank.

"Open it," Jason told Victoria. One-handed, she inserted the key into the lock and unhooked the industrial-sized padlock from the door. She handed the key back to the boy and debated making a run for it. One swift kick to the balls, and she and Trinity could take off. Jason handled the gun like he couldn't bear to touch it. She doubted he would shoot them.

Leo she had no doubts about. She'd seen the killer in his eyes.

Her wrist and arm screamed every time she took a rough step. Running would make her pass out from the pain. Besides, where would they run? Back to the cabin to the two men with shotguns? And she couldn't leave without Seth.

Jason gestured for Trinity to slide open the shed door. A faint light spilled out. Victoria looked inside and caught her breath. Trinity made a small sound in the back of her throat. On a filthy mattress at the back of the small shed lay a woman. Her hair was long and black. With streaks of gray.

Isabel.

Victoria glanced at Jason. He looked as confused as Trinity. The boy didn't know why the woman was there. "Do you know her?" she asked him. Jason gave a brief shake of his head.

The woman moaned and shifted on the mattress. Victoria stepped up into the shed and darted to the woman, kneeling on the floor next to her. She brushed the long hair out of the woman's face, and Isabel's eyes opened. A split second of fear shone from her eyes until she focused on Victoria. She relaxed and her lids fell shut. Victoria's hand stroked through a wet mass in her hair. Blood. She could feel the wound starting to crust on the woman's scalp.

Someone had hit her in the head. *Leo?*

"Is she all right?" Trinity asked. She hovered over Victoria's shoulder.

"I don't know. She's been hit in the head. She woke and saw me but fell back asleep."

She shook the woman's shoulder. "Isabel? Isabel? Wake up."

"You know her?" Trinity whispered.

Victoria nodded. She looked back at Jason, watching from the shed door. "She needs a hospital. She has a serious head injury." *Maybe.* "I can't get her to wake up. Do you know how she got here?"

Jason shook his head again. The teen looked horrified.

"Jason, do you know why she's here?"

Jason looked pleadingly at her, turmoil rolling in his gaze.

She tried again. "Jason, what is going on with your father?"

The teen's shoulders slumped. "I think he killed those girls. The ones last week."

Trinity sucked in her breath. "Your father? Why? Why do you think he did it?"

"Because I found some pictures on his camera. I was going to use it and I scanned through some of the pictures saved in the memory and saw pictures of those dead girls. Brooke was one of them." His voice wavered on her name. "I wasn't supposed to be using his equipment."

"Why didn't you go to the police?" Trinity asked. She looked heartbroken, her crush on the boy disintegrating. "How could you cover it up?"

"They were just pictures, you know? They didn't mean that he'd done it. I couldn't figure out what was going on. And then I found the skulls . . . I didn't know what to think. How could my father be a murderer?" His voice cracked on the word.

"Skulls?" Victoria asked. "Three of them?"

Jason nodded. "I stuck the skulls and the camera in my bag. I wanted to go to the police but I didn't know what I'd say. And what if he didn't do it?"

"Is that why you were avoiding him?" Trinity asked.

"Yes, he'd discovered his stuff was missing and he was on the warpath. Grandpa thinks he's a big wimp, but when he gets mad he can be kinda violent." Jason wouldn't look at either one of them. Victoria wondered what pain Leo had inflicted on the boy.

"You need to help us get out of here," she said in a hushed tone. "He's killed before. He'll do it again. I don't know why he got me to come out here, but I don't think it's to give me a present." She looked at Isabel. "I think he plans to kill all of us."

Tears streamed down Trinity's cheeks. "No," she whispered. "This isn't happening." She looked at Jason. "Come with us. You don't want to stay here with them."

Jason looked from Trinity to Victoria and back. "I can't. I can't do that. He'll—"

"He'll what? Hit you? Do you think he arranged for me and Isabel to be here so he can throw us a party? Your father is a cold-blooded killer, Jason!" Victoria clenched her arm tight to her chest, her wrist throbbing. "We have to get out of here now."

A shadow loomed behind Jason. "Hello, Victoria. Did you get to chat with your mother again?"

Victoria wanted to cry.

"You ladies need to change your clothing," Leo ordered. "There're some lovely white dresses in that box." He gestured to a cardboard box in the corner of the shed. "You." He pointed at Trinity, who shuddered. "There's black hair dye in there, too. I want your hair black. Now."

"What?" Trinity gasped.

"Hair. Black. Now." Leo stared at her. "Get moving."

He was re-creating the tableau. Panic immobilized Victoria at Isabel's side. The white dresses. Three of them with long black hair.

That was how he planned to kill them.

"Where is Seth?" she asked.

Annoyance crossed Leo's face. "He's busy. Change your clothes. Now." He didn't move.

She glanced at Jason. The teen looked miserable.

"Don't look at him. It's about time he learned to grow a spine. I was younger than him when I figured it out." He slapped the teen on the back. "Time for you to grow up and face your roots, son." He pointed at Victoria. "This is what we call shameless. She's the type of woman who lives only for herself. She doesn't care about anyone around her. She can't please a man in marriage. She tries to pretend to be a man."

"What utter bullshit," Victoria spat.

Rage crossed Leo's face. "You can't speak to me like that."

"I believe I just did." This prick had pushed all her buttons. "What are you going to do about it? Make me drink some poison and pose in the woods to make yourself feel powerful?"

Leo stepped inside the shed, his shotgun still at his side. Victoria stood up to meet him. She'd rather go down with a fight than cower in a white dress.

"Dad." Jason put a hand on his arm. Leo slapped it off and continued toward Victoria, his face irate. Jason stepped back hesitantly, and then abruptly turned and silently leaped out of the shed and ran. Leo took two more steps toward Victoria.

"Put on the dress. Dye her hair. You've got ten minutes." He held her gaze. His pupils dilated in the dark cabin, and his stare drifted down to her mouth. A slow smile stretched his lips.

He's aroused. She wanted to puke.

He glanced at the unconscious woman on the mattress. "She's not much to look at, is she? You had no idea you came from such garbage, did you?"

Leo sent the note about my mother?

"She's not garbage," Victoria said quietly.

"You needed to be taken down a notch, going around with your snooty airs. You're nothing special."

Victoria blinked. "I'm what I make of myself, not who I'm born of. What makes you think she's actually my mother?"

He threw back his head and laughed. "You really do know nothing. Of course she's your mother, little sister. Dad would never let me forget it."

Sister? Dad? Victoria felt like she was falling, everything spinning in slow motion around her, but her feet were firmly on the floor as she stared Leo in the face. Her inner sense of self cracked and shifted. *Who was Leo?*

Leo grinned at her. "Yes, we share a father. But not that whore for a mother." He prodded at Isabel's head with his shotgun. "He got her pregnant then gave you away. There were lots of adoptions going on back then. It was easy to slip you in. Dad always knew where you were, what you were doing, and got off on shoving your success down my throat."

Leo was her half brother.

She had a killer's blood in her veins.

Not if she had anything to say about it. She shook her head at him.

"Oh, yes. It's true. Dad said your adoptive parents were thrilled to get a baby girl. I don't remember any of it. I was only six or so. But I recall all the young women who came and went. Some stayed at the church for months, having nowhere to sleep. Some stayed only a few days. Dad never let me talk to them. He said they were all whores."

He used the word "whore" to a child?

"'Whore' is used in the Bible, you know. Perfectly acceptable." Leo smirked.

"So is 'thou shall not kill,'" Victoria stated.

Seth blinked, trying to clear his vision.

No. This isn't happening.

He'd barely swallowed any of the liquid Leo had forced into his mouth. He blinked again and the porch boards came into focus. There was no way he'd taken enough to be having any symptoms.

You don't know how concentrated he'd made it.

He couldn't have swallowed more than half a teaspoon. He shook his head, fighting the mild fuzziness that'd tried to nest in his brain. More likely he was noticing symptoms from his blood circulation being cut off at his wrists and waist. He wiggled in the chair, trying to make room for the blood to move back where it should be.

What was Leo going to do to Tori? Drag her up here with the shotgun and threaten to blow a hole in her stomach if he didn't drink? What would he do? Would Leo really kill her? And if he didn't drink, what was keeping Leo from putting a shotgun blast in his head? He was screwed either way.

The fog tried to overtake his head again. Part of him wanted to give in, to simply close his eyes and fall to sleep. But he had to fight. Before Leo came back he had to figure out what to do.

Footsteps sounded behind him. Too light for Abbadelli. He twisted his head. *Jason!* The boy fell to his knees and attacked the knots in the ropes.

"He's going to kill them, just like he killed those other women. I knew he'd done it. I should have gone to the police right away as soon as I saw those pictures, but I didn't know what to do." The boy's words spilled from his mouth in a rush.

"Ahhh." Seth let out a sigh as the rope around his waist released. Blood rushed back to his head, clearing the cobwebs. Pressure from the rope had impaired his circulation. "Where's your gun, Jason?"

"It's right here." He set the black pistol on Seth's lap as he worked on the knots around his wrists. Seth looked at the useless gun; he couldn't feel his fingers. *So close but so far.*

Jason suddenly snatched the gun away.

"Jason?" The older Abbadelli's voice came from the doorway of the cabin. Seth looked over his shoulder, feeling his blood pressure skyrocket. Cesare Abbadelli stood with his shotgun pointed at the boy. Jason had his legs planted apart and the handgun pointed at his grandfather, his finger on the trigger.

Holy crap.

"Put the gun down, boy," Abbadelli ordered.

Seth saw the quiver in Jason's hands. Did the boy even know how to shoot? The old man seemed steadier on his feet than he'd been earlier. With a shotgun you didn't really need to aim. At these close quarters, simply pointing it in the right direction would permanently take care of either him or Jason.

"No, Nonno. I won't let you kill him."

Seth saw the teen's Adam's apple bob nervously.

"I don't plan to kill anyone."

"But you killed those women all those years ago, didn't you? The ones in the first circle?" Jason asked.

Abbadelli seemed to age twenty years with the question. "I had problems. Problems I couldn't tell anyone about. I was ashamed, but I couldn't stop myself."

"It's not too late," Jason pleaded. "You can turn yourself in. You're an old man, they wouldn't treat you too bad." His arms shook.

Abbadelli gave a harsh laugh. "They'd fry me, boy. At my age the best thing a man can do is pick the time he decides to leave this earth. I've had a long life, and I regret a lot of things. But what your father has done can never be undone. The police are too close. Leo is going to have to pay for what he's done."

"He's going to do it again, Nonno. He's going to dress them in white dresses and dye Trinity's hair black. We've got to stop him!"

White dresses? Tori? Like the death circles?

Abbadelli looked at Seth. The old man's brown eyes were tired. All the spit and fire Seth had seen earlier was long gone. Abbadelli was a shell of his earlier self. "Can you stop Leo?"

"Let me out of this chair, and I'll do my damned best." Seth wiggled in the chair, trying to loosen his hands. Abbadelli nodded at Jason and lowered his shotgun. He leaned heavily against the frame of the doorway.

Jason attacked the knots while Seth tried to hold still. After an eternity, the rope fell away and spikes jammed their way up Seth's nerve pathways in his arms. He leaped out of the chair, rubbing at his hands. Jason offered him the gun. He shook his head; his fingers couldn't aim the small gun. "I'll shoot myself."

Abbadelli held out the shotgun, his eyes downcast. *That size weapon he might be able to handle. Point in the general direction and pull trigger.* Seth clumsily tucked it under his arm, clasping it to his side, still working the circulation back into his hands. He stood for a second, studying the old man, who seemed to fold in on himself. "Victoria really made something of herself," Abbadelli said quietly. "I don't know what happened with Leo."

His words spun in Seth's head. Why would Abbadelli care about Victoria?

Jason tugged on his arm. "Let's go. Hurry up. We've got to stop him."

Seth jogged down the porch steps after the teen, and followed him into the dark. He glanced back at the porch and saw Abbadelli lift the flask from the porch railing to his lips.

Seth didn't stop.

From far off, he heard a siren.

Victoria stood in front of Trinity, blocking Leo's lecherous gaze as the teen changed into the dress. The dresses weren't dresses. They were shapeless shifts sewn from white sheets. And there were at least a half dozen in the box. Victoria didn't want to know how many there'd originally been. Trinity had turned her back and slipped the shift over her head, pulling her jeans and shirt off underneath. Victoria did the same and then followed Leo's directions to help with Trinity's hair.

Leo didn't seem too upset by Jason's absence. Victoria prayed he'd gone for help, but Leo blew it off, saying the boy had gone to hide under his bed.

Isabel had awoken two more times. Mumbling incoherently both times. Victoria worried for her. Her doubt about Isabel's identity as her mother was nearly gone. She'd known in her gut the moment she'd seen her step into the street that she was looking at herself in thirty years. Minus the cigarettes.

She'd much rather claim the bond with Isabel than with Leo.

Or the bond to the Santa Claus with the shotgun who was her father.

It hadn't sunk in. She remembered bits and pieces about Cesare Abbadelli from her childhood. He'd always had a pat on the head and a kind word for her. And then her family had left. Had her parents known she was Cesare's daughter?

She doubted it. Her caring parents would never have removed her from his immediate circle if they'd known she was his daughter. She wondered if he'd fought their move to Portland.

One-handed, she tried to evenly move the black dye through Trinity's hair. The chemical stench filled the cabin. There was no water to rinse it off with. Nothing to wash the dye from their hands. They weren't imitating the ethereal girls from last week. This looked like they'd played in ink. Sloppy. The mess made Leo angry.

"Dad?"

Leo's face brightened at the sound of Jason's voice outside. "Damn you, Jason! I need a bucket of water," he yelled back through the closed door.

"Okay," the boy called back.

Seth heard the sirens more consistently as Jason filled a big bucket of water outside the shed. Hose in his hand, the teen glanced anxiously at him. "What's going to happen?"

"I need a distraction. The sirens are getting closer and Leo's going to hear them soon. It's going to be a fire truck responding to Victoria's call about Trinity's car, but maybe there'll be some police too. We need to hold Leo for them."

"What about locking him in the cabin? Can you get the women out?" Jason asked.

Seth thought for a second then shook his head.

"Jason!" Leo yelled from inside the shed.

"Coming, Dad!" he hollered back. Jason turned off the hose and threw it aside.

Seth grabbed his arm. "Listen. I want you to throw the water at him and then hit the ground no matter what. If I have to, I'll shoot him in the leg to slow him down."

Wide eyes met Seth's, but the teen nodded.

They had one chance.

What would he see when Jason opened the door?

Seth moved back into the darkness as Jason stepped up to the shed door and rapped with his knuckles. "It's me, Dad."

There was a pause and the door opened inward, spilling a weak light out into the wet night. Seth couldn't see inside the shed. He took three steps to his right, crouching and straining to get a glimpse of Tori. Jason stepped up the single big step inside, the bucket sloshing in one hand, his pistol in the other. Shadows moved inside.

Where was Tori?

Seth crept closer, his hands tight on the shotgun. He could feel all his fingers now and had faith in his ability to pull the trigger. But could he do it if he was pointing the weapon at a human?

To save a life he could.

He could see Leo, his back against a side wall, his shotgun pointed at his own son as he moved forward with the water. Jason would have to get closer to surprise his father with the water. Tori and Trinity were at the back of the cabin, covered in white gowns and . . . black paint?

"Set it down," Leo ordered. "And give me your gun."

Seth saw Jason halt.

He wasn't close enough.

Jason set the bucket down in front of his feet and held his gun out to his father, the handle first. Leo reached for the weapon.

Jason moved a step closer and soccer-kicked the bucket, sending the bucket and water flying over Leo's legs.

Leo yelled and Seth leaped into the doorway, weapon aimed at Leo's center mass.

"Drop it!" Seth yelled at Leo.

Leo's gun swung in Seth's direction. "Never!" Two black holes stared at Seth from the muzzle of the shotgun. Leo's crazy eyes challenged him from the far end of the weapon.

Seth fired.

Leo's left shoulder and upper arm vanished in a red mist. His body slammed against the wall, and he slid down to the floor. Jason fell to his knees next to his father, his hands scrambling to stop the bleeding.

Seth heard screaming. Trinity had her black hands over her eyes as she screamed from a crouch on the floor. Victoria bent over her, her good arm wrapped around the girl, her wide gaze locked with Seth's.

The sirens grew louder.

Weak-kneed, Seth sat down heavily on the shed's step. He looked at Leo. His shot had caught part of Leo's neck. Seth's shotgun clattered to the floor of the shed.

He no longer needed it.

CHAPTER THIRTY-ONE

Three days later

Seth held tight to her hand as they walked between the firs. Her left hand and wrist were in a brace, her scaphoid and radius broken from her fall. At least she wasn't left-handed, but she might as well be. She couldn't do anything—cut a steak, shampoo her hair, or type efficiently on her keyboard. She felt like an invalid with Seth as her caretaker. Sure, having him shampoo her hair was fun, but dictating her reports to him was simply frustrating.

He hadn't complained once.

After Leo's grisly death, she'd been focused on comforting Trinity and Jason. Nothing Victoria could do could erase that memory from Jason's sight. His mother had appeared from Idaho the next day, packed him up, and taken him home to her new husband and young sons. Trinity said he'd texted a few times, complaining that his toddler half brothers were pests, but Victoria suspected he'd quickly grow accustomed to a caring family.

The shed had revealed a history of horrors. The investigators didn't know how many bloodstains from different victims they were going to find in the mattress. Unlocking the lockbox had opened a Pandora's box of death. Old square black-and-white photos and fading Polaroids revealed women in various states of bondage and death. No current color photos graced the box. It was theorized that Cesare had gotten too old to act as an angel of death in recent years. The newest items in the shed were in a plastic grocery bag. Investigators found six pairs of women's shoes, six cell phones, and a few purses.

Cesare had created a small graveyard under the firs. A hundred yards from the house, they'd found the first of the graves. This one had been recently disturbed, the woman's skull missing.

"I bet that's the skull that Leo threw through my window," Victoria had said to Callahan. "I figured out yesterday that it didn't match the photos or X-rays I'd taken of the missing skulls."

"So that tells me Leo was aware of the graveyard, too. I wonder if Cesare knew his son had discovered his dark side," said Callahan.

"From what I heard that night, Cesare was oblivious to anything about Leo," added Victoria.

Police and investigators had been at the cabin nonstop since the first fire truck had arrived late that night, expecting to help pull a car out of the water. Instead the first responders had been led by Seth to the cabin, where they tried to revive Cesare

Abbadelli, who'd consumed an estimated thousand milligrams of phenobarbital. The old man had been unresponsive and his body had shut down within hours, following the identical path of the young women killed by Leo. His autopsy had revealed a body riddled with cancer; Seth estimated he wouldn't have lived another six months.

Leo was dead at the scene. There was nothing the first responders could do for him.

Investigators had found eleven graves. So far. Victoria had been unable to join the team unearthing the graves. Part of her wanted to be here, making certain every little detail was handled appropriately. The rest of her wanted to never set foot near the cabin. Ever.

The graves exposed young woman after young woman. So far there'd been two exceptions. One young man and an older woman. According to Jason, Abbadelli's older son and wife had "left town" years ago. DNA comparisons had been requested to see if these two sets of remains showed a genetic connection to Leo.

The rest of the Pacific Northwest police departments were digging into every cold case of missing young women, flooding the Oregon medical examiner's office with requests. With all the publicity, Victoria had strong hopes that the last two women from the old circle would be identified. Esther Cavallo had pointed out that in the sixties and seventies the church had been known for its outreach program for runaways and women in "difficult" circumstances, receiving referrals from agencies in downtown Portland where women went to seek shelter. Possibly Cesare Abbadelli had used this program to search for women who fit his "type." Women who wouldn't be missed, women who needed a strong shoulder to cry on.

He must have stockpiled victims in his shed before creating the white circle in Forest Park. Could he have managed it alone? Callahan hadn't been certain. He could have drugged the women into compliance. Or he could have had an accomplice. Scratch marks in the corners and around the doorframe of the shed spoke of the terrors of the women locked in his hellhole. The shed had been through extensive strengthening at one point, with heavy-duty boards nailed and glued into impenetrability. It was a prison cell.

Isabel had healed from her head injury. Leo had surprised and attacked her in her home. She didn't remember anything after being hit in the head. She had no memory of the shed, which Victoria thought was extremely lucky; her own shed memories would last a lifetime. She'd visited Isabel in the hospital, explaining how Leo had claimed she was Isabel's daughter. The older woman had stared at her for a long time. "It's possible," Isabel had admitted grudgingly. "Abbadelli put my baby girl up for adoption. I wanted out of there. At first I'd been thankful for a roof over my head after getting away from a boyfriend who liked to beat on me, but Abbadelli gave me the creeps. I was happy to leave the baby behind. I didn't want any memories of that man." She'd offered to give a DNA sample for Victoria to compare.

Victoria hadn't taken her up on the offer. Yet.

Maybe someday she would.

Dr. Campbell had agreed to postpone his retirement a few weeks to lend a helping hand as a deputy examiner and offer advice as Seth took over his position.

Seth was now Victoria's boss. And bossy he'd been. "Don't lift that," "Don't do that," "Let me do that" were the phrases she was utterly sick of hearing from his mouth. She'd moved into his hotel room while her house was cleaned and renewed from the fire damage.

Next week they were flying to Sacramento to meet Eden.

Oddly Victoria wasn't nervous. She'd developed a fondness for teen girls that she was positive would extend to Eden. She was an extension of Seth. How could she not instinctively love her?

She hadn't been out of Seth's sight for three days. He'd said that when she'd walked away from him that night with Trinity, his heart had feared he'd never see her again. Now he frequently touched her arm, reassuring himself that she was close by. He'd been back in her life for a few days, and she couldn't imagine her future without him.

Today they'd visited the recovery site. She'd fought the urge to give direction over the shoulders of the diggers. Instead she and Seth had hung back, watching the investigators crawl through the house, shed, and woods. The gigantic scope of the investigation made Victoria's brain spin. And the main characters were dead. The police might find answers to lingering questions, but there'd never be anyone to punish for the crimes.

At least Brooke had survived. She'd slowly regained function of her brain and body. To Trinity's relief, she'd known her best friend. But her short-term memory was shot. Her doctors were optimistic that she'd return to full health over time. She'd revealed to the police that she'd communicated with the photographer through his Facebook professional page. He hadn't been in her list of friends, where investigators had first sought a common ground between the victims; he'd been in her "Likes." It'd been a moot point, because the page had been removed the day of the deaths.

Seth had finally dragged Victoria away from the site, pulling her down a path away from the bustle of the scene. For once, it wasn't raining. The sky was a depressing gray, but was holding tight to its water for the moment. Victoria breathed in the ripe wet scent of the trees and damp undergrowth.

"How could Cesare hide his true colors from so many people? And present himself as a spiritual leader?" she asked.

Seth paced silently beside her for a long moment. "I think people saw what they wanted to see. At one time, his personality must have been pretty charismatic to convince people to not see through his façade."

"And those who did, didn't report him. I hope Jason gets over his guilt about not going directly to the police with his suspicions about his father and grandfather."

"He's lucky no one else was killed by Leo. That level of guilt would have messed him up for life." He didn't add how close the both of them came to losing their lives.

"Do you think he'll always wonder if he has an evil side, directing some of his actions or waiting to come out of his personality at the wrong time?" Victoria said slowly.

Seth stopped and turned her to face him. "You do not have rotten blood in your veins. You are living proof that a good heart can overpower anything that nature throws in your genes. You are not Abbadelli or Isabel. You're Victoria Peres, forensic anthropologist extraordinaire, dragon-boat queen, high-school teen hero, and my Tori." He pulled her into him, carefully avoiding crushing her hurt wrist. "I love you, and I never want to be in the position of wondering if some crazy nut has hurt you again. I plan on not letting you out of my sight for a very long time. Maybe never."

She squirmed in his embrace. "Never? That has a bit of a compulsive implication about it. I don't know if—"

He cut off her teasing words with a kiss, pressing his lips against hers. She opened to meet him, seeking his heat and reassurance. She moved closer, loving the strength and hardness of his body next to hers. Soft drops of rain hit her cheeks, bringing back memories of their first kiss. *Their first kiss this time around.* A rare second chance at being together. She wasn't going to waste it. They'd been given a precious gift, and she would embrace it with everything she had.

"I love you, too," she spoke against his lips.

If this was an example of how Seth needed to keep her in his sight, she was the luckiest woman in the world.

ACKNOWLEDGMENTS

This book wouldn't have happened without the pestering of my developmental editor, Charlotte Herscher. During the edits of my previous novel, *Buried*, Charlotte told me she found Victoria Peres to be a fascinating character and suggested I write the next book about her. I immediately replied, "No. She intimidates the hell out of me. And the other characters are scared of her." Charlotte didn't accept that answer. She wanted to know why Victoria unsettled me, and what had made her into a cold person who pushed away the other characters.

Her questions stuck in my head. I wrote three chapters of *Alone* with Victoria in a secondary role, but in my head I heard Charlotte's voice ask, "But *why* is Victoria like that?"

Victoria took over the book. And I loved discovering her past.

Montlake Romance is a wonderful team, and I'm extremely fortunate to have a home with them and to work with people who are enthusiastic about my books. Thank you to Lindsay Guzzardo and Kelli Martin, my editors extraordinaire. More thanks to Jessica Poore, author team angel, who *always* knows the right answer.

Thank you to my kids, who put up with a constantly distracted mom and are proud to pimp my books to their teachers. Thank goodness I married a man who is tied to his laptop as much as I am. He understands me.

ABOUT THE AUTHOR

Photograph © Yuen Lui, 2010

Born and raised in the Pacific Northwest, Kendra Elliot has always been a voracious reader, cutting her teeth on classic female sleuths and heroines like Nancy Drew, Trixie Belden, and Laura Ingalls before proceeding to devour the works of Stephen King, Diana Gabaldon, and Nora Roberts. She has a degree in journalism from the University of Oregon. Now a Golden Heart, Daphne du Maurier, and Linda Howard Award of Excellence finalist, Elliot shares her love of suspense in her Bone Secrets series: *Hidden*, *Chilled*, *Buried*, and now *Alone*. She still lives in the Pacific Northwest with her husband and three daughters. Keep in touch with Kendra at www.kendraelliot.com or through Facebook.